ISBN 13: 978-1-940014-01-2

Library of Congress Catalog Number: 201313946245
Printed in Canada
First Printing: 2013
17   16   15   14   13   5   4   3   2   1

Cover and interior design by Aurora Whittet

Wise Ink, Inc.
53 Oliver Ave S
Minneapolis, MN 55404
www.wiseinkpub.com

To order, visit www.itascabooks.com or call 1-800-901-3480. Reseller discounts available.

This is a work of fiction. Names, characters, places, and incidents either are the product of the author's imagination or are used ficticiously, and any resemblance to actual persons living or dead, businesses, companies, events, or locales is entierly coincidental.

Bloodmark

Endorsements

"*Bloodmark* is like the Baskin Robbins of paranormal books—a little something for everybody. Partially period piece, it also has elements of fantasy, light horror, and YA paranormal with engaging romantic elements. Well within my 'buy this book now' range, *Bloodmark* easily fits in the 'buy an extra copy as a gift' zone."
—**Joe Alfano, "Zombie Joe" of *Wicked Little Pixie* blog**

"*Bloodmark* certainly doesn't disappoint. A strong-willed, independent women, Ashling is an intensely appealing heroine. I couldn't put the book down and I've never been so sad that I couldn't rush out to buy and read the next book in the series."
—**Katy Gerdes, contestant on *Project Runway* Season 3**

"*Bloodmark* is a fast-paced, beautiful blend of the emotional rollercoaster of first love and the fear of what's around every corner, told through gorgeous descriptions and characters. The book is engrossing."
—**Leslie Rich, Hounds of Finn**

"I was drawn into the beautiful world of Bloodmark within just a few pages. Whittet's first novel in the series perfectly blends all of the elements I love in a good book: suspense, mystery, strong characters, and most important (for me), romance. The gripping romance between Ashling and Grey quickly made Bloodmark an undeniable page-turner. Looking forward to the other books in the series is an understatement."
—**Jessica Flannigan, editor of LivetheFancyLife.com**

Bloodmark

Aurora Whittet

There are moments in life when you truly realize you are in the presence of love. My mother was pure love. She shared it with everyone she met and taught us to feel the wind in our faces and the rhythm of the earth. We lost her on March 28, 2013 and now when we feel lost, all we have to do is close our eyes and feel the wind in our hair to know she's still here.

*For my son Henry, you are my sunshine,
and Brian, you are my soul mate.*

Contents

1   *Acceptance*   1
2   *Curiosity*   11
3   *Untamed*   23
4   *Animal Kingdom*   31
5   *Broken*   39
6   *Lost*   47
7   *Sightings*   59
8   *Caged*   73
9   *Attraction*   87
10   *Missing*   103
11   *Free*   113
12   *Promises*   123
13   *Wild Animals*   141
14   *Fake It*   159
15   *Reasons*   173
16   *Nightmares*   185
17   *Eyes of the Night*   193
18   *Encounter*   207
19   *Embrace*   223
20   *Stolen*   241
21   *Captors*   255
22   *Darkness*   265
23   *Wild*   277
24   *Survivor*   289
25   *Bloodmark*   305
26   *Lies*   317
27   *Perfect by Nature*   327

1
Acceptance

"Are you ready, Ashling, my love?" Mother asked.

"I've been ready for ages," I replied.

"It's a three-hour drive, so don't get too excited just yet." She smiled.

"Can't we run there? We could do it in about an hour." Just the thought of shifting to my wolf form made my pulse quicken with anticipation. It had been weeks since my brother, Mund, had visited and we could run free. I missed my red fur and four feet.

"That would hardly be the proper behavior of a lady," Mother said. "We want to make a good impression, don't we?"

I knew she was right, but I still yearned for the freedom of it. I had never left the cliffs, and the impending journey filled my soul with yearning. I wanted desperately to be part of our pack; I felt a hole inside myself where my pack should have been. I was certain Father was going brand me with the Boru Bloodmark and accept me into the pack. I should have been branded as a baby, but he had refused. I still didn't know why. Without his Bloodmark on the back of my neck, I had no lineage and no family, no past and no future. I was the only daughter of King Pørr Boru and Queen Nessa, and no one even knew I was still alive.

Mother was an elegant beauty with long, strawberry-blonde hair she always kept expertly woven into braids. For being over seven hundred years old, she appeared to be only in her early forties to human eyes. She was beautiful, yes, but her unending love for all living creatures was the essence of her spirit. Mother watched over the humans as though they were her own children and protected them from whatever evil lurked in the shadows. She was everything a queen should be. Sometimes I vied to be refined and demure like her, but my wild nature and free-flowing opinions prevented that. Still, I adored the earth she walked upon; it was her love that made the sun shine.

We traveled from the southern tip of Ireland's coast to the center, past the city of Cork, the Galty Mountains, and through the city of Cashel. The Rock of Cashel sat on the outskirts of the city limits, though the entire city was Father's kingdom. The ruins of the medieval castle were built into the limestone terrain, and it couldn't have been more beautiful. I had only seen photos of it in tourist books Mund brought me, but to finally see it as we approached left me awestruck.

I eagerly jumped out of the car, nearly knocking into the guard who held my door. He was wearing a green Rock of Cashel tour-guide jacket—to inform human tourists of the Rock of Cashel's "history" while deflecting their interest at the same time. His sleeves were rolled up, exposing his Boru Bloodmark tattooed to the underside of his wrists, a Celtic knot with two wolves' heads; it was the heart of our pack.

He snorted his disapproval at me as he held out his hand for Mother. "My queen," he said.

"Thank you, Dillon," she replied.

He looked at me again with a frown before looking back to her. "Follow me, m'lady." His criticism should have bothered me, but I was too excited.

Mother and I left our trunks with our driver and walked through the old, patinaed gate and followed him down the small, winding staircase into the dark underground. We stepped around the signs notifying tourists that it was unsafe beyond that point and continued down another flight of stairs into the deep earth.

I didn't see them, but I could smell the guards as we approached a solid stone wall. The only marking was the Boru Bloodmark carved into stone. Mother put her hand on the mark, and the wall began to open, revealing a hidden door. The ancient magic of our kind pulsed with the unified heartbeat of our pack. In this place, we were one. We stepped into the underground labyrinth of the Boru Kingdom, hidden underneath the earth for over a thousand years. Human generations had come and gone, but our kind stood watch over them.

"Who's Dillon?" I asked as we continued to follow him through a grand carved-limestone doorway.

"He's the head of the guard," she said. "This is my bedchamber."

Mother's bedchamber was exquisite in every detail. Two guards carried our travel trunks into the room and set them down. I was curious to see other werewolves, and I watched them intently. I had spent my whole life with just Mother and visits from my brother Mund. I barely even knew my other brothers.

"When can we see Father?" I asked.

"We must freshen up before your father receives us. Now hurry, love, he is expecting us," Mother said.

I slipped on an ivory satin dress—simple, but I knew Mother would approve. "Who's going to be there?" I asked.

"I believe all packs loyal to the Boru will be there." Mother began weaving my wild, red hair into braids like hers. "You'll meet the Swiss Kingerys, the Spanish Costas, the Cree Indian Four-Claws of Canada, the African Sylla, the Scottish Killians, the Welsh Kahedins, and my family, the Greek Vanirs. And of course, your father and brothers will all be there."

I had seen Father only a handful of times and my brothers even less. I was nervous to live up to their expectations. "What if they don't like me?"

"Like you?" Mother smiled. "They will love you."

A light knock came to the door, and my heart pounded with anticipation. My brother Mund grinned. "Ash, you look lovely," he said. I couldn't stop smiling.

Mund was my favorite brother; he visited me monthly as long as I could remember. He was handsome with dark-brown eyes and his shoulder-length, wavy brown hair. He looked no more than eighteen years old, but I knew him to be nearly four hundred. Wolves only began showing age when they were badly injured or when they missed a full moon without shifting, and Mund had been lucky in that respect. Despite his age, his style was sophisticated and modern, from the cut of his light-gray suit coat to the tips of his white, collared shirt. He kissed us each on the cheeks before continuing. "Father wants you both to join him in the War Room."

Mother frowned. "Why does he not first receive us in our family chambers?"

"Flin summoned us."

Flin was my eldest brother and Father's first in command. I met him once, but he didn't approve of me. Mother had said it was because Flin was envious of my power to shift into a wolf from birth, unlike the rest of my kind, who had to wait until adolescence. I knew that was why they hid me in the countryside of Ireland for fourteen years; I was an embarrassment.

"This is not proper etiquette," Mother said, "but no matter. We shall go to him. Father is a busy man." She gave my hand a little squeeze as we walked down the stone halls of our underground kingdom. The limestone walls were carved with our history. I ran my fingers over the rough texture, feeling the cool stone and, with it, the energy of the pack. For the first time in my life, I felt a connection to them.

We followed Mund into a large, round room filled with books, maps, and priceless paintings by the masters—all items the humans assumed had been lost over the centuries. We protected the humans' past just as we protected their future.

Father's thick, spicy scent filled the room. He leaned over a large map on the center stone table. He was strong and stocky, and his reddish-gray hair was swept back, but it was his full red beard that the legends all spoke of; he was a warrior king. Today, he was dressed in traditional linens and leather with a fur hide draped down his back like a cape. He wore a large copper Celtic belt buckle at his waist. His appearance was intimidating; if I didn't know he was my father, I might have trembled in his presence. I hadn't bonded with him as I had with Mother and Mund, but I could still smell his emotions—his fear washed over me as I entered the room.

A very refined man stood next to him, dressed in a fine suit with a velvet jacket. He was near Father's age in appearance, though I couldn't be certain how old he really was. Standing in Father's presence made my palms begin to sweat; I was excited and scared at the same time. I felt as though I could faint from my anxiety. I wanted to stare at him and study every feature of his face—I barely knew him, and I often forgot what he looked like. Most of all, I wanted to rush into Father's arms and cling to him, but Mund's hand on my shoulder kept me in my place with him and Mother as we waited to be addressed. I knew it was proper to wait, but what place did etiquette have with my own father? It felt like an eternity, but patience wasn't a virtue I seemed to possess. Finally, Father looked up at Mother. "Nessa," he said, "you remember Lord Beldig Kahedin."

He was the father of Tegan, Mund's wife. I heard many stories of his greatness in battle. Mother smiled as Lord Beldig kissed her cheeks—first left, then right. "My queen," he said.

"It feels only yesterday since our Mund married Tegan," she said.

"Already a decade has passed," he replied. Time was nothing to our kind.

"May I present our daughter, Ashling," she said, gesturing for me to join her side. I stumbled my first step forward but quickly recovered.

"I am honored," he said. "You look so much like your mother."

"Thank you, sir."

I blushed and looked away, suddenly distracted by the silver chains, shackles, and knives displayed on the far wall. They weren't commonly used anymore, but I knew what they were for—torture devices used on wolves who broke the laws of our kind throughout the centuries. If pure silver touched werewolves' skin, even for a moment, it would render us temporarily mortal and it would be impossible to shift into our wolf form until the effects wore off. The longer we would be in contact with the silver, the longer the effects took to wear off. If silver got in direct contact with our blood, the effects were instant and brutally painful. It made my skin crawl just to think about it.

"What business brings you today?" Mother asked. "I trust the Kahedin pack is well?"

Lord Beldig looked as nervous as I felt; he glanced at Father before answering. "The price of a bride."

There was a tense pause. "Has Brychan found a mate?" Mother replied. Her words were strained; something had changed.

"I have offered Ashling's hand to Lord Beldig's son and heir," father said.

As the words sunk in, I felt my heart sink. Father didn't want me at all; he had sold me in marriage to his ally's son. I couldn't stop my hands from shaking. My own father had betrayed me. My eyes welled up with tears, my misery reaching epidemic proportions.

"She is yet a child of fourteen," Mother said.

"Old enough by our laws," Father replied, turning his back on us.

A young male werewolf entered; he appeared to be in his mid-twenties and smelled of black tea and leather spices. Brychan was a darker, more unrefined version of his sister Tegan, though they shared the same beautiful olive skin. He had startling dark-blue eyes, and a slight beard shadowed his face, giving him an even more rugged appearance. His dark-brown hair was slightly messy around his sharp, masculine features. He was taller and more muscular than Mund and wore a full suit that was tight across his chest. He was handsome. I couldn't quite read his expression, but he seemed amused by something. He leaned casually against the giant globe at the side of the room.

"Lord Brychan, your father and I have come to terms," Father said to the man. "I present Princess Ashling."

Brychan looked at me for the first time. My lips quivered with fear and my hands still shook. I'm sure I looked like a scared animal to his inspection, not the bride he had come to bargain for. His posture didn't change, but his eyes softened; for a brief moment, I wasn't scared of him.

"Pørr?" Mother interrupted.

Still Father didn't look at me. "It is done," he said. Mother froze at his words. I knew she was angry—I could sense her emotions—but she knew her place and wouldn't question him again. "Ashling, greet your soon-to-be-husband."

I couldn't move—I was too scared. Father had just sold me to the highest bidder as if I were nothing more than cattle. His eyes narrowed on me, and the vein in his forehead started to bulge out of the surface of his skin.

"Do as you're told, child."

"No," I said, wiping the tears from my face with the back of my hands.

He crossed the room in less than a heartbeat and roughly placed his large hands on my shoulders, digging his fingernails into my flesh. He leaned in close and whispered in my ear, "You are my property, and you will do as I say."

"I will not." My voice was calmer than I could have hoped.

His hand clenched to strike me down for my disobedience, but Mund shielded the blow with his forearm. I flinched from the forceful impact that vibrated through Mund. "Perhaps she is too young to make such a decision," Mund said. "I will take charge of her until her eighteenth birthday, at which time, Lord Brychan, you can state your claim as her betrothed."

Before Father could argue, Brychan said, "I agree to your terms, Prince Redmund. I trust her safety to you."

"I will keep her safe," Mund said. "Tegan and I will look after her at the cliffs."

I could see Father's anger in his hideous expression. Mund's disloyalty was a disgrace to him. "Nessa, you will resume your position here at the Rock," Father said.

"Husband, my king, I will fulfill my duty to my daughter until she is wed. You know where to find us." Her words were soft, but I knew the choice she had made and she would not forgive him.

She wrapped her arm around my shoulder and began leading me from the room when Brychan stopped our path. He studied my tear-stained face. His expression was cold, but his touch was gentle as he put a ring in my hand, closing my fingers over it. "Until we meet again," he said.

"Thank you," I whispered. I knew it was only because of his agreement that Mund had won. Brychan had chosen to let me go . . . for now. He bowed, releasing my hand.

I followed Mother and Mund down the hallway, where we met my brother Quinn. "I need you to load my and Tegan's trunks with Mother and Ashling's," Mund told him. "We'll leave at once." Quinn didn't question his elder brother. He quickly kissed Mother's cheek and ran to complete the task. He looked more like Mother than I did, the same light hair and blue eyes. He was the youngest of my brothers.

"Go straight to the car before he changes his mind. I will meet you there," Mund said to Mother and me.

We turned and walked swiftly to leave. "Hurry," Mother said. Her pace quickened as we retraced our footsteps out of the castle and into the daylight. Mother and I climbed into the backseat of the pewter Bentley as Mund and Tegan got in the front. We sped away.

"Ashling . . ." Mund said. I could see him watching me in the rear-view mirror. "Brychan is a good man, strong, loyal, and of the Kahedin house. He'd be a good match for you. An honorable match."

"But I don't love him, I don't even know him."

"There are different kinds of love, Ashling. A love that grows over time with friendship and a binding love that is instant and unstoppable. Both loves are true—just because you didn't immediately bind with Brychan doesn't mean he's a bad match."

Mother held my hand. "The choice is yours in time, *m' eudail*." She often spoke in Gaelic when she said terms of endearment. It made the simple words "my dear" that much more beautiful on her lips, but none of it made me any less angry or sad.

I cried on the way home, staring into the depths of the diamond ring Brychan had given me. It was surrounded by black metal and blue sapphires. It was a beautiful ring, but I didn't want anything to do with it. It could only remind me of my awful father.

2
Curiosity

Two years had passed, and I hadn't seen Father since. Not once had he visited, not one letter did I receive. I never knew why he hated me so or why my very presence put him on edge. I didn't know him. As the High King of our packs, Mund said it was Father's duty to remain at the Rock and lead our kind, but I knew better. He was afraid of the power that flowed through my veins—because I was the only wolf to ever be able to shift from birth, he hated me. Perhaps it was jealousy. Still, was I such a hideous beast that I shouldn't even be a member of his pack? I still felt shame for not screaming all the things I felt the day he tried to damn me into an unwilling marriage with Brychan. If Mund hadn't stepped in, I would have been Brychan's wife today . . . his property.

The only wolves I could trust were Mother and Mund. I was even a bit leery of Tegan, as she was Brychan's sister. Even though she was also Mund's lovely wife and she was carrying their first child, I barely knew her. She wasn't terribly easy to get to know, but I was slowly getting comfortable with her. She had moved here only two years ago; before, she lived at the Rock with the rest of my brothers and their wives. I was just glad to have Mund around. Today, I was making my way up the cliffs to watch for his return from the Rock—I missed him terribly.

I resented my father. It disgusted me how easily he could cast me aside, and thinking of it filled my stomach with acidic anger. Still, Mother chose me—even though her place was next to him at the head of our kingdom, not out here on the edge of nowhere. Her love for me was deeper than her duty to the crown. Living out by the cliffs in a mere cottage was no way for a queen to live, but I knew my mother liked the peace of the ocean.

Reaching the edge of the cliff, I leaned into the crisp, salty wind, letting it hold me up. I spent most of my time here; I longed for the freedom of it. We were Old Mother Earth's children, her wolves, and no place settled my wandering mind back to her as did the treacherous cliffs by our home. My emerald satin dress blew in the wind along with the wild hurricane of my curly, red hair. It was liberating, letting the wind and Old Mother cleanse my soul and clear my mind. My body was one with nature.

I closed my eyes and crept closer to the edge, my toes wrapping over. The hem of my dress caught and tore on the sharp rocks, but I didn't care. I wanted to feel the exhilaration of the wind and the danger. I wanted to feel something other than loneliness. I had been waiting for three weeks for Mund to return; I was bored out of my mind without him. I could smell him on the wind—it was faint, but it was there. He would be home soon. I could feel his anxious mind. I could only imagine he yearned to reunite with Tegan.

In every way, Tegan was viewed as a perfect woman in our culture. She had lovely olive skin, the deepest blue eyes, and the most radiant dark-brown hair that flowed down her back in perfect braids. I often attempted to imitate her elegance, from the delicate way she moved her wrists to the soft sound of her voice, but I was nothing like her. I was more like Mund, rough and opinionated. Maybe I was that way because I spent most of my time with him instead of in the house with Mother and Tegan, learning to be "accomplished." But I didn't want to be contained.

I wanted to be free to think, to learn, to question, and most of all, to find love—not to be forced into a marriage by my father, a political pawn to be traded at his will.

Mund's scent was becoming much stronger—it would not be long now. I ran home through the puddles and tall grass, my bare feet meeting the earth to the tempo of my heart. I looked over the hills and saw Mund's white 1948 Jaguar XK120 still miles away; it was a convertible that made him look like a knight in shining armor. I absorbed anything he had to say, and a lot of it was about his love for classic British cars. I wanted a vintage American muscle car. Even though our culture believed a lady shouldn't drive, Mund taught me anyway, and I loved the feeling of that steel beast in my control.

As Mund closed the distance to the house, I climbed to the roof of the wooden shack and hid, waiting for my chance to scare him. He was coming home in time for the Beltane celebration, marking the beginning of summer. The nearby village was mostly Christian, but they still honored the old traditions. What they didn't realize was we lived them; we were the characters of their legends.

I watched as Mund climbed out of his car, carrying brown-paper packages. I pounced from the roof onto his back, but he didn't miss a step. He swung me over his shoulder with barely any effort and continued on his way to the house.

"Ash, you lack stealth," he said as he dropped me on my feet.

I couldn't stop smiling. His dark-brown eyes studied my rough appearance, but not with any sign of disapproval. My dirty, bare feet had tarnished his white shirt. "Sorry," I mumbled as I dusted him off.

He reached out and messed my hair into a puffy red cloud. "I missed you too," he smiled as he handed me one of the packages.

The door flew open with a thump, and Tegan ran out and melted into his arms, Mund's packages falling to the ground. It pained them to be apart. Their souls were bound infinitely to each other—they were true soul mates. I envied their love.

I wasn't even permitted to talk to a male who wasn't family. I was "sheltered"—or more appropriately, *caged*. As Mund and Tegan soothed their pains of separation, I went unnoticed collecting the packages strewn at their feet. I left the two lovers outside as I entered our modest cottage and dropped the gifts on the rough-cut wooden table in the center of the room. I stood in front of my mother, and she looked me over—my messed hair, ripped dress, and dirty feet.

She shook her head and smiled. "My dear Ashling, not another torn dress."

I don't know why she bothered trying to dress me as a lady when I was clearly a wild animal in a sixteen-year-old girl's body. Sheepish, I smiled, scrambled up the ladder to the loft, and changed into the one thing I truly enjoyed wearing: raw leather scraps. I'd wrap their smooth texture around my petite frame and create simple outfits. I loved the fact I was using all of what Old Mother offered, from the animals' flesh we ate to their hides for my clothing. I viewed it as respecting nature and the loss of a life. But really, I liked it because I knew if Father could see me, he would be furious. Mother didn't approve of it either, but today she was tired of my feisty energy and didn't protest.

I plopped myself on the bare floor in front of the fire as I carefully unwrapped the gift from Mund. Inside was a classic copy of Jane Austen's complete works. Mund knew I was currently reading my way through seventeenth- and eighteenth-century classics. If Father knew Mund disobeyed him and let me read, he would be furious. Sometimes he would send someone from the kingdom to spy on us. He didn't think ladies should read, as it might give us "ideas" and "free will"—just as it had two years earlier when I refused to marry Brychan. The problem with an ancient culture of immortal beings is their inability to embrace change. My kind clung to the past, their fear resisting any change. A lady was to be accomplished in many manners of things but never to have ideas of her own. Women were to be controlled. But I decided I wasn't.

I settled in to read my new treasure, letting my mind wander wherever this story wanted me to go.

I awoke the next morning on the floor by the nearly burned-out fire. I yawned and stretched and watched Mother, Mund, and Tegan eat raw lamb flesh for breakfast. My stomach growled as the delicious scent filled my nose. I snatched a fresh morsel as I flipped open the book to where I had left off.

"Come, love, we have to go show our support of our humans," Mother said. Mother employed a few farmers who sold our livestock in the town market. Mund said we had to behave like humans, and being a small part of their culture ensured we would go unnoticed. I wasn't interested in interacting with the humans.

"I'll pass," I said, going back to my reading, but Mother pulled it from my fingers and delicately set it on the table.

"It is our duty to Old Mother," Mother said.

I groaned.

"Come on, Ash, just follow us around looking sullen, and you will perfectly play the part of a teenage girl," Mund said laughing. I rolled my eyes and started to follow. "Are you really going to wear that?" he said, gesturing to my leather skirt, top, and boots. I stuck out my tongue.

"Mund, my darling," Tegan said lightly, pulling him out the door before he could protest farther.

I dragged behind, following Mother, Mund, and Tegan. I never felt a connection to the humans—most of them seemed to avoid us. Even in their eyes I was a freak, and they didn't know I was a werewolf. I didn't belong in the human world, and I wasn't even accepted in my own pack. Without the Boru Bloodmark, I was alienated. Still, I never felt alone. Mother and Mund were my family, and that bond could never be broken—Bloodmark or no Bloodmark.

"Mund, would you purchase some lamb today? It will do nicely to support the neighbors," Mother said. "And Tegan, do you think we could use some more potatoes?"

Tegan's beautiful face flinched for a brief moment before returning to perfection. "We still have to throw away the last bag we purchased."

We didn't eat human food—we could, we just didn't like to. It was bland, and the cooked meats were rancid to our tongues. Fresh animal flesh was always preferred, and we never spent time with the humans without eating first. Human blood smelled all the sweeter to us—a temptation we had to learn to overcome. Sometimes I wondered if it was all part of Old Mother's plan, the temptation was part of the lesson, to love and protect something that you desired so desperately to possess.

"Well, let's buy some potatoes anyway," Mother said. "We have to keep up appearances."

Both Mother and Tegan always wore satin gowns, far overdressed for our tiny community of farmers. Not that my leather scraps were any more suitable. Dunmanas Bay wasn't exactly the fashion capital of the world. For the most part, we stayed out of the day-to-day dealings with the humans, just keeping a watchful eye on them and protecting them from harm. Of all the humans, I preferred watching over the children. My soul connected with their open hearts, and I felt my higher purpose when I was with them. I was quite certain a few of them actually knew what we were. The adults were ignorant to us but still subtly fearful of our differences. We walked on the dirt road into town, and I watched Tegan and Mund holding hands as they interacted with the townspeople. Gracious and giving to all of humankind.

I slipped away down another path toward the fountain. I suppose it was selfish of me, but I didn't want to be there. I yearned for my life to begin, yet I still dreaded a marriage to Brychan. With that as my future, what life was left for me? A little boy with curly black hair and bright blue eyes smiled at me as I passed. I smiled back, and he giggled and trotted after his mother. I recognized him; he was the O'Learys' son. He always put a smile on my face. I sat on the edge of the stone fountain, watching the birds dance as I stared up at the dark clouds that rolled overhead. A storm was coming. Suddenly, I smelled something on the cool wind—a werewolf.

My eyes flashed open as I searched for the source. A strange man dressed in a vintage brocade suit coat leaned against one of the buildings about twenty-five feet away. It was as though he had fallen through time.

His green eyes glowed even in broad daylight. I was curious to get a better look at him. Other wolves weren't allowed in this territory. His beard was trimmed close to his tanned skin. He appeared to be in his late twenties with long black hair and a hard jaw, but something about him seemed much older.

As I walked closer, his eyes lit up with interest. I was intrigued by him. I wanted to know more about him, where he came from. Most wolves still didn't travel great distances alone, but where was his pack? He was so fixated on me that he didn't even blink. My skin prickled, making me feel uneasy.

I heard my name in the distance and turned as Mund ran over, carrying a shank of lamb. When I looked back, the stranger turned and disappeared behind one of the buildings.

"What are you doing wandering alone?" he said.

"There was a wolf, just there." I pointed. His eyebrows went up, which was the expression Mund used when he thought I was making up wild stories. "No, I saw him and he saw me!"

"Ashling, other werewolves aren't allowed in this territory." Mund smiled as he wrapped his free arm around my shoulders and steered me toward home. Sometimes he made me feel so foolish, but I knew what I saw.

"I know," I said, "but he was there. He was tall with long black hair and glowing green eyes."

The sun had begun to set as we walked on the worn dirt road toward Mother's cottage. Mund came to a stop facing me in the near darkness, but I could see him clearly. "Are you certain?"

"Yes. He wore a black brocade jacket."

His face went pale, and I could feel his fear. Mund quickly grabbed his phone and showed it to me. "Was it this man?" he asked with bitterness in his voice. I could almost taste his anger.

As I looked closely at the image, I saw the same intense green eyes. "Yes, that's him."

The lamb fell to the ground. Before I could even question, Mund dragged me home to Mother's cottage.

"They found us," he said.

"Who found us?" I asked.

Mother grabbed the old wooden lockbox from above the mantle and wrapped a red hooded cloak around my shoulders. "It's time to go," she said. I followed them outside to a tarp-covered SUV in the shed. Mund never drove it; it always just sat there collecting dust. He yanked the tarp off, sending the dust fluttering into the air.

"Tegan, Mother, after you," Mund said. "Careful, my love." He gently helped Tegan as Mother and I slid in the backseat.

"What about all our stuff?" I asked as I turned to see our travel trunks in the back, and then I knew. We didn't intend to return. Mund had us packed and ready to flee at any moment. He had prepared for this day. "What's going on?" I begged, breathing in their anxiety.

"The man you saw is of the Dvergar pack, the Boru and Vanirs' oldest enemy," said Mund as he stepped into the driver's seat and started the engine. "He is Adomnan Dvergar, the eldest son of Crob. They are treacherous murderers who have forsaken their vows to Old Mother. They have been searching for you for years, and they have every intent of taking you from us at any cost."

My throat was dry. I couldn't fathom what I had to do with any of them.

"We are going to your father—he'll know what to do and he will keep you safe," Mother said. I didn't feel any comfort in her words. How could I possibly trust my father after everything he'd done? I could feel Mother's fear, it mirrored my own, but Mund was filled only with anger. He reached across and placed his strong hand on Tegan's as she cradled her pregnant stomach. The darkness consumed the car as we left the only home I had ever known.

We sped through the night to the Rock with the full moon lighting our way. We traveled the road through the Galty Mountains, and my memories started flooding through me, filling me with dread. The Rock wasn't a beacon of safety for me, and Father wasn't my savior. He would probably demand I marry Brychan immediately. Every unfamiliar shadow seemed to mock me as we grew closer to Cashel.

"Why are the Dvergars our enemy?" I asked.

"In the eleventh century, Adomnan Dvergar's grandfather, King Uaid, murdered my sister Calista Vanir at Carrowmore on her wedding day," Mother said. "He had wanted to possess Calista's power as a seer, and he took her last breath when she refused to share her gift. He broke his vows to Old Mother to protect life, severing him from the packs."

Mother's breath caught in her throat, the memory was still raw almost one thousand years later. Tegan reached back and squeezed Mother's hand. The horrible truth of our history loomed over me, sending chills down my spine.

"His darkness didn't end there," Mund continued. "Uaid corrupted his entire pack. They began a murderous rampage of entire villages of our sacred humans, devouring their flesh. They painted the earth in blood. Our great-grandfather, Donal Boru, sacrificed his life to take Uaid's, but Uaid's eldest son, Crob, replaced his father on the throne. And Uaid's younger son, Verci, set out to destroy what was left of our pack. The Dvergars began attacking smaller packs and exterminating them on their quest for domination, and they showed no mercy.

"Adomnan himself led the attack on the Kahedin pack in the seventeenth century as they worked their way from Iceland toward the Boru throne. They wanted to destroy everything the Boru stood for, and that included all our allies. I fought Adomnan and his brothers to protect the Kahedin pack, and we won, but not before nearly eighty of us died at their hands. I watched as he tore children apart with his bare hands. I have never witnessed something so brutal. . . ."

My stomach knotted to hear the pain and fear in my brother's voice, and rage poured through me at the grotesque murders on the Dvergars' hands. Adomnan was a terrible creature, and the more Mund spoke of him, the more my fear and anger grew. If I fell into their hands, I could only imagine what they would do to me before they finally got Father to trade something for my life—if I were to survive at all. The thought of it made me want to vomit.

As we raced into Cashel, my nerves got the best of me. Every emotion I felt when I left the Rock two years earlier bubbled to the surface, rage at Father and Brychan clouding my thoughts. How could I trust Father to protect me now? Would he finally take me in his arms, comfort me, and tell me all the things a daughter yearned to hear, or would he betray my trust in him yet again?

We entered the darkened castle to the secret underground world. Mund escorted Tegan to their chamber to rest, and I followed Mother to Father's War Room. I remembered the way as if it were yesterday. It was there, in that room, that Father had last betrayed me. I shook my head at the memory.

"Pørr," Mother said.

He looked up from the ancient scrolls on the table before him. Anger consumed his face. "Why have you come?"

"Adomnan Dvergar found us," Mother said.

"Seize her," Father commanded his guards as they rushed forward, grabbing me. I was stunned to have their rough hands grasping my body, nearly crushing my bones. I should have known he would abandon me. Fear trickled through my blood.

"Stop, Pørr!" Mother shouted. "Have you gone mad?"

He didn't even dignify her with a response. "Lock her away," he told his guards.

Anger pulsed inside me like a shockwave. They dragged my body out of the room as I struggled and screamed against them. Mother ran after me—I could feel her fear, and I needed to protect her from all of them. I bit into one of the guards' hands, drawing blood, but several more guards blocked her path.

"Ashling," Mother said, her voice quivering and tears staining her porcelain cheeks. I fought as hard as I could to get to her, but her screams began to fade as they dragged me farther into the fortress. I finally stopped struggling against them and let them take me wherever they chose, instead focusing on memorizing the labyrinth of halls for my escape.

They dropped me on the cobblestone floor and slammed the heavy wooden doors shut. I could still smell them standing outside the locked doors. I looked around my new cage, yet another enormous room that had been built on the blood and backs of our people. It was a hand-carved stone room, filled with books from floor to ceiling. The history of the human world was hidden in this limestone room, the only surviving copies of thousands of books, scrolls, runes, and hieroglyphics. Every language through history was trapped in this one room. Just one room out of hundreds, our endless world below the earth's surface. This was the sanctuary of our pack, gathering place of our elders, and the tomb of Calista Vanir—yet I felt no comfort.

3
Untamed

My anger boiled to the top. Like the animal inside me, I felt wild. Locked up in that empty limestone room was bloody infuriating. I listened, but no sounds came. Neither Mund nor Mother came to free me. I was alone. I paced back and forth, agitated. *The only daughter of the great and legendary King Pørr Boru.* What an honor that must be, I laughed. I was treated as a pet. The look in my mother's eyes broke my heart. My father was a monster.

The sounds from the street outside the stone wall trickled through an iron grate high above my head. The grate was old and rusted and forgotten, just like all the books that inhabited the library. For a fortress that was seemingly impenetrable, the small opening could be its greatest weakness. I was sure my small body could fit through, if only the grate was weak enough to fail. I ran at the nearest pillar and leaped against it in one swift movement, ricocheting to the ledge of the vent grate and tearing my leather skirt.

From the grate, I could smell the grasses swaying in the wind, even the spray of the ocean miles away. The fresh air swirled in through the vent, and it consumed my mind, calling to me like a command to come home to where I truly belonged. I didn't belong here, locked up in a musty old castle; I belonged on the cliffs with the wind and the ocean in my face. I was trapped in a stone tomb of fools.

Father wasn't going to protect me. I shook my head angrily. I'd have to protect my bloody self. I yanked the iron grate off the wall with all my strength, cracking the edge of the stone, dropping it loudly to the floor, but no one stormed in to see what the frail little princess was doing. I laughed; they didn't know what I was capable of. Staring down the dank tunnel, I couldn't see any hints of the morning light at the end. I crawled through the dark, moist vent, barely shimmying my body through, but I crawled out onto the grass and limestone outside the castle walls that surrounded the Rock. The passage wasn't even blocked on this side, like an open invitation to enemies. I shook my head at the arrogance of my father. He had to have known this was here, but he didn't bother to bar it.

I glanced at the city of Cashel. Through it was the shortest path home, but I didn't want the guard to see me flee. So I took the long way around the cemetery on the north side. The feeling of the rocks under my soft boots reminded me of home. The edge of freedom waited there for me, and I ran to it. Away from my duty, away from Father, from everything they thought I should be—and I would never be what they wanted. I fled from the city like a fugitive. My boots were so thin, it felt as though my bare feet were meeting the ground with each stride. When I was finally out of sight, I began running faster, away from human eyes. Miles away from duty, over the countryside of Ireland, through the mountains of Comeragh and Galty through cattle pastures and scattered farmhouses. In a mere hour, I ran 136 miles, and I could finally see the coast.

The rocky edge looked treacherously inviting, it was my salvation; I yearned for the adrenaline of the wind and Old Mother's spirit. I ran right to the end of the earth and leaned forward, letting the wind hold my body, suspended between sky and earth. I breathed in the salty air and closed my eyes as the wind blew my menacing hair all around my face. I leaned farther into the wind, past the point of sanity. It was exhilaratingly easy to get lost in the adrenaline.

I flopped down on my back in the tall grass, completely hidden as I watched the clouds drift by. I closed my eyes and breathed in the ocean. I wanted to always feel this way, but Father's deception crept into my mind. He just wanted me to sit still and look pretty. I hated him. But who was I without him, without his Bloodmark? I was just an untamed, wild animal with no family to claim. Without a Bloodmark, I wasn't recognized as a member of our pack, and I could never marry. Even Brychan couldn't marry me until Father tattooed the Boru Bloodmark on my neck. I closed my eyes and rested as the warm sunlight eased my wandering mind.

"I have waited a long time to possess you, Ashling."

Adomnan bent down and stroked the side of my face. I tried to squirm away from his touch, but he grabbed a handful of my hair and nearly tore it out as he forced me to look at him.

"They tried to keep us apart, but you were destined to be mine." *There was an evil twist in his smirk, and I closed my eyes so I didn't have to see it. Crob's two other sons, Eamon and Bento, stood next to Adomnan, though Adomnan was about a foot taller than each. Bento, the youngest of them, looked innocent; his brown eyes were softer, more understanding than Adomnan's harsh green eyes. Bento's hair was cut short, and he wore a simple shirt, nothing fancy like Adomnan's.*

"Are you scared yet?" Eamon said, chuckling at my vulnerability. His shaggy dark hair fell slightly over his left eye. He was stockier than the others. His green velvet coat stretched over his back, bringing out the green flecks in his blue eyes. I noticed the shape of his nose—strong and angular.

I hated the way they looked at me, as though they were starving. Their eyes devoured me, and I shivered from their unwanted inspection.

Only scraps of leather covered my modesty, and I wrapped my arms around myself protectively. They talked in hushed whispers that were absorbed by the wind.

The confusion and drowsiness left my mind in a blur, but through the whipping wind and the rustling grass, I heard someone approaching.

I couldn't recognize their scents, so I didn't know who—or what—they were, but they must have been wolves by how swiftly they were closing the distance between us. Had Father sent his guards to collect his wayward daughter? They were closing in from the north, trapping me between them and the rocky cliffs.

I crept up in a crouch, barely visible above the grass, with my hair dancing around my face like flames. I felt confident and ready to fight, but the sight of Adomnan and his two brothers stole all my resolve. Panic raked through me.

It wasn't just a dream, it was a warning. I didn't need to be reminded what would happen to me if they caught me. All the stories Mund had told me were enough to make my heart pound with fear. I knew in that split second by the smirk on his face that he could plainly see my fear; I couldn't beat him. He was faster, bigger, and so much stronger. I wanted to scream for Mund, but he was over a hundred miles away. I felt frozen with fear.

"My beloved," he cooed.

I could smell human blood on them. I felt sick to my stomach, and anger filled my soul.

"My lady, I have searched for you for so long. I'm sorry to have kept you waiting," he said, standing only a few feet away. There was fresh blood still on his lips.

"You're disgusting," I said.

Adomnan lunged at me, grabbing a clump of my hair, ripping it from my scalp. I screamed in pain and leapt into the air, ripping through my clothes as I shifted to my wolf form and Old Mother's love and blood flowed through my veins. I landed several yards away as a small red wolf with blazing golden eyes. Without a conscious decision, my body was running. Self-preservation was fueling my adrenaline. I knew I had to get to Mund, or I would be just a pawn in someone else's game.

"Why are you running, Ashling?" Adomnan taunted.

I turned a daring glance back at them, faltering my gait. They were shifting, three large black wolves at least twice my size were coming up from behind. I pushed myself forward, my heart pounding like thunder in my body.

I was running faster than I had ever run before, and yet it seemed like slow motion. I knew I couldn't outrun them for long. I wondered how long it would take to die. Mother would mourn for me, but would Father even notice I was gone? Or would Adomnan try to trade me back to them in return for something far worse?

I slipped on loose rocks, and my left flank hit the ground, ripping at my flesh. I could feel Adomnan and his brothers gaining on me, and the pain in my leg vibrated through my every step. I just had to ignore the pain. The leg would heal quickly while I was in wolf form with Old Mother's blood in my veins. I knew the terrain well enough to gain some ground through the mountains, but they were still close behind.

I pushed my body harder than it could sustain; the exhaustion burned my muscles as I continued to run. If they caught me, I would be too weak to fight back. Their howls sent chills down my spine as I finally reached the edge of Cashel. I slowed down as I entered the city, knowing I was safe from them, they didn't belong in the kingdom. I glanced behind to gloat at them, but they weren't stopping. At a full run, they were pursuing me, quickly eliminating the ground between us. I scrambled through the dirty alleys of Cashel toward the kingdom, my nails ripping at the cobblestone streets as I ran for my life. Their hot, stinking breaths were only seconds behind mine.

It would not be today. It was not my day to die. I was not ending like this—scared and running away. Anger fueled my last desperate steps to the gates.

They must not have realized how close they were to Father's castle. Even if they killed me, his guards would gladly kill them before they ever reached the edge of the city. A smile curled at my wolf lip as I rounded the final corner, skidding slightly.

I leapt through the welcoming gate and shifted to my human form, proud and naked as the day I was born. My hands and feet welcomed the cold stones of the Rock. I straightened from the crouch to stand before my enemies. My hair flowed down my pale skin. I threw a knowing look over my shoulder—they dared not enter here.

At the back of my mind, a question still nagged at me. Was I truly safer inside the kingdom or outside? I pushed my thoughts aside.

Their glowing eyes were all but hidden in the shadows, their growls close to a hiss. I knew the guard would quiet their chatter and chase them from the city. I gave them a throaty laugh and flashed a crooked smile as I dashed down the stone stairs to the entrance of the underground kingdom.

I didn't care how they were to be punished . . . I was more concerned with Father's retribution for my escape.

As I entered the main halls of the castle, I could hear yelling. It echoed off the walls with a thunderous roar, but the stone echo made it impossible to make out what was being said. I heard my father's voice, the heavy alpha weighed down my mind. He was still angry. I wondered if he had discovered me missing. Mund was probably trying to cover my tracks. The only time he ever disobeyed Father was for me. I had to know what was going on. With all the yelling, they would never hear me enter.

I knew I had to hurry to get to Mother and Mund, but I had to get dressed first. I giggled, turning into a side room through a small stone archway. I saw the red coals of the fire in the hearth still burned from supper the night before. Our great Boru family painting hung above the eight-foot-wide mantel, proclaiming our family's domain over the kingdom. I was only about three years old, but I remembered it. They couldn't convince me to shift into human form, I loved my four legs. So there in the family painting of perfection: my beautiful mother in all her glory; my powerful and proud father; my four strong brothers all dressed in their finest clothes, jewels, weapons, and adornments; and one tiny red wolf pup in the foreground, ruining the tranquility of the portrait.

I looked like the family pet. I shook my head at the memory.

At the end of the long, thin room was our travel chests. Centuries old, the chests were decorated with jewels of every variety from all over the world. Oddly, their beauty was nothing compared to what was inside each of them. Quickly I opened mine, revealing many family heirlooms and jewels.

My things, gifts from my family over my sixteen years. All priceless pieces of history. A rose-gold, leaf-shaped wrap-ring covered in tiny glimmering diamonds stood out among the large gems and jewels. Mund had given it to me for my sixteenth birthday. He had been so proud; he knew I would love it. It sat next to Brychan's ring that signified his claim to me—the symbol of my doom, in one gaudy ring, waiting to smother the life and breath from my body and soul.

I lifted off the top shelf of jewels and carelessly set it to the side to access the clothes below. There in the bottom of the chest were all the appropriate choices of gowns—beautiful greens, ruby reds, and cream silks—all gowns of importance, all picked out by Mother. The appropriate attire for a lady of royalty, but I had hidden several leather outfits below all the stuffy gowns. I put on similar handmade leather boots and a simple short leather wrap skirt with rough-cut edges and metal peg closures on my left hip. I tied a piece of soft leather around my chest, creating a strapless top from the supple fabric. And as a final adornment, I wrapped my right wrist with extra leather laces in shades of brown and black, creating a cuff. Now all I had to do was sneak into the throne room and find out what Father's new strategy for punishing me would be.

4
Animal Kingdom

"*Redmund!*" I heard my father bellow, his thunderous voice vibrating in my ears and cutting through all the clutter in my mind. I needed to get to Mund and Mother. I wasn't a child anymore, and this time I would protect them. I slammed the trunk closed and broke into an easy sprint, winding through the halls, into the labyrinth.

The long, twisted passages would get the best tracker lost. Certainly no enemy would ever get to the center—alive, that is. The darkness was welcoming; the candlelight barely kept me on the path. But even though I had never been to the center, I knew the way. It was in my blood, I was born to find it. As I grew near, I could hear the collective breathing of the council as the argument continued.

I came to a halt and walked slowly to the giant doors created by our ancestors from the wood of the ships they sailed during the ninth century, hand-carved with grotesque wolves to scare the strongest of opponents. Honestly, they even intimidated me. I barely noticed the guards on each side of the door; they were like pieces of furniture—always there, always silent, barely moving, and they didn't even look at me.

I had never seen the throne room or met all the packs. I barely even knew my own father. I nervously gnawed on the inside of my cheek. Part of me wanted to just turn around, run away, and take my chances with Adomnan.

I paused, calming my breathing. Still staring straight ahead, I nodded once to the guards, and the doors opened with a creaking welcome to the throne room. The most elegant and oldest room in the kingdom, I had heard of its splendor, but seeing it for the first time took my breath away. Every stone was hand-cut and engraved with the runes of our people. They told the tales of Old Mother's protectors. The engraved stones went stories and stories up, all the way to the high ceiling and yet far beneath the earth's surface.

Calista's sarcophagus was at the center of this underground tomb, surrounded by silk drapes hung from the high ceilings. The smell of frankincense filled the air. Every thought and detail of an ancient culture was still alive and pulsing down here, unlike the tourist-filled streets above.

The council filled the room, but with all the yelling, no one heard me enter. I'd never met any of them before, but I knew the tales Mund had told me. The Swiss Kingerys were easy to spot with their golden spun hair. The Spanish Costas had dark hair and bronze skin. The Welsh Kahedins, Tegan and Brychan's family, had a dark hair and olive skin. Like warriors, the Canadian Four-Claws had long dreadlocks with feathers woven in their hair. Mother's family, the Vanirs, were the most beautiful of all; most had the golden skin of the Greek, but Mother was porcelain. The African Syllas were taller than most everyone in the room, and their clothing was closer to mine than that of the royal Kahedins.

I slowly walked the endless length of the room with my head held high. I wasn't going to cower from Father anymore. Father stood in front of the Boru throne. Carved from wood, the armrests were two ferocious life-size wolves. The vein in Father's large forehead looked as though it might burst. He looked old today, much older than he had seemed before.

"You have no right to voice your opinion here! You must serve the king's rule," my eldest brother, Flin, screamed in Mund's face.

"Flin, you're a bloody fool," Mund said.

The room was filled with hushed whispers from the council.

"If it weren't for you intervening, we would all be safe," Flin said.

"You should be ashamed of yourself!"

"Silence!" Father said. He turned away from them and sat in the mighty throne. "I will decide."

As I walked past the Four-Claws, the feathered woman turned and watched me, but I didn't dare look at her. I was nervous, but I couldn't let any of them know it. One by one, I could feel their stares burning into my skin.

"You don't know anything about her or what's best for her," Mund said.

My pulse pounded and my mouth was as dry as the desert. As strong as I wanted to appear, I was suddenly terrified.

"You still have to learn your place, Redmund," Father said.

"I know my place," Mund said.

Quinn was quiet, but he stood proudly next to Mund. His light-blue eyes stared at the floor, and his furrowed brow clearly gave away his disgust in the conversation. The council was eerily quiet, but I could feel their stares. I studied Mund; his dark brown eyes were solid masses of anger, and his jaw was tight and set at an inhuman angle. He had never pushed Father this far. He usually just took his place as the second son. Mund's thin, muscular frame shook with his emotions.

My brothers' wives and young sat in stone silence. Gwyn sat next to Tegan, unflinching to the chaos only feet away. There was almost no resemblance between them, even though they were sisters. I met Gwyn once when she visited with Quinn. I loved her spiky blonde hair; I imagined it was her rebelling. Flin's and Felan's wives were quietly reciting Latin poetry. It was unreal how they could tune out everything around them.

Father lunged out of his seat and struck Mund in the face, the sound thundering through the room. My nervousness twisted into horror as

Mund spat blood on the floor.

"Stop, please!" Mother said, defiantly standing between Mund and Father. Father just grabbed her like a doll and threw her out of his way, knocking her to the floor. She wept at his feet, holding her already-swelling cheek.

Rage pulsed through every cell in my body, and I forced my feet to move forward once again. Mund and Quinn stood in front of Mother. "You will not touch her again," Mund threatened.

A deep growl came from Father as he narrowed his eyes at Mund. I dragged in a ragged breath, burning my deprived lungs with the fresh air.

A new scent swirled through my thoughts, briefly distracting me, and my instincts turned my head to see glowing black eyes in the shadows. Definitely wolf. I didn't know his scent, and I couldn't see his face, but he watched me.

My mother let out a cry when she saw me, and I rushed into her arms. I felt her pain as if it were my own pain to bear, and it filled my soul with the deepest sadness. I almost looked away, afraid to see her so vulnerable, but her mournful eyes held mine. The burning ache in my throat stopped me from speaking.

She wrapped her arms around me, holding me so close, I felt as though I were becoming a part of her. I closed my eyes as I breathed in her beautiful scent—fresh rain and lavender. I always loved the way she smelled and the warmth of her arms. I wanted to avenge her, but she didn't release me.

"She endangers us all," Flin said, pointing down at me. It felt like a death sentence.

"It can't be the only way," Mund said.

"She must leave," Flin replied.

"Do you want to sacrifice her to a fate worse than death? They know she lives," Father said. "She can't stay here."

My mind was whirling around in all the confusion. Death. Sacrifice. I was grasping to understand, but I didn't understand at all. Was this because of Adomnan? Was I being punished for being outside the walls?

"She endangers everything we've spent centuries building," Felan said.

"We have to protect her from herself," Flin said.

"She's just a child," Quinn replied.

"If they capture her, we will all die," Father said.

My mind was thick and heavy. I demanded to know what was happening, but no words came out. My mother's arms wrapped around me tighter, as though she had heard my cry.

"You can't send her away," Mother said.

"She goes," he said, looking at me for the first time, "to save us all."

Looking into my eyes, Mother said, "*Tha gaol agam ort.*"

"I love you too," I whispered.

Mother slid a ring on my finger, but I couldn't concentrate on it. I was too distracted by the chaos around me. Everything was happening so fast. Father ripped Mother away from me.

"Get your hands off her," I said forcefully. My voice was icy.

He looked surprised by me, but I didn't care and I didn't have time to think. He was tearing my family apart. I started advancing on him as one of his guards grabbed me around the waist, knocking the air from my lungs. He dragged me farther away from Mother. I tore at his flesh, kicking and fighting as hard as I could to break free. My anger twisted into adrenaline, and I broke free from his grasp as I lunged back to my mother. Before I could even take a step, a second guard grabbed my throat, nearly choking me. Tears stung my eyes. I saw my mother slipping away from me. I felt as though I couldn't win, but I kept trying.

Out of nowhere, the black-eyed man from the shadows seized me and dragged me onto a motorcycle, holding me tightly in front of him. I screamed as loud as I could for Mund, but I couldn't see him anywhere. Everyone's eyes were on me as they watched my life being torn apart, but they didn't try to help me, they only watched. I tried to free myself, but I was held firmly in place. His motorcycle roared to life.

"You have betrayed me," Mother screamed at my father.

Her words broke Father's hardened face as he looked at me. I felt as though he was seeing me for the first time, seeing my tear-stained face and wild hair.

"It is done," he said. My heart sank with his words. I was nothing to him.

Mund ran to my side and placed something in my hands, but I was too numb to care. "I *will* come for you, I promise."

"You know where to find me," the man said to Mund.

Suddenly we were driving through a doorway I hadn't seen before, winding through catacombs in a sea of darkness, driving so fast that I couldn't comprehend what direction we were traveling. The light from the bike only cast a few feet ahead of us, making the tunnel seemed endless.

I welcomed the stillness of the dark as I would welcome death. We broke into the moonlight on a dirt road far from the city limits, followed only by a cloud of dust.

I cried to the moon, but the stranger said nothing. I sobbed so hard, he had to hold me on the bike. I shivered in the cold wind that whipped me with my wet hair, stinging my face. The rain began to fall. My tears danced with the raindrops in a grave melody.

The bike slowed to a stop. There was nothing around and no scents of life. This was where I would die. His boot hit the ground with a thud, grinding the dirt and rock to nothing. He was off the bike before I even realized he had moved. A silver blade hung at his hip. His gloved hand protected him from the poison as he wrapped his fingers around the handle, staring down at me. I squeezed my eyes shut, hoping my death would be quick and merciful. When the blow didn't come, I peeked at his hard, black eyes; they were filled with uncertainty.

I waited a long time, but he didn't hurt me. Instead, he handed me his leather jacket without a word. I slipped on his warm coat, and my body stopped convulsing from the cold. My tiny frame nearly drowned in his coat, but I didn't mind. I couldn't help but breathe in his scent of musky earth, wood, and gasoline.

"I'm not going to hurt you, child," he said.

He was much older than I, closer to Father's age, but much taller and thinner. As frightening as I thought Father was, this stranger was even more so. His long black-and-silver hair was soaking wet to his shoulders, and his black T-shirt was getting drenched, but he didn't seem to notice the cold. He slid me to the back of the seat, and we sped off.

We drove in silence. I was thankful for the warmth of his jacket, but I didn't trust him. I still had no idea where we were or where we were going, but I let the rhythm of the bike soothe my mind as I watched the world whip by. There was nothing but the ocean and grass as far as I could see, and the occasional outcrop of limestone and cattle pastures.

I allowed my mind to let go and just be there. I would have to bury the pain deep to forget, if I were to survive this. I knew someday I would have to deal with these feelings, but right now, I was content burying them. My mind and body were numb.

5

Broken

We entered a small coastal village on the eastern side of Ireland.
It was more rustic than modern in appearance—livestock-filled streets
were a way of life here. It reminded me of home, and I hoped he would
leave me here. I could live among these quiet people, protect their village,
and find my purpose. The bike slowly crept down the dirt streets, the
livestock scattering out of the way and turning to look at us.

A small Irish man with wide-set shoulders and drab hair was staring
at me. I wondered what he was thinking from the vast expressions that
twisted his face. Mostly it looked like concern.

From far away, a deep howl echoed through the sky, but it was close
enough to even make the stranger in front of me sit straighter on the
bike. The eerie sound made the hair on the back of my neck stand on
end—it was Adomnan hunting me.

"Hang on," he said, "they're coming for you." I wrapped my arms
around his body and buried my face into his back. Another howl answered the first call, and the people began to scramble back into their
homes, gathering their children and as many animals as they could. I

smelled their fear, and it called to my soul to protect them.

On the other side of the village, we reached a cliff, and the ocean came into view. The bike leapt forward in a thunderous jolt, and we slid down the side of the cliff toward water. His leg scraped the ground, and he fought to keep control of the bike. The howls were closer now, and I felt my pulse pounding in my ears. I was certain they were already in the village searching for us. The bike ripped up rock in a storm behind us.

"Willem!" he called to a man at a dock. Willem, whomever he was, frantically started untying the ferry and barking out commands to two dockworkers. When I caught his scent on the wind, I was certain he was a wolf too.

We neared the dock, but seven large wolves erased the earth between us. They saw me and howled as the pack closed in on me, their prey. I couldn't tear my eyes away from the fierce rage in Adomnan's green eyes.

"Cast off!"

"Bloody hell, hurry!" Willem said.

The ferry engines gurgled to life, sending bubbles to the murky surface as it started moving farther away from shore. We weren't going to make it in time. I was frozen stiff with fear and adrenaline.

"Let them take me," I said. "Save yourself."

I hung my head with acceptance of what was to become of me, but I made the right decision. No one should die for me; he owed me nothing.

He laughed so hard, he shook the bike and me with it. He caught me by surprise; I didn't even know what to say. Was he straight-up crazy? Just what I needed—to be traded by my own father to an insane old man to save me from Adomnan. I wasn't certain whom of the three I trusted more.

"I don't give up that easily," he replied.

The ferry was at least fifty feet out in the water now. Willem looked as panicked as I felt. The two humans with him were revving the engine. What was my captor thinking? This was insanity. We would hit the water and drown or have to swim back to shore to them. I shuddered at the thought. Both options seemed rather bleak to me.

"Please—don't die for me."

He laughed again. "I don't plan to," he said.

He hit the throttle, and we sped down the wooden dock toward the water. We drove up a ramp and soared into the air. We floated between earth and sky for what seemed like an eternity. The wolves howled and pawed the dock just moments behind us as we barely landed on the ferry, cracking the boards under the bike's weight. We slid across the deck, and I lost my grip, slipping off the bike, cracking my arm into the metal rail. I cried out in pain as the bike came to a stop. The pain vibrated through my bones. He was next to me in a moment, looking at my arm, mumbling again. I couldn't make out a bloody thing he said.

The humans were stunned with fear staring at us, but they quickly resumed their work. I watched the wolves as they grew smaller in the distance. This was the second time I had gotten away from Adomnan. The pain from my arm blurred my vision, and my head was spinning. If I shifted, it would heal in minutes, but there were humans on board, so I would just have to endure the pain.

I looked at the strange man before me. His Bloodmark was a four-point Celtic shield burned into the flesh of his wrists. The blood-red color was unmistakable. He was thin, but obviously strong. He was good looking for his age. His dark jeans were ripped, and there were cuts on his legs. I stared into his black eyes, hoping to find some truth there.

He placed his hand under my arm and pulled me to my feet. He stood there watching me. It was more than I could endure. I felt overwhelmingly self-conscious, and I blushed as the rain cascaded down on us.

"Thanks for the coat," I said.

He just kept staring at me as if he were waiting for me to transform into a leprechaun. I hated the silence.

"Who are you?" I said.

"Baran," he replied. He smiled and walked away.

That was it? That was all he was going to say? One word? What the heck was wrong with him? Definitely crazy, I decided. But I wasn't going to stand for this. I was going to get some damn answers.

I marched right up to him, ready for a fight, but he turned on his heel just as I approached, and I nearly walked right into his chest. He smiled again, looking down at me.

"Come have a seat out of the wind," he said, gesturing toward the covey behind the captain's area. "I'll be right back."

He walked away to the motorcycle, picking something up. Returning, he sat down, crossing his long legs out in front of him. "Or stand if you prefer," he said.

I was still standing. Feeling quite dumb, I sat down, leaving plenty of space between us. However, this decision did leave me in the wind and rain, drenching me, but what little was left of my pride wouldn't allow me to move any closer.

He shook his head. "My name is Baran Killian. I am a very old friend of your mother's. I was born to the Killian pack of Scotland, but the Killians were exterminated in the seventeenth century. My nephew, Willem, and I are the last of our pack."

He was quiet, lost in thought. I knew the legends of the Killian pack. They used to be one of the most powerful royal packs, but I had never heard of Baran. Why hadn't anyone spoken of him before if he was a trusted ally?

"Your father has bestowed you as my ward."

"To take me where?"

"I can't tell you just yet," he said, nodding toward the humans who were obviously trying to listen. They were suspicious of us but didn't ask questions. "It's not safe. But I vow to protect you."

I sighed and studied my hands. The dark shape on my right ring finger caught my attention and stopped my fidgeting. I remembered Mother putting it on my finger. I recognized it immediately—intricate Celtic knots carved by Ragnall Boru for his betrothed, Calista. It had slightly tarnished with age, and as long as I could remember, it had had a place on Mother's hand. A wave of sadness rolled through me, and I wept as I studied the ring both Calista and my mother had worn.

Baran wrapped his long arm around my shoulders, pulling me to him, out of the rain. I buried my face in his chest and cried. "There now, child, it will be all right," he said. His tender response only made me sob harder. I hadn't expected this rough-looking man to give me any comfort, and I showed him all my weakness. I didn't know how to deal with my feelings; I just felt broken. "The worst is over now."

"I don't feel I am strong enough to survive."

"You're stronger than you know. The legends speak to this."

"What legends?"

He placed the hand-stitched leather book Mund had given me in my hands. It felt at home in my fingers, as if it had been there every day of my life, though Mund had just given it to me at the Rock.

"Once you've read this, ask me again," he said and stood up. "I have to speak with Willem. We'll talk more soon." With that, he walked away.

I studied the book; it had the most beautiful handwriting, but most of it was in ancient Greek. It would take me months to translate. My answers were hidden in a language I didn't speak. It was frustrating. As I paged through, I noticed I could read the parts written in Old Mother's language, the language of the Bloodmoon. Old Mother's language was the one thing Mund was adamant I learn, and this book would tell me why.

I was cold, soaking wet, and irritated with everyone. Instead of spending years teaching me the language of the Bloodmoon, Mund could have saved us both time and just told me what this stupid book said. Everyone was always trying to protect me from something, but making me ignorant didn't protect me from anything. I curled up into a ball, hugging my knees to my chest, and closed my eyes, hoping I would wake to find it had all been a bad dream.

With the ferry bobbing on the rough waters and the fear that still pulsed through my veins, my mind didn't allow me to rest, but soon we were on land. I slowly sat up and looked around. I saw Willem first, standing at the dock, writing something down for a portly, bald man. They continued to converse quietly.

Willem turned to me. "Ahhh, you're finally awake," he said.

My stomach did all the talking with a loud grumble. He smiled and tossed me a heavy package. "Eat up. Baran will be back shortly."

I hastily unwrapped the butcher paper and started shoving the meat in my mouth, not even tasting it. I think it was dried venison, but I was too hungry to care. There was a constant aching pain in my heart that the meat wouldn't ease. Willem stood before me, and he put his palms to my cheeks.

"That is the saddest face I've ever beheld. You could break the very heart of me."

"Thank you," I said, smiling a little before shoving the last piece of meat in my mouth.

"Any time," he said with a wink.

The loud thud of footsteps drew my attention back to the dock. Baran had changed his clothes. He was fresh and clean again but rugged all the same. He carried a black plastic bag, and he smiled when he saw me.

"We're in Queensborough, outside London," he said, handing the bag to me.

I peeked inside. It was a black leather motorcycle jacket with a mandarin collar and crisscross stitching over the sleeves. It was simple but elegant. I took off his jacket and slipped on the new one. It fit perfectly. I smiled at him.

He looked embarrassed suddenly. "I wanted mine back," he said. I almost laughed, but I handed him his jacket. "It's time for us to go. Take care, Willem. Give my love to Khepri, and I'll contact you when we're safe."

Willem nodded, and if I knew him better, I would have said he was sad to see us go. Baran ushered me to a waiting cab.

"Heathrow Airport," Baran said to the cabdriver.

As we drove away, I looked back for Willem, but he was already gone, probably on his way back to Scotland. It must hurt them to be apart, as it had always left a hole in my soul being away from my family. We were pack animals, and living a solitary life was against our ways. We were meant to be one with each other.

I was too distracted to notice the drive as we arrived at the airport. I stood on the sidewalk, waiting for Adomnan to come for me. I smelled the air, but I didn't smell anything out of the ordinary, beyond Baran and I. We were the only animals here.

He rushed me into the airport with smooth, long strides. I almost had to run to keep up with his pace. He knew his way through the airport with ease, and he had all the proper paperwork for me. I just followed him like a lost puppy. If he moved, I moved. We drew the attention of the humans, but trying to be discreet wasn't really an option for the two of us.

Once seated in first-class on the airplane headed for New York City, away from everyone's questioning and judging eyes, I finally thought to ask, "Why are we going to New York?"

"We land in New York. Then we will get my bike and drive to my home." He studied my face for a moment and corrected, "I mean, our home."

I tried to smile, but there was nothing left. I felt empty or too full of emotions I didn't know how to deal with. He took my hand in his.

"You will be posing as my niece. You lost your parents, and I'm now your guardian. You will start your junior year in high school in a little over a month. You'll have to try to fit in."

I turned away from him, looking out the window into the foggy unknown. I didn't know how to fit in. My cheeks turned red, and my vision blurred with tears. I didn't want to let him see me cry again. I wasn't a child anymore.

I heard the flight attendant stop bustling about and lean over to me. "Are you well, dear? Can I get you anything?" I tried to smile at her and shook my head.

Her voice was saturated with empathy. I wondered if Baran could hear that in her voice as plainly as I could. If he did, he gave no indication. "She's lost her parents, but she'll be fine. Thank you for asking," he said. "I'll take a water, please."

She handed a short plastic cup of ice water to Baran and touched my shoulder. "Oh darlin', you just let me know if there is anything I can do to help you two," she said. With that, she finally wandered away.

I wished it were easy to leave everything behind. How could I tell my brain to stop hanging on to my heart and to just let it go? I should have been excited for my first flight, but I couldn't feel anything as I watched the city disappear under the clouds. I was too angry, scared, and lonely.

6

Lost

The ten-hour flight went by so fast, I didn't have time to collect myself or my thoughts. But I knew I had to gain a little self-control. The captain interrupted my self-indulgent thoughts, asking everyone to take their seats and buckle up as the plane prepared to land in New York. "'Bout time," Baran said. "I'll get you home real soon, safe and sound."

It sounded too good to be true. It was only a matter of time before the tiny bit of reserve I had broke and there would be nothing left for him to protect but a pile of blubbering tears. I had to hold it together, or this whole battle would be for nothing.

He wrapped his arm around my shoulders, and his strength almost gave me strength, but not enough. We walked through the crowded airport, and there were blurry faces all around us, empty space where their faces should have been. It was like walking through a sea of soulless people. Were they soulless, or was I? I wanted to be home by the sea. I wanted to be with my mother. Everything I knew was gone, and everything I had was taken away. Everything had somehow changed, and I still didn't understand why.

We exited the airport into the rain. I looked up into the sky and let it wash my tear-stained face and calm my mind. I started spinning around, letting it wash over me—cleansing my soul, setting me free.

Baran's motorcycle waited for us outside. I studied the black Harley. I had to admit that his bike made a statement no one would dare argue with. It had a presence like he did. We left the brightly lit, concrete city behind on our five-hour drive to the coast of Maine. We drove on the blackened roads of a foreign land. We passed cities, farms, and the great wide open. If it hadn't been for the crisp wind in my face, I might have believed this was all an illusion, but the trip was over quickly in comparison to the last few days. We arrived in the small coastal town of York Harbor after dark. We parked in front of a historic-looking house with an open porch and a widow's walk on the roof. The house loomed over us as we walked inside.

His house was immaculately clean but cluttered with books. I felt strangely comfortable surrounded by his things. "This is home," he said. "Your room is this way."

He showed me to a closet door in the center of the house, just off the kitchen. He pulled a silver handle that opened up a hidden doorway to a wrought-iron spiral staircase. I gulped down my fear as I followed him. At the top of the stairs was a small bedroom and bathroom. A bay-window seat was on one end of the room and the bathroom on the other. It was a little creepy, but it felt safe. Only a bare bed and a five-drawer dresser were in the room.

"I'll get you some bedding."

I took a seat in the window, resting my face on the cool glass, watching the nocturnal animals as they scurried about their evening business. I didn't look up when I heard him enter. I was too bitter about my situation to care what he wanted. Baran set sheets and a large comforter on the bed.

"I'll see you in the morning," he said. I heard his footsteps as he descended the stairs. I was wary of my new home, but the tiniest part of me was excited. Maybe I could build a life here. I grabbed the black comforter and wrapped it around my body and sat back down.

I was so angry with everyone. Why didn't Mother fight harder, why did she let Baran take me? Had she finally given up? Even Mund let this happen. I could expect as much from Father, but it hurt to think Mund and Mother would allow this. Maybe it was time for me to learn to be on my own. I had yearned for freedom and adventure my whole life, and here it was in front of me, waiting for me to grasp it. I just had to have the courage to do it.

The next morning, I studied the room by the light of day. It wasn't a bad room; boring, but private. I yawned, taking in a deep breath. I hadn't showered in days, unless the rainstorm counted. I hopped in the cast-iron tub to take a shower. The warm water felt good on my dirty skin.

I was finally clean, and the idea of putting dirty clothes back on was out of the question. I wrapped myself in a giant towel and ventured, the metal stairs frigid under my bare feet. I found a plate of cooked bacon in the kitchen and snagged a piece of the salty meat, surprised to find I liked it. I searched for Baran, wandering through the living room; the room was as clean as the others and utterly masculine. The smell of burned wood was prominent from the fireplace. A large bookcase was filled with books that poured out of the full shelves to the floor. The coffee table was cluttered with papers, a few open books, and a pair of boots.

I continued from the living room down a long hallway, and I entered the office with four walls of solid bookcases. The books in here appeared to be much older, like books from Father's library. Some were stacked haphazardly, barely on the shelves at all. A large wooden desk sat in the center of the room, and it was covered in stacks upon stacks of books and scrolls. Behind it was a stately chair, almost throne-like. There was a stack of old tapestries and Turkish rugs in the side of the room. I glanced across the hall to the bathroom. It looked uninhabited.

I continued down the dark hall past two stark, empty rooms, opening the last door to a large dark bedroom. His room was like a well-organized antique store. It must have contained his family's most-prized possessions. His large four-post bed was unmade, his black sheets hanging off onto the floor. Even more books were stacked all over the bed and floor. I wondered what answer he was searching for.

I dug through a stack of pants in his closet until I chose a pair of tan canvas work pants and slipped them on. They rode low on my small hips and were a foot too long, but they would have to do. I saw an open drawer of white T-shirts and slipped one over my head, tying it at my waist.

I walked back to the kitchen for more bacon and took a seat at the table. There wasn't a single photo displayed in the entire house. It was unnerving, as if he had something to hide. I had met his nephew Willem—why were there no photos of Willem and his wife?

I glanced out the window to see a blue four-door sedan. It didn't seem like something Baran would drive, but then whose car was it? I turned around to the sound of the front door opening. A blonde woman with big blue eyes watched me from the doorway. She was short with cute freckles all over her round face and little nose. Her hair was cut short to her chin. She looked young, but her eyes gave her away. She was much more mature in life and age than her round face alluded to.

She smelled good, almost savory. My mouth watered at the thought. I had never tasted a human before—I knew our purpose was to protect them—but their scents tempted even the strongest of our kind. The woman studied me as I did her. I felt self-conscious of my appearance and began to fidget with my shirt.

Her pink baby-doll shirt offset her light-blue jeans that crinkled as she set her purse down on the entry table. "Good morning, dear. I'm Claire. I work with your uncle at his shop."

What shop, I wondered. I didn't know what Baran did to pose as human. She took a few steps toward me, extending her hand out in the standard human greeting. Her scent crept back into my nose. I tightened up, standing perfectly still, wide-eyed, trying desperately not to react to her scent. I couldn't think with her scent in my head. I closed my eyes tight, trying to block her from my mind.

Nervously, she giggled, and I heard her take a subconscious step back. I had to get control and respond. She was going to think I was deranged.

It was obvious she was uncomfortable in this odd situation—only she didn't seem to realize why she should be scared of me.

She started to talk very quickly, but it was easy for me to understand her. "Baran asked me to pick you up this morning and take you to the shop to meet up with him. Are you ready to go now, or shall I come back later?" She didn't even wait for my response. "I'm sorry to have bothered you." She started toward the door in a rush.

"No bother," I managed.

She glanced back over her shoulder at me, and I forced a smile. It worked. Her face lit up like sunlight. "Oh good. Baran said you might be sad, with the loss of your parents and all, but here you are smiling and everything. What a trip you must have had."

She babbled the whole way across the small town of York Harbor. We passed houses and storefronts and arrived at a large mechanic's shop with an immaculate showroom. Everything in York Harbor was so different from my home at the cliffs. The chatter had quieted; Claire must have asked me a question, but I wasn't listening—I was concentrating on not killing her. I looked over at her, and her car door was open. She seemed to be waiting for me to get out. I jumped from the car and followed her to the second open stall, where a custom-built matte-black motorcycle sat getting new tires.

Baran knelt, loosening a bolt with a lot of grunting, but it was all for show. I knew he could easily lift the bike with one hand and toss it across the street if he had wanted. He looked up at me and answered Claire. "Claire, thank you for bringing Ashling. I'd like a word with her."

"Sure thing," she said, and she darted away like a rabbit into the building. Though we were meant to protect them, she sparked my predator instinct to chase. Baran was studying me when I finally brought my attention from the scent of Claire's blood to him.

"Nice clothes."

I felt my face turn as red as my hair. "Sorry. I didn't have anything to wear. I hope you don't mind?" I kept my eyes on the floor, suddenly embarrassed to be dressed like this. I wanted his acceptance, and I didn't know how he would react to me rifling through his things.

He laughed, filling the tall ceilings with his thunderous sound. "Had I known I'd be bringing you back with me, I'd have prepared better for you," he said, still chuckling at my expense. His tone turned serious. "Claire is a test for you. You're doing well, but you need to do better. I can see it in your eyes. You need to hide your desire, bury it deep. Don't let me down." He paused, studying my face. I didn't dare meet his eyes. I was ashamed to be reacting to Claire's scent so deeply. I knew the forsaken wolf packs ate humans, but all other packs ate livestock. I preferred wild game myself—the hunt was so much more rewarding. "Well, you can't run around in my clothes forever. So I've asked Claire to take you shopping for whatever you need to be comfortable here."

Despite my anxiety, I smiled at him. "I *forgot* to bring any money while I packed for the trip."

He snorted out a laugh; at least he appreciated my sarcasm. "Oh, I have that covered." He handed me a wad of American money. It was so colorless in comparison to most of the world's money, but the texture was almost like cloth in my fingers. "This should get you started. Please return Claire to me in the same condition I'm lending her to you." He closed my hand around the money with a smirk and went back to grunting on the bolt.

I followed Claire's scent into the main building and found her barely able to sit still. She rushed over to my side, grabbing up my hands and dragging me out the door and back to her car.

"Just think, Ashling—shopping on work time and a makeover too!"

"Makeover?"

"Oh sure, honey. Baran said to help you with all the lady essentials. So I thought we'd go to the spa first. Hair, mani, pedi, makeup, then hit the mall. He said you needed some things for your room too. And then who knows where the wind may blow us."

"What's a mani and pedi?"

"Oh heavens!" she said. "You've never had a manicure and pedicure? Honey. It's a good thing you have me."

Her energy made my skin twitch. The day was a horrifying blur. After several hours of what I gathered to be the ritual sacrifices of the American woman, I was starving, but she didn't returned me to Baran until dusk. I had to have had at least a dozen shopping bags of clothes, shoes, and makeup. I did sneak into a bookstore when she was distracted and picked up a few of my favorite classics.

My hair was shaped into ringlets of red curls but still wild. I had makeup on my face. I wore a short denim jacket over a paisley-printed, knee-length, flowing dress and tall, dark-brown boots. I could feel Baran's steel gaze as he looked at me.

"You look nice, Ashling," he said. "But the boots? I'm not sure they're appropriate for a girl of your age."

"What don't you like?"

He glanced at Claire, who gave him a dirty look, and he started back-pedaling. "No, no . . . you look . . . "

"Beautiful," a broodingly handsome young man said as he stepped around the motorcycle. I hadn't seen him there. His shaggy dark hair was unkempt around his chiseled face, and his sideburns grew long down his cheeks, perfectly shaped into points, making him look dangerous, even wolf-like. His almost-eerie green eyes were piercing . . . and they made no effort to conceal his surveillance of my body. His smile was an interesting mix of sweetness and temptation. I wanted to reach out and touch his lips and run my fingers over his sweet flesh. I couldn't explain it, but I wanted to be near him.

His obviously fit body was covered in a black long-sleeved T-shirt, spread tightly over his chest. The sleeves were pulled up to reveal tattoos on the undersides of his wrists, but I couldn't make them out. The tattoo on his left wrist was partially covered by a brown leather cuff.

I was surprised to find myself desperately intrigued by him, from his dark denim jeans to his black cowboy boots. He was ruggedly handsome. His scent was hard to detect with all the oil and exhaust. I felt my face flush from his insistent gaze. He walked up to me, wiping his hands off on a shop rag, tossing it nonchalantly into a bin as he passed. He reached out his hand and claimed mine in his big, warm hands, bringing it up to his lips as he kissed the top of my hand. My heart was beating so loud, I was certain he would be able to hear it, but he didn't seem to notice. He looked up at me over the top of my hand. His eyes were a daring invitation I was willing to accept.

"What's your name?" he asked, still holding my hand, drawing my devoted attention.

I straightened myself up. "Ashling," I replied.

"Ashling. That's an unusual name. But seems right for a vision like you."

"That's enough, Grey," Baran said.

Grey snuck a mischievous glance at me. "Is it?" he said before winking and letting my hand go. It was instantly cold, and I missed his warmth. "How about you climb on the back of my bike, and I'll take you for a ride?" He gestured toward its sleek frame.

Baran swiftly closed the distance and stepped between us. "Beat it, kid. Before I kick you to the curb."

"Don't ruffle yourself, Baran." He turned to me again. "She'll be safe with me," he said, offering me his hand again around Baran's body. I giggled despite my best judgment, and Baran grabbed the back of Grey's shirt, spinning him around toward the bike.

"We're closing up, Grey. You're done working for the day, you better get home."

"All right. I'm out," he said. He kicked the bike to life, and a thunderous rumble echoed in the garage, but it was nothing compared to the beating of my heart. "I'll be seeing you." He drove off, leaving us in an awkward quiet. I was afraid to speak, for what might come out of my mouth. I rubbed my fingers over the spot his soft lips had touched my skin, longing for him to return.

Baran was grumbling around me as he collected all my bags and put them in his pewter Land Rover. He closed the last stall, locking up. "Thanks again, Claire. See you tomorrow."

"Glad to help you any way I can," she said. "It was so very nice to meet you, Ashling, dear."

"You too, Claire." I smiled. And with a wave of her acrylic nails, she drove off.

"You getting in?" Baran asked.

"Sure," I said and climbed into the Land Rover. The ride home was silent, except for the grumbles from Baran's side of the vehicle. I wondered if he typically liked Grey. More importantly, what was he? Grey seemed more animal than human. He wasn't a wolf, but I couldn't get his scent. It was masked by the gasoline.

I had never seen anyone like him. I reacted to him in a way I had never felt before. I felt as though I was encountering a lost piece of myself when I was in his presence. I wanted to . . . well, a lot of things that I wanted to do had crossed my mind in those short seconds. I blushed at the thought. I wondered if I would see him again. I was sure he felt it too. Or maybe he was just getting on Baran's nerves and it had nothing to do with me.

We pulled into the garage at Baran's house. Unsurprisingly, it was filled with collector cars. In the far corner of the garage was a tarp-covered motorcycle. I found myself wondering why it was tucked away like a secret.

Baran carried my stuff up to my room, and the sea of bags exploded all around the small space. As I began to unpack my new treasures, I realized I had forgotten to buy hangers. That would be a project for tomorrow. Tonight, all I wanted to do was think of Grey.

The smells of tomatoes, spices, and cheese began to waft upstairs, interrupting my thoughts. I followed my nose downstairs to find a pizza on the kitchen table. I had never tasted pizza. I had seen it and even smelled it, but it was never something we ate.

"Time to eat," Baran said.

"You eat this?" I said.

"Yes. And you need to learn to eat it too. You can't just go running around killing livestock and wild game whenever you're hungry. And you certainly can't eat humans."

"I don't make a habit of eating humans, for the record," I said, taking a slice of the cheese-smothered pizza. I quietly devoured it, despite its less-than-appealing flavor.

"Ashling, there are a few rules," he said as he sat back and crossed his arms over his chest. "We have to protect ourselves. I've spent many years establishing myself here, and we're lucky the humans don't suspect what we are."

"Why are you living here? Why didn't you stay in Scotland with Willem?"

"The Killians lost their lands long ago, so I followed my sister here, and I grew attached to *some* of the humans here and stayed to protect them."

"But . . . they aren't yours to protect. Shouldn't you be in Scotland protecting your humans?"

The way he stared at me made me uncomfortable. I wanted to look away from his penetrating gaze, but I couldn't. "All humans are ours to protect; it doesn't matter if they come from our lands or they are strangers to us. It is our duty to Old Mother."

I sighed and stared out the window.

"It is important that you understand we're in hiding. For your safety. You can't draw attention to our primal ways."

"Yes, sir." I rolled my eyes. I was so tired of being told what to do and talked down to like a child.

"That means no hunting humans. Period. It's unnatural and against our vows to Old Mother Earth."

"But I don't!"

"No livestock or wild game."

"What?" I said.

"And no shifting under any circumstances, no running, and we have to eat like humans all the time while you're here. No excuses for any of them to notice us. There can be no wolf tracks in the woods, either. The game warden tags and tracks the wolf population here. We have to be careful not to disrupt their balance. The humans are delicate creatures."

I couldn't believe what he was saying. Without my wolf form, I was mortal. I would start aging as a human if I didn't change with each full moon. My pulse pounded, and the hair on my arms stood on end.

"I know it's going to be hard for you. But what we don't need is the game warden all in an uproar about wolf sightings. Or the disappearance of livestock—or worse yet, missing people in the paper."

"I don't eat humans!" I was enraged at his refusal to hear me. I didn't hurt humans. I didn't understand them, but I would never hurt them—I could feel Old Mother's love for them. His insistence that I could be a potential danger to them was nothing but insulting.

"And another thing—steer clear of Grey Donavan."

"So I'm a prisoner? I can't go anywhere. I can't shift. I can't eat. And now I can't even have friends, even though I'm supposed to be blending in? Is there anything else I can't do, master?" My icy voice dripped with sarcasm as my emotions boiled to the surface.

"I didn't say you couldn't have friends, just not him."

"I can pick my own friends, thanks."

He abruptly stood, sending his chair flying back. I flinched away from his movements as he yelled down at me. "Damn it, Ashling, I've made my decision on this. You will not go hanging around that boy. Do you understand me? This is for your own good."

"I've heard those words a lot in my life," I said, silently adding Baran to the list of people I hated.

"You will listen to me," he said.

"You're worse than my own father," I said, turning my back on him. The insult was meant to cut him, but I didn't stay to find out. I went up to my room, leaving him to yell at himself. Who did he think he was, ordering me around like a prisoner? It was as if he locked me away in a tower and there I was to stay. His little pet. If I were such a detested creature, why did he take me in? I could survive on my own. I didn't need my father, and I certainly didn't need him.

I plopped down on the edge of my bed among the explosion of my new clothes. I picked up the ancient journal from Mund and studied its weathered appearance. How could this old thing answer any of my questions? Had everyone gone stark raving mad? It was in ancient Greek and the language of the Bloodmoon. How could it have anything to do with me? I tossed the journal to the corner of the room with spite.

7
Sightings

The next morning, with nothing better to do, I walked across town to Baran's shop. I didn't want to see him, but I didn't know what else to do, and boredom won. It was about a fifteen-minute walk in the brisk, coastal air. I knew now why Baran liked it here—it reminded me of home in Ireland, and I supposed it reminded him of Scotland as well.

As I approached his shop, I decided to ignore him, and I snuck in to chat with Claire. I enjoyed her endless chatter. I saw her talking to a customer, so I took a seat on the purple sofa in her office. Everything that wasn't nailed down was purple. The chair cover, picture frames, cell phone, desk calendar—the woman liked purple in an unnatural way.

Picking up the fuzzy picture frame, I saw Claire smiling back at me with her arm wrapped around a teenage girl with wavy brown hair and olive skin, but she had the same freckled nose and big blue eyes. I leaned forward and put it back.

"And who are you?" a sharp female voice said.

The same girl from the photo stood in front of me. She smelled a lot like Claire, but not as tempting, which was good, considering the small space she trapped me in. Her eyes were even bigger in person. She was almost odd looking with her strong features and thin nose, but it made her pretty. She was wearing a light-blue plaid flannel shirt tied at her waist with blue jeans. Her thin lips were pursed together, waiting impatiently for my reply.

"Ashling Boru," I said. "I'm Baran's niece."

I held out my hand to her, and she laughed, plopping down on the sofa right next to me. "So you're who my mom was babbling about all night," she said, looking me over again, this time without disdain. Finally she smiled back at me, satisfied with her inspection of my blue jeans and black tube top. "I'm Elizabeth Elliot, but you can call me Beth. Claire's my mom."

"Nice to meet you."

"You sound weird. Where are you from?"

"Ireland."

"When did you get here?"

"A few days ago."

"Where are your parents?"

"I lost them," I said.

"Oh, um, I'm sorry. I didn't mean . . ."

"It's okay."

"My dad's gone too," Elizabeth said. We sat in silence as we both reflected on our joint losses. I suppose that was what made her so sharp and strong; loss does that. A lot of Claire came out of her too, like the never-ending questions and chatter.

"Hey, so, I'm running some errands around town today. Do you want to come?" she asked, showing the tiniest bit of self-consciousness under her hardened exterior.

"I'd love to," I replied.

"Great," she said, jumping up. "I'll tell my mom, and we'll be off." She disappeared for a moment and came back smiling. "Let's roll!"

I followed her outside to an old, rusty truck. I was pretty sure the only thing holding the bumper on was the plethora of stickers there. We drove around town, running her errands, and she continued a constant flow of chatter the whole time about her job at the café south of town where she waited tables, her mom, and school. Then we stopped at the park to just hang out.

"Beth, what grade are you in? And how old are you?" I asked.

"I'm sixteen, and I'm in the eleventh grade. I can't wait for it all to be over. How about you?"

"I think Baran mentioned something about being a junior."

"You're a junior too!" She laughed. "I hope we have classes together and lunch too."

"I'd like that."

The rumble of a motorcycle caught my attention. We both looked up to see Grey driving down the street in a black leather race jacket with white stripes on the sleeves. "What do you know about him?" I asked.

"Grey?" she asked.

"Yeah. I met him yesterday, and Baran was clear he didn't want Grey hanging around."

She laughed. "His dad's the game warden—they live about fifteen miles north of town. He's one of those guys who's so smart he's stupid. Like, too smart for his own good, I guess. I think he gets bored, so he gets in trouble for something to do. He's seventeen, and he's in a band. Half the girls in school are in love with him. He's only ever gone out with Lacey, but I heard they broke up again."

"Oh . . ." I replied, trying not to seem as though I cared too much.

"Yeah. He's pretty damn hot, though."

I laughed nervously. "Are you friends with him?"

"Ha! Hardly. I don't think he even knows I exist."

I didn't understand her response, but I just nodded. I couldn't see why they wouldn't be friends, but I had so little experience with anyone other than Mund and Mother that I didn't understand the delicate balance of teenage friendships. "I'm glad we're friends, Beth," I told her.

"Me too. Do you want to hang out on Friday?" she asked.

"That would be great."

"Cool. I'll stop by around seven thirty."

After making a stop to pick up some hangers, Beth dropped me off at Baran's house in the early afternoon. I didn't want to be cooped up in the house, but Beth had to work, and I didn't want to go back to Baran's shop. Still, I hated being confined. I flopped down on the front porch swing, hanging my legs over the edge, letting my shoes slip off and hit the floor. There wasn't anything worth doing in this tiny town.

The wind lightly moved the swing in a smooth and inviting rhythm. I gave in to my buried feelings and let my mind wander to my mother, her beautiful smile—and oh, how I missed the way she smelled and the sound of her laugh. Mund was probably better off without me. He always found himself in trouble because of me. Though I adored him, I was probably his greatest flaw. He always felt the need to protect me, to a fault. He always put everyone ahead of himself. With me gone, Tegan and Mund could finally concentrate on the wolf baby they had on the way instead of worrying about me.

I knew I had to figure out what to do with the shabby, old journal, but the idea of translating ancient Greek and the language of the Bloodmoon was daunting. But as Mother would say, there was no time like the present. I sat up quickly, hitting my head on something that also seemed to be surprised by the sudden smack. I rubbed my forehead as I studied the blond boy in front of me. He was good looking . . . well, except for the grimace of pain on his face.

"Sorry about that," I said.

"Oh, I'll live, I'm sure," he smiled, still holding his forehead. "Do you mind?" he asked, gesturing toward the open spot on the bench next to me.

"No, not at all, please have a seat."

He sat down, and after the color returned to his face he continued with what I imagine he had come to say in the first place. "I thought I should come introduce myself to my new neighbor. Well, that was before you attacked me. Now, I'm not so sure," he said with a wink. "My name's

Ryan. I live just there." He pointed, leaning in close to my body. I could feel every pulse of his heart, and my throat tightened with the smell of his skin. I leaned away for fresh air. Luckily, he took the hint and leaned back to his side. He was the definition of a good American boy—tan, muscular, blond hair, brown eyes. He was good looking, in a safe way, but he had a contagious smile. He asked all the usual questions. They all did really, as if it were their nature.

"I play in a band," he said.

"That sounds fun."

I felt so awkward and embarrassed trying to talk to him. His deep brown eyes were pouring into mine, and he was still leaning too close. I wonder if it were this hard for human girls to talk to human boys. Or if they felt just as stupid as I did.

"Yep. We practice tonight at seven-ish in the garage, if you want to stop over later and watch me play." I could plainly see the hope on his face. Despite the fact I head-butted him and I was socially awkward, he still seemed genuinely interested in my company.

"Maybe I will." I smiled.

"It was nice to meet you, Ashling."

"Likewise."

He was lingering next to me. Did I miss some human tradition? Was I supposed to do something else? My nerves were raw and my palms were sweaty. I just needed to get away from him. "I guess I best get inside."

He turned on his gleaming, perfect white smile and walked down the steps toward his house as I went into mine to hide. For someone who knew no one, I sure seemed popular. It didn't make sense—they should be afraid of me. They should, deep in their subconscious, have a flight reaction to my predatory nature, and yet they kept bringing themselves to me. Perhaps they could tell the difference between the wolves loyal to Old Mother and the forsaken, or maybe they were just blind to what they couldn't see. We were their connection to Old Mother, and without that bond, it was possible they were as lost as I was. As if we needed one another to survive.

The clock chimed five. Baran would get home soon. I searched the cabinets and found the makings for meatballs with gravy. I had no idea if it would be edible, even to humans, but I was going to try. Maybe if I buttered him all up, he would be more open to me spending time with Ryan.

I wished desperately I had gotten Beth's number she could have gone with me to Ryan's. Then I wouldn't have felt so self-conscious. What if his friends didn't like me?

"Sure smells like human food in here. What's the occasion?" Baran asked suspiciously.

"I thought I'd take your advice and try to like human food," I lied. He nodded in return and dished up. I mimicked his movements, trying not to draw attention to myself. It didn't work.

"So I hear you spent the day with Claire's daughter."

"I did."

"Good for you. She's a smart girl."

I let out the breath I had been holding. At least I wasn't in trouble yet. We lulled into the silence of chewing while I gathered up my strength. "So I thought after supper I'd go hang out with Ryan next door." I waited for him to yell and forbid it.

"Sounds fine. Be in the house by midnight." He stood up and rinsed his plate. "I'm going to my office. Let me know when you leave."

"Sure."

I was stunned. He didn't freak out about Ryan, so that meant he did have something against Grey. That was a mystery I was going to have to solve.

After cleaning up the kitchen and checking my reflection in the mirror about thirty times, it was already half past seven. I wanted to be late, but not miss it. I decided not to change my clothes. It might look as if I were trying too hard. I walked to the edge of Baran's office and said, "I'm going to walk over to Ryan's now."

He didn't even look up. "Sure."

I darted out the front door toward Ryan's house. I clearly heard the music in the air and a thick, masculine voice singing out, piercing the night. I entered the side of the open garage, lingering at the edge. I let the music wash over me. The voice made my skin tingle and the hair on my arms stand on end.

I glanced around the space filled with teenagers and spotted Ryan playing a bass guitar. Next to him was an African American boy with dark eyes playing the drums. His hair was cut almost to his scalp. He had his shirt off, and his dark chest was covered in glistening sweat.

The voice penetrated my thoughts again, and I searched for the sound. My eyes snapped to the lead singer—it was Grey. Our eyes locked, and my heart surged. His vintage guitar hung at his hip as he sang. He smiled at me, and I fought the urge to get closer to him. A girl with bleached-blonde hair whipped her tanned face around to burn a hole in my skull with her eyes. Her long, straight hair was down to the middle of her back, and her blue eyes nearly sparkled with hate. She was tiny and boney, and she looked how I imagined an American princess would look. But to me, she looked unhealthy.

She was obviously angry about how Grey had reacted to me; I could see it on her face and smell it on her skin. I suppose she was the girl Beth had talked about. I smiled back at her, but her stone face didn't soften. Instead she abruptly stood up, catching everyone's attention as she stalked toward me like a cat.

The thought of turning and running was in my mind, but my legs didn't listen. I wasn't scared of her—I could easily take her life, but I didn't want to hurt anyone. I was certain she was going to lash out at me like Medusa, but the song ended just in time. Ryan ran to my side with a huge smile on his face and his guitar slung around his back.

"You made it!" he said.

I managed to peel my eyes away from the miniscule girl to Ryan's happy face, smiling back. "Thanks for the invite. You guys sound fantastic."

"Awesome," he said, wrapping his broad arm around my shoulder and pulling me farther into the garage. They all watched me, and it made me want to hide. "How about some quick introductions. Everyone, this is my new neighbor, Ashling Boru. She just moved here from Ireland and lives across the street with . . . " he paused, "your uncle?"

I nodded.

"Ashling, this is everybody."

They laughed, all except the blonde, who I was certain would rather see me dead than welcome me to the group. Her name was Lacey, and she was quickly flanked by a dark-haired, hearty-looking girl named Nikki. Nikki was nondescript, except for her full red lips.

Then came a series of names, though I knew I would have to be reminded of who was who. In the audience, there was Emma, Kate, and Kelsey for girls and James and Clint for additional boys. I would have to place the names with faces again later. For now, I just smiled. Ryan introduced the drummer as Eric and then introduced Grey as the vocalist and lead guitar. Grey gave me a wickedly handsome smile that nearly stopped my breath.

"We've already met. Haven't we, love?" he said with a wink. I could see Lacey's face contorting. I laughed, though I didn't know if I was laughing at him or her.

"We did? I just don't remember," I replied.

This brought the smile back to Ryan's face. I took a seat, and the band started playing again. A girl with black curly hair turned around to face me. She looked a lot like the drummer, same beautiful black skin. She had an innocent smile, but her eyes were oddly intense.

"Hi, I'm Emma," she said. "Eric's my twin." She pointed him out behind the drums. Lacey gave us a dirty look.

Emma laughed. "Don't mind her. She just hasn't eaten in a decade. Makes her kind of bitchy. Besides, she's just pissy because Grey winked at you. She asked him to take her back again tonight. He said no. You should have seen it! I thought her head would explode. But he said no, which is good because she's nuts-o. Plus, she cheats on him, he breaks up with her, she begs him back, and like a silly puppy dog, he takes her back time and time again. But tonight, he turned her down. For the first time ever." She studied me for a moment before continuing. "I just ignore her. Otherwise everyone else is pretty cool."

Emma was quiet for a while, watching the band, but I saw Lacey eyeing me from across the room. That scrawny little twig seemed to think she could fight me. What a laugh that would be. I could break her in half—in my wolf form, anyway.

"I think Ryan likes you," Emma said.

"Oh?"

"Look at him watching you. It's cute."

"I guess I hadn't noticed," I replied. It was Grey I couldn't take my eyes off of. There was something unnatural about the way I was drawn to him, and it was strong enough to create bad blood between Lacey and me in a matter of seconds. I didn't need help making enemies—I had a lifetime of practice at that. But here I was, my second day in the States, with a twig as my adversary.

"That's it for tonight. I gotta roll," Grey said, unplugging the microphone.

Lacey lingered near Grey, waiting for his attention. "Grey, honey, how about you give me a lift home?" Lacey asked, batting her eyes at him. I was trying not to pay attention or at least look as though I weren't paying attention to them, but I couldn't help it. I had to know his answer.

"Not tonight, Lace. Get a ride from Nikki or call your mom."

"Come on, Grey, please?"

"I said no, Lacey. Let it go."

"Grey!" she said as he walked right past her toward us. Lacey's eyes burned with hate, and all of it was focused on me. "Where are you going?"

He kept his eyes on mine and didn't turn around. She screeched an unholy sound and stomped out, ramming her shoulder into mine, but I didn't look away from Grey's intriguing green eyes. They almost glowed in the light, and his sideburns pointed right to his delicious lips. I wanted to reach out and run my fingers over them to feel how soft they were. My body warmed at the thought.

"Sorry about that, ladies," he said.

I had to drag my eyes away from his lips. What was wrong with me? I had to get ahold of myself. I didn't even know him. And he certainly didn't like me that way. He was just using me to get Lacey to move on. Why was I getting all worked up around him?

Kelsey and Emma gushed over the music as Eric, Ryan, and Grey listened to every word, but Grey continued to watch me out of the corner of his eye. I must have had something on my face. I flipped my hair to create a shelter from his eyes and tried to concentrate my mind back on the conversation and away from his penetrating gaze.

"What are you up to tomorrow, Grey?" Ryan asked.

"Heading up to the falls to work with my dad. Might do some jumping. You?"

"Mom's got me helping at the café. Maybe on Friday we should all hit the movies?"

Kelsey said, "Sounds great. Let's all meet at the theater at seven o'clock?"

"Fun," Emma replied.

"You in, Ashling?" Grey said.

I glanced around nervously. "Okay."

"Should I pick you up then?" he asked.

I wasn't going to admit I was already obsessed with him. No way was he going to win me over. He was just trying to get Lacey in an uproar, but it was me who couldn't take my eyes off him.

I wanted to scream "Yes!" but instead I simply replied, "No. Thanks. I'll meet you all there." I smiled at everyone. "Thanks for the fun night. I'll see you all Friday at seven. Goodnight."

"It was great to meet you," Emma said.

"You too," I said. I quickly turned to walk home. I could feel all their eyes on my back. If I had wanted, I could have heard what they were saying about me, but I was blocking it out. I didn't want to hear it. I wanted to stick with hope, the hope that they liked me. It would be nice to actually have friends.

I stepped up on to the porch with a glance back toward Ryan's house. Grey was sitting on his bike watching me. He smiled his perfect smile that would keep me up all night. I stepped inside as he waved and drove off. I sighed as I shut the door.

"Nice timing, Ashling," Baran said from in the darkened living room. I couldn't see his body, but his wolf eyes glowed in the dark. It was startling even to me.

The clock chimed twelve times.

"Glad you could make it."

"I made it. What's there to discuss? You don't have to hound me all the time."

"Is there anything you want to tell me?"

I smiled innocently. "Not that I can think of."

"Ashling. This doesn't need to be so hard for you. If you learn to obey my rules, we will get along fine. I know Grey was there."

"I wasn't my fault. I didn't know he was going to be there. And what's the bloody big deal? He's just a human."

"I don't want to be constantly wondering where you are and who you're with and if you're safe. It's my duty to protect you, but I'd like to be able to continue living our lives without me having to follow you around."

"I was just across the street. Right where I said I'd be. What's the big deal?" I said.

"You don't pay any attention to your surroundings. Did you sense me or smell me? I was in Ryan's garage. You need to hone your senses to constantly be aware if there are other wolves or threats near, for your own safety. Can you do that?"

"Can I do that?" I repeated sarcastically. "Of course I can do that. I am a wolf," I sneered.

"I can't always be there for you. I can't go to school with you like a bodyguard, so I want you to spend some time tomorrow working on that. Practice listening, picking out one conversation from a larger group. Smell things that are farther from you. Familiarize yourself with my scent and the humans around you. You will need to be able to tell the difference between a friend and foe in seconds."

"Yeah, I get it."

I stomped away to go to my room. I was tired of everyone thinking I wasn't good enough. I must have done something horribly wrong in another life. I was constantly under inspection, always coming up short. *Your hair is too red, they'd say. You're too wild for a lady. You're not good enough as a wolf. You can't pass for a human. You're too opinionated. Know your place, Ashling!*

My bloody place was wherever I wanted it to be. Bunch of harpies. They can all bite me, I thought angrily.

I flopped down on my bed. Maybe he was right, though. If I didn't want him following me around all the time, I could have a little freedom if I harnessed my wolfy skills. Then eventually I wouldn't need protection from Baran, Mund, Mother, or any of them. I could take care of myself.

I would prove it to him. I would prove it to everyone.

Walking over to the window, I peered out on the nocturnal creatures. An owl in the tree right outside my window watched me carefully while never taking his true attention away from a couple of rodents that scurried in the bushes. He was waiting for his supper. I could learn restraint from watching him. Poised, motionless, yet alert to everything around him.

Suddenly he called to the creatures of the night—a warning cry— and flew away, leaving his supper behind. Searching the trees for what would have caused him to forfeit his meal, I saw a large shadow moving through the darkness. It looked like a wolf, but it couldn't be.

A knock on the bedroom door caused me to jump and look away from the window. "Come in," I said. The door swung open, and Baran stood there, filling the doorway. When I looked back out the window, the shadow was gone, as if I had imagined it. Could it have been a wolf, or was it a werewolf? Or was it a human? Maybe it was just a shadow.

"Ashling, I just wanted to apologize for our fight. It wasn't fair to you. You did do what I asked. I worry about you," he said.

What had the shadow figure been outside my window?

"Ashling, are you listening?"

It could have just been a dog. Or could it have been Adomnan? I shuddered to think what would happen if he found me. And yet I had no idea what he really wanted from me. Maybe it was just the trees and my eyes were playing tricks on me. But I swore I saw something . . . and it moved. Didn't it?

"Are you okay?" Baran asked.

"Oh yeah. Fine. Just thinking, I guess."

"Very well . . ." he hesitated. "Goodnight then." I was too distracted to respond. He shut the door behind him, leaving me once again looking out the window at nothing. I would have to sharpen my senses and stay focused. Remembering what Grey had said about his plans, I laughed. Maybe I would even head out to the falls. Might be a good place to think, test my senses, and enjoy the *view*. I giggled.

8
Caged

I leapt out of bed as the front door closed behind Baran. I was ready to take on the world, and I desperately needed to shift into my true self. Baran didn't have to know. After a sleepless night filled with thoughts of Grey, I was ready to reconnect to Old Mother in the forest and start listening to all of her creatures and memorize their scents, their way of life. And I would be able to spy on Grey. I yearned to see him again.

I knew it was unnatural to be so obsessed with a human or any man, for that matter, but I felt something different with Grey.

I dressed quickly in my leather skirt, tie-top, and boots and ran downstairs. My stomach protested as I passed the kitchen. I was starving, but bland, stale meat wouldn't do. I wanted warm flesh. I would have to avoid humans and livestock on my way to the falls because my restraint was wearing thin.

I carefully smelled the air, but Baran's sent was already fading. The city wasn't awake to see my escape, but the animals were stirring for their breakfast and mine. My mouth watered at the thought of eating. I started running, but only as fast as a human could, in case someone was awake to see me. I couldn't keep the smile off my face as I ran. The houses flew by faster and faster to the edge of the forest, and once secluded in the forest's trees, I ran as fast as my legs could carry me. The trees whooshed past me, and the animals froze in terror. I could smell their fear, but I didn't stop. I followed my ears to the waterfall and climbed a cliff above the pond. It was a good place to hide, with good plant cover.

I lay down among the plants and rocks and settled for the morning. If I were lucky, my breakfast would come to me while I was listening. The animals had started to forget my presence as they entered the clearing for water. Slow, cracking branches came from the east, but the birds continued their song. Whatever it was, it smelled of mushrooms and fresh mud. Definitely not a predator. A pair of boars, perhaps?

I peeked my head around the rock to see two small boars drinking water. I listened to the sounds from the other side of the pond. Something was drinking there too. It was large and seemed nervous with almost a twitch to its flesh. I could smell male pheromones and hear the blood pulse through its veins. I slowly stole a glance at a twelve-point buck standing in the pond, drinking but constantly checking his surroundings. He must have smelled me on the wind.

I rolled onto all fours. I would have to get my clothes off before I shifted, or I would be running back home naked after dark. Nothing says "I broke the rules" more than showing up at home naked, not that it would have been my first time for either. I stifled a laugh as I slid out of my clothes. I shifted my weight to reach the knot on my back, and a leaf cracked. The tiny sound was enough to alert my breakfast of my presence. My eyes darted to my prey; his head was up, ears were moving. My next movements would determine if I would get to eat today.

I untied the top and gently put it on the ground. I hunched back on my legs, coiling, and pounced off the rocks across the pond in my wolf form. I felt my warm blood flow through my veins, and my mind was at peace.

The deer started to run as I hit the water. I misjudged the distance, about four feet short. But the muddy bottom of the pond was on my side, making the deer slip, and I sunk my teeth into his throat, silencing his cries. The warm blood ran over my fur as it trickled down my throat, satisfying my hunger. The sounds of the forest had gone quiet again. All its inhabitants were hiding. Watching. Waiting.

After devouring half of the deer's meat, I left him for the critters to finish off and become a part of Old Mother again. I jumped back into the water to rinse the blood from my fur as I swam back to the other side.

The warmth of his blood and flesh made me tired. I jumped back up the rocky cliff to my hiding spot, pushing my clothes under an overhanging rock with my nose. Circling twice, I lay down, curling into a ball to rest.

My morning nap was suddenly shattered by the sounds of a large truck and men talking. The sun was late in the sky. I crept to the edge of the rocks toward the noise. It was too far off through the trees to see anything, but they were making enough racket that even the dead could have heard them.

"Set that one over there on the left."

"Got it, sir."

"Where in the hell did Grey run off to?"

My heart pounded with fear and anticipation. I could smell him—he was close. I searched the waterfall and the pond for him, but not a ripple was out of place. Why did my survival instincts not wake me up? I was a werewolf; I should have heard him coming miles away. A rock clattered from below where I hid as Grey climbed up into view. He saw me and froze but not with fear. He almost looked excited, but there wasn't time to figure out the inner workings of his crazy mind. I threw myself off the cliff too quickly and skidded down the last few feet, ripping my flesh. The pain pulsed through my limbs. I ran through the trees, but he was following close. I could hear his footsteps. I knew if he could still see me, it wouldn't be safe to run too fast. It would cause too much suspicion. I just had to out-maneuver him until I was out of sight.

My fascination with him had affected my ability to protect myself.

Anger coursed through my veins, shooting through me like a steroid, but he was still gaining on me. Impossible. I was going to have to break the rules. I couldn't let him get too close. I glanced behind to see his smiling face. What did he have to smile about? Maybe I should just turn around and take a bite out of his ass. Then he would have something to smile about, I snickered to myself.

I turned, breaking left through the dark canopy of the trees. Faster and faster I ran from his sight. Only small slivers of light broke through the trees to the ground, giving it an ominous look, light versus dark, good versus evil. Glancing back, I couldn't see him anymore. He was gone and I was free. As I looked forward, my eyes began to water as a cracking sound registered in my mind, followed by the slamming of metal. The pain rippled through my body, and I whimpered as my nails tore at the metal-bottomed cage and I fell onto my side.

Trapped.

I looked through the bars; I was surrounded by cages. There had to be fifteen metal cages out here, all set and ready to catch large prey like me. I had run right between them. I must have passed about five of them before smashing my shoulder into this one. I licked my shoulder as I remembered the pain that had already started to fade.

There was a slit of light right outside my cage shining on the dented lock. If I could just reach it, I could set myself free. And this would all be a bad memory.

Who did Grey think he was, running with wolves as if he were afraid of nothing? I was a predator, he was my prey. Sure, my sole existence was to protect him and his kind, but he didn't know that.

I shifted back into my very naked human form and shivered from the cold metal under my legs as I slipped my thin hand through the bars. The light hit my skin, and I marveled at how my pale skin looked in the ominous light. It almost glowed around the edges.

I had to get this unlocked, I reminded myself. Then I would be free. I pushed on it with all my strength, but my hand slipped, and the metal lever cut deep into my fleshy palm. I cried out from the pain and licked my palm as I would if I were my animal self. My saliva would numb the pain until I shifted again.

I reached through the bars again . . . I almost had it. Just a little harder, but it was such a difficult angle. None of this would have happened if Grey wasn't so stupid. I fumed at his absolute disregard for his own safety. I caught Grey's scent coming closer, and I quickly pulled my hand back inside.

"What the hell?" Grey said. As he came running over, I shifted into a wolf.

He fell to his knees to unlock the cage. "I'm so sorry, miss—are you okay? I don't know what happened. But I'll get you out." Then he looked up into the golden eyes of a wild animal—my eyes.

Grey sat back pretzel-style, letting his hand fall from the lock to the ground, but his eyes never left mine. His eyes were glowing around the edges, and his scent was musky and earthy. It made me feel warm and content. I wanted to touch his face, to ease the worried lines between his eyes, to rub my lips ever so lightly across his and feel the warmth of his skin on mine.

"But I saw you."

I cocked my head to the side, watching his movements, trying to read his expressions. Mostly concern. Could it be concern for his mental health? Thinking he saw a woman, only to be confronted with a red wolf? Or concern for the wolf herself? He turned his head to match the angle of mine. He seemed to be humanizing me.

I winked at him, and he smiled and winked back.

"I know what I saw, Red. I know what I saw."

What did he know? He was just a human. He thought he knew what he saw, but he didn't know anything. Then again, neither did I. My mind whirled through the possibilities for these cages—were the victims to be destroyed? His smile faded. He looked almost expectant, as though he thought I would change before his eyes, but I could outlast his curiosity. I could stare at his perfect face all day. As though he sensed my decision, Grey stood up.

"Look, I know I'm not supposed to let you go, but I can't leave you here. You're far too beautiful of a creature, a vision. So you better not hurt me when I set you free. . . ." He sighed. "Geez, I'm talking to her like she's going to talk back," he said to himself. Grey unlocked the cage and stepped back, letting it fall open. There was an ocean of space between us, but I felt unable to cross it. "Go ahead, you're free," he said.

I hesitated. I wanted to be with him to ease his worry, but I decided to save my own skin. I leapt from the cage toward him, knocking him over into the dirt. He groaned from the fall. I stood with my front paws on his chest as I felt the rise and fall of his breathing. Still he showed no fear. He reached up and touched my shoulder, feeling the soft fur of my neck between his fingers. I leaned into his touch, drowning in my desire.

I licked his cheek and ran into the darkness. I ran from fear and from the passion that swarmed in my stomach like bees. The salty tang of his skin remained on my tongue, taunting me.

I had to get back to my clothes and get out of here. Luckily, I didn't hear him following me. The sounds of the forest were silent as the creatures watched me flee from my greatest fear, a *cage*—whether the cage was a cold, metal box or the oppressive societal position of a woman in my culture. Forever beneath another. Even in marriage, she was never an equal. Trapped as a servant, all thoughts and opinions stripped from her. All because her father sold her in marriage. A servant to her father, a servant to her husband, a servant to the world. That was not the life I chose. Those were not my rules. I was through following the rules of someone else's game.

I quickly shifted into human form and put my clothes back on. I sat down to slip on my boots when I heard Grey arguing with someone as they entered the clearing.

"Damn it, Grey, where have you been?"

"I was . . ."

"I don't even want to hear it. You were supposed to be here helping us set up the cages!"

"I know, it's just that . . ."

The older man squared his shoulders to Grey. He was probably in his forties, but his skin looked older than that, weathered. The sleeves on his khaki-colored shirt were rolled up over his elbows, he wore leather gloves, and his hair matched Grey's.

"It doesn't even matter what your excuse is, Grey! You always have one, don't you? Absolutely unreliable."

"But Dad, I had to . . ."

"Had to what? Be a failure?"

"No," Grey said, as he squared his body up to his dad in silence. His whole body was rippling with rage. Except his eyes. They gave him away with a deep sadness. No wonder Grey seemed so rebellious, with a father like that. His father's hand was ready to strike him down for his defiance. In that split-second, I decided what I had to do before it even registered in my mind.

I jumped to the ground silently, out of sight, and I walked toward them calling ahead, "Grey, do you think you guys could give me a lift home when you're done working?" I paused for dramatic effect. "Oh, you must be Grey's father. Hi! I'm Ashling. I got myself all lost in the woods, and Grey was nice enough to help me. So sorry I took him away from his work for so long." I put on my sweetest, most innocent smile. Grey looked confused but seemed willing to accept my lie, for now.

His father's expression went from rage to confusion to acceptance, even almost friendliness, though he seemed warily aware of me. "Good day, Ashling. I've heard so much about you around town."

"My greatest apologies for keeping Grey from his work, sir." Looking up at him through my lashes, I smiled my way into his thoughts. Simple creatures, really. I was quite sure a man like Grey's father liked his women to be quiet. A lot like my father, I mused. I could play that role if it meant getting Grey out of trouble, although now I had to explain my presence in the woods to Grey. I hadn't even consider that. He was never going to let this go. Yet there I stood, protecting him. Like a fool.

"I'm Grey's father, Robert Donavan," he said. "I'm glad Grey was able to help you out. A pretty little thing like yourself, *lost* in the woods?

You could have been eaten up by a big bad wolf. I'm glad my boy was there to save you," he said slapping Grey on the back. He said "my boy" as if he owned Grey—it was a fatherly assumption I knew all too well. It disgusted me. I had to fight my urge to tell him what I really thought of him.

"Oh yes, sir," I agreed. What was I doing, I wondered. I should have just stayed hidden. Instead I had to put my little nose where it didn't belong, and Grey was smiling at me. I wasn't that good of an actress to have him being all cute over there, looking at me. "I'll just go sit by the water and watch the animals until you're done working, Grey. I promise to stay out of the way, sir," I said. Grey had his father's chin and strong nose but very different eyes. Robert's were harsh and uninviting. He studied me suspiciously, and I smiled with all my charm, and he smiled back.

"That is out of the question. We can't have you out here in the woods alone. There are all sorts of wild animals out here. There were wolves seen just the other day. Grey, you take the rest of the day off and get her home safe."

"Oh no, sir, that's not necessary. I can wait. I would hate to be a bother." I winked at Grey. I was out of my bloody mind.

"I will hear no more about it. Grey, you take her home, and we can pick this work up tomorrow. We'll head back to the office. Nice to meet you, but next time let's do it in civilization, shall we?"

"Thank you so much. You're too kind," I replied.

Robert walked away, looking over his shoulder at me, leaving me standing next to Grey with a river of lies between us. I figured I had only seconds before he'd seek the truth, which I could never tell him, but that would always separate us.

Grey studied my face and eyes for a long time before fully and obviously taking in my whole body. It was easy to hear the appreciation he had for my body by the sound of his heartbeat. But it was only a physical attraction, not emotional. The best I could hope for was that he would be thankful for my help. Beyond that, there would never be anything between us. He could never feel for me the way I felt for him. The taste of his skin lingered still on my tongue, and I wanted desperately to touch him. I bit my lower lip, breaking the skin; the pain helped slow my raging pulse.

"Shall we?" he asked, gesturing toward the south.

I walked next to him, but neither of us spoke. I caught a glimpse of him watching me out of the corner of his eye, and I looked down at my feet, trudging along, kicking leaves with my boots. I would never be good enough for someone like him.

He surprised me by reaching over and wrapping his fingers with mine, weaving them together. The warmth of his skin radiated against mine. I looked down at the woven tapestry of our hands, fitting perfectly together. I glanced up at his face, but he was looking ahead, allowing me a tiny bit of privacy in this intimate moment.

I had never held the hand of a man before; never such an intimate touch as our palms together. I was sure he had done so much more. Mund would be furious if he knew. I was never allowed to be alone with a male who was not family, and yet Grey's hand touched mine. It felt as if it had always been there, as if I had been waiting for it. I tightened my grip; I wanted this feeling to last forever. Even if I knew we could never be.

Just for this moment, he was mine.

"So were you out here spying on me?" he asked with a wolfish grin on his lips.

I laughed and tried to pull my hand away, but he didn't let go. He started rubbing his thumb over the back of my hand, leaving a blazing trail of warmth behind each stroke.

"If you wanted to see me again, you could have just asked," he said.

"I wasn't spying on you," I said, unable to hide my smile.

"Well, that's disappointing."

I breathed in his masculine scent, and my skin tingled. Every part of me wanted him. I tried to tell myself I was no good for him, but I couldn't stop my desire. It was overwhelming, and it didn't make any sense.

"Who are you?" he asked.

"I don't know what you mean."

"Who are you, really?"

"You know who I am."

"Do I?"

We fell silent while his words echoed in my mind. He knew something wasn't natural about me. And my nerves twitched with warning. I should run away from him, but there was nowhere in the world I'd rather be.

When we reached his motorcycle, the sun was nearly down and what light remained cast mysterious shadows across his face. He hesitated to let go of my hand, fidgeting with my fingertips, and I was in no hurry to let go of his hand either. So we just lingered that way, but finally he let go, letting my hand fall back to my side. Grey mounted his bike in one fluid movement as he glanced back at me over his shoulder.

"Hop on and let me take you for a ride." His ridiculously cute smile curved up at the corners of his lips. It was impossible not to smile back as I slid right up behind his warm body and I wrapped my arms around his chest, pulling myself closer. I wanted to feel all of him. I rested my face at the nape of his neck, breathing him in.

The bike roared to life, as did his pulse. I felt overwhelmed by the need to be with him and to be touching him. I was losing control and I knew it, but I didn't care.

I don't know what direction we drove or how long it took to hit the road. All I knew was how it felt to have my arms wrapped around him, and it was all over too soon. He parked in front of a diner, and my arms reluctantly released him, long after it was appropriate. He slid off the bike and held his hand out to me. I slipped my hand into his as he led me into the diner. We sat in the back corner booth, and he slid his body next to mine. He seemed as eager as I felt to have our skin touching.

A current flowed through my veins every time we touched, and I never wanted it to end. It was a stolen moment, hidden from the world, from rules that weren't ours, from the inevitability that I would never feel this again.

He brushed my wild curls out of my face as he let the back of his hand lightly brush my lips. I exhaled sharply. Mund had described mates binding and how the overpowering essence of love was instant, but this was incredible. There wasn't a doubt that it was happening to me, at this very moment. Every inch of my body burned for him.

"So what were you really doing alone in the woods today?"

Finally it came, as I dreaded it would. What could I ever tell him that wouldn't send him running away? The truth was forbidden. If I let him try to decide, then I wouldn't have to lie. I could just go along with whatever he dreamed up. My nervousness gnawed at me, and I began fidgeting with the napkin-wrapped silverware, unable to meet his probing green eyes.

"I got lost."

He laughed. "I doubt that. There is more to you. Anyone can see that."

"No," I whispered.

"Don't you see how everyone reacts to you? They flock to you."

"They are just being polite."

"Can't you see how every guy you meet falls over himself to be in your presence? Just to be near you?"

I shook my head, trying to get his words out. He couldn't say these things to me. I realized then, even though I barely knew him, I loved him with every fiber of my soul, as though we were created from the same material . . . but this could never be. I was immortal, and an immortal couldn't bind with a human. They were sacred to Old Mother. This was forbidden. But from the moment I met him, I wanted to be his. It didn't make sense, we didn't even know each other, but I was unable or unwilling to resist him.

"Ashling . . ." he paused. "*What* are you?"

The question took my breath away, and my body went rigid. I could tell him everything right here, spill every secret, and watch him run away, to never see him again. I could lie and convince him to stay, but then what would we have? A relationship built on lies. I didn't know what to do.

Without a word to say, I hung my head. Defeated.

He put his finger under my chin, raising my face back up to meet his eyes. "Ashling, I don't know if you are some sort of goddess sent here to torment me, or if you are sent by the devil himself. I know nothing about you, and yet I feel as though I have known you my whole life. I don't know how, but . . ." he hesitated."

"Grey?"

"I love you," he said.

His words melted any resistance I still had; any sense of duty or reason were gone. I leaned forward and pressed my lips to his, kissing him. My first kiss. His lips were gentle yet urgent, and they pulsed with his promise.

Breaking our kiss, I smiled up at him. "I love you too," I said. It was so soon to say such things. I barely even knew him or anything about him, but I knew it was true. Everyone would say it was superficial love, a childish love, that we couldn't possibly know what love was or how it felt to be in love, but they would be wrong. Every part of him joined tightly to my soul, and there was no turning back. He kissed me again, holding me too tight as he wrapped his hand at the back of my neck, pulling my face closer to his. My heart felt as though it might explode. Passion pulsed through my veins, and I felt myself losing control, but I had to pull away before I was completely lost to him.

"Grey, if you ever change your mind, just tell me, and I won't bother you again."

He looked at me, disbelieving, and shook his head. "That won't happen."

I would love him for all of my days, even after he stopped loving me. I would always be his. And I would remember every moment, as long as he wanted me. I lay my head on his chest, listening to the rhythm of his ragged breath, and he buried his face into my wild hair, breathing me in.

"You smell spicy, like bottled passion," he said, taking another deep breath. "It lingers in my mind long after you've gone, and it urges me back to you."

"Oh?"

"My spicy little redhead," he said, burying his nose into my hair. I felt his breath on my neck, and I loved the way it felt to be wrapped in his arms. I yearned for more.

9

Attraction

Grey dropped me off a block from my house so Baran wouldn't know of our secret rendezvous, at least I hoped. I felt as if I were in a dream, but the raw feeling on my lips anchored the memories to reality. I jumped up to my windowsill, slipping into my room without a sound. Baran was in the house—I could smell him. I got into the shower to wash Grey's scent from my skin. I didn't want to, but I knew Baran would catch his scent.

His advanced sense of smell would make it impossible to keep our secret, but why would he forbid me to be around Grey, unless he hated him? Grey even worked for Baran. It didn't make sense. If he could just see how Grey made me feel or the look on his face when I smiled at him, maybe then Baran would understand and he wouldn't try so hard to keep us apart. I didn't know why Grey loved me or why I loved him, but that was just it. It didn't matter why. He loved me, and that was all I needed to know. I quickly threw on a sundress and slipped downstairs.

"Hi, Ashling. I didn't hear you come in," Baran said. "Your friend Ryan stopped by, asking if you needed a ride to the theater on Friday. He said he'd be happy to pick you up."

"Oh. That was nice of him."

"He's a good kid," he said, nodding. "You be careful around them, Ashling. They are fragile creatures—you could kill them easily," he said. "I am going into Canada on Friday to stretch my legs and hunt. I don't suppose you'd like to come?"

I blushed. "Maybe next time. The movie would be a good opportunity for me to blend in."

He nodded. "I've searched the area. There are no signs of other werewolves. I'll be back Sunday. You'll be safe, but stay in town. The game warden is setting traps. You'd hate to wake up with a tag in your ear and a GPS collar."

His sense of humor was disturbing. "No problem," I said. Baran studied my face, waiting for me to crack and tell him the truth, but I hurried to the door. "I'm going to thank Ryan for offering me a ride." I darted out the door.

I walked across the street to find Ryan in the garage, tuning his guitar. He smiled when I entered. "Hey, neighbor," he said.

His smile was oddly contagious; I couldn't stop myself from smiling back. He quickly stood next to me, lightly touching my arm. I felt awkward suddenly and took a step backward. I didn't like him being so close, it made me feel trapped, but he closed the distance again. He seemed friendly and harmless, but I was terribly uncomfortable.

"Thanks for offering me a ride," I said stepping backward. "But I already have a ride, so I'll meet you there."

"Cool. Okay," he said. "If you change your mind, you know where I live."

His fingertips grazed mine, and I felt panicked. "I'll see you around. Thanks again, Ryan." I ran across the street from his unwanted attention.

His movements were magnetic; when I moved, he'd move. Maybe Grey was right—were they drawn to me? I hadn't met a single human who didn't want to be near me. With the exception of Lacey, but even she seemed curious.

Going back into the house, I walked to Baran's office door and knocked.

"Enter," he said.

"Can I ask you something?"

"What can I help you with?"

"I keep noticing that humans are drawn to me . . . sometimes desperately trying to be near me. I don't understand why."

He sighed. "They didn't teach you anything. They tried to protect you from the world, but who will protect you from yourself?" He shook his head in disgust.

"Teach me what?"

"Don't you understand? You're different."

"I know that. I'm a werewolf, not a human. I got that part," I said.

"No, more than that. You know that no other werewolf in all our history was born able to shift into a wolf at birth. Transformations come at the age of change with puberty, but you were able to change from birth. You became a danger to our secret and to yourself. You didn't understand when and where you could transform. So your father took precautions to keep you away from humans."

"Okay . . . why would a human want to be near us?"

"They used to rely on us for protection and their connection to Old Mother's elements, but the bond between werewolf and humankind was broken long ago. They no longer sense us as loyal. It's now the natural state of predator versus prey. But you, Ashling, you are a dream to them. So alluring that they have to be near you to understand if you are real."

How could this be? I felt no different than any of the other wolves. I felt nauseous and out of control.

"The Elder Gods say you are stronger than all of us, a potent essence born of Old Mother's love. That is why the humans are drawn to you. It is a pheromone you give off that they don't even realize they are smelling."

"So I stink? That's why they want to be near me?!"

"Don't be a child. You know my scent?"

"Yes."

"You are able to detect who I am by it—it's my pheromone. The humans don't realize they smell it, but it clouds their minds. Every pack's essence is different. Killian's base element is protection, and every wolf's scent is unique. Some are stronger, some weaker."

"What is the Boru element?"

"The Boru are wisdom, but yours is different. It's spicy and sharp. It lingers long after you've gone, like an endorphin high. They seek you out so they can feel it again. I know your scent, I can smell it from about a mile. So can they, it's just that they don't realize it. They just know they need it."

"So they don't really like me? It's just a chemical reaction?"

"They are fragile creatures, and without our balance and connection to Old Mother, it's like a piece of their soul is missing. Without her, there is no harmony, and they have lost their integrity and ability to positively affect all those around them. As though they no longer know how to love."

Fear gnawed at me. Was Grey only reacting to my scent, or did we truly have a connection? It didn't make any sense. Why didn't Mother just tell me about any of this? Or Mund? How could he keep this a secret?

I was different among humans because I was a werewolf, and I was different among wolves because I was born a wolf and my scent was stronger. Just what every girl wants to hear—that she stinks and doesn't fit in.

"Do wolves react to other wolves' scents in the same ways as humans?" I asked.

"No, certainly not. We don't respond with false attraction, but when we choose a mate, we will never choose another. We only bind our souls to one, for life."

"Could a wolf bind with a human?"

"A human's soul can't bind with a wolf's. They don't feel anything outside their own bodies."

He was wrong. My soul danced with Grey's and our energy connected. I saw it in his eyes. "Why am I different?"

"No one knows for sure, but I was there when you were born during the counsel gathering at Carrowmore under the Bloodmoon. All the packs of the world gathered at Old Mother's sacred tombs to worship the humans she lost. Many have rested there since 4600 BCE. After those terrible wars among humans, Old Mother created the Elder God werewolves—like your grandmother, Mother Rhea—to form the packs and protect Old Mother's humans. We gather there every eighteen years to pay our respect to their souls and to air grievances between packs, and the elders decide our fates. And it was there that your mother gave birth to you where Lady Calista's blood burned the earth.

"Some say you were spun from Old Mother's soul, but all talked of the prophecy. It was written over nine hundred years ago in Calista's blood, and it hasn't been seen since. I suspect that journal Mund gave you is hers. Legend says a girl of snow-white skin and crimson curls born of Calista's blood holds the fate of the world. So every pack in the world became interested in you. Some offered betrothals, some attempted to kill you, and some tried to possess you and your undeniable power. So your father faked your death in order to keep you safe. It wasn't until Adomnan found you that anyone knew you were still alive. Which is why I am hiding you here."

"How could I hold everyone's fate?"

"I'd bet that journal has the answers I cannot give."

"The journal is in ancient Greek and Old Mother's language!"

"Well, if you want to know, you better start translating it. That'll give you something to do this weekend to keep you out of trouble," he said, smiling.

"Great," I muttered as I ascended the stairs to my room.

At least my secret rendezvous with Grey wasn't exposed. I loved him, and I didn't care what any prophecy or pack law said. I would never love another the way I loved him. Although it may have been a misguided love, there was something strange about Grey. Some sort of a warning. I knew it was careless to give all of myself to him, but I couldn't convince myself not to.

I shut my door and turned to see Grey crouched in my open window.

I gasped. My love was crouched like a predator of the night, waiting to devour me. His green eyes glowed, and my heart pounded with anticipation.

"I just had to see you again," he said.

I rushed to his side and grabbed his face, kissing him as he wrapped his arms around my waist crushing our bodies together. Every cell in my body felt alive as we kissed. Passion filled me as our lips collided and my body warmed to his touch. He pulled away, looking deep into my eyes. I lightly ran my finger over his moist lips, desperately wanting to feel them on mine again.

"I have to go," he said, "but I'll pick you up tomorrow."

"Goodnight," I whispered.

He leapt from the window into the tree and was lost in the shadows, but his scent remained. I grabbed a bottle of perfume and sprayed it erratically, hoping it would mask my secret encounter. I searched for him, yearning for his touch, but I was alone and my lips were raw from the attack. How long it seemed until I could be in his arms again, an eternity of waiting.

I stood as still as stone all day, watching the clock tick, waiting and wondering if he would come. If Grey chose to be smart, he would forget he ever met me, but even after just one day, he was already a part me, and I was anxious to see him again.

The sound of a motorcycle turning on my street interrupted my semi-psychotic thoughts, only to start a new string. Should I meet him on the porch, as if I'd been waiting? Or should I make him ring the bell? Should I act as if I were busy? That was probably better than the truth— that I had stood waiting like a fool for hours.

Grey rang the doorbell, forcing me to decide if I would hide alone or if I would live my life. I opened the door. His hair was messily styled to several points that complemented his side burns. He wore an unbuttoned gray dress shirt with a light-blue screen-printed tee. I stared at the print on his T-shirt of a light-gray shield with a wolf head. The design made my skin crawl. His dark jeans were held on with a black belt, low around his hips, with a strange-looking silver belt buckle. It almost looked like a weapon. I shivered. I knew if the silver metal touched my skin, it would make me temporarily mortal.

Grey reached out, slowly running his fingers across my collarbone, sending tingles down my spine. "You've never looked lovelier," he said. His fingers lingered on my skin, leaving a burning trail everywhere they touched. "Shall we, love?" he asked, offering me his arm.

"Thank you," I said with a smile.

We walked outside, and he slid on the bike, giving me his hand as I slid on behind him, wrapping my arm around his chest. I'd missed the warmth of his skin. I'd missed everything about him. How was it possible to be this stupidly in love with someone I didn't know? And to trust him without any concern? But I did. I trusted him with my life and loved him with all my being, as though we'd been together for centuries.

The drive was over too quickly, and we arrived at the parking lot across the street from the theater. I could see everyone in the entryway in little cliques waiting for us. Lacey's jaw dropped so far, she must have been able to taste the floor. That would have made me laugh, but the hate in her eyes changed my mind. Ryan looked upset too. I had told him I had a ride to the theater; I just hadn't elaborated with whom. Why did we have to endure this? We could just run away together, instead of making a spectacle of ourselves.

"Maybe we should just take off," I said.

He laughed. "I was thinking the same thing."

I spotted Beth in the corner, separate from the rest of the group. She wasn't friends with them, but she seemed like she would be a kindred spirit to Emma. I needed to get her in the group. Beth was abrupt and loud, but she was super sweet if people would give her a chance.

"Come on. Let's get this over with," I said. Grey held my hand, binding us together.

"Hey, guys," Grey said. "Did you pick a flick?"

Everyone stared at us, scrutinizing our every move. I gnawed at my lip from nervousness before Emma finally said, "We were thinking we'd see the chick flick." All the guys groaned—they obviously hadn't been asked to vote. I laughed.

"I know, right?" Emma said, smiling.

"I'm up for a chick movie," Grey said, gently squeezing my hand.

"Good, it's settled," Emma said.

"Hey, Emma, you know Beth, right?" I asked as I grabbed her hand, pulling her with me toward Beth in the corner. "You guys are in the same grade, right?"

"I don't think I've ever had a class with you, Beth, have I?"

"Maybe in elementary school," Beth said. I could tell she knew Emma, she just didn't admit it.

"Oh yeah! Weren't you in Mrs. Anderson's first-grade class?"

"Yes."

"Cool. Me too," Emma said. "Come sit by me, and we can talk schedules this semester." Emma grabbed both Beth's and my hands and started dragging us into the theater.

Lacey had cornered Grey, and they were obviously in a heated debate about something. I suppose they were talking about me. I grabbed Grey's hand when I walked by, pulling him away from her.

"Let's pick out our seats," I said.

"Thank you," he whispered in my ear.

We all took our seats in the center of the theater, and Lacey took her seat right behind Grey. I supposed so she could try to burn a hole in my head with her eyes. I wished she would stop being so mean—maybe then we could even be friends. Grey and I didn't try to find each other—it was fate. She had to understand that, right? Otherwise, she could make my whole experience in high school a horrible one. Girls could be really catty and mean, at least that was what Tegan had said.

"So Ashling, where are you from?" Lacey said.

I turned around and smiled. "Ireland."

"Don't you mean a whorehouse?" she said. My mouth fell open. Tegan was right.

"Lacey, why don't you shut up?" Grey said.

Lacey scowled at him, but she didn't say anything else to me. I never learned the art of being a mean girl. Which I had always thought was a good thing, but now I wasn't so sure. She would likely try to make all the other girls not be friends with me, slowly weeding me out. Or she'd spread ugly rumors about me. I would rather just punch her and be done with it. That was how it always worked with Mund and Quinn. Wrestle, fight, swear, high-five. Easy. Girls . . . girls were complicated.

But I wasn't going to let her intimidation get between Grey and me. I wasn't going to let her affect my mood and happiness. She didn't have that kind of control over me. I was going to be so sugary sweet to her that she couldn't possibly be mean to me. She would have to be my friend then. I would fight her anger with my friendship.

Emma and Beth were becoming fast friends, whispering to each other during the movie. Grey leaned over and kissed my cheek. He was everything I had ever dared to dream about, but my instincts were still looming in the back of my thoughts. He was a mystery, but his green eyes always gave him away. There was something there, something dangerous. Luckily the movie was bright and vibrant, so he wouldn't notice that my eyes glowed in the dark. I had to close my eyes only a couple of times to protect my secret.

Once the end credits started rolling, Grey and I excused ourselves before Lacy could stop us. I quickly hugged Beth and Emma on our way out, and we ducked out the side door, running hand in hand across the street.

"Where to?" Grey asked as we hopped on the bike.

"Somewhere we can be alone," I said, refusing to meet his eyes.

"Let's go to my place—my dad's gone for the weekend," he said. Without waiting for a reply, we were already driving down the road to Grey's house. I wasn't sure where he lived or what secrets he might have been hiding in there, but I was eager to get him alone.

We crested the north side of Portsmouth, heading back toward York Harbor. I felt uneasy not knowing where we were going, but the idea of being completely alone with him made my emotions simmer with expectation. My heart pounded so loudly, I was sure he'd hear it over the rumble of the motorcycle. Grey shivered. Was he scared too? I was a predator.

We drove down a dirt road, twisting and turning deep into the forest. The starry sky was barely visible when we stopped in front of an intimidating slate-gray house with black shutters. It was completely dark, not a single light welcomed him home—just a dark house in the middle of nowhere. The moon barely lit our path. As we stepped on the porch, motion lights went on all around the property, causing the birds to scream in anger and fly out of the trees into the night sky, like a swarm of angry bees. Startled, I shoved him into the door, using myself as a shield to protect him from whatever may still lurk in the shadows.

"It's okay. You can let go now," he said, smiling.

He must have thought I was crazy, but he only smiled as he smoothed the wild tendrils around my face and pulled me into the unlocked house. It seemed unlikely anyone would come this far to break-in, but it was strange that they didn't bother to lock the door. Even Baran locked the door, and he was a wolf.

My eyes easily adjusted to the darkness inside the house. A large black staircase started directly in front of us; it beckoned me upstairs, but my body was firmly in place. I wasn't going up those stairs. I couldn't fathom why, but it made the hair on the back of my neck stand on end.

Grey flipped a few switches, illuminating the darkened spaces, casting exaggerated shadows on the walls and ceiling from the intricate, carved creatures all around us, as though we were surrounded by their screaming souls. I swore I could even feel their fear. An icy chill settled on me.

"Do you want something to drink?" Grey asked.

I shook my head as I studied the carved faces all around me. How could he live here? It was unnatural and frightening.

"Do you want to see my room?"

I nodded.

He led the way into a parlor with a massive fireplace at the center of the wall. A hideously ugly wallpaper depicting slain wolves covered the walls, but what scared me to the core was a large gray wolf hide on the floor in front of the fireplace. Its head was missing. It made me want to throw up, but Grey continued gently pulling me into his room.

I couldn't get the wolf out of my mind. The poor creature was dishonorably displayed in their home, and it had been beheaded. If its body wasn't returned to ash, its soul could never return home to Old Mother. It was unthinkable. His dad was a game warden; didn't he respect animals more than this? Wasn't he supposed to protect them? But then I was supposed to protect humans, I reminded myself.

We entered a brightly lit bedroom with dark gray curtains that puddled on the wood floor. A giant king-size bed covered in charcoal-colored comforters was on the far end of the room. All his wall space was covered with mismatched bookcases made from cinder blocks and raw-cut lumber. Books covered every conceivable place—it reminded me of Baran's organizational style. On the other end of the room stood his guitar and amp.

"So . . . this is where I crash," he said.

"It's nice," I said, glancing back out the doorway into the parlor. The look on my face must have shown my fear, and Grey shut the door, closing out the darkness that lurked.

"Sorry. The rest of the house is pretty dark. It's historic. I know it looks intimidating, but you get used to it."

"It's different," I said. "What do your friends think of it?"

"I've never brought anyone else here before."

"Really?" I asked, unable to hide my shock.

He slipped off his collared shirt, revealing his tight T-shirt and muscular arms. He discarded it over the guitar stand, causing his scent to swirl around the room, making my head spin. His scent was strong and intoxicating. Every breath I took eased my worry and urged me toward him. I wanted all of him.

"Yeah, I don't know. Just never had anyone I wanted to bring here before."

"Oh." I said.

"Sorry I don't have a chair to offer you," he said. "We could sit in the parlor if you prefer."

"No, I like it in here," I said.

I walked calmly across the long room to his bed, trying not to trip, and sat on the foot of the bed. My lower lip quivered in anticipation as I waited for him to join me. His expression was a mixture of concern and excitement. He sat at the head of the bed, resting against the headboard.

"I want to know everything about you," I said.

"What do you want to know?"

"Are you from here? What do you like to do? Where's your favorite place you've ever been?"

He laughed. "Let's start at the beginning, shall we? I was born and raised here in Maine. My dad's family built this house in 1810. His family came from Ireland before that. They came here for work. I don't know what I want to do yet. I love playing my guitar, and I know I want to travel. I haven't been a lot of places. Just around here, I guess. I'd love to see Scotland, though. I'm drawn to it, for some reason."

"What are you thinking?"

"Nope, now it's my turn."

"But . . ."

"No buts," he said with a smirk. "How big is your family?"

"Big," I said with a laugh. I knew it was safer for him if I just lied, but I couldn't lie to him. I knew telling him Father and Mother were alive was risky, but I couldn't stop myself. I wanted desperately to be a part of his world. "There's Father and Mother. He's a large, red-haired, bearded man, and Mother is an elegant beauty. And I have four older brothers, three of whom are married and one engaged. I'm the baby. Flin is the oldest—he's a redhead too. He's married to Bridgid; they have a couple of boys. Then there is Mund, married to Tegan. They have a baby on the way, and he's my favorite brother. Felan's married to Cadence, and they have a son too. Quinn and Gwyn are engaged, and then there's me."

"Why is Mund your favorite brother?"

"He always looked after me, and he spent time teaching me things. I know him the best, I suppose. You're going to love him."

He just nodded. I could tell all the names were still swarming around his mind. It was a lot to absorb.

"Do you have any siblings?" I asked.

"No, I'm an only child, just me and my dad," he said. He seemed lost in that moment. I crawled up the bed to be closer to him and touched his hand, tracing his knuckles in figure eights. I felt nervous to ask him, but my curiosity got the best of me.

"Grey, what happened to your mother?" With the words already out of my mouth, I couldn't take them back, and the feeling it sent up my spine left me shaking. I suddenly felt that I didn't want to know the truth. There was a dark energy that surrounded the memory, and I could feel it seeping into my bones, as if she were crying for my help.

"She died."

"How?" I asked.

He started playing with my hand as he thought. Each moment that passed caused the crease between his eyes to deepen. Even worried, he was still handsome. I wanted to kiss his lips until he surrendered and his smile returned.

"She was killed by a wolf." His voice dripped with hate.

I gasped. "That's horrible. I am so sorry."

"It's okay. I was barely two when it happened. My dad told me about it years later. Which is why we work so hard to trap the wolves and track them in the woods. So no one else gets hurt."

I was the one thing in the world he hated most, the horrible creature that took his mother's life. I was a fool to think this could work, a human and a wolf. He would be bound to hate me for all eternity. I pulled my hands away from his, resting them in my lap. I should leave, I thought. I didn't belong here, I wasn't good enough for him. He deserved so much more than an animal like me.

"You look so worried. It's okay. I'm okay," he said, pulling me back to him and crushing me with his big arms. I didn't resist, though I knew I should, for his sake. Instead I ignored my conscience, resting my head on his chest, and I listened to him breathe.

My kind killed his mother, and here he was, comforting me. I was a masochist. Or a sadist. Or both.

"This was her wedding ring. It's all I have left of her," he said, holding out a diamond ring encased in silver. I leaned away from it, terrified to even let it touch my skin.

"It's lovely," I said. The design was appealing enough, but just the sight of the silver ring made my hair stand on end. "It must remind you of her."

"Do you miss your family and home?" he asked, putting the ring back in the drawer. I was relieved.

"I do. I hated it here at first. All I wanted was to go back home to Ireland, but then I met you. Though you might be better off if I did go back," I said.

"I'm glad you came."

His lips captured mine in a deep kiss, smothering my mind, leaving only his scent dancing through my thoughts. He pulled me onto his hard chest as his hands wove into my hair. He wrapped my red mane around his wrist, gently pulling my head back. My body tingled, pricking my skin with desire. I wanted desperately to cry out, but only a small sigh escaped my open lips as he kissed my exposed neck, nibbling at my delicate skin.

I could feel the waves of heat roll off him as they crashed into my burning flesh. My body yearned with need. He incapacitated me with desire. His hands roughly caressed my shoulders as his mouth devoured my raw lips, forcing his delicious tongue into my mouth.

My lips barely parted as he began his conquest. With each stroke of his tongue, my heart nearly leapt out of my chest. I wanted nothing more than to be a part of him. He pulled his lips away, resting his forehead on mine as he breathlessly panted for air.

"You're dangerous," he said.

Worry filled me with self-doubt. I shouldn't endanger him like this, but I couldn't keep myself from him. I was addicted to his touch.

"I'm losing myself to you," he said.

"I went crazy from the moment I saw you," I said.

He smiled, and I laid my head on his shoulder, snuggling into his body for warmth. His body was as warm as mine. He had to be at least 102 degrees like mine. I wanted to lose control with him. Our heartbeats slowed and calmness came over his body as he held me tightly. There was nothing I could imagine that could have filled my soul with such light. I started to drift off to sleep with his arms wrapped around me. I felt him kiss the top of my head as he pulled the blankets over us.

"Goodnight, my love," he said.

10
Missing

I woke up still wrapped in his arms. It was the deepest sleep I'd had in weeks. We had hidden away from the world all night in each other's arms. He was still asleep, and I gently slid myself out of his embrace and crawled to the edge of the bed. I started to slip my bare feet down to the cold wood floor. He must have taken my shoes off for me while I was asleep, and I glanced around the room for them.

Grey grabbed my hand, pulling me beneath him, and heat radiated off his skin. "Where do you think you're off to?" he asked with a wolfish grin.

"I didn't want to wake you, so I thought I would look through your books," I said, pushing at him with a smile. "Now if you do not mind, get off me."

He didn't move a muscle. My hands were still on his chiseled chest, feeling his warm skin through his thin T-shirt. My pulse quickened, covering my cheeks in a deep blush. I wanted so much to kiss him, but then I would be letting him win. I couldn't let that happen so easily. I pushed at him again, a little harder, but still he didn't budge. He was unnaturally strong for a human.

"Grey, I asked you nicely to let me up."

"And I quietly rebelled."

His grin turned into a full smile, just as it did that day in the woods. He was awfully smug for someone threatening a wolf. I lifted my head up toward his face as though I was going to kiss him, and he took the bait, letting me move. I licked his face from his chin to his cheek, leaving a trail of moisture behind. He looked completely mortified, but I had to laugh.

"Sick," he said, pulling his weight off me to wipe his face.

"I asked nicely," I laughed, pinning him down this time and resting my chin on his chest. I took in a deep breath of him.

"So was it my turn to ask the next question?" he said.

I opened my eyes to see he had been watching me. "Nope. It's mine." I grinned.

"Okay. Is there anything else you want to know about me?"

"Why do you like me?" I said.

"That's a silly question. You know why."

But I didn't and I needed to know. What was it that drew him to me? Was it only a pheromone? Or was it something more? Was his attention only fleeting? Was this just puppy love?

"Ashling, stop worrying. I love you. That's all there is to it. Love. Do you need an explanation? Because I don't know that I can give you one. It's something I just know."

"How do you know?"

"I can't see it, but I feel it." He smiled. "Now, come on. Before we miss it."

He tossed me off him like a rag doll, and I flopped back on the bed. He was already waiting by the door. He slipped a clean white T-shirt over his head, giving me a glimpse of his bare skin.

"It's the best time for a ride."

I jumped off the bed and followed him from the safety of his room and quickly out the front door. I savored the feeling of my bare feet in the dirt. We hopped on the bike and took off through the fog, cutting our way down the dirt road and leaving a swirling trail behind us. Grey sped up, taking turns through the fog with ease and precision, far faster than he should. I let go of him and leaned back with my arms wide open and just let the mist and freedom take over. It was deliciously reckless.

He drove the bike with one arm as I slid my right leg over his lap and pulled myself around in front of him, locking my legs behind his back, straddling him as we sped down the road. I kissed his succulent lips and nibbled at his bottom lip before lying on the gas tank between the handlebars. Whether I deserved him or not, he was unmistakably mine.

We drove onto the beach, but not a soul moved this early. He pulled my hips into him as he lifted me off the bike and carried me to the water's edge. My body tingled with need, and I could feel his heat. He set me down where the water could envelop my toes.

He smiled at me, stopping my breath. I was caught in his gaze.

"My turn," he said. "So how many guys have you dated?"

"You mean other than you?"

He gave me a quizzical look, and I realized we had never actually said we were dating. I was mortified. "I . . . I . . . did not mean anything by it."

"Yes, other than us. How many guys have you dated?"

"I have never dated anyone else," I said.

He looked shocked, as if I were lying. I wished. The reality was sad, but it was still my reality. I was never allowed to date or to be alone with a man who wasn't family, but that didn't mean I was broken.

"Never?"

"I wasn't allowed to date."

"Why?"

"Father just said no. I wasn't even allowed to be alone with a boy who wasn't family." I laughed at the irony. At that moment, I sat alone on the beach with Grey, whom I had just spent the night snuggling with. Father would have a stroke if he knew. The vein in his forehead would burst right out of his big forehead. Mund would be mad too, but at himself for not fulfilling his duty to protect me. I was definitely rebelling against everything they had taught me, but I didn't care. This was my chance to finally live my life.

"You didn't hang out with boys who weren't family? Not even friends?"

"Nope," I said. "Just hung out with Mund and sometimes Quinn, but they're my brothers."

"None of your brothers' friends either?" he asked.

"Father tried to set me up with Brychan once. One of his friends' sons. But I didn't want to marry him."

"Marry him? You're sixteen."

"Yeah. Father thought he was a good choice," I said. "I disagreed."

"But you're sixteen."

"Actually, I was fourteen at the time, but we wouldn't have been married until my eighteenth birthday. It was more of a betrothal."

His nose crinkled up in disgust as he sat quietly watching the water rise up over his feet and back out to sea. I wasn't betrothed now. I was free to love anyone I chose, and I chose him.

"Why didn't you want to be with Brychan?"

I saw the truth in his eyes. "Don't you mean, why did I choose you instead?"

He smiled, flicking sand on my feet, but the sea just washed it away. He was just as neurotic as I was. We both couldn't seem to see in ourselves what the other one saw.

"Grey, I choose you. I will always choose you. I adore everything about you. But why do you want to be with me? You have so much more experience than I do."

"I fell in love with you the moment I saw you walk into Baran's shop that morning. You looked so entirely silly and sexy at the same time, wearing his Carhartt pants. I wanted to love you and protect you. I felt compelled to always protect you from any harm and be by your side, always. I can't explain why," he said. "I've only ever dated Lacey. And that was on and off since we were children. Her mom was one of my mom's friends. So after my mom died, Lacey's mom would baby-sit me when

Dad was gone for work. Lacey and I are polar opposites. Over the course of our dating, we spent more time broken up than we did together. She always said I was too distant. And I didn't talk to her, but I never felt comfortable talking to her. The last time we broke up was . . ."

"Was what?" I asked.

"It was stupid."

"What happened?"

"Well, it was because she wanted to have sex, and I told her no. I know it sounds dumb, but I didn't want to waste it on someone I didn't really love. And she had already cheated on me so many times."

"That's not dumb."

"It's kind of embarrassing."

I leaned over and kissed his cheek, and he pulled me into his arms, layering kisses on my earlobe and neck as we lay there, watching the sky as morning approached. The beach was beginning to populate with people who watched us curiously.

"Let's get out of here. It's feeling too crowded," he said.

We drove down the beach where the water made the sand dark and wet, past everyone's prying eyes. It would be hard to hide our relationship now that we made it so public, but I didn't care. I would stand next to him and fight any battle.

The drive to my house was almost painful. I knew it meant he was leaving me there for the day. I hated the idea, but it was inevitable. He said he had stuff to do before his father got back. He came in to use the bathroom, and I found myself plotting how to keep him. Not that I couldn't live through the day. I just wanted him to stay. He walked across the living room to where I sat and straddled me. He kissed my cheeks, first one then the other, followed by my chin, nose, and forehead. Then he stood to leave, but I wanted a kiss, a real kiss. I grabbed his arm and pulled his face back down to mine, kissing him until there was no breath left in either of us. He panted breath back into his lungs as he slightly tripped on his way to the door.

I spent the rest of the day and night dreaming of him. I couldn't get him off my mind, and Sunday evening came before I knew it. I sat at the kitchen table, sketching the slain wolf from Grey's T-shirt. I shaded in the wolf head, making it darker and more intense. There was something trapped in its expression. Was it fear?

The front door swung open, and Baran stumbled in, cussing in the language of the Bloodmoon. It was obvious he was enraged. I darted into the living room. His movements were murderous, and I was frozen in fear. Did he know I disobeyed him?

I started to back away from his fury, but his anger vibrated through my spine. I felt unable to speak and even more afraid to move. I watched him pace back and forth around the room, flinching every time he looked in my direction.

I smelled a human's scent on him, one I recognized, but I couldn't remember whose it was. It was accompanied by several wolves' scents, a melding of unknowns, but one I did know.

Mund.

Panic started to take over, and my hands were shaking. If anything happened to Mund, a piece of me would die with him. He was all I had for so long. I couldn't imagine living in a world without him. He was my only friend.

"Baran?"

He turned to me as though he noticed I was in the room for the first time. Pure hate poured out of his eyes. The door opened again, and Mund stumbled in. He was dirty, and his shirt torn, but it was him. I jumped past Baran into Mund's arms, knocking him off the porch and onto the ground outside. All my fear disappeared. Despite Baran's still raging voice, Mund laughed.

"I missed you too, kid," he said as he stood up, throwing me over his shoulder, carrying me into the house. "I told you I would come for you." He set me down on my own two feet and took in the sight of me. I was still wearing an oversize sweatshirt and a pair of hole-filled blue jeans.

"What?" I asked.

"It's just odd to see you wearing anything but sheep hides."

I shoved him playfully. "Just trying to fit in," I said.

"You didn't buy those with holes in them, did you?"

I grinned.

He shook his head and turned back to Baran, who was still pacing. "Let's talk through this. What happened before I met up with you?"

I jumped on Mund's back, but he tossed me on the sofa. "Come on, Ash, this is serious," he said. I didn't get to see him for weeks, and this was the welcome I got? I rolled my eyes and listened to their conversation.

Baran stopped moving and stared right through us, as though he were reliving it. "I went up into Canada to hunt, but on the way, I picked up a trail from a pack of wolves headed south into Michigan. So I tracked them. I picked up four scents. Two male, two female, and they were in a hurry. A human was tracking them. He moved on foot at speeds that matched, if not surpassed, theirs.

"I caught up to them to find only three remaining, and the remaining male was injured. The human had captured their companion. We tracked him, but it was too late, and the trap was set for us. That was where you picked up my trail and followed it to us, only to risk your own safety."

I pulled my knees up to my chest and wrapped my arms around them. "What happened to the others?" I asked.

"Their companion, Leon, was dead before we got to him. The other three made it out alive. They headed back up into Canada," Baran said. "I didn't get a look at the Bloodsucker, but I will never forget his scent. Did you get a good look at him?"

Mund shook his head. "No. I kept my eyes on you."

"The rumors are true—they're back," Baran said.

Mund shrugged and reached over, messing my hair into a snarly mess as he walked into the kitchen. "I see you haven't changed a thing since I was here last," he said, opening the fridge and scanning its contents.

"I get by," Baran said.

"You're drawing again, Ash, that's great," Mund said. I jumped up in a heartbeat, but my sketchbook was already in his hands. He looked at the drawing, then snapped his eyes up at me in dread and anger. "Do you know what this is?" he said, shoving the sketchbook in my direction. I shook my head no.

Baran pushed past me to see the drawing. "Where did you see this?" I shook my head.

"Where did you see this?" Baran asked again.

"I don't know," I said. My heart pounded in my ears. "I dreamed it."

He disappeared into his office and reappeared back again. He opened a large, hide-bound book, flipping through the hundreds of pages too quickly for a human to see any of the content. He removed a thin sheet of paper to reveal the same image I had drawn.

"The Bloodsuckers, as they are known, are the hunters of wolves, the original clan of human men Old Mother called on to hunt the forsaken packs. But when they started drinking wolf blood from our still-beating hearts, they absorbed our power and lusted for it and became Bloodsuckers. They began exterminating all werewolves from the earth. Our sacred blood gave them inhuman strength, speed, and sense of smell. The power corrupted them, and we became the hunted," he said. "Most of what we know about them is just legend, but it is said if they drank the blood of an Elder God, they would corrupt all the human race. Without the love of animals, there is no measure for humanity. They were supposed to be extinct, but now . . ." he shook his head.

"After that human killed Leon with a silver blade and set the trap for us, and with Ashling's drawing, I can't assume it's just coincidence any longer," Mund said. "We have to take precautions. I will send for Quinn—we'll need him. We have to keep Ashling safe."

Baran studied my wide-eyed face. "I think you should join the school with her, Mund. Then you can stay close and protect her."

"I agree," he said and sat on the sofa. His spine stiffened, and he sniffed the air. "Baran, are you in the habit of letting humans in the house?"

"I don't know, am I?" Baran asked.

"Grey dropped me off after the movie, and I let him use the bathroom," I said trying to sound innocent.

"I told you to stay away from him," Baran said.

Mund interrupted, "Who's that?"

"Brenna's son," Baran said.

"Bloody hell," Mund said. "Really?"

"Who's Brenna?" I asked.

"None of your damn business, Ashling Boru. I gave you one rule to follow this weekend, and you couldn't even do that. You will spend the next week locked in your room while you think about what you have done."

I looked to Mund to save me from Baran's unfair ruling. But he shook his head at me and said, "You best go, Ash."

11

Free

Who was Brenna? And how did Baran know her? That's what I really wanted to know. Grey never said what his mother's name was. Just that she died and how she died. I shivered remembering what he had said. Was Brenna why Baran didn't want me around Grey? Or was there more to him and his secrets? I was old enough to hear what was bloody going on. Though, I shouldn't have lied about where I saw the design . . . but I didn't want to bring Grey into this, yet here he was. The center of all of it.

If Grey's father was a Bloodsucker, then his father probably killed Leon. His job would be the perfect cover and would explain all the traps. But if Robert was a Bloodsucker . . . was Grey? Was Grey's sole purpose in life to hunt me? Kill or be killed?

That sure was some kind of twisted Romeo and Juliet crap.

What kind of relationship ends well when the families are mortal enemies? I could name so many literary examples that all proved our love would be our demise. But for my entire life, I was told I wasn't good enough, that I wasn't part of the pack, so their rules didn't apply to me. My life was my own. I just had to figure out what Grey was.

I knew Grey wasn't a killer. He let me go that day in the forest. He didn't know it was me, but he chose to let me go. I spent the night at his house, alone, and he didn't hurt me. It didn't make any sense. Unless I was the bait, and the trap was set to catch my family too. I couldn't believe he would hurt me. I believed he loved me as much as I loved him. I needed to stop scaring myself. The self-torture bit was getting old. We loved each other.

Was his father a Bloodsucker? Robert was a very dominating, old-fashioned man, and there was the house, the carvings, the wallpaper, the wolf rug . . . my skin crawled with the memory. If his father was a Bloodsucker, maybe Grey chose not to be and that was what caused the friction between them.

Footsteps on the stairs interrupted my theories. Mund stood in my doorway, studying my angry face. He knew my moods as well as I did.

"I am sorry, Ash," he said. "This is hard. We just want to do what is best for you and to keep you safe."

"I guess."

"So you have to understand that his wanting to keep you away from Grey is to protect you."

"Do I?" I asked. "I don't understand why Baran has some weird grudge against Grey and why that should affect me. Isn't it my choice? Isn't that what you always told me?"

Mund smiled back at me. I hated when he did that. He acted as if I were throwing a fit like a child, but I wasn't a child anymore, and I was right.

"You know it isn't that simple."

"You can't protect me from everything, Mund."

"Ms. Boru, will you please hear me out?" he said with an exaggerated accent.

I almost laughed. He walked across the room and sat on the bed next to me, as still as a statue. What was he playing at? I mean, it was Mund. He was tricky, like a fox. Although he was a wolf, but whatever.

"Ash, what's with this boy? Are you taking this stand because you really like this one particular human? Or is it because you want to stake your independence? Help me understand."

I sighed. "I love him, Mund. When I open my eyes, all I want to see is his face. He makes me happy, Mund. He really does," I said.

He wrapped his arm around my shoulders, comforting me. But he couldn't fix this with a hug. I wanted Grey, that wasn't going to change. My eyes welled up with angry tears, but I didn't let them fall. I looked up through the puddles in my eyes to see Baran, but he wouldn't look at me. I thought he was my friend.

"Baran?" Mund said.

"I don't know about this."

Mund laughed. "Do you think I want my baby sister dating some punk? No. But I can't come home every day and see her cry either. Besides, you don't want to see her mad."

Baran grunted.

"I'm joining the high school. And if we know when and where they're together, we can keep an eye on them. It's not like he'll hurt her. You told me yourself, he's a good kid," Mund said. "I think we should trust her to make this decision, not make it for her."

"What about Brenna?" Baran asked.

"That's doesn't concern Ash, Baran, and you know it. And Grey was as much a victim in that as Brenna was."

I pulled away from Mund, wiping the dampness from my eyes. I wanted to push Baran for details on Brenna, but then I risked making him angry again, and Grey was more important than my curiosity.

"You heard her, Baran. You know how she feels."

Baran simply nodded his head. They were going to let me see Grey. I wanted to howl to the moon, for my love, my victory, but something about Baran's face made me leery. He turned and walked back downstairs without another word, leaving Mund and me in the aftermath of Hurricane Brenna. Though I didn't yet know the damage.

"Mund, does that mean I can keep seeing Grey?"

"I want you to be safe, but I can feel the love you have for him. I don't understand it. He's just a human, but if he makes you happy now, I'm okay with that. Now get some rest. We have to start translating that journal of yours, and school starts next week."

"Thanks, Mund. Grey and I really love each other," I said. "I can't wait for you to meet him."

"He may love you for the rest of his life," he said, "but you will mourn him for the rest of yours." I knew he was trying to make me realize my mistake in falling in love with a human, but I wasn't listening.

The week flew by without a single visit from Grey, and I didn't have his phone number. Baran promised he would tell Grey to stop by the house if he saw him at the shop, but he never came. It was as though he had vanished. The separation was physically painful. My stomach was tied in knots, and I was constantly nauseous. I would have gone crazy if it wasn't for Mund making me study ancient Greek and the language of the Bloodmoon. I had to translate every individual letter to get a word, and each word to get a sentence. It was monotonous, but it filled my time with something other than worry.

The labor had been worth it. I knew it was the journal of my aunt, Lady Calista Vanir, and it was filled with prophecies. Every one I researched from the early entries had come true: wars, conquests, marriages. It was frightening and intriguing. Her last entry was in her own blood, just as Baran had said it was, but it wasn't even a sentence. Mund said before she died, she had written the words using her own blood, handed the journal and her wedding ring to my mother, and said, "This oracle is for the dream—she will need it." She turned back to her mate, Ragnall, and said, "I will always be yours." Then she died. It was tragic and poetic.

Claim her, rule them all. The last thing she wrote.

The prophecy predicted the birth of a baby girl with snow-white skin and crimson curls at Carrowmore's Bloodmoon of the Vanir family line. She would unite the packs and bring balance and love to the humans. How could I ever unite the packs? I was just one wolf. How could one person change the fate of the world?

Every wolf in every pack around the world knew of the prophecy all these years—except me. I was frustrated with my entire family. How could they protect me by making me ignorant? They didn't trust me enough to tell me my purpose. I was born of her bloodline on the earth where her blood spilled at Carrowmore's Bloodmoon. I was her dream, and still they kept the truth from me. I was appalled by their distrust.

It did partially explain why Father was trying to find someone he trusted to claim me. Brychan was a gentleman and Tegan and Gwyn's brother, a trusted family ally, but why couldn't he just tell me that?

Baran said other packs were trying to abduct me or kill me, and that was why they hid me away from the world for so long. But was Adomnan determined to kill me—or claim me as his? It was frightening to even think about. I constantly felt the cold sweat of fear waiting for him to attack. He didn't come, but my fear remained.

A week passed without any sign of Grey. It made me incredibly sad, but my nervousness at starting school scared me nearly as much. On the morning of my first day, I rushed around the house, getting ready. Mund was ready far quicker than I, and he was completely at ease. Considering he was over four hundred years old, he looked remarkably like a seventeen-year-old boy. He hadn't aged a day since he first changed, but he shifted with every full moon, unlike Father, who lived closely among the humans before he took the throne and aged as a mortal with every Bloodmoon he missed.

Mund bought a heroic-looking white-and-silver motorcycle that waited for us in the driveway. I followed Mund outside to find Grey waiting for me on his motorcycle. I was excited to see him, but his smile brightened my mood, and I jumped on his bike.

"See you at school," I said to Mund, and Grey and I drove away. Mund was clearly annoyed, but he would get over it. I wrapped my arms tightly around Grey's chest, letting his warmth radiate through me.

"So that was your brother, huh?"

"Yep. That's Mund."

"He sure doesn't like me," Grey laughed.

"He's just hard to get to know. You guys will love each other in no time."

"So he's joining high school? I thought he was married."

"Yeah, he is. He's just not finished with school," I fibbed.

"Huh . . ." he said.

"Where were you all week?"

He was quiet for a while. I almost thought he hadn't heard me, but then he finally responded. "I'm sorry about that, Ashling. I had a fight with my dad, and I couldn't leave the house. I hope you're not mad."

I hugged him tightly. "Nope, just glad to have you back in my arms."

"Me too."

We arrived at the school with Mund right behind us. I spotted Emma, Beth, and Eric chatting by Beth's truck, and Lacey was watching for Grey's arrival. Lacey was ready to attack. It was amazing how she looked so evil dressed all in fuzzy pink. Such a contradiction. Maybe if she'd eat something, she wouldn't be so crabby all the time.

Mund came up and flanked me on the right. Oh good, I came with my own personal bodyguard. Just what every boy wants in a girlfriend— an over-protective brother. I tried to stifle my hysteria, but a small giggle escaped. They both turned to look at me, only to catch each other's glances and continue their stare-off.

If I actually had known where I was supposed to go, I would have walked away from them both, but I had no idea where to go. Luckily Beth ran over, smiling.

"Good morning, Ashling!"

"Hi, Beth. How are you?"

"Great! Ask me why!" she said.

"Why?"

She beamed back at me like a child at Winter Solstice. "Clint asked me to the dance!" she said. "I'm so excited . . ." And she was, so much that she hadn't even noticed my good-looking brother standing next to me, staring at her as if she were possessed.

"That's great, Beth." I smiled back, ignoring him. "But what dance?"

"The homecoming dance, of course. I've never gone before, but it's supposed to be awesome," she said. "You're coming, right?"

"I have no idea," I replied.

"Hey, what's your first class? I have English."

"I don't have my schedule yet. Where's the office?"

"I'll show you," Grey said, smiling and taking my hand before Beth could reply.

"Show the way," Mund said.

"Beth, if I don't see you before, I'll see you at lunch. Okay?" I said.

"Definitely!"

I walked across campus with the two most important men in my life. The hostility rolled off them both, but they turned on the charm as soon as we entered the school office. Not stupid, over-protective boys, but charming, good-looking men. The transformation was disturbing. Two middle-aged women sat behind the counter, already being enchanted by their antics.

"What can we help you with this morning, Grey?"

"These are new students, Ashling and Mund Boru," he said, gesturing toward us. He gently pushed me ahead of Mund.

"Welcome to York Harbor," she said, placing a stack of papers in front of me. "Here you go, dear. It looks like your first class is with Grey. He can show you the way."

"Thank you," I said.

"And for you, dear," she said, turning her attention to Mund. "Here is your schedule. You are in World Events this morning, across the quad. Here is the map, from where we are standing now."

Grey and I turned to go.

"Oh wait. Grey, you'll need this pass, so you aren't tardy." She handed him a pink slip of paper and turned back to Mund, who wasn't listening at all. He was watching me. I smiled big, waved, and walked out. I knew I would pay for that later, but right now I was escaping with all my skin still intact.

"What class do we have first?"

Grey glanced down at the schedule. "We are both in English with Ms. Erickson."

The halls were empty, as classes had already started. The idea of walking in late made my stomach churn. Everyone would notice us and have a long time to stare at me before I could hide. I wasn't looking forward to that.

"Do we have any other classes together?"

He leaned up against the lockers, looking rebellious, and glanced over our schedules. "Yep, fourth period," he said, pulling me toward the door. "They'll hardly even notice us slip in."

The teacher was already doing introductions when we entered, and everyone stopped and stared at us. The only person I recognized in the class was Lacey sitting in the front of the room. All the other faces were new to me. Grey walked to the teacher and handed her his slip. "Sorry I'm late, Ms. Erickson. The office asked me to show Ashling to class." I smiled on cue. "Where should I park?" Grey asked.

She looked down at her seating chart. "Grey, you are assigned to the back table, by the window. As for you, Ashling," she said, turning her attention back to me, "how about you tell us a little about yourself while I decide where to seat you."

I turned red under the class's scrutiny. I wanted to die. This was far worse than any execution in all of history. I just wanted to sit down, but my path to freedom was paved by my story, so I quickly summarized. "My name is Ashling. I'm from Ireland. My brother and I moved here this summer to live with our uncle." Hopefully that was enough information to earn myself a chair.

"Welcome," Ms. Erickson said with a smile. "Why don't you take the seat next to Grey at the back table."

I wanted to run, but that would only make them stare more. I slowly took my seat next to Grey, and the students were forced to turn their attention back to Ms. Erickson. I felt a sense of relief wash over me. One down, six periods to go.

I had my next two classes with Beth and Kelsey, which was a friendly relief. Fourth period was with Grey, as promised, but I wasn't as lucky this time. I had to sit next to Lacey. At least they were individual desks.

Mund caught up to me at lunch. Grey took his seat at the table, and I tried to sit next to him, but Lacey shoved me out of the way as I started to set my tray down. She took the seat next to Grey.

I wanted to reach over and smash my lunch tray into her face, but I calmly walked around the table to sit across from Grey.

"Grey," Lacey said, "would you like to take me to the homecoming dance?" She batted her hideously perfect blue eyes at him. I couldn't believe this was how she was going to play this. She was going to ask him out right in front of my eyes. She was a banshee.

Grey continued looking into my eyes as he answered the pest, "Lace, I'm in the band." My heart fell. That wasn't a true no. He was intentionally not answering the question. "Ashling, you'll be there right?" he asked.

What did that mean? How could I answer? He had doomed me to no date, but if I said no, then Lacey would be there and I wouldn't. High school was harder than I thought it would be.

"You will, right?" Emma said.

Now I was trapped. "Yep. Sounds fun," I lied.

"Great!" Emma said.

Mund was openly staring at Grey. Knowing Mund, he was sizing him up, deciding how to fight him. In case the time came. Though I don't know why he was concentrating so hard. A fight between a wolf and a human—the human didn't stand a chance.

The bell rang, and we were sent off to our afternoon classes. They went by in a delightful blur, but seventh period was just what I needed, art class with Beth.

High school was painful. How did they do this every day and not die inside? The constant judgment of peers and boring nature of the classes was excruciating. I had no real interest in any of what they taught. Mund and Mother taught me, and I had a tutor for many years. The stuff they were teaching here for juniors was stuff I'd learned when I was ten.

"So you're dating Grey?" Beth said.

I smiled.

"He never really said much before you showed up. He was incredibly quiet for someone so popular. I mean, he dated Lacey on and off, but he never paid attention to her like he dotes on you. It's cute."

I blushed. "Oh . . ." Changing the subject because of all the ears around us, I said, "So this dance thing—what do you wear?"

"We'll need to go shopping and buy dresses. Not super formal, but semi-formal. Cocktail dresses and suits for homecoming, and gowns and tuxes for prom in the spring. Can you help me pick one out? I'm no good at dresses."

"Only if you help me," I said. "We should invite Emma, Kelsey, and Kate."

"That'd be fantastic."

"You should mention it to Emma."

The final bell rang, and we were free. Beth and I darted out of the class, running right into Grey, who had been waiting in the hall. I shivered, whether from impact or the mere sight of him, I wasn't sure.

"Bike's parked out the side door," he said. Adrenaline pulsed through my veins, and my skin tingled with delight.

"Beth, be sure to talk to Emma. How about Saturday?" I waved and ran out the door with Grey.

12

Promises

I yearned for Grey's touch and wanted so much more. I loved the way he smelled, the mischievous look in his eyes, the little smile that played at his lips. I couldn't stop kissing him. I had permission to date Grey, but I was certain Mund would be furious that I ran off. But Mund couldn't contain our love, and it was my life.

Grey drove us deep into the forest down a dirt path worn by his tire tread. He parked in front of a giant old oak tree. It was maimed and misshapen, but to me the old oak was perfect. It was one with the river, fed by it as well as threatened by its power. A beautiful relationship they had taken many years to create, the little details humans never saw. Grey was different. He saw them too.

"My mom used to bring me here. We'd climb up high as we could and hide for hours," he said.

"It's beautiful."

"I don't know why I keep returning here, but I feel like I'm closer to her," he said, running his fingers over the gnarled bark.

"Care for a climb?" I asked.

He leapt up onto a branch, farther than a human should be able to jump. I noticed it, but chose to ignore it and carelessly leapt up after him. We climbed up high into the tree. He stopped on a worn branch, and we both lay down, looking up into the sky, with our legs intertwined. Grey was different today—quieter but yet protective and aggressive around Mund.

"Grey, what did you and your father fight about?" I asked.

"He came home angry, and then he found your shoes in my room," he said. "So he took out his frustration on me. I'm not supposed to bring anyone to the house."

My face burned bright red. I hoped his father wouldn't tell Baran. I was already in enough trouble for letting Grey in the house, much less spending the night at his house unsupervised. I wish everyone would just trust us to make the right decisions instead of always assuming the worst.

"I'm sorry."

"I don't mind being in trouble, for you."

I leaned in to kiss his lips, rubbing mine lightly over his, tempting him to move. He leaned in, but we lost our balance and fell toward the ground. He wrapped his arms protectively around me and tried to grab the passing branches. His hand was being ripped up by the rough bark. I should have been protecting him—he could die from a fall like this.

His hand locked on to a branch twenty-five feet from the ground. His shoulder cracked as it popped out of the joint, but he didn't cry out in pain. His other arm was wrapped around my waist, and my legs were wrapped around his waist as well. Adrenaline raged through my veins, and I felt myself becoming a part of him. Every part of me wanted more of him.

"Let. Go. Of. My. Sister. . . ." Mund said below us.

"Mund?" I said. I hadn't realized anyone else was out here. He was a great tracker and unusually quiet, but I was shocked that he found us so quickly.

"Ash, get yourself out of that tree immediately."

Before I could respond, Grey let go of the branch, dropping us down to the ground with ease. He set me back on my feet, placing a hand on each side of my face, kissing me on the forehead, heating my entire body.

Mund cleared his throat.

"Bye, Grey. See you tomorrow at school," I said.

I could feel the anger rippling off Mund, and I could smell his fear. I grabbed Mund's arm, pulling him back down the dirt path. He wouldn't turn around or take his eyes off Grey. What kind of man-issue was this? Was he threatened? Grey was human, what threat could he pose against Mund, of all creatures? But Mund was more territorial and defensive than I had ever seen him before.

"I'll be there," Grey called after me.

The tension between them was unbearable. In the blink of an eye, Mund shoved Grey into the tree with his forearm at Grey's throat, nearly crushing him. My brother had lost his mind. My lust was replaced by panic.

"I don't trust you," Mund said, pushing harder into Grey's throat. Grey stared back at him, unfazed. "Stay away from my sister."

"That's up to her," Grey said.

"Mund, this isn't funny," I said.

"Did you not hear me?" Mund asked.

"Oh, I heard you," Grey said.

"Mund, come on. Let him go. Mund, please!" I cried, pulling at his arm, but he was stronger than me. Mund released his grip on Grey and took a step back. "Grey, are you okay?" I said, checking for injuries, but Grey stilled my hands and kissed my palm. "It's okay, love. He was just looking out for you."

"Are you sure you're okay?" I asked.

"Sure thing."

I didn't delay getting Mund out of there. I pushed him all the way to the parking lot as he growled. It was dangerous to be that close to an angry werewolf, but I didn't care about myself—I just wanted them to both be safe. Thankfully, Grey hadn't tried to fight back. I would figure out what was going on later, then I would kill them both myself.

Once Mund had me on his motorcycle, he ripped through town to add as much distance as he could between me and Grey. Baran looked furious, pacing on the front porch as we pulled in the drive. Mund followed me up the stairs, blocking my exit. I had no choice but to walk toward Baran. He opened the door, but I was afraid to go in. On the porch, they couldn't kill me, but inside I was a goner. My feet disobeyed my brain and led me in to my execution.

My palms were sweaty with fear, but I was equally mad. "Mund, what the bloody hell was that about? You had no right to behave like that. If Mother would have seen you . . ." I shook my head in disgust.

"Mund, what is this all about?" Baran said.

Mund's hands shook as he spoke. "I don't know how, but their souls are binding."

"He's human," Baran said.

"It's impossible, I know—a werewolf can't bind with a human, but they are."

"You must be mistaken," Baran said.

"It's not complete yet, but we have to keep them apart. If she binds with him, eventually he will die and she'll be alone for eternity. No wolf will marry her after her soul is bound to another. Especially a human."

They talked as if I weren't even in the room. As if they were deciding the fate of a prized cow for breeding. I could bind with whomever I chose. I loved Grey, and I knew our souls connected. He would age and leave this earth, but a short time with him was worth a lifetime alone.

"There's something about that kid, Baran. He smells human. But he moves like an animal. I saw him drop eighty-plus feet from a tree with her in his arms, like nothing. He grated his hands on the bark, but when he landed, his hands weren't bleeding. There was no damage to his skin. And you should have seen the look in his eyes when he kissed her. He was challenging me."

I looked at my clothes; there should have been blood all over me, but there wasn't a drop. Mund was right, there was something different about Grey, but it didn't change the way I felt about him. So what if he was some kind of creature from children's stories? So was I . . . except I didn't know what kind of creature Grey was yet.

Baran sat down on the edge of the sofa. "I've seen it too. He does things no human can do. The question is, what is he and what do we do about it?"

"Do about what?" I said.

They continued as though I hadn't said anything.

"The real question is, which parent did he get it from?" Mund asked.

"Yes, that is the real problem," Baran said. "He could have any number of strengths from her, but without the proper supervision, he could be a threat."

"What are you two idiots babbling about?" I said.

I slapped my hands over my mouth. I shouldn't have said that. They glared at me.

"Ashling . . ." Mund said. He was clearly disappointed.

"Don't you dare scold me, Redmund Boru! I'm not a child. I deserve to know what the bloody hell you're talking about and why you behaved so poorly today. He's my friend. You had no right to attack him. I trusted you."

They both looked astonished. I was already in trouble, but this time, I was getting my answers. I steadied myself for a fight.

"Ashling, there are things you don't know and can't understand about Grey and his mother. That I don't even fully understand yet," Baran said.

"Well, maybe I'd understand if you would just tell me what was going on."

"Ashling, it doesn't concern you right now," Baran said.

"Doesn't concern me? Are you stark raving mad? This is my *life* you're discussing. My happiness. My forever! This does very well concern me."

Baran gave me a dirty look, but I didn't care anymore.

"My life."

"May as well tell her, Baran. She's too stubborn to let it go," Mund said. "You haven't seen her angry yet. Trust me. It isn't pretty."

"Can she keep it secret?" Baran asked.

Mund nodded.

"Very well. Grey's mother, Brenna . . . was my sister."

He waited for it to sink in. I kept my face as calm and plain as I could, but I'm sure my eyes revealed my confusion. *Grey's mother was Baran's sister*, I repeated over and over to myself, but it just didn't make any sense.

"She was the only other survivor of the attack in Scotland. During the attack, she was raped. She was only eighteen years old. I tried to protect her, but there were too many. Your father and his packs saved our lives. But it was too late—Brenna was pregnant with Willem.

"Knowing the right her attacker had by our laws, that he could claim both her and the child, Brenna hid in the United States while I raised Willem. We saw Brenna from time to time, but I lost touch with her for about two decades. When I finally found her in York Harbor, I was too late—she was already dead."

Baran continued, "I found her in her human form—dead in the river, decapitated, and all the blood was drained from her body. It was the worst thing I've ever endured. She'd fallen in love with a human, Robert Donavan, and I found two-year-old Grey hiding up in a tree. He had her eyes and her mischievous smile. I stayed here in York Harbor to keep an eye on him. I think it is what Brenna would have wanted. I was afraid he'd become a werewolf and have no one to trust, but puberty came and went, and he never changed. He has extraordinary strength, precision, and speed, even advanced healing like a wolf, but he never shifted."

The weight of his story bore down on me, and my confusion was thick.

"If you loved her and stayed to protect him, why are you so afraid of me being with him?" I asked.

"Because we don't know what he is. And frankly, he doesn't know what he is. Maybe I just haven't let myself see it. I've studied his life; his father locks himself up in that house for days at a time. I've seen Robert's violence, speed, and strength. It's inhuman too, though he's not a wolf. So if Grey is more like his father than his mother, he could be dangerous.

He could be a Bloodsucker."

"What does that have to do with me?"

"Everything," Mund said.

"Grey's not going to hurt me," I said.

"Ashling, you have to be careful. He's as strong as I am, but he's not a werewolf, and he may not even be human. He might be some sort of hybrid. What if he hurts you?" Mund asked. "I could never live with myself if something ever happened to you."

"But he won't. You said it yourself. Our souls are binding. We love each other. He can't hurt me."

I thought we had already had this fight, and I thought I had won, but here we were again. Except this time, I understood what they were talking about. I understood Robert was strange—I thought so too. He made the hair on the back of my neck stand on end. But Grey was different . . . he was nothing like his father.

"Ashling, do you even understand how dangerous it is for you on a normal day, much less when you choose your friends so carelessly?" Baran asked. There was an icy spike at the end of his words. It was meant to cut me, but what Baran and Mund didn't realize was the massive amounts of time I had already spent pondering my life with Grey and what his mortality meant for me. I already knew that one day I would be destined to live without him.

"Yes. Adomnan hunts me, and I'm supposed to unite everyone."

"Without you to unite us, we remain a lost civilization, and the humans will have no future," Mund said. "If you risk your life so carelessly, you endanger us all. Protecting you isn't just about you; it's about protecting our family and protecting the humans. We are all servants to Old Mother, even you. You are one of her wolves."

"I'm not trying to kill myself. I love him. That's never going to change. I understand your fear for my well-being, but you need to understand my fear of living without him. I know he's not a werewolf, nor is he human. I am not threatened by him, and neither should you be. You both agreed to let me make my own choices. So let me. I will respect your wishes and let you know when and where I'll be. But I expect you to trust me too."

I felt a sense of satisfaction in saying what I did. It made me feel good. I finally stood up for myself, for what I believed in, and it felt right. I had the right to love. And I had the right to fight for it.

"Agreed," Baran said.

"Fine," Mund said. "But we have one more subject to discuss."

What else could there possibly be left to batter to death? It was like kicking a dead horse. It was already dead, what was he trying to prove? I would get to be with Grey. There was nothing left to discuss.

"What's that?" I asked.

Baran said, "You shouldn't have sex until your souls are bound to one another and you've been branded. It's tradition. Mating will bind you with his soul for eternity. Which you might think is what you want now, but your soul will be bound to that other life. If you don't choose wisely, you risk losing yourself."

"What do you mean, losing myself?" I asked.

"The humans go from one mate to another, leaving pieces of themselves behind. Until there is nothing left. You only have only one chance," Mund said.

"Ashling, it is important you understand this. By mating with him, your soul will be matched with his for eternity, and even after he dies and you move on, your soul will never be free of his," Baran said. There was a deep sadness in his eyes. I couldn't explain it, but just speaking those words broke him somehow.

"I understand," I sighed. "Grey is picking me up for school tomorrow and hopefully every day, so if you could both be on your best behavior, I'd greatly appreciate it."

"Ash, I'm sorry," Mund said. "I shouldn't have let my emotions get the better of me today." His head hung low. He was ashamed. He was a gentleman, but he had acted purely on emotions and physical strength. It was a disgrace to him.

I walked over and stood on my tiptoes to hug him. I couldn't stand to see him this way. "I know you love me and want the best for me. So let me choose it."

"I'm not promising to like him, Ash, but I'll give him a chance."

"That's all I ask," I smiled. My brother was overprotective, but I loved him just the same.

I excused myself to my room to think. Baran's sister, Brenna, was Grey's mom, but Grey didn't know he was half werewolf and half human. How could he not know? Did wolves kill her for betraying her own kind? Was it a betrayal? Do we really have the choice of whom we love? I spent all this time fighting for a choice, but did I have one? Or had fate already chosen Grey for me?

Downstairs, I heard the front door open and quiet voices talking.

"I wanted to apologize for our disagreement," Grey said.

"I'm sorry, I overreacted," Mund said.

"Mund was just upset that his sister grew up right before his eyes. We're just looking out for her," Baran said.

"I understand," Grey said. "I should have spent time getting to know you, Mund. You are important to Ashling, so you are important to me."

"Is there something else you came here for, Grey?" Baran asked.

"I would like to ask your permission to date Ashling. She is everything to me. So with both your permissions, I would like to date her," Grey said. I could almost imagine the look on his face.

"If that's what she wants," Baran said.

It all rested on Mund. This one moment would determine everything. If Mund said no . . . I couldn't even imagine it. There would be no force on this earth that could keep me from Grey, and Mund knew that. He had to know I would never accept his decision in place of mine.

I don't know how he responded. He must have nodded.

"Thank you both. I appreciate you seeing me tonight. I would like to pick Ashling up for school tomorrow."

"That will be fine," Baran said.

I heard the door close as Grey left.

Grey asked permission to date me. He walked into a house full of werewolves and never once second-guessed his choice to fight for me

. . . just as I would always choose to fight for him. Only one question remained, did he know what I was? Or what he was, for that matter? He must have some idea he wasn't normal—but I knew deep within me that together we were limitless.

I was no longer going to accept being moved around like a pawn. I would make my own decisions. My life would be legend. I wouldn't be held down by whom I used to be and how I used to be controlled.

The rest of the week was uneventful. Mund didn't attack anyone. Grey and I didn't run off together to antagonize them. Grey picked me up for school every day and walked me to all my classes. We didn't get to spend a lot of time together, though, because his dad kept him busy. But finally Saturday arrived with the sound of giggling. Beth, Emma, Kelsey, and Kate met at my house. Emma had an unnatural obsession with Mund, who was desperately trying to avoid her. I started to notice a trend in the humans around me. They seemed to be fearful and avoidant of Mund and Baran, but they were drawn to them if I was in the room. Something about my presence eased their natural fear.

The girls and I planned to go shopping for homecoming dresses. I wasn't sure where we were going or what I was supposed to wear to a semi-formal . . . or even what a semi-formal was. I wore dresses all the time, but Beth said I looked like a hippie.

Mund darted past me on the stairs to my room. "Save me," he begged. I turned back around to see Emma following him. Mund had fought many battles, and yet here he was, running from a human girl. She had no sense of self-preservation, but she was too sweet of a soul to be eaten by a wolf.

"Let's get going," I said, ushering her with me.

The girls ran around in frenzy, grabbing their purses and shoes and whatever else they had left lying around, and the five of us piled into Kate's van. They chattered the whole way to the dress shop about everything possible. Boys, more boys, clothes, dresses, chocolate cake, more boys. I hardly kept up with them.

"So what's up with Grey?" Kate asked.

"Yeah. So are you guys exclusive?" Kelsey said.

"Exclusive?" I asked.

"Yeah, like, not dating anyone else?" Kate said.

I nodded, and they all squealed.

"Any juicy details?" Kelsey asked.

"Nope."

"Come on. Is he a good kisser?" Kate said.

They were all staring at me. I couldn't help it—their excitement got the best of me, and I spilled. "You have no idea! It's like being lifted up to the heavens and looking down on the stars."

They all giggled.

"So what kind of dresses are we looking for?" I asked, changing the subject with the only thing they were more interested in than Grey.

"Cocktail dresses," Kate said.

"I want to find something blue," Beth said. "Maybe a sweetheart neckline to enhance the girls." Beth gestured toward her chest. Kelsey giggled.

"That would be pretty on you," Emma said.

"I want mine to be classic, like Audrey Hepburn," Kate said.

Kelsey said, "I'm thinking dramatic and bold."

"Metallic and fitted but feminine," Emma said.

"What about you, Ashling?" Beth asked.

I didn't have a clue what I wanted. I had never been shopping for dresses. Mother had dresses made for me that were considered appropriate. I never had a say in what I wore.

"You guys will have to help me pick something out, I guess," I said.

"You know we will," Beth said.

After trying on nearly every dress in the store, Kate, Emma, and Beth had found theirs. They seemed to know exactly what they were looking for. But Kelsey was nearly in tears—she couldn't find what she wanted. Kate tried to calm her, but it wasn't working. I walked through the store again and found an employee.

"My friend is looking for something flowing and jewel-toned." I smiled.

"I know just the one, it came in yesterday. It's not supposed to hit the floor until tomorrow, but I'll make an exception for you," she said. She came back with a beautiful dress, and Kelsey's face lit up like a light bulb.

Finally all my friends had their dream dresses. It felt good to see them all smiling and happy. Their emotions affected mine. If they were sad, I could feel it. It was overwhelming, and it was hard to not let their emotions take over mine. Their human emotions had a stronger effect on me than the emotions of my own kind.

"Didn't you find one you like?" Beth asked.

I laughed nervously. "I guess I haven't tried any on yet."

"Well, now it's your turn," Kate said.

"What style do you like?" Kelsey asked.

"I'm not really sure. Something soft, flowing, and organic," I said.

They all ran around the store, searching for the right dress for me. They paraded dresses past me. There were pink dresses, bubble dresses, and dresses with bows, but I didn't like any of them.

Then Beth walked over timidly, handing me a single dress. It was a cream-colored, one-shoulder dress with an iris print of green, teal, and gold and a handkerchief hem. Flowing, feminine, and just what I wanted. I tried it on, and it fit just right.

"It's lovely!" I said, hugging Beth.

We headed to the counter to pay. Beth and I stepped up to pay as the others went to check the area for food establishments. Beth's dress rang up $350, and she turned a shade of purple.

"I don't have enough," she said quietly to the cashier. "I only have $225. I'll have to buy a different dress." Her sadness crashed into me, nearly making me cry. She glanced around the store, looking for a dress she could afford. She wouldn't look at me or the cashier. She was clearly embarrassed.

I pushed my dress forward to the cashier and said, "Ring them both up on me."

"Oh no, Ashling, you can't. I couldn't."

"You can't have a second-choice dress for our first dance."

"I can't take your money," she almost cried.

"You aren't." I smiled. "You're letting me do something for my best friend."

"Are you sure about this?" she asked.

"About what?" Kate asked as they all came back in. Beth's face lost all color. She didn't want to tell the others she didn't have enough money. That was social suicide. It wasn't that the other girls were mean. It was just one of those things everyone would always remember, she would always remember.

"Oh, Beth forgot her credit card today, so I'm spotting her the cash," I said. "Now where are we going to eat? I'm starving." I winked at Beth, changing the subject quickly and easily. She started to breathe again.

"The pub is open. They have burgers and stuff like that," Kate said. "The café on the beach is already closed." She shrugged.

"Great," I said as we followed Kate. Beth mouthed "thank you" to me. It was a simple gesture, but it made me feel like a hero.

After I gagged down dinner, we all sat laughing and talking for a long time as the restaurant started to fill up with regulars. Our booth faced the bar, so we had a good stage for people-watching. I learned what a cougar was, and it wasn't a wild animal, that was for sure. It was certainly a learning experience. The girls taught me all the different types of drunks, but all I saw was waste. Waste of life, time, and money.

The bar was full in no time. A group of eight college-age guys were hanging out at the bar, drinking beers and watching us. They all had the football-player build, muscular and stocky. Good-looking guys by the other girls' accounts, but I disagreed. Everything that came out of their mouths made them even less appealing, and the more they drank, the more they stared. It made me uncomfortable.

A woman with ratted-up fake-blonde hair and fake fingernails sat next to one of them, petting his shoulder and chest, trying to get his attention, but he was obviously not interested in her advances, at least for the moment. He was preoccupied with Kelsey. No one needed my keen senses to feel the vengeful rage that filled her as she was continually ignored.

The woman whispered in his ear as she stared at me, and I felt the challenge in her. Something had changed in her, and it wasn't in our favor. The pheromones they gave off filled my nostrils with poison, and the hair on the back of my neck stood on end.

"We should head home," I said.

"I agree," Beth said.

"No, let's hang out a little longer," Kelsey said, glancing at the guys at the bar. "I don't have a date for the dance yet."

"It's getting pretty late," I said.

"Yeah," Emma said. "Let's get going."

"Ten more minutes," Kelsey replied.

"No, I think we have to go," Kate said. She grabbed her keys.

I stood up and threw cash on the table to cover the check. "Let's go," I said, waiting for them to all file past me to the door. Kelsey was the last to go, and she smiled at the guys before turning to leave. An open invitation to follow. Was she stupid? That was like a chicken dancing in front of a fox and wondering later why it was dying. The others were already outside as I pushed Kelsey out the door. We caught up to them by the van, where three guys blocked their path.

The other guys followed Kelsey and me; we were surrounded. We couldn't get in the van, and we couldn't go back to the restaurant. If the girls ran and separated themselves, I wouldn't be able to protect them all.

"Get out of my way," Beth said. I could hear wavering in her voice, but she was trying to be strong. The other girls clustered behind her. Even Kelsey finally understood the gravity of the situation she had created. There were more of them than us, and they were drunk.

"Going somewhere?" the leader said to Beth, batting her hair off her shoulder as his woman came around his large frame, hanging on him like a viper. The smile on her face almost made me look away.

"Leave us alone," Emma said.

The woman smiled, but her eyes were cold. "Honey, why don't you pick one of them for us."

"Don't you want to come with us?" another egged us on. "We'll show you a real good time."

I'll show them a real good time with a swift kick to the balls, I thought. If I were alone, I would have ripped them apart, leaving their dead carcasses on the unforgiving ground.

"No. We don't like you," Kate said.

"That's not the message we were getting in the bar," I heard from behind me.

"It's the message we are sending loud and clear now," Beth said.

"I like her," the woman said. "I could enjoy breaking her."

He ignored her and responded to Beth. "You have something to say to me, little girl?" he said, stepping closer to Beth.

"No, but I do," I said. The girls all turned to me with fear in their eyes. I walked around them, slipping the keys out of Kate's hand as I shoved the guy blocking the sliding door of the van. "Get in!" They quickly all jumped in, I tossed the keys in after them, and I slammed the door shut. My movements were far too fast for a human's, but I hoped no one noticed.

The guys closed in around me, closer now. Angrier. They thought they had the upper hand on me, but I was the monster in this story. The girls screamed for help and begged me to get in, but I didn't dare open that door. It would endanger their lives.

The woman shoved her scrawny hands into my hair, pulling it hard at the base of my skull. It hurt but not enough to give her the satisfaction of crying out.

"That was stupid," she said. "Now you're all alone."

Her lover's breath moistened my skin. It was disgusting, but I wasn't afraid of him or any of them. The alcohol on their breaths saturated the air. They were all drunk. I took a step forward—only inches from her face. My face contorted into a fierceness I had never felt before.

"We'll give you a head start, go ahead," he said, gesturing for me to run.

"Run," his buddy taunted.

My lips parted, and I showed my teeth as I partially smiled. Rage erupted inside me, and a fierce growl emerged from my throat.

"You aren't running?" he said.

"Oh. Should I be?" I asked. My sarcasm flowed freely, and my saliva ran through my mouth, making me hungry. I wanted to taste their blood, spill them open all over the ground, and feel the wet warmth of their flesh. Each of them with a unique flavor, marinated in alcohol. A buffet of stupid creatures waiting to die in front of me. The animal inside was consuming the girl. It was only a matter of time before I lost all control. I closed my eyes and let the primal need wash over me. I was only an animal after all. I licked my lips as I looked into the depths of his soul, but I couldn't find anything worth sparing.

I leaned forward and whispered into his ear, "One step closer, and I will devour your flesh while you still breathe."

He was scared—I could smell it on him. My promise was sincere. If he didn't act on his fear, I wouldn't be able to control myself much longer, and I would have their evil blood on my hands. He wouldn't be able to let a scream slip out before I sunk my teeth into his flesh. I concentrated on Beth's voice as I desperately tried to stay in control. She was the only one not screaming or crying; she was on the phone with emergency. That would be my way out. If I killed them right now, the girls would see it. If I let the attackers take me and killed them later, the police would question how I got away and what happened to them. If they just left, the girls would wonder why. But if I could just keep myself from being a stupid *animal* until the sirens came, no one would suspect anything.

"Are you going to be my first?" I asked him. I could feel my lust for blood taking over my thoughts.

"Let's get out of here," he said. "She's not worth it."

"Run, my little lambs," I said, laughing as they started to run away. I wanted to chase. I *needed* to chase. It was in my blood, but the police cars raced into the parking lot, surrounding them. I had to play the part of a scared girl, I had to stop the beast inside.

The van door flung open. "What were you thinking, Ashling!" Emma sobbed onto my shoulder. "I was so worried."

She was just the distraction I needed to separate myself once again from the animal inside. My true self. I wrapped my arms around her limp shoulders and let her cry on me, holding her tight, for fear she would fall apart. The girls mashed around us in one big group hug as we watched the police put the men and the woman in handcuffs. Only I could hear the leader thanking the police for arresting him.

He pointed over at me, saying I was demented. Warning them to be careful. His eyes locked with mine, and I burned my glare into his. He jumped into the police car when the door opened. The handsome, young police officer looked back over our way suspiciously. I gave him my biggest, saddest puppy eyes, and I bashfully glanced away, turning my attention back to my friends.

"I'm sorry, you guys. I saw a chance to protect you, and I didn't see any other way. Please forgive me," I said, covering my inner smile and victory. "It was stupid." I shook my head for effect. In truth, I was proud of myself. It was my purpose to protect Old Mother's humans from harm, and now they were my friends too.

"I'm so glad you're safe. Did they hurt you?" Beth asked.

"I'm fine." I smiled. "I promise."

The young police officer sauntered over to question us. The girls told the story perfectly. I just stood back bashfully and watched him. His blond hair wisped over his tan face, and the girls whispered about how cute he was in his uniform. Though I hadn't noticed all the details they had, he wasn't really my type, but I caught him stealing glances at me. Eventually I smiled in return, causing him to drop his pen. Normally I would have laughed, but it didn't seem like the place, considering what had just happened. They answered all his questions, and Kelsey even asked him to the dance. He declined but still gave her his card, in case we thought of anything else.

"Miss Boru," he said, turning toward me. "May I please have a word with you?" He gestured for me to walk with him toward his cruiser, and I did as instructed. We stopped out of earshot of the girls and the other officers. He studied me from head to toe—trying to discover if I really were crazy or not, I imagined. The men were petrified, which did make the officer suspicious of me.

"Is there something you need?" I smiled up into his golden face and his unusual brown eyes. He smiled back, almost dumbfounded. Perfect white teeth. His mother must be so proud, I mused.

"I just wanted to personally make sure you were uhharmed. What you did was brave, but you should never endanger your life like that." He started fussing over me, checking my arms for bruises. Finally as he moved my hair, I winced. "Are you all right, miss? I can *personally* rush you to the hospital."

"Oh no. I'm fine," I said, smiling.

"Well, Miss Boru. I'll let you out of my sight, this time. . . ." He pulled out another one of his business cards, but this time, he flipped it over and jotted something on the back. "This is my personal number in case *you* need anything. Any time of night or day," he said.

"Thank you, Officer Thilges."

He straightened himself up taller, puffing out his chest. "You can call me Gavin," he said. "Now you get those other girls home safe, you hear?"

I hid the card from the others. I didn't feel like explaining it. Besides, Kelsey was in love with him. Well, as in love as her fleeting emotions made her capable of being. We piled back into the van for the ride home, and she gushed about how handsome Gavin was. In my culture, age was nothing; in her culture, the ten-year gap was significant. Kelsey was the only one not shaken up—she was also the cause of all of it. Someday, that girl was going to learn *some* life lessons the hard way. I shook my head.

"Ashling, that was incredibly stupid what you did back there," Kate said. "But thank you for protecting us. I don't know what we would have done without you."

I let them recount the whole night, and the embellishments were already starting. Clearly Beth and I were the heroes of the story. I was officially high school lore, as Kate put it. I didn't admit it to them, but I was scared for their lives.

13

Wild Animal

Grey was sitting on my front porch when Kate dropped me off. Distress was written all over his face. He looked as though he had spent the last few hours pacing. I almost expected to see a worn patch in the decking where he had walked back and forth. The wrinkle between his furrowed brows was prominent and really cute, but also troubling. A look of relief washed over his face as I walked up on the porch. I reached out to touch the side of his face, and he crushed my body with the fierceness of his embrace.

"Ashling," he said. "I don't know how, but I felt you were in danger. I rushed over, but you weren't here. I didn't know what to do. I didn't know where to go. I didn't know how to tell your brother what I was feeling. How to explain to him you were in danger."

"Grey, it's okay. I'm here now."

"Are you okay? What happened?" he asked.

"The girls and I had an unpleasant encounter with some disturbed souls."

"You were in danger, weren't you? I felt it. I felt your fear."

"*They* were afraid. . . ."

"How could I feel that?"

"I don't know."

"Every moment we are together, I feel closer to you."

"Me too," I replied.

"Next time, I'll find you. I'll protect you," he said. His handsome face was strong and confident. His lips were set in a stern line as love washed over his face, mixing with his determination.

"I believe you, but trust me, we were okay. . . ." I said. "I love you."

His face softened and the worry washed away. "I want to be a part of *your* forever," he said.

"You already are," I said with a smile.

"I love the way you feel in my arms," he said, holding me tighter to his chest, lightly running his fingers through my wind-blown hair. Each stroke sent tingles over my skin, intoxicating me. I breathed his masculine scent deeper into my lungs, hungrily devouring his essence.

"So, do I get to see your dress?" I could nearly hear the smile on his face.

"No. You have to wait until the dance. Speaking of, why didn't you tell Lacey no?" I asked.

The smile left his face. "I'm sorry about that. I thought it best not to tell her no there in public. She has an ugly side to her, a vengeful side, and I didn't want her coming after you."

I smiled. "Well, I think she has finally met her match."

"So have I," he said. He crushed my lips with his, igniting my body with his touch. He ran his hand over my hipbone, lighting caressing my skin. I pressed in hard against him, feeling his rock-hard body, and I gasped as he bit my earlobe. I nipped at his lower lip, gently catching it between my teeth. His green eyes sparkled with passion.

I captured his lips with mine again and kissed him with all the ecstasy that flowed through my veins. I wanted every part of him.

Suddenly, Mund opened the door and caught sight of us. He tensed at first, but he didn't say anything. I knew he could feel the emotions flowing through our bodies, but he said nothing about it. He didn't agree with my choice, but he was strong enough to stand by and let me choose it.

"We were just going to sit down and watch a movie," Mund said. "Why don't you join us, Grey?"

Without waiting for Grey to respond, I grabbed his hand and pulled him into the house. It was strange, the way everyone described him before he knew me. Even Baran was nervous about him. And yet, with me, he was sweet and protective. I needed to learn more about soul mates, the prophecy surrounding my birth, and where Grey fit in. I wondered if it had to be a wolf that claimed me, or if Grey could do it? We could run off and get married, and he could claim me. And life would be happy. How simple that would be.

But life was never that simple. I sighed.

Baran and Mund had chosen *An American Werewolf in Paris*. If nothing else, they had a sick sense of humor between the two of them. I wondered if Grey would pick up on the oddness of the movie selection while he sat in a house full of werewolves. It seemed ironic to me. Baran even made popcorn; I was starting to think he *liked* playing human, or perhaps he had gotten so good at it over the years that didn't even realize he was doing it.

Baran sat in the leather chair, and Mund sat on one end of the sofa while Grey sat on the opposite end—as far apart as they could be. They left a giant spot in the middle between them for me. Enough room for three of me, actually.

It felt like a test. If I had to choose between my beloved brother, who protected me for sixteen years, or the love of my life, whom would I choose? The only friend I ever had, or the only love I would ever have? I wouldn't choose, because I would never have to. They both loved me. I took my seat on the floor in front of Grey. He leaned forward, wrapping his arms around my shoulders and resting his chin on my head as we watched the movie.

He fit so perfectly in our lives. I really didn't know why Mund and Baran were so afraid of what he was. He was a part of me.

Grey jolted during a fight scene, and I looked up at him, touching the side of his face. "You aren't scared, are you?" I asked, smiling.

Suddenly, he jumped back away from me. "What the hell!" he said. "Your eyes are glowing in the dark."

Instantly Baran was on his feet, and Mund grabbed me, spinning me behind him as he growled.

"Stop!" I cried.

Grey was standing in front of the sofa, and his eyes were glowing like ours. There was more wolf in him than they realized. I smiled at the thought. I wondered what color he would be if he were truly a werewolf. Gray like his name, or dark, chocolaty brown like his hair?

I stepped around Mund toward Grey, but Mund pushed me back between him and Baran. "No," Mund said.

Grey's eyes turned cold, and I could feel his rage rippling to the surface. Grey looked so much more animal than human. "Let her go," Grey said.

"You have no place here," Mund said.

"What?" I said, looking at each of them. "What is the matter with all of you?" I shoved Mund back into Baran with far more force than necessary and walked over to Grey. I was getting good at fighting back. Grey's tension eased, and he sat back on the sofa. I knelt in front of him, my back to the TV, my eyes surely glowing. I rested my hands on his.

"You okay?" I asked.

"Your eyes glow in the dark," he said. "So do theirs."

I smiled ruefully. "I know," I replied

"I've never seen someone's eyes glow in the dark before. Except my own."

Baran sat back down, watching us. Though he looked casual, I knew he was ready to fly out of his seat at any moment. Mund stayed standing, his posture rigid. Why did this have to keep happening? I wasn't a delicate flower. I wouldn't just shrivel up and die or anything. Grey touched the side of my face.

"Yours are like the color of candle-lit, warm honey. Beautiful, actually." I felt like warm honey in his hands. His compliments made my heart soar.

Mund growled, but we ignored him.

"I know mine glow, and I thought I remembered my mom's eyes glowing, but it was so long ago that I figured I'd imagined it," he said, shaking his head at the memory. "But then here you are. All of you . . ." his voice trailed off.

"Indeed," Baran said.

"Ashling, I know I said I didn't care what you are, and I don't. It doesn't change anything I feel for you. Whether you are heavenly or not, I'm yours, but I do need to understand," he said, looking at all of us.

Baran looked worried, and Mund looked furious. Was I the only one unfazed by this? It seemed only natural that Grey would figure out something was different about us. Especially when more of us were together. I didn't care if he knew what I was, I wanted him to know, but I didn't dare speak first. The look on Mund's face could silence me in a heartbeat. He was afraid of telling a human what we were; we could be chased out of town with pitchforks, or far worse.

"I think the time has come, Grey. You should know what I am," Baran said. "We are more than mere animals. We are werewolves, shape shifters. The eyes of the night."

Mund spit on the floor. He was furious and frightened. He paced between the two exits, the front door and the kitchen. I knew he didn't agree with Baran's judgment, and he wanted to pull rank with his royalty, but he didn't. He just paced back and forth, his eyes trained on Grey's every movement. Adrenaline pumped through my veins, bringing every cell in my body to life. I held my breath as I waited for him to respond.

"Werewolves . . ." Grey said.

"Yes," I replied.

He stood up, pulling his hands away from mine. Mund was instantly at my side, and in that split second, he backhanded Grey into the door. The sound echoed all around me, sickening my stomach. Grey licked the blood from his lower lip and turned his back on all of us as he put his hands on the doorframe for balance. The muscles in his back pulsed with strength.

"What do you eat?" he asked. There was an accusation in his tone, and Mund growled in return.

I stayed sitting on the floor to not further upset them all. "We prefer to catch our own wild game, but we can eat everything humans eat," I said.

"You don't eat humans?"

"No, Grey. We do not. There are some who have forsaken their vows of protection and do kill humans, but we do not," I said.

"So the legends are true? Werewolves are real?"

"Yes, the legends are true for the most part. We live forever. We shift form at will. We are supreme beings. We protect the balance of life and protect all humans from danger and from each other," Baran said.

"You're being careless, he's not one of us," Mund said.

"He has a right to know. If he's going to love Ashling, he should understand what we are and what he's committing his life to." Baran continued, "Our appearance is varied, usually by our genetic makeup, matching our hair color. Our physical stature in our wolf form corresponds to our stature in human form, and other similarities cross over, such as hair color and eye color. Ashling, for instance, is a small red wolf."

Grey smiled at me shamelessly. "I've seen you," he said. I didn't take my eyes off Grey, but by the sounds in the room, Mund swallowed his own tongue. "The little red wolf that day in the woods . . . I knew it was you."

I nodded. He touched his cheek where I had licked him that day.

"Werewolf," he said.

"You're the one running with wolves, you fool." I playfully batted at him.

"He's seen you?!" Mund roared, advancing toward Grey, but Baran stepped between him and us.

"Care to explain?" Baran asked me.

"I was at the falls, trying to learn the different sounds and scents of all the animals, when I got caught in one of the game warden's traps.

Grey set me free," I said, smiling at him. "I had been running through the woods, and Grey ran with me. Stride for stride." I couldn't hide my admiration for him.

Their faces wore every emotion: gratefulness, anger, and fear. I had been reckless, I knew that, but I wouldn't change it. My reckless behavior brought Grey to me.

"What were you thinking, Ashling?" Mund said. "You should never have been in the woods by yourself. What could have happened?"

"Grey was there."

Mund glared at us. "You're a trusting fool."

"Mund?" I said.

"You shouldn't trust so easily," Mund said. Then he turned his angry stare on Baran. "And neither should you. I know you want to trust him . . ." He turned his back on us.

"Grey, we are putting our faith in you. You have to understand that you can never tell anyone about us, or you risk endangering Ashling's life," Baran said.

"I understand," he replied.

"Is that bloody good enough?" Mund said. "You're going to trust this half-breed with her *life?* I know he's Brenna's son, but that doesn't make this right!"

Grey turned his attention on Mund at the sound of his mother's name. He watched Mund carefully. I wonder how much he really knew about his mother and about us. There was an eerie quiet to him.

"Mund . . ." I said. How could he be so mean after everything Grey had done to protect me and how much he clearly loved me? He treated Grey as if he were still a stranger.

"You understand this, *wanker*—she's my sister, and if you hurt a hair on her head, I will bleed every drop of blood from your body," Mund said.

There was a quizzical look on Grey's face, as though he knew something more than he was saying. He stood up and offered his hand to Mund. "Agreed," he said, waiting for Mund to shake his hand. But Mund didn't accept it; he only growled in return. "Look, I get it. She's your baby sister, and you're having a hard time letting go of the fact that she's growing up." He paused, studying my face. "But you understand this—I love her and I am a permanent fixture in your life as long as she wants me here. So get used to it."

Mund's growl deepened. It was a warning, but Grey ignored it, turning his back on him. Was it arrogance, or a misguided trust in Mund? He was oddly unaffected by what Baran had told him, and it was troubling that he didn't have a stronger reaction, as though he were the one keeping secrets.

"So can I see you as a wolf?" he asked.

Baran answered for me, "No. There's more you need to understand, Grey. If you are going to be a part of her life, you need to understand she is in hiding right now. There are some *dogs* from our world that are trying to take her from us, so you'll need to help us keep her safe."

"That I can do," Grey said, scooping me up from the floor into his arms as if I were a child, holding me tightly to his chest as if I weighed nothing more than a feather. "As long as you want me."

"Good. Now can I finish my movie?" Baran asked.

Grey sat down on the sofa with me in his lap, and I rested my head on his shoulder. Mund stayed standing by the front door. He was too shocked to move, and I was too angry with him for overreacting about this whole thing, but I had to admire him for loving me so much. No matter how mad I was, I was still touched by how much he cared about me.

I listened to Grey's heart; it was steady and unyielding, like his love for me. He was watching me instead of the movie, studying my face, though I couldn't fathom what he was seeing.

"You really are my little wild one," he whispered in my ear. I hid my smile, but I liked the way he said *my*. I liked the way it sounded on his lips. Before I met Grey, I could never have imagined the depth of love and how much it would change me.

The movie ended, and Grey said his goodbye to me—three times before finally driving off. Which left me with Mund again. He had to get over the protective-older-brother thing. It was getting old. I was a big girl, and I didn't need a babysitter any more.

I shut the front door quietly and stood, waiting for them to get it over with. But Mund didn't say anything; he only held his face in his hands as he sat on the edge of the sofa while Baran still sat in his chair.

"Thank you," I said.

"Ash, please be careful," Mund whispered through his hands.

"I know, I know. The prophecy," I said.

He looked up at me with pain in his eyes. "Ash, it's not like that. I don't care about any prophecy. I only care about keeping you safe."

"Right."

"Be fair," Mund said.

"Fine. Then you be fair. I love him. End of story."

"Well, now he knows what we are," he said. "If we aren't dead by morning, he's probably a keeper." I laughed despite my annoyance with him. Even when he was being melodramatic, he still had a sense of humor.

Luckily two weeks passed without any fights. Grey spent every day at our house or at Ryan's practicing. Either way, we spent every evening together. Laughing, hugging, even stealing a kiss or two when no one was looking. School blew by without even having to notice. I just kept smiling and saying hi to Lacey, and she just kept ignoring me—the best of both worlds.

I worked on translating the journal and found poems of love from Ragnall to Calista. I found a pressed thistle, which was a sign of strength, and drawings of the ring on my finger. One passage I translated caught me by surprise.

Spring 1048

The visions come more often of Ragnall's and my demise. Our wedding brings my death. Uaid's betrayal. The red one, the dream, she will come from my blood to save us all. With her snow-white skin and crimson curls. She is the missing element that will bring balance back to the earth.

She wrote of her own death two years before it came to pass in 1050. She knew Uaid Dvergar would kill her, and yet she still married Ragnall and died. For love? Or for me? Why would she accept death for the idea of someone coming over nine hundred years later? She knowingly sacrificed herself . . . for the dream of *me*.

Could I have made such a sacrifice for the sake of love? I couldn't truly know until I was put in the situation. I couldn't say how strong I would be, how hard I would fight, or how much I could really sacrifice for the ones I loved. It was humbling to finally understand the sacrifices that had been made for me.

Another entry also captured my attention. This one I didn't share with Mund or Baran. This one I kept to myself. They wouldn't understand.

Winter 1048

The Dream will be all-powerful with her love by her side. Finding this wolf is of the utmost importance. He is the key to her . . .

The entry was incomplete and abruptly stopped midsentence, the ink smudged on the last word. But I knew it referenced a wolf . . . a wolf who would be my love. If Mund knew the prophecy spoke of a wolf love of mine, he would fight harder against my choice to bind with Grey, a human. This entry would be mine alone. I tore it out of the journal, hiding it in my copy of *Pride and Prejudice.* Mund hated fiction—he'd never open it.

Maybe she was wrong about the prophecy. Or maybe it was never about me and they were all mistaken. All of the *maybes* made it hard to think. I wished Mother were here; she would hold me tight in her steel grip, safe from worry, and braid my hair while singing a sweet song. She would tell me to stop running wild as she delicately washed the dirt from my face. I missed everything about her, though I could still feel her love and strength in my heart.

The day of the dance finally came, and it coincided with Samhain, the end of summer. It was an important ceremonious day for our kind, but I had a dance to go to. The girls had nominated my house for getting ready. Baran was less than thrilled about having so many hormone-charged humans in the house again, but he still agreed. He said he would stop back before we all left for the dance. Mund also decided to hide elsewhere until he absolutely had to come back in to get dressed.

Kate and Beth were the lucky ones with dates. At least the rest of us had each other to hang out with, though. I wasn't sure why I was going— Grey would be playing up in the band. I would be alone all night, and Lacey would be there, hopefully without incident. She had been ignoring me for weeks, so that seemed promising.

The girls sculpted their hair into beautiful up-dos, but I didn't have a clue what to do with mine or how. This was one of those moments when I found myself looking around and realizing how completely unfeminine I really was. I could hardly put mascara on without poking myself in the eye.

"What do you ladies think?" Kate asked, spinning around, showing her perfect hair.

"Beautiful," Emma said.

"Truly lovely," I replied.

"You haven't started your hair, Ashling," Kate said.

"I don't know what to do with it. And even if I figured that out, I'm not sure I'd know how to accomplish it." I laughed nervously. I hated feeling inadequate. I could dance nearly every classical step, I could weave silk, speak the language of the Bloodmoon, and recite classic poetry in Latin. I was even learning ancient Greek, but could I do my own hair? No. Every part of being a girl that should come naturally was foreign to me.

Kate squeezed my shoulder and studied my dress. "With the shape of your dress, I think we should do something asymmetrical." She began moving my hair around expertly, creating a side sweep. "Let's straighten your hair. It'll be beautiful, but still a little wild. What do you think?"

she asked.

I just nodded. I had no idea what she was talking about, but I trusted her style. The others continued on their own hair and makeup while Kate straightened my hair, section by section. I watched her transform me into someone I didn't even know. The girl in the mirror was smooth and refined, wide-eyed and beautiful. By the time she was done, my hair was exquisitely shaped around one side of my face.

"Oh, Kate . . ." I said.

"You're welcome. Emma, can you help Ashling with makeup? You're a pro."

Emma smiled. "What do you want me to do?" she asked as she started digging through a large makeup bag, pulling out dozens of strange little containers.

"Not sure really. Something simple."

"How about we play up your eyes and do a simple nude lip," she said, more to herself than to me. "A lightly smoky eye, but in golden tones."

After Emma and Kate finished their work, I looked like a woman. I had to admit, I loved the feeling of being dressed up.

"Clint and James should be here soon," Kate said.

"Will you help me?" Emma asked Kelsey as she held out a flower corsage she'd purchased herself. Kelsey easily pinned it on to her bodice.

"My mom bought me one too," Kelsey said.

A horn honked outside, sending us all running to the window to peer out. There stood James and Clint in front of a black limo, smiling proudly. Beth and Kate rushed out to greet them, and Kelsey, Emma, and I followed. It was going to be my first ride in a limo. Everyone was ready to go, but I felt out of place. I wasn't as dressed up as the others, and I didn't have flowers as they all did. I wished I would have known—I could have picked something up.

Mund walked out the front door in a light-gray suit with a white dress shirt and a white tie. He looked striking. And if Emma's gasp wasn't enough to convince him he looked good, nothing would.

"I was just wondering about you," I said.

He smiled, opening the limo door. "Ladies, your chariot awaits," he said. Emma giggled as she hopped in. Mund pulled a container from behind his back, revealing white orchids. "I thought you could use this," he said, pinning the delicate flowers into my hair.

"Thank you, Mund."

"Let's go!" someone called from inside the limo.

"Where's Baran?" I asked. "He said he'd be here."

"Something came up."

"What?"

"Nothing to worry about," Mund said.

Nothing to worry about? With them, it was always something to worry about, but I decided to wait and give it my full attention later. Tonight was about enjoying this human ritual, the homecoming dance.

We arrived at the dance about twenty minutes after it had already started, making our grand entrance. The darkness made me nervous, but luckily the strobe lights made it impossible for anyone to notice our glowing eyes. The gymnasium was decorated with paper streamers and gossamer. It seemed the entire senior high was actually there, even Lacey. I could have spotted her a mile away . . . even if she wasn't standing in front of Grey, jumping up and down, screaming like a groupie. She was dressed in a nauseating pink strapless dress with a bow on the side, as though she were a little pink present, her bleached-blonde hair piled on top of her head.

The song ended, and Lacey and Nikki headed off to the refreshment table. The dance floor cleared, leaving an opening from Grey at the front of the gym to me at the very back, standing alone. He wore an exquisitely tailored black pinstriped suit coat and pants with a white dress shirt, collar tips flipped up, and a loose, straight-cut black tie. He looked delicious, and my heart was beating so loud in my ears, I couldn't hear anything around me. All I could see was him. They started playing another song, and his voice penetrated my mind. It felt as if my blood were being replaced by an intoxicating drug, tingling every inch of my body. His guitar swung at his hip as he walked the length of the gymnasium toward me, singing. His jacket swayed with each step of his strut, enticing my soul.

I couldn't hear the words he was singing; my erratic pulse thundered through my body as I watched the movements of his perfect lips. I knew everyone was watching him, but I didn't see any of them. Only Grey. He fell to his knees, sliding to my feet with six bright-red roses in his hands. His lips curved up into a mischievous little grin, and his eyes were wild. He studied every inch of me from the top of my head to the bottom of my toes.

"May I have this dance, my lady?" he said.

I slipped my hand into his and let him lead me to the center of the dance floor as he sang to me. Everyone watched us, but to us, the room was empty, only our love remained. The song came to an end, and the room stopped spinning—or we stopped moving. I wasn't sure which. He leaned forward, kissing me on the cheek.

"Love you," he said as he winked and ran back up to the stage.

I had to escape. Everyone was staring at me, and it made me apprehensive. I darted to the bathroom for shelter. I needed to breathe and have a moment to myself away from the scrutiny of their prying eyes.

After regaining my ability to think and breathe on my own, I relinquished my hiding place and exited into the hallway, where I promptly ran right into Lacey. Her face matched the color of her dress. "I hate you!" she said, ripping the roses from my hands. Petals fell all over, creating cascades of red that covered the floor. It looked like blood. The glorious flowers were destroyed, but I knelt down to scoop them back up.

"You're nothing more than a fling," she sneered. "He'll dump you when he's done using you up! He'll come back to me, you know."

I looked up at her contorted face. "I'm sorry you feel that way," I replied, and I went back to collecting all the petals from the floor, trying to put back together what she had destroyed. Lacey slapped the broken flowers from my hand. With the second assault, anger started to flow through me, and my vision flickered, but I had to hold the wolf at bay. No matter how much she deserved my wrath, I had to remain calm. This wasn't the place to lose control.

Standing up, I put myself face to face with the little waif of a girl, looking her right in the eyes as she continued her verbal assault. "Why don't you go back where you came from, you *dog*!" she said.

At some point, people had started to notice what was going on and were beginning to circle around us. I almost laughed at the spectacle she was making. And to think, I had hid in the bathroom so I wouldn't be the center of attention. Now here I stood, in the middle of a silly fight over a boy, just like a teenager. I finally got what I wanted, to feel like a normal sixteen-year-old girl.

I stood in a pool of broken flowers as Grey walked over to us. He wrapped his arm around my waist and started to pull me away from Lacey and her hate. She grabbed my arm, pulling me back, then pushed me with all her might into the wall. I hardly felt the impact, but rage churned in my body.

"What the hell, Lacey," Grey said.

"She's not good enough for you, Grey. She's not like us," she said.

"You're right about one thing," he replied. "We're not like you."

"Little cat fight?" Mund asked, suddenly appearing.

"Hardly," I said.

Grey said, "Come on, let's get some fresh air." He led the way out the front doors to the picnic tables, leaving Lacey in her embarrassing mess of pink and red.

"You okay? Did she hurt you?"

"I'll be fine," I said.

"I'll buy you more flowers," he said.

I poked him in the nose with my index finger and smiled. "I don't need flowers. I only need you." He smiled back, kissing my forehead, and we gazed up at the stars in silence.

Suddenly, Mund ran out to us. "We have to go," he said.

"Why?" I replied.

"Baran."

Instantly both Grey and I were up and ready to run. Emma came out after Mund. "Where are you going?" she asked, batting her eyes. Her infatuation with him was starting to annoy me.

"Ashling isn't feeling well. So we're going to take her home," Mund said. "Will you be a dear and tell everyone?" He knew how to put on the charm when he wanted to.

"Oh yes," she said. "Feel better, Ashling. *Bye,* Mund. . . ."

We made our way to the side of the school, out of sight. "We have to run," Mund said.

"Okay," I replied.

"Can he keep up?" Mund asked.

"Yes," I said, slipping off my high heels.

"We have to get home to Baran—something isn't right," Mund said to Grey. "I trust you."

Grey nodded. With one shoe in each hand, I started running for home with Mund and Grey flanking me on either side. Flying past houses at incredible speeds, I could see Mund watching Grey's agile movements. It had to blow Mund's mind to see a human with such strength and agility.

We reached the house in a matter of minutes. Bursting through the front door, the rush of a human's scent washed over me. Mund recoiled from it, blocking both Grey and me from entering any farther. He was instantly on the defense, only a split second from shifting at any sound.

"What is it?" Grey said.

"The Bloodsucker," Mund replied.

Grey looked confused and worried. I remembered what they had said about the Bloodsucker killing a wolf to trap the others. Was this a trap? As scared as I was, Grey looked worse. His face was pale, and his palms began to sweat.

Baran leapt into the living room as a giant salt-and-pepper gray wolf. He was a dire wolf, alpha in every sense of the word despite his current position as a nomad. Robert lunged in after Baran with a large silver blade, barely missing Baran's back leg. Baran snarled at Robert and slowly backed up closer to us, keeping a cautious distance between Robert and us. Robert's expression changed from enjoyment to rage when he finally saw his son. I could only stare at his silver blade; one prick of our skin would make us temporarily mortal. Fear crept through me as I finally realized it was Robert's scent that I had smelled that day on Baran. Only it hadn't registered as Grey's father then . . . but there was no doubt that Robert was a Bloodsucker.

"Get out," Mund said to Robert.

The authority rang off each word Mund spoke, but Robert didn't move. He stared from me to Grey and back again. Neither Mund nor Baran seemed to notice the difference in Grey, but he was motionless in his father's presence.

I was sure Robert recognized me from the forest, and he had concluded that the shoes left in his son's room were mine. He was the Bloodsucker and Grey was his son. Dread filled my mind, slowing my reactions.

His father was a murderer, his mother the victim. That was what Baran couldn't say earlier. I could feel the truth vibrating in the air. Robert was bred to kill our kind. It was his sole purpose on this earth, and his son was my love and my executioner.

"Grey, what are you doing here?" Robert said.

Mund finally realized the situation. He was desperate to pull me away from Grey's side; I could see it in his eyes. But he didn't dare move and give Robert a chance to attack Baran. It was all happening so fast. I didn't know how to make it stop.

Grey held my hand tightly, straightened his posture, and he faced his father.

Robert choked back a twisted laugh. "Do you realize what she is?!"

"I love her."

"You can't *love* a filthy dog." Robert spat out the words.

"I love her," Grey repeated.

"It's time for you to leave," Mund said to Robert.

"Not without *my* son," he said, his words cutting.

"I'm staying with Ashling," Grey said.

"They are nothing more than a pack of wild dogs! Infesting the human race with their disease!"

Grey didn't respond. He stood his ground next to me, intertwining our fingers, holding my hand firmly with his. Mund looked as though he were about to rip out of his skin to silence Robert, but one movement from him could set off events with consequences we hadn't even imagined.

"You listen to me, boy—if you stay here, you renounce everything your mother stood for. You will shame her life," Robert said.

Grey hung his head in disgrace. He actually believed the heinous words that came from Robert's evil mouth.

"Your mother died to protect you from this filth," Robert said.

Baran growled and snapped at Robert, and I could feel his bitter rage at Robert's lies. Grey wasn't looking at anyone, his eyes cast to the floor. I felt desperate. After several long seconds, he said, "I'm sorry, Ashling." Before anyone could say anything else or look at anyone, he was gone; the love of my life turned and walked out the door without even giving me a second glance. In one moment, everything changed. The shoes fell from my hand, clattering on the floor. My cold, empty hand ached for his touch. One simple lie destroyed everything.

14
Fake It

The sobs came from somewhere deep inside. I fell to the floor, unable to hold myself up. Baran lunged at Robert, chasing him out through the back door. But Mund stood guard by my side; he needn't have, there was nothing left. No reason to breathe. Grey was gone, and I was empty. Each breath my body took cut my soul. I couldn't move; I just lay there on the floor, tears streaming down my face.

I cried so hard, I started to gag. I wanted to die. I never wanted to feel again. This was the worst pain I could endure. Wasn't I good enough to love?

I smelled Baran return, but I couldn't see him through my tears. I only heard murmurs of their conversation. I wondered if he caught Robert. Would Baran hurt Grey? The thoughts tore me apart—loyalty to my family, or to my love for Grey? Was this really the choice Grey had made? The deep, unrelenting pain in my heart thickened and slowed with each beat.

"I want to die. . . ." I said, barely a whisper.

"No, Ash," Mund said.

"I can't live without him."

"You can and you will," Baran said.

"He made me feel like a princess," I cried.

"You *are* a princess," Mund said, smoothing my hair out of my face. "You don't need him to make you feel anything."

But he was wrong, I did need Grey. I had never lived before I knew Grey—he was my match and I was his.

"I knew he couldn't be trusted. He's a murderer," Mund said.

"I should have known better," Baran said. "I knew something was wrong with Robert, but I didn't want to see what it was. I was too busy trying to be Grey's friend to see him clearly. And then he was so different with Ashling. I thought she had brought him to life, but I overlooked the obvious danger."

Like a jolt of lightning, my body suddenly heaved under pressure, and a small whimper escaped my lips. Grey. Someone had struck him across the face, but my face stung from the pain. I doubled over from the overwhelming feelings. His emotions were changing quickly. More intense than my own feelings in my own body, his took over every cell, consuming me.

Mund was at my side. "What is it? Are you alright?"

"No . . . no. It's nothing," I said. But it was something. Something was wrong with Grey. I felt his emotions shift quickly, and his anger pulsed through my veins. My face still stung from the impact. "I'm going to lie down," I said, excusing myself to my room. I felt sick to my stomach. Grey's father was beating him—punishment for being with *me*. Why could I feel him so strongly now, when I couldn't before? Why, now that he had chosen to not be with me?

I gasped for air on the cold floor of my room. Every assault on Grey's body registered pain on mine. My ribs felt bruised and my face felt swollen, but no visible wounds showed on my skin. Every pain, every impact, every nauseating blow, was mine to endure. He didn't fight back, I could feel it. He just took the punishment upon himself. His sorrow rippled through me. I crawled to the window seat, resting my tear-drenched face on the cushion, gasping for air, waiting for the pain to stop. "Grey . . ." I whispered.

How could he leave me? Only to be beaten? He had betrayed me. He betrayed me for the love of his mother, I reminded myself. Robert had lied to him, but Grey had still made his choice. I couldn't tell him his own father was nothing more than a liar. He had to figure it out for himself. I couldn't force him to love me, even if I wanted to.

It didn't make sense that I could feel actual physical pain through Grey. Neither Baran nor Mund mentioned physical pain from being connected like this. Only emotions. We hadn't finished binding, but I could feel what he felt deep in my bones. His father was punishing him for loving me, and I hated Robert for it.

A shadow moved outside, hiding among the trees, just out of sight. Whatever it was, it wasn't about to show itself, and I was in no mood for games. I shakily stood up, opening the window. "GO AWAY," I cried to the moon.

When I looked back, the shadow was gone.

Baran and Mund burst into my room, questions shooting out of their mouths faster than I could process in my broken state. Blinking back the tears, I crumbled to the floor in the fetal position, weeping. I felt Mund scoop me up, and he hummed mother's lullaby as he rocked me back and forth like a child. My entire body felt lifeless in his arms, and my stomach recoiled from the nausea.

"I can feel him," I said.

"The emotional connection comes quickly for some bonded pairs," Baran said.

"No. I *feel* what he feels."

"You're feeling the emotions he's feeling. It can be very overwhelming at first," Mund replied.

"You don't understand. I felt him being beaten. I felt every hit, every blow. I felt it."

"What?" Mund said. "It's impossible."

"Nothing is impossible with Ashling, is it?" Baran shrugged.

"It's never happened before, not that I know of," Mund said.

"Our little Ashling transcends all reason, realms, and realities."

I floated in and out of their conversation. I heard them say horrible things about Grey and his father, but I was too numb to respond. Mund even suggested leaving Maine to seek refuge somewhere else. Had I the will, I would have refused, instead I cried myself to sleep.

My tears spilled over my cheeks, and the floor shined like glitter. I ran my finger into the surface of the dark liquid. It was warm as it pooled around my fingertip. It was so beautiful, but what was it? I lift my hand up to inspect the shiny substance that covered my hand, and I quickly realized it was blood. It was all around me. Red and glistening in the tiny bit of light from the open doorway. Was it my blood? My body shook with fear.

"Ashling, Ashling, shhh now. It's all right. I'm here," Baran said as he crushed my limp body into his hard chest. The dream felt real, and the tears were still on my face, but was it a dream, or was it a warning? I gagged air into my lungs as I cried.

"*Ylva,* my little she-wolf, I'm right here," he leaned down and kissed the top of my head.

The sun was bright; it was midday. How long had I been asleep? Had Baran been sitting next to me, watching me dream? Watching the tears seep from my sleeping eyes and the pain ripple through my helpless body? I wonder if he thought I would perish from this earth in front of his eyes.

I tried to speak, but my throat was raw.

Baran said, "Take it slow. I'll go get you some water."

He was back before I pulled myself up to sit. He carefully held the cup at my lips and let me drink. Mund burst into my room with Quinn on his heels.

"Ash!" Mund said, running to my side. He crushed me in a hug.

"Ashling," Quinn said softly. "It's so good to see you."

Tegan waddled in with Gwyn's assistance. The baby must have been due any day—even nine months pregnant, she almost glowed. Had the rest of the family come? I desperately hoped Mother had come. I wondered what she would say about this life of mine. I watched the doorway, but she didn't show.

They must have all hated me for needing them to leave their lives and come here to take care of me—an emotionally broken teenage werewolf who found the only human who wasn't only half wolf but half Bloodsucker as well. That sort of tragedy bordered on absurdity. Now that I was back with the living, they could all go home. They shouldn't have had to been here to see my failures. I had managed to destroy a lot of lives, including my own.

Tegan sat on the edge of the bed, smiling at me. "Hi, Ashie," she said.

"Hi," I choked.

"It's good to see you. I've missed you." Her voice was so sweet, like songbirds chirping. "I wanted you to be with me when the baby comes. Since you couldn't come to us, we came to you." I touched my hand to her stomach, and the baby kicked.

"Did you feel that?" she asked. She smiled so beautifully, the joy was clear on her face. She would be a wonderful mother.

I had to be strong for her. I wouldn't cry anymore. I would hide my emotions from them and carry on. Eventually the pain would numb. I couldn't let Grey see me like this either. I couldn't let him see how he had broken my heart. This pain was mine. I had to put myself back together, for everyone, but most of all for myself. Grey had made his choice, and I had to respect that. It was his choice to make. I promised him I would let him go if he chose, even if it killed me. And I knew I should try to find the wolf Calista wrote about . . . maybe there was another love for me. Or at least the partner I was meant for. But how could I ever love another?

"Ashie, do you want Gwyn and me to help you clean up?" Tegan asked.

"No. I can manage," I said, slowly climbing out of the bed, but a wave of nausea made me dizzy. Gwyn wrapped her strong arm around my shoulders and helped me walk to the bathroom without a word. I hardly knew Gwyn. She visited us at the cliffs only a handful of times, but she didn't know me. Still, she was here, helping me.

"Thank you," I said, "I can take it from here." I gave Gwyn a weak smile and closed the bathroom door after her. I stared at the disheveled girl in the mirror—I looked like hell. My hair was matted and knotted together. I looked gross and worn out. I hated how low I had let myself sink, but I felt helpless to change it.

Tears streamed down my face, but I muffled my cries with my hands so the others wouldn't hear my pathetic pain. I climbed into the shower still wearing my dress and sat down, letting the water run over my face. I rocked back and forth as I cried. The faces of everyone I had disappointed ran through my head. I was a burden. Nothing had changed; I was still the same outcast on the edge of Ireland.

"Ashie," Tegan said, entering and shutting the door behind her. "Sorry to intrude on your space, dearie, but I thought you might need a friend right now." She sat on the edge of the tub, getting her beautiful silver dress wet. She wrapped her arms around my shoulders, holding me tight. I rested my head on her knees as she cried with me.

I don't know how long we stayed like that before she finally let go and started washing my hair, then shut off the water that had grown cold. She grabbed a towel and wrapped it around me.

"I promise not to tell the others I saw you cry," she said, squeezing my hand. "I know it hurts, and I can't say it will go away. But I know you're strong enough to survive it."

"Thank you," I said.

"Come on. Let's get ourselves dried off."

She picked out my clothes and left me to change. She quickly returned and sat on the foot of my bed, studying me. I was embarrassed for her to see me this way.

"I wish I could join the school with you, but I can't with the baby due any day, and I need Gwyn here with me until the baby comes. Mund insisted Quinn also stay home, but Quinn, Gwyn, and I will be here waiting for you every day. We could try to switch you out of your classes with Grey, if you want?" she said.

"No." The idea of never seeing Grey again hurt nearly as much as having to torture myself by being near him. "Tegan?"

"Yes, dearest?"

"Do you think he still loves me?" I asked, looking up into her bright, extraordinarily blue eyes.

She smiled back at me. "Ashie, I *know* he still loves you."

"How do you know?"

"I just do. You've never seen yourself the way everyone else sees you. I've watched you for many years as you've grown. You don't see how everyone adores you."

"Everyone hates me."

"They don't hate you. You have to understand; we are stuck in a very old, traditional world. And you and I are different from them, because we don't *want* to just stand still and look pretty. You are powerful and a dreamer. They just don't understand you yet. Someday, you will see what you really are and what the rest of us see in you."

I didn't really believe her; I didn't see any strength in myself, only weakness. I was too weak to resist Grey, too weak to fight Adomnan. I would always be the weak one in my family.

"Thanks, Tegan." My reply was halfhearted, but I did appreciate her unending love.

"Do you want to go to school tomorrow?"

"I'm ready."

"Okay. Get some rest, and I'll help you get ready in the morning," she said and left the room, leaving me alone with my haunted thoughts.

I didn't move. I just sat there watching the clouds float by. I had let everyone down, but I kept thinking the same thought over and over again. *I love Grey.* He was all I could think about.

I was such a selfish fake.

Nightfall came, and I wrapped myself in a blanket and leaned my head against the cold windowpane. A shadow moved in the tree line again. Whatever or *whomever* it was, it had returned. It had to know I could see it, but why then did it not come for me? Why wait? I was here for the taking. There was no fight left in me. But it only watched. And so did I.

It never came out of the shadows. All night long, I waited, as did the creature in the shadows. We just watched each other as if we were participating in a never-ending staring contest. There was something comforting about its presence. My own personal stalker, lucky me.

Tegan helped me get ready for school the next morning. She styled my hair and gave my face the perfect natural glow. She handed me a simple dark-denim strapless dress and my brown boots.

"It's getting colder out," she said, handing me a cropped green sweater. "Mund will be there all day with you. If you don't feel right, you can come home sick. I'll be here."

"Thanks, Tegan," I said, forcing a smile for her.

We walked into the kitchen, where everyone waited. They looked as though they were afraid to move or that I may break, but I wouldn't. Not in front of anyone. I could survive this, Tegan said so. Forcing another fake smile for them, I walked over to Mund. "Ready?" I asked.

"Good morning, Ashling," Baran said. He looked as sad as I felt. "I think it is time you have a car of your own," he said, handing me a set of keys.

"It's in the driveway," Quinn said.

That was my cue to go look out the window and be excited. So I did, for their sake. In the driveway sat a vintage 1965 Ford Mustang in poppy red. It was the car I had always dreamed of. I had a picture of it on my wall back home. Any other day, I would have truly been excited, but today I gave him all I could muster.

"It's lovely," I said.

"I thought you shouldn't have to wait on anyone anymore," he said. "Now get to school before you're both late." He didn't like being mushy, but it was obvious I had grown on him over the last months.

"Mund, do you need a ride?" I smiled. A real smile. It felt good even if it was only for a moment.

He laughed. "No thanks, Ash. I'll follow you there." He pointed out the window to a new stone-white Jeep. Of course he had to buy himself a flashy vehicle too. I rolled my eyes and walked out to my new car. The leather-covered steering wheel felt good in my hands. I looked around— no sign of Grey. Not that I expected him to come pick me up, but a little bit of me had hoped.

Despite the new car, I couldn't remember the drive to school. Autopilot took over. I'm not sure what roads I took to get there, but I knew Mund walked into the school with me. My friends saw us and rushed over with the usual list of questions. It seemed no one knew Grey and I had broken up . . . if that was even what had happened.

"Good morning, Ashling," Ryan said, moving in next to me. I didn't like his close proximity, but there was a comfort in his presence. "I didn't get a chance to tell you, but you were gorgeous at the dance."

My eyebrow involuntarily went up, and I gave him a quizzical look.

"I mean, you're always beautiful. And you are today too, actually," he said. "Crap . . ."

"Thank you," I said, freeing him from his social suicide. "Do you mind walking me to class?"

"Yes. Definitely. Should we wait for Grey?"

"Nope," I replied.

Ryan didn't need any other explanation to walk alone with me to class. He fell in step next to me. I knew it was cruel to get his hopes up even the slightest, but I needed his company. And his silly flirtations kept my mind off Grey temporarily. It was a nice escape. Too bad I wasn't attracted to him.

We stood in the center of the hallway talking, trying to avoid going into our classes as a group of girls walked by and giggled. Ryan was the captain of the football team, which meant girls swooned for him, but Ryan hardly noticed them. He kept his eyes on mine, chatting about this and that . . . I wasn't really paying any attention. Suddenly he stopped talking and froze midsentence. I turned around to see what had scared him and saw Grey walking down the hall toward us.

He looked so good but so jealous. He was dressed in a pair of ripped black jeans and a faded black T-shirt. His black biker-boots clunked as he walked toward us with a slight chime of the buckle, it almost gave him a Wild West look. I almost expected tumbleweed to blow by. The very sight of him made my pulse quicken. I wanted to run into his arms and smother him in kisses, but instead I focused on keeping my face straight, appearing to be unfazed by his presence. I turned my attention back to Ryan, giving him a radiant smile. It worked; Ryan smiled back.

"See you at lunch, Ryan," I said loud enough for Grey to hear me as I cut in front of him to walk into class, where we shared a desk. The next hour would be horrible, but at least I knew I was having an effect on him. I took my seat and kept my attention at the front of the room. Ignoring him as he sat down.

"Hi," he said.

I chose not to reply. Instead I flipped open my book to the page written on the chalkboard. I wanted so much to talk to him, to hear his voice, to touch his hand. Ignore him, I attacked myself. You can't give in. He broke your heart, remember?

"It's nice to see you," he said.

"Oh," I replied as I pretended to read.

I could feel his pain at my rejection. He pointed his body forward, but his eyes didn't leave my face. I had just hurt him. And why? Because I could? That was petty, but it felt good too. I wanted him to see how he had hurt me. I wanted to scream at him and shake him and say, *Why didn't you love me like you said you would?* I wanted to slap him across the face until he admitted he still loved me back.

But most of all, I wanted him to be happy.

I gave him a weak smile, and a single tear rippled down my face. I quickly wiped it off and went back to pretending I were reading. I didn't want to hurt him. I just missed him. He returned the half smile, but his heart wasn't in it. All through class he watched me. I felt as if he were trying to memorize every detail and burn my image in his mind. The bell rang, and I wanted to reach out and hold his hand, but he was already out the door.

School was a numbing blur filled with snippets of Ryan's presence. Every time Ryan sat by me or walked with me, Grey looked as though he might rip Ryan's head right off his body for daring to talk to me. It was strange to see Grey so jealous. He was almost a completely different person now. He looked more dangerous than I had remembered him, and yet when he looked at me, the anger melted away, For that brief moment before he forced himself to look away, we were one again. He was *my* Grey again.

School was finally over, and I found myself sitting in my Mustang with the engine running. Mund had taken off a few minutes ahead of me, expecting me to immediately follow, but I just couldn't get myself to put it in gear. It was sleeting icy, crappy rain. Just how I felt—cold, painful shards of ice streaming into my life. I could hardly see the school's outline from where I sat, but I knew everyone had already evacuated the parking lot in a hurry to get home. Mine was the only car left in the empty lot.

I laid my head on the cold steering wheel; I just had to clear my head before I drove home. Just a few minutes to myself. I felt nauseous and I couldn't think about anything but Grey. I'd successfully pretended I was okay in front of everyone at school, but now I had to go home and put on an even better show for the others. They knew me better; they would see right through me.

My car door swung open, and I jumped halfway into the passenger's seat. Through the sleet, I could see Grey, soaked to the bone. Icicles had started forming on his wet hair and eyelashes, and dark circles were under his eyes. He looked sick. How long had he been standing outside?

"What are you doing, Ashling? Go home."

"What am I doing? You're the one soaking wet. What were you doing? Spying on me?" I demanded.

"Just go home."

A hand came out of nowhere and yanked Grey away from the door into the icy rain. I couldn't make out either of them anymore, but they were fighting. I leapt out of the car toward them; every drop of ice felt like a tiny knife on my delicate skin, but I didn't care. I reached the fight to see Mund and Grey staring at each other.

"Stay away from her—you're nothing," Mund yelled.

"Maybe you should do a better job of watching out for her," Grey said. Mund's eyes narrowed, and suddenly he swung and punched Grey right in the jaw.

I swung around and dropped to the ground, screaming in pain. My jaw felt broken. I lay on the ground, holding my face as the rain soaked through my clothes. The pain in my jaw was excruciating and debilitating.

They rushed over, but I didn't care. They could just finish their fight and kill me. I no longer wanted to be a part of this world and all this stupid fighting. I closed my eyes, hoping for the end. Welcoming it.

But it didn't come.

"You're killing her," Mund said.

"How can she feel that?" Grey asked, rubbing his own jaw.

"Stay away from her."

"How can she feel that?" Grey said again.

But Mund didn't respond. He scooped me up and carried me away, and Grey did nothing to stop him. Neither did I. Mund laid me in the passenger seat of my car, and I watched Grey disappear into the rain as Mund drove me home. My jaw ached and burned from the pain.

"Once we get home, you'll need to shift to heal your jaw," Mund said. "I'm sorry I hurt you. I forgot. I was just so angry." He kept repeating he was sorry until long after we had gotten home. I knew he was sorry, but it hurt too much to move my jaw to say so.

The whole house was in an uproar about the incident. Asking what I was doing. Was Grey hurting me? Had he stopped me from coming home? Baran was furious with Mund for leaving me at school and for hitting Grey.

Tegan wrapped her arm around my shoulders while everyone was yelling. Even Gwyn was part of the fight. "What were you thinking?" she said to Mund. "You should never have hit that boy."

"He's not a human, he doesn't deserve our protection," Mund said.

"All humans need our protection," Gwyn said.

"You need to heal," Tegan whispered in my ear.

I didn't want to heal. The pain almost felt good; it reminded me I could feel. But I didn't want to see the sad look on Tegan's face. "Please," she said. Her hands were shaking, and I could feel her sorrow.

I patted her hand, went up to my room, and shifted into my fury form. The shift tingled through my body as it began repairing. I had to admit, it was good to be back in my true body. It centered my thoughts back to Old Mother.

I wasn't mad at Mund. I wasn't even mad at Grey. But I was furious with his father.

I may be a wild animal, but he was a killer.

15

Reasons

Tegan stayed up all night with me. She was still worried. And though I didn't fully understand why it had hurt in the first place, my face didn't hurt anymore. She sat on my bed, telling me stories, and I sat in the window, watching my shadow stalker. It was there again—despite the icy rain, it sat, watching me. I wasn't listening to her. The voice in my head drowned out her voice.

I could feel the depths of Grey's sorrow, and it weighed down my mind. Making everything around me seem murky. Why couldn't he see the only way we could heal was together? He had his reasons for not being with me, and I had mine for not telling him the truth about his mother. At least I think I had reasons. As much as I kept telling myself I wasn't mad, I knew I was. But lying to everyone else worked, so I figured I might as well lie to myself. Unfortunately, it wasn't working.

I was left here calling out his name, yearning for his love. Missing the soft feeling of his lips on mine. The agony of losing him crushed my heart. Each breath I took felt as though I were drowning in sadness, desperately clawing for the surface, only to suffocate from the poison of fear. I was trapped in anguish. I wanted to close my eyes and give in to the pain. I wished I could let him go, but I didn't believe I had lost Grey for good. No matter how hard this lie pulled us apart, I was destined for him. He was my love.

"Ashie!" Tegan said. She looked angry; she must have asked me something. I wasn't being a good friend to her, but I just couldn't keep my mind straight.

"Sorry," I said.

"It's morning."

I looked out the window at the sunrise. "So it is."

I sorted through my clothes and put on jeans and a black sweater. I pulled my hair up into a high ponytail, smoothing it to the tail, where it exploded in a puff of red hair. I just wanted to survive the day and not have to think about Grey, but his face was burned into my memory. Without a word, I walked out to my Mustang and drove to school. I knew Mund was surely following me, but I didn't look. I didn't need to. He would never make that mistake again.

I didn't bother walking to my locker, since I knew Ryan would be there. I was in no mood to smile and play nice. I wanted to break something and yell and scream and punch Grey right in his perfect jaw, but that would only hurt me. It was a cruel irony.

I continued down the hall. I felt like a hollow carcass with no will to survive. I walked into my first class of the day. The room was still dark and empty, but I didn't bother turning on the lights; I welcomed the darkness. I sat in the back of the room, alone. Tegan was wrong, I wouldn't survive this. Not really. It wouldn't be me who made it out the other side. I would be someone else, going through the motions of the living.

I was meant to fulfill a prophecy and nothing more. I wasn't meant to have Grey. I stole him. I knew in the beginning it could never be, but I lied to myself and fell in love. I deserved this pain. In the aftermath of his passion, I was nothing more than ash. I had given all of myself to Grey, and there was no way for him to return it to me.

"Ashling, you're crying. . . ." Grey said.

I looked up into his big green eyes. Still, even now, I couldn't hear him coming, I didn't have any sort of defenses against him. His big, warm hands wiped away my tears, and I melted at his touch. I was helpless to him. An addict. I would do anything just to have him touch me again, love *me* again.

His face was healed. His jaw should have been broken, but here he was, good as new. It didn't make sense, but it didn't matter now. He didn't want me, and seeing him only ripped my heart open again.

"Don't cry, love," he said. "I'm not worth your tears."

"You don't know what you're worth to me," I said.

He sat down next to me but said nothing. Was this what it was going to be, just him staring at me for the rest of the semester? It was unbearable. Being apart didn't make any sense. It didn't have anything to do with *us.* It was all a lie. I felt crazy inside. I wanted to burst through my skin and disappear into the air, but my earthly body remained. What did he want from me? I had nothing more to give.

What was he doing yesterday in the rain, watching me? It wasn't like I didn't know the way home, but he had obviously been watching me. He studied my face now too. He was staring at my lips.

"I'm sorry for everything," he said.

"I'm not. I love you," I said.

I bit my lower lip, and his pulse quickened. He wanted me as much as I wanted him. The realization stunned me and warmed my body. I ached for his touch. Impulsively, I captured his lips with mine, and he let me kiss him. His tongue pushed into my mouth as I wrapped my arms around his neck. I was overwhelmed by the emotions running through my veins, but I refused to pull away from the kiss. It was my only chance to get through to him. Our love couldn't be contained by any mortal power.

"Grey and Ashling sitting in a tree, K-I-S-S-I-N-G!" someone sang.

But we didn't stop. We just continued to devour each other. Trying to get a lifetime of passion from one kiss. A lifetime of love in one moment. I could hear whispers and giggles, but I didn't care. He loved me and his lips were on mine. It felt heavenly.

The lights flickered on. "Mr. Donavan . . . Ms. Boru," our teacher said, "go to the principal's office immediately."

I started to pull away from Grey, but he grabbed the back of my head, pulling me back into the kiss. He refused to let go. He dug his fingernails in my scalp as he grasped to hold on.

"Now," Mrs. Erickson said. Grey released his grip on me, and his eyes were wild with passion. I could feel his warm breath on my face, and I felt flush.

My breath came out in bursts as I panted to calm down. Every part of me tingled from his touch, and I had lost all ability to think. Grey's lips were red from the roughness of our kiss. They looked delicious, and I want them back on mine. I had to force myself to look away before my overwhelming need to have him took over my ability to make decisions. I walked quickly out of the classroom with Grey right behind me. I was embarrassed and yet not remotely ashamed.

Once we were safely down the hall, I abruptly stopped, turning toward Grey, who stopped only inches from my face. Our short breaths mingled together as we lost ourselves in each other's eyes, drowning in our love and sorrows. Our lips were only inches apart. A slight breeze could push us together. Any excuse to touch each other. I could kiss him right now, and I knew he would kiss me back, but I had to know.

"Do you want to be with me?" I asked.

"You know I do."

"Then be with me," I said.

"I can't."

"Why?" I said.

He sighed. "Because of my mother."

"She was a *wolf,*" I said, anger dripping from my voice. I couldn't stop the words.

He didn't move for a second; he just stared. But then I felt anger rippling through his body, and he took a step closer to me. "She was *killed* by them."

"She wasn't killed by one, she *was* one."

I didn't know her story yet, but I felt the truth when the words left my mouth. It was the secret Baran kept hidden. It was the lie Robert told. I could feel the truth in my bones. I had no way to prove it, but it didn't make it any less true. I shouldn't have blurted it out at Grey—he deserved better than that—but I wanted to hurt him. And the truth always hurt the most. I wanted it to cut him and make him realize he had trusted a lie. He left me for a lie from a Bloodsucker. He didn't want to face the truth, but that wasn't good enough for me.

Even if he never forgave me for it, he deserved to know.

"What do you know about it?"

"A lot more than you," I said. "Ask your precious *father* for the truth."

Grey's anger consumed his body, and he shook uncontrollably. His hands balled into fists and straightened again. My lower lip quivered as his eyes burned into mine. He grabbed my shoulders, pushing me back into the wall, slamming my body into the tiles. I heard the tile crack from the impact, but it didn't hurt. He placed one hand against the wall on each side of my head, creating a human cage around me. His breath was ragged and almost animal-like. I was torn between passion and anger. I wanted to kiss his lips that were just about touching mine—and I wanted to slap sense into him.

"How dare you disgrace her memory," he said.

I shook my head. "No, Grey, you do. When you listen to a lie instead of your heart. You've always known the truth, haven't you?"

He leaned in, eyes narrowed as he closed in around me. I didn't resist his trap. I wasn't afraid of him. I lightly caressed the side of his face. "Grey . . ." I whispered. He seized my lips in a passionate kiss. I wanted to be with him, but at what cost? I needed him to face the truth. I turned my face away, breaking our kiss. "I have to go," I said, and I shoved him away from me.

I ran down the hall, away from his touch. I couldn't keep letting him consume my mind. I couldn't just give him parts of me—it was all or nothing. I needed to close myself off to him. It hurt too much to feel this way.

I waited by Beth's locker until the bell rang. I needed a girl's help. A normal human girl's. I couldn't possibly tell her the whole truth, but maybe that was better. I would get a normal perspective on relationships. Lacey walked by with a smirk on her face.

"It didn't take long for him to get bored of you, did it? You're just trash," Lacey said. She just kept walking as if I didn't even exist. I spotted Emma and Beth walking down the hall toward me. They both looked concerned by my expression.

"Grey and I broke up. His dad won't let him see me," I said.

"What! Why?" Emma said.

"What a dumbass," Beth replied.

"What can we do?" Emma asked as she wrapped her arm around my shoulders.

"Let's skip class. I really can't be here right now, and your company would be the best thing in the world."

"Skip?" Emma said.

"Hell yes!" Beth said. "Let's go. We'll take my truck."

Beth led the way, orchestrating our escape out the door. It was far too easy to just walk away. No one seemed to notice. We were invisible. I quickly walked a few cars over and left a note for Mund. I slipped it under the windshield wiper and jumped in Beth's truck.

Emma was babbling, filling the space between us with her nervousness. Beth slammed the truck into drive, and with that, we raced out of the parking lot to our freedom. Beth drove us across town to an enormous old stone church with a massive stained-glass window. Its presence loomed over the edge of the woods as the gatekeeper to the forest. I slowly opened my door and slid out onto the cobblestone parking lot. The church was nearly alone out here, and it would have been if it weren't for the hundreds of souls keeping it company in the adjoining graveyard. The hand-carved tombstones were as weathered as the church itself.

"I'm not sure we should be here," Emma said.

"Come on," Beth said as she dragged us through the archway into the sanctuary. She shut the old doors behind us with an echoing creek. My eyes easily adjusted to the darkness. The church was filled with pieces of the past. Only shards of light streamed through the colored glass, creating mosaics on the floors.

"Which way?" I asked.

"We'll go upstairs," Beth said, leading the way up a darkened staircase. We followed after her without a word. I could feel Emma's heart rate increase through her palm. The old church must have made her uneasy. I didn't mind the looming architecture and dark corners. It reminded me of the Rock. What a foolish child I had been then. The selfish worries of a child. I still yearned for human blood even now, as my friends' scents swirled around me, but not as I had before. My love for them overpowered any instinctual desires I had. I finally felt a love for them that Old Mother had intended all along.

We entered a room with large windows facing the forest behind. Beth shut the door, giving us privacy, but there was no one here. Beth plopped down on the floor, and Emma quickly sat next to her. I didn't know how to start telling them how I was feeling or what had happened. Where could I even begin with a tragedy such as this?

"So . . . what happened?" Beth asked.

"I don't know," I realized. "Grey's dad forbade him to date me."

"Why?" Beth asked. Leave it to her to cut the crap and get to the real issues.

Because I'm a werewolf, because Grey's greater purpose is to kill me, because his father is a Bloodsucker, because his mother died . . . none of these were things I could tell them. What was I thinking when I decided to vent to humans when I could never tell the truth?

"His father doesn't like my family, I guess," I said, finding words to explain without revealing anything I shouldn't.

"But your brother is so delicious," Emma said with a giggle. Beth shot her a dirty look, and I almost laughed.

"Grey is actually listening to his dad?" Beth asked.

"Yeah. He broke up with me," I said. "But then he kissed me today in class. In front of everyone, but he claims he can't be with me. It doesn't even make sense. I want so badly to be with him, but I don't want to be the girl who can't stand to be alone. I just don't know what to do."

"Oh, Ashling . . . that's terrible," Emma said.

"Who the hell does he think he is?" Beth said. "What a pig."

"If he kissed you, that means he still loves you and still wants to be with you. Maybe all he needs is some convincing to show him what he gave up," Emma said.

"No way. He deserves to hurt for this," Beth said.

"When it was good . . . it was so good," I said.

"And now?" Beth asked.

"Now there is nothing left of me. I need him."

"You don't need any man. Ever. You are just as amazing as you were before he broke your heart. Don't ever let him tear you down."

Hearing her words, I cried. I knew she was right, but wasn't love the reason we all lived? Without love and compassion, the world was a desolate place. Beth leaned forward, taking my hand in hers.

"He's making a stupid mistake. A mistake that has nothing to do with you."

"She's right, Ashling," Emma agreed. "You can't beat yourself up because he's not strong enough to stand up to his dad. That's silly. And that's not the Grey we know. He'll fight for you."

"You can have any guy you want—don't get stuck on him," Beth said.

"I want Grey."

"What I meant is, you're amazing. You can do better than him."

"He made me whole," I said. Tears streamed down my cheeks in salty waves of desperation. My body convulsed in heaves pouring out my sorrow. My friends wrapped their arms around me in a protective embrace. I heard their reassurance, but it all seemed so far away. I wasn't safe anywhere as long as I was without Grey. Every glance, every touch would break my heart again, my soul wept for our love.

"I don't like feeling like this."

"He'll come to his senses," Emma said.

"Do you want me to beat him up?" Beth asked.

I laughed through my tears, and I shook my head no. Beth and Emma laughed with me. I held my dear friends tight as I let the laughter overcome the pain and win the race, for today at least.

Suddenly, the hair on my neck went rigid as the faint smell of a wolf drifted into my nose. With the scent mingled with the musty smell of the church, I couldn't make out the wolf's identity. Had Adomnan finally found me? Was this where it would all end? My fear vibrated through the room, and the girls responded to my quietness.

"What's wrong?" Emma whispered.

Footsteps outside the door silenced her. Both Beth's and Emma's bodies subconsciously cringed away from the door for fear of what lay on the other side. The door swung open with a heavy thud against the bookcase, revealing Mund. He looked emotionally wrecked.

"Mund?" I asked.

"Tegan is in labor, she asked for you. She needs you," he replied. "I need you."

He turned and motioned for me to follow. I ran down the halls after Mund, only as fast as I dared. My friends followed behind me. We opened the church doors to the darkness. It was already evening, and the crisp air bit at my exposed skin. It seemed as though time had stopped while we sat in the church, but it had certainly carried on without us.

"Thank you," I said quietly as I hugged my two friends. "I'll see you tomorrow."

Mund was so nervous, his whole body visibly twitched as we drove home. I could smell his fear. His love for her was so deep, it shook his core from its foundation. The only thing that could kill him . . . was his love for her.

"How is she?" I asked.

"I don't know . . . I don't know," he said.

I reached over and touched his hand to reassure him.

"I need your help, Ash. She needs you."

"I know. I'll take care of her," I smiled.

I wasn't sure how, but I would, that much I knew. I had been with Mother as she was a midwife for many births. It was something I had always admired about her. She was calm and reassuring to them, and they looked to her for strength. Mother always wanted me with her to talk to the babies before they were born. I seemed to relax them. I had never done a birth alone before, but Mother said my presence painted a dark room in sunshine.

We ran into the house, and Mund led the way to their room. Baran sat next to the bed, dabbing a cloth on Tegan's pale face. I rushed to her side and placed my hand on her rock-hard stomach. She opened her eyes and smiled weakly.

"I'm here, Tegan. It's going to be okay," I said. The worry erased from her eyes, and she breathed in my scent.

"I know," she replied, "but I don't think the baby is moving."

I slid my hands to the sides of her abdomen, feeling for the baby. No movements came, and I could hear the weakened beat of the baby's heart. "It's your time, little one," I whispered to her stomach. "We are waiting for you."

Tegan watched me wide-eyed. Her worry was contagious, and Mund looked stricken with pain. I rubbed my hands over her stomach protectively as I whispered, "I will protect you."

"Oh," she said, "the baby moved!"

"I think this little one is ready for us now," I said.

Tegan nodded slowly, and Mund wrapped his arms around her shoulders and hugged her tightly. Even in the scariest moment, they looked perfectly matched.

The birth went quickly after that. A lot of screaming, as always, but the radiant baby appeared on schedule into my welcome arms, and I presented her to her glowing parents. She looked like her mother, but strong like her father. They named her Niamh, but I decided to call her Nia. Her name meant "radiance," a good Irish name that matched her perfect little face. Nia nestled in Tegan's arms, Tegan wrapped in Mund's, picture perfect. I left the family to bond.

We now had something more important to protect than the prophecy, more important than my life. I had to protect Nia.

16

Nightmares

Days turned into weeks as Samhain passed and my family celebrated the beginning of winter. It was already November and the darker half of the year. Grey hadn't spoken to me, not once, but he was always there, always watching. I thought about my life up to this moment and what I once found important. I had a broken heart that miraculously was still beating, but I had a new perspective. Everything changed the moment I saw Nia. I would always be her ally and protector. When she first opened her eyes and saw me, she knew me.

Everything felt different now. I didn't know if it was the talk with Beth and Emma, the birth of Nia, or just a change in myself. I felt surprisingly aware of who I was becoming. Beth was right; I didn't need Grey to survive, but he was a part of me. Humans couldn't understand the deeper connection and loyalty of a pack. We live for the pack, we are the pack, and we can't survive without the pack.

Grey had to feel some of the pack emotions in him or a connection to Baran. He must be yearning to be a part of the pack, to feel whole. If I could just make him see what he really was, he would know his true place was with us. Even if he weren't a werewolf. He was a member of Baran's pack—he belonged with us. He belonged with me.

I looked out the window into the dark and realized I was looking at my shadow friend. It was there again, watching me . . . always watching me. Every night, there it sat. Who's watching whom, I dared to wonder. It was almost an eerie comfort night after night. I came to expect it to be there, that shadow of mine. It was odd no one in the family had noticed my shadow out there. Neither Baran, Mund, Tegan, nor Quinn had seen it. Or had they, and they just didn't want to scare me? I sat down in the window seat, curling up into a ball with my fuzzy blanket, and drifted off to sleep.

I woke up in the center of an empty, dark room. My hands were bound behind my back, tightly restraining me. The marble floor was cold under my bare skin. I dragged my broken body to the corner, and I cowered there. Light only seeped in from the open doorway.

Adomnan walked in, and his footsteps echoed off the walls. He stood over me, laughing, delighting in my pain. Blood dripped from his hands onto the floor. My body shook from fear. Light illuminated half his face, leaving the other half menacingly in the dark. His wicked expression felt like a nail in my coffin.

"Please," I said.

He slapped me across the face with the back of his hand, cutting my lower lip open with his ring. My face stung, and I licked the sweet, warm blood off my lip, sucking the cut, trying to hide the scent from him. What did he want from me? I had nothing to give.

He had already taken everything from me, everyone I had ever loved. Their blood was still on his hands, glistening in the light. The sickening smell of it filled the room. He grabbed a handful of my hair, forcing me to look up into his ugly green eyes. "You will look at me," he snarled.

I screamed out in agony.

I woke from the dream, still screaming. I slapped my hands over my mouth, smothering the sound. It felt as if he really had me. Was it possible Adomnan was coming to me in my dreams? Could he actually haunt me in my own mind? The dreams were coming more often now.

The shadow in the trees was closer, at the edge, almost breaking into the light. Its eyes glowed a brilliant green in the darkness, like Adomnan's.

Baran burst into my room. "Ashling, are you okay?" he said.

I stood up, shaking like a leaf.

"I've got you," he said, pulling me into his strong arms.

I wrapped my arms around his waist, and I pulled myself tighter against his strength. I clung to him like a lifeline away from my horrible dream that threatened to eat me alive. I heard the others come in, but each left silently.

I clung to Baran. He was the father I never had. He was everything to me that my father never could be. And I loved him for that and so much more. He chose to love me. He chose to protect me. He didn't have to, and yet here he was, wasting his time on a lost cause like me.

"I thought you were dying," he said.

"Adomnan found me in my dreams, and he killed everyone to get to me," I whispered. "Everyone."

"That will never happen," he said. I looked up into his chiseled face; his dark eyes were strong and true.

I looked out the window. My shadow had returned to his original post. I almost couldn't see him, but he was there. Was it Adomnan, was he finding a way into my head? If I could feel Grey's physical pain, it could be possible that Adomnan was sitting outside my window, eating away at my sanity. Maybe that was his plan, to destroy me from the inside.

Whether the shadow was Adomnan or not, the dream had to be a sign. He was close. I hadn't dreamed of him since before Grey and I were together. Was he actually the reason I had been safe, and without Grey in my life I was left unprotected? But Grey wasn't mine anymore. I had a greater purpose—to protect Nia and my pack. Maybe I didn't have a werewolf love. Because Grey wasn't a wolf. Maybe he was supposed to be, but Brenna made the wrong choice. Maybe the fate Calista wrote of was interrupted by Brenna's choice to mate with Robert, and all of fate stood differently now.

My fate wasn't tied to some old prophecy; it was tied to my soul. And my soul was free—I had to believe that. I had to fight. I wouldn't let Adomnan hurt my family or break Old Mother's heart. He wouldn't spill our sacred blood anymore. I decided I would make my own fate.

"Baran?"

"Yes?" he replied.

"Why . . ." I paused, gathering my strength, "why are you here with me? Why are you still protecting me? I'm not a member of your pack."

I couldn't look at him to ask the question. I didn't want to know the answer, and yet I had to know. I snuck a peek at his face through my shield of hair. The lines and age of his face showed plainly as he considered my question.

"Old Mother created three who were the wisest of us all. They had been around for centuries before the others. The power of the three together was meant to bring unity to the earth and create one pack led by your maternal grandmother, Rhea Vanir; Uaid Dvergar; and your paternal great-grandfather, Donal Boru. Mother Rhea, Uaid, and Donal were three sides of the Triquetra; mind, body, and soul. Mother Rhea was the nurturer. Many legends speak of Donal's wisdom, and Uaid brought strength to the packs. Together, they united our kind, and we all benefited from the Elder Gods standing together. Old Mother had intended them to protect the balance of life and protect her most glorious creation, the humans.

"But out of their formation, a hierarchy of the packs was created. The Elder Gods, the royal packs, the noble packs, the servant packs, the nomadic packs, and the forsaken packs. In that order of importance."

"We aren't broken into groups like that."

"We are, Ashling. You have just never been allowed to see the others before. You were surrounded by what they wanted you to see. Who they wanted you to meet. You, Ashling, are of the royal pack. Not only are you royal, but you descend from both Vanir and Boru Elder Gods, making you and your siblings an even higher-elevated status in the pack hierarchy. I am of Killian. Killians were once royal, but we are nothing more than nomads now. We lost our lands, and with it, our humans to protect and our status."

"I don't understand," I said.

Baran was still as night. "Before my father's royal lands were taken, he swore our lives to the aid and protection of Rhea Vanir and all her offspring. When only my sister and I remained, we had no choice but to serve your father in exchange for his protection. But I still serve Mother Rhea, and I belong to your mother, and so I protect you. As you are of their blood."

"So you protect me because you have to?" I said. I knew it was childish, but I wanted his approval and his love rather than to be his burden.

"Yes. I protect you because it's in my blood. I could never deny the duty of my blood. But I care about you because I choose to, just as I have always loved your mother and I love you as though you were my own child. Because I choose to. You are as much of me as I am of you. Though I am no longer of your station and should not cross this boundary, I can't stop myself from caring for you. You have wiggled your way into my heart."

"How can there be a boundary for caring?"

"*You* are supposed to only interact, marry, and befriend wolves within your royal status, with the possibility of royal or noble mates upon your father's discretion. But you aren't even to speak directly to lower packs. It's lowering yourself to our level."

"And you believe that?"

"I choose to play their games."

"Well, I choose to be your friend," I replied. The indignation poured from my lips.

Baran tried to hide his smile. "Ashling, you should know and understand your place. You need to understand the ramifications of the things you defiantly *choose* to do. Even if Grey were truly a wolf and one of us—which he is not—you couldn't love him. Killian is no longer of royal blood. You wouldn't be permitted to even speak to him. And he would be stoned to death for even daring to look you in the eye. It's best it ended now, before your father and the counsel learned of it. They would kill him for the offense."

That my own family would kill Grey was more than I could bear. "What is wrong with these people?" I said. "You're my friend and my only protection, and you aren't supposed to be allowed to talk to me? Why would they send me with you if we aren't even supposed to speak?"

"Your father asked me to protect you because I'm hard to track and even harder to kill."

"Why?"

"I'm a dire wolf, Ashling," he said. "The Killian pack was created to protect, so I'm nearly twice the size of your father and twice as strong."

"Then why didn't you protect your family?" I asked.

A sad smile crossed his face. "I was just a boy then, not nearly full grown." He sighed. "I lost everything that day, my brothers, my parents, my pack, and my lands. When we lost our status, I even lost my betrothed."

"I'm sorry," I said.

"And so am I," he said. "If it weren't for your father, Brenna and I would be lost too."

"I hate my father."

"Don't hate him. I don't agree with the laws, Ashling, but you can't change the whole world in a day."

"Well, I don't agree with any of it," I said.

"Ash, you shouldn't say such things," Mund said, entering the room. "You endanger Baran's life when you do."

"But these laws are ludicrous," I said.

"I agree. Baran is a trusted friend to me and Mother, and he can be your friend. But just remember where you are and whom you are with so you don't endanger his life. I'm sorry you have to learn all these lessons now. Father decided you had to be hidden from everything in order to keep you safe until you were sold in marriage. I am sorry I failed you. I should have taught you more. There was never enough time."

"Mund, I don't want to be sheltered anymore. I want to know everything. I want to find my place among these ashes of life. I want to make a difference."

"Good," he said. He messed up my hair, then walked toward the door. "I always knew you would change our world—but you have to be smart, Ash. Learn Father's rules, so you can break them. I'll be glad to be by your side when you do it." And with that, he was gone again.

The whole world was against me, but I would overcome this. I would make them all see they had been wrong. There wasn't anything wrong with me. If I fell now, it was because I let myself fall. I wasn't going to let Father and his stupid rules drown me. I knew what I wanted and I knew who I was, even if I had to fight the whole world. I felt empowered.

"Do you think you can get some more rest?" Baran asked.

"I can. Sweet dreams, Baran."

"You too, my little *ylva*," he said with a smile, and walked out the door.

My only remaining guest was in the shadows outside. The energy that flowed through my veins made me want to jump out my window, march right up to that shadow, and tell it to bloody shove off. Who did it think it was, standing out there, waiting every bloody night? Was it actually Adomnan, or some other wolf he sent to watch me? Adomnan had a twisted soul, but he was patient. But what was he waiting for? Was he waiting for me to make the first move? Maybe that was part of the trap. Well, he could just keep on waiting.

I could just surrender myself and let this all be over, but I wouldn't do that. I would never surrender. I would never be Adomnan's pet, I could never endure it. I had to flee before he attacked my family; I would have to run away to free everyone from me.

Did Grey actually think he could live without me forever? We were bonded to each other. There was no way to live apart now. We were meant to be, and there was nothing his father could do to change it . . . or my father, for that matter.

The sun was on the horizon, and my shadow was gone with the night. Figuring I wouldn't be able to go back to sleep, I decided to get up and get ready for school. It was the last school day before the winter break . . . I could do one more day. I quickly got ready, straightening my hair, and grabbed my black leather jacket on my way downstairs. No one was up yet. I walked as quietly as I could to the kitchen, tossed a bagel into the toaster, and opened the fridge.

"Looking for something?" Mund asked.

I spun around to see him sitting at the table. Had he been there the whole time? He was already ready for school as he studied my appearance. I had to admit, it was very dark for something I would normally wear.

"So . . . you look different," he said as he tossed a tub of cream cheese to me.

I turned away, busying myself with my bagel. "Yeah, I feel different today," I said as I shoved my bagel into my mouth.

"How has it been going with Grey?" he asked.

"He won't speak to me," I said.

"Are you sure you don't want me to rough him up a little?" he said with a smile.

"I can handle it myself, thank you," I said. "I'm off to school."

"Me too," he said, standing up and following me to the door. "I'll see you there."

"Yep."

I arrived at the school, and grounds were dead silent. I was forty-five minutes early for school, and not a single other car was in the parking lot. Mund didn't follow me directly—he stayed to kiss his family goodbye. He seemed to trust me more now. I finally had a moment to myself where no one was hiding in the shadows, waiting to eat me alive. Just then, I heard the rumble of a motorcycle approaching and watched Grey pull up next to my car.

17

Eyes of the Night

I couldn't believe he was still riding his motorcycle. It was so cold, but there he sat in all his masculine glory. His messy hair was even wilder. His brilliant green eyes were greener. His lips were more inviting. The longer we were apart, the stronger I felt the pull toward him. My desire was written plainly across my face.

He dropped the kickstand but stayed seated on his bike. His eyes probed into my soul, as though he had asked me to dance. I got out, walked over, and stood next to him; I couldn't walk away. He was intoxicating to me. I needed him, but I couldn't get any closer either. I would be in his arms again. Everything about him made my skin tingle. If only he could see what he really was.

"Grey?" I asked.

"I just had to see you," he said.

The pain in his green eyes was clear. I knew he missed being mine. We hadn't been alone together since our last kiss. Either Mund or the teachers had their eyes on us at all times. We had gotten in a lot of trouble for that stunt, but I didn't mind. Our classmates began to fill the parking lot around us. No one seemed to notice the odd stillness between Grey and me.

"Are you okay?" I asked.

"I am now that I'm with you," he said, half-smiling at me.

Mund's scent drifted through the air. He wouldn't be happy I was standing here with Grey. I heard him approaching, every step calculated and planned. He was casual in appearance, but the stiffness of his back and the tension in the air were heavy.

"What is this half-breed doing here?" Mund asked.

"Mund, don't," I said.

Grey and I were frozen in the center of a lie, unable to do anything but stare at one another. Mund seemed cold as steel to me, while I could feel the heat rolling off Grey's skin. When I was away from him, I swore I was going to avoid him and let him live. Then when he was here, I could hardly keep my wits about me. His presence filled my mind, clouding out any rational thought and leaving the overwhelming desire to be near him.

Emma and Beth walked over, breaking my concentration. Emma was upset, but Beth looked as if she were going to burst with anger and smack Grey right in the face. I loved her spitfire attitude. None of us moved and no one said anything. It was eerie and unnatural, but everyone around us pulsed with energy.

Suddenly, the charge in the air was thick with the threat of danger . . . something bad was coming. Grey jumped off his motorcycle and pushed me toward Mund and the girls, putting himself in front of me. I was sandwiched between Grey and Mund. What could possibly make Grey turn his back to Mund? He had to sense the rage inside Mund and have some sense of self-preservation. What could possibly make him endanger himself? I searched the crowds of students and didn't see anything out of the ordinary, but I could feel it in the pit of my stomach. How did Grey sense what was coming before Mund or I did? I intertwined my fingers with Beth and Emma's, giving them a quick squeeze of reassurance. I didn't know what was coming, but I knew it wasn't good.

The crowd parted, and out walked Adomnan, flanked by Eamon and Bento. My heart sank to the ground at the sight of them. They looked completely out of place here. Dressed in fine velvet jackets, dark jeans, and collared shirts. They looked decadent and dangerous at the same time. It was a beautiful juxtaposition, worthy of a painting by a master.

I could feel everyone watching now. Their curiosity and whispers broke into my own thoughts, muddying the waters of my mind. Adomnan's smile was pure evil. There was no mistaking his happiness at our reaction.

Grey stood so close in front of me, I could feel his hair when the wind blew.

"This isn't the place, Adomnan," Mund said.

Adomnan just smiled.

"You need to leave."

"What? No hello for an old friend?" Adomnan asked.

I wanted to vomit. Just looking at his face made my skin crawl. He scared the shit out of me.

Bento twitched with anxiety. He seemed uncomfortable with all the humans seeing them. He must not have trusted Adomnan's ability to keep the situation from escalating. But it was Eamon who looked the most out of place; he watched me with curiosity. His attention wasn't on all the humans around, his brothers, Grey, or even Mund. He studied my appearance, from my straight hair to my leather jacket.

"Beth, Emma . . . why don't you guys go into school? We have to talk to our old friends for a moment," Mund said. I let go of their hands, and they slowly and reluctantly walked toward the school.

"Playing with your food, Ashling?" Adomnan said. "A little beneath you, don't you think? They are food, after all. And what does his little fleshy body think he can do to protect you from *me?*" He gestured toward Grey, appalled by his mere presence but not directly speaking to him.

We didn't move, and I didn't take his bait to start the fight. I didn't know how strong Grey was or what he was capable of, but I didn't want to find out either. I didn't want him to get hurt. If he died, I would die.

With our physical connection, his fighting could kill us both.

Adomnan continued to egg me on. "What would your father say about your new little friend? I could save your father the trouble and kill him right here, if you want. It would be more humane that way. Your father would instead use the old punishments and stone him to death over several days or use him as bait in the Bloodrealms. I could do it quickly for you, as a personal favor."

I lunged forward at Adomnan, trying to break past Grey to rip him apart. I wanted his flesh in my hands and his blood on the ground. I wanted to exterminate him like the rabid dog he was. But Grey sensed my movements before I even made them and blocked my path, holding me to his side, though his eyes never left Adomnan's. His concentration was superior to mine. Mund had leapt down and was between them and us, a light growl tearing up from his throat.

"I told you Adomnan. This isn't the place," Mund said so firmly it felt like a decree from the Elder Gods themselves. "Grey, please escort Ashling into school. I'd hate for her to be late for class."

"Mund, no. I'm not leaving you," I said.

"Disobedient," Adomnan said, shaking his head. "I could *train* her for you, Redmund." His voice was dripping with cruelty, and his mouth twisted into a sick smile.

He disgusted me—I would never be his. I would die before I would submit to *him,* of all creatures on earth. He had to know I would die fighting, but maybe that was his plan after all. I suddenly felt like throwing up. Mund was shaking with rage, there were so many of him that I couldn't focus on his form. He was nearly going to shift. Panic rippled through me, and I didn't know what to do.

"Aren't you a charmer," Grey said to Adomnan.

Grey turned me toward the school and nudged Mund on the way. The nudge was just enough to get Mund to move with us. Mund walked backward, never letting his eyes off Adomnan. My legs felt as though I were walking on gelatin, but Grey's strength held me together. His arm was wrapped around my back as we walked into the school; his arm felt so right there. Protected in the cloak of his arms. The parking lot had emptied, and they were gone, but their scent remained. It was only a matter of time before they really did come for me. Today was only a warning.

"Thank you," Mund said to Grey. "For a moment, I wasn't sure I could control myself, and this wasn't the place. So thank you. But do everyone a favor and stay out of it. You'll only get yourself killed and hurt Ashling in the process. You aren't one of us." Before Grey could respond, Mund ushered me away, leaving Grey standing in the hallway. No matter the distance, no matter how many people were around, I was alone if I wasn't with Grey. It would always feel that way. A love lost.

"They found us. They will come back," Mund said, dragging me down the hallway. His face was stricken with worry and anguish. "I'm sure they have already followed our scents to the house. Tegan and Nia are there. With Tegan and Gwyn protecting Nia, that leaves Quinn to . . ." Mund said, not able to finish his sentence.

"Go to them. Make sure they are safe," I said. He shook his head no, but the panic on his face was plain. I knew he was torn between love for his family and his duty to protect me. I placed my hand on his shoulder to comfort him. "Come back for me when they are safe."

He nodded and was gone. My hand lingered in the air where he had just stood. I hoped Mund would make it home in time, before Adomnan dared to show his ugly face. And what if he smelled the baby? Mund told me how Adomnan had went on a murder spree, killing all the babies of his enemy's packs. He had nearly as many babies on his death list as adults. It made me sick with worry. I felt so overwhelmed. I wanted to help my family, but I didn't know how.

I realized Mund had left me in front of the nurse's office just as the door opened and the portly little nurse jumped back startled.

"Ms. Boru, can I help you with something?" she asked.

Half-smiling, I replied, "Yes, ma'am." I held my stomach for dramatic effect. "I think I don't feel well."

"Oh golly," she said as she swooped me into the small office, her tone completely changed. "Go lie down on bed four. I'll be right there with a bucket."

She was waddling around the office in frenzy. I didn't hear a thing she said to me. I just lay there on bed number four and watched nothing and felt everything. Maybe there was something Calista had written that I had missed. Or maybe I translated it wrong. There had to be an answer to this . . . a foretold moment that could help me. Or maybe that stupid old journal didn't hold a lick of truth. Maybe it was left to torment me. There was no way to know what or who to trust anymore. I needed a break from this madness. At least it was the last school day before break and the Winter Solstice.

"Her temperature is one-o-two!" the nurse said. She was on the phone. Great. She must be talking to Baran. Just what I needed right now. And my temperature was always 102 degrees. "Okay . . . okay. Great."

She hung up the phone and stared at me with her big eyes. She must have thought I was about to burst into flames like a phoenix and turn to ash. I had always envied the phoenix, with her ability to start anew. Instead I was a wolf, feared by man.

"Ms. Boru, your uncle will be here to take you home."

"Thank you."

"I'll be back in a few minutes. You'll be okay, won't you, dear?" she asked. I nodded, and she waddled away, her paisley dress waving goodbye to me. It was clearly too much paisley for one person.

I was finally alone again, I sighed.

The door slammed open and Grey darted in. His scent filled the room with his delicious pheromones, swirling through my senses. "You have to come with me," he said. What was he doing here—trying to torment me further, or trying to be my knight in shining armor? "Now." The urgency in his voice sprang me from the bed, and I was at his side, breathing in his scent.

"What's going on?"

"They're in the school. I can smell them."

"There's nowhere I can hide—they can smell me too."

"Not when you are touching me," he replied. What on earth had come over him? First he turned his back on Mund, and then he stands between Adomnan and me when he was directly ordered to stay out of it? Now he was convinced his scent hid mine. He had to be stark raving mad.

"Didn't you notice the strange look the calm one gave me when I held you?" he said.

"Eamon?"

He shook his head. "I don't know. Not the chatty one. And not the twitchy one. The other one."

"Eamon."

"He was watching your every move, but when you tried to get past me and I grabbed you, he finally broke his concentration and was distracted by the scent in the air. At that moment, I noticed it too. They can't smell you over me."

"They're here in the school?" I said as I finally caught their scent. It was barely there, but I could smell it now. They were getting closer.

"But you're safe with me," Grey replied, wrapping his fingers with mine. "As long as we are together, all you have to do is hold my hand."

My skin pulsed from his touch and tingled all the way up my arm and spider-webbed across my chest. Consuming my whole body in his warmth. We sat down on the bed, still holding hands. He seemed calmer now, the deep furrow of his brow relaxed, and there was even a hint of a smile on his lips. Why was I always infatuated with his kissable lips? I had to get my mind back on my safety and the safety of my family—and get my mind off all the parts of Grey I wanted to kiss.

"Why can't they smell me?" I asked.

"I don't know," he said. "And I don't care why. I just need you to be safe."

His hands were rough on my delicate skin, but it was utterly arousing. I was trapped in that moment. So many emotions poured through me. My emotional turmoil raged like a bull crashing into itself.

200 · *Aurora Whittet*

"I can't live without you, Ashling. I tried."

Did he actually just say the words I had been dying for him to say? I finally got my wish, yet it wasn't enough to heal the hurt I had endured. I was still bloody angry at his betrayal. I thought all I needed was for him to come back to me, and yet here I sat, and it wasn't enough. I was still angry.

My breath rasped in my throat. "I love you, but I just can't forgive you so easily." I looked down at his hands—they were shaking in mine. I was hurting him. The pain was clear all over his face. "I'm sorry, Grey. I'm not sure I can trust you."

I stood up, letting his hand drop back to his side. I walked to the window and slipped outside, silently dropping two stories to the ground. The ground sponged with my weight, releasing the smell of the frozen earth. I started running for home. I heard the thump of something falling behind me. I turned back to see Grey leaping up from a crouch; he looked just like a wolf in his movements. He was by my side in the blink of an eye. I ran harder than I had ever run before, faster than I thought I was able. My cheeks grew wet with my tears, and I rubbed them away.

He matched my pace, running next to me, side by side. He reached over and linked his fingers with mine. The heavens opened up and the sky cried with me. As though Old Mother was weeping for my soul and washing away my pain. Old Mother always reclaimed what was hers.

I caught Mund's scent across town, and we followed it north to my home. There was no sign or scent of Adomnan as we neared the house.

We leapt up onto the porch as Baran's Land Rover screeched into the driveway. The smell of burned rubber filled the air. Mund appeared from inside, standing over us. The look of disapproval on his face was overwhelming. I would regret this memory if Grey hadn't been in it. Before Mund could say anything, Baran appeared behind us, and his large shadow cast over all of us.

"Care to step inside?" Baran said through gritted teeth.

We all obeyed. I dropped my gaze to my feet, and there it stayed.

"Can anyone explain to me why I had to drive all the way to the school, only to catch your scent leaving the school, then to have your scent die out instantly in the middle of the street? I thought you were dead. Don't you ever, ever do that to me again," Baran said.

"I'm sorry," I said.

"Sorry? Sorry!" he said. "Then why do you keep disobeying me? Do you want to die?"

"No, Baran it's just that . . ."

He interrupted me, "Damn it, Ashling, how can anyone be expected to keep you safe when you are told to stay at school and then you leave?"

"Baran," Grey stepped forward. "We had to flee, they were in the school."

"Do you think you can protect her, Grey? You know, I like you, kid, and secretly I'm rooting for you. But it's time to grow up here. This is life and death, not playtime at the park. Those are werewolves out there, and they will stop at nothing to get Ashling. You are nothing more to them than a moist, fleshy wall between them and what they want. How long did you think you could stand there before they tore you apart?"

"I don't know. I'm not one of you, but she means as much to me as she does to you, maybe even more, and I am hollow without her. I'd gladly die for her," he said, his voice unwavering and strong. It sent a shockwave through my body.

"You will likely get your wish," Mund said, taking a step closer to Grey, their noses almost touching. "I told you to butt out. Did I not make myself clear?"

I was tired of all the testosterone and fighting. It was exhausting. Tegan walked into the room with the sleeping baby swaddled to her. It was like a little baby hammock made of pink silk. It complimented the ivory silk dress Tegan wore. Looking at her, you would never know she had ever given birth.

"Baran, Mund, if you boys are done having your macho contest, please join us in the kitchen. I'd like to have a word with you. In the other room, please." She smiled lightly and walked back out of the room with Mund right behind her. Baran followed quietly, leaving Grey and me alone in the living room. Grey cleared the ten feet between us in one beat of my heart and knelt before me.

"Ashling, I know you aren't ready to forgive me. I let you down, but I won't give you up. I'm yours." He bent his head toward the floor in a bow. "I'm yours."

"Do you even know how much you hurt me?" I nearly choked just saying the words.

"Would you both care to join us?" Tegan said from the doorway. "We are having a family meeting, and that includes you both."

Looking at Grey, I grabbed his hand, and he followed me to the kitchen. I looked around the kitchen at my family—Baran, Mund, Tegan, Quinn, Gwyn, Nia . . . and Grey. They were so much more than I ever realized. They were strong and fearless, and they all sacrificed things for me. I owed each of them the world.

Baran's jeans were dirty with oil and grime. His black T-shirt stretched across his chest with every cautioned breath. The resemblance between him and Grey was unmistakable too. The same thin, muscular structure; dark hair; and badass beauty.

"Well, we knew this day would come, and it has. The Dvergars found our Ashling. It took them far longer than I had imagined, but now we need to decide how we are going to react to their presence, as a family," Tegan said.

"Tegan's right. I'm sorry for my making decisions without consulting all of you, as I should have," Mund said. "If Ashling chooses Grey after all he's done to destroy her, that is her choice, and I respect it. I am not Father, and so if you want Grey to be a part of this, it is your decision *alone,* Ashling, and your weight to bear." Mund paced back and forth between us, the frustration clearly visible in his tense posture. "Grey," he said, "I need you to understand something."

Grey nodded.

"As much as I can clearly see you love Ash, you have to understand that without her, we are all lost. Whoever claims her at her eighteenth birthday will rule over us. This isn't just about the two of you and your wayward love story. It's about an entire lost civilization reclaiming our right to survive." Mund placed his hand on Nia's head, lightly caressing her curly hair, and she cooed in her sleep. "There is a lot at stake, and I need you to fully understand if you stay in this room now, you are not only bound to Ashling, you are bound to all of us, and all of our fates reside together, with her."

Grey knelt down, once again, in front of my family, bowing his head to them. "I belong to Ashling," he said. There was no question that what he had spoken was true and from the heart, but no one moved for what seemed an eternity as they waited for Mund to decide. Finally he placed his hand on Grey's shoulder.

"As you should."

The air whooshed out of my lungs. I felt relieved that Mund accepted Grey, though I didn't trust myself with him yet. He stood back up and stood by my side. I lightly grazed my fingertips across his face. He turned to face me with a crooked smile, and his green eyes glowed with love and pride.

"I think we should leave," Mund said. "We could hide for a time with our allies, the Sylla in Africa, while we plan our next move."

"Maybe we should call the banners of all the Boru packs and protect Ashling at the Rock," Quinn said.

"We could hide with our father at Castle Raglan," Tegan said, and Gwyn nodded. "The Kahedin pack would protect us."

The smell of fear filled the room, suffocating me. I was furious. Adomnan was ruining everything. This wasn't what I wanted to happen. "What about Grey?" I said.

"His place is here," Quinn said.

Baran stood quietly watching my family bicker about where we were going next. His silence was eerie. I knew he had an opinion, but he chose not to share it. Every emotion rippled over my skin, but anger was the strongest.

"We leave at nightfall," Mund said.

"No. We don't," I said. "We don't run. We fight. There is nowhere I can go that they won't find me. There is nowhere left to hide. Don't you all see—this is where we make our stand."

Baran smiled. "I was never one for running."

"Ash, are you sure?" Mund asked.

I looked at my family, and the strength of their love was enough for me to believe. I finally belonged somewhere. I had a family, friends and home, and that was worth fighting for. Grey smiled at me, that wolfish grin I loved so much.

"We stay and we fight," I said.

"Then I follow you," Mund said.

"And I," said Quinn.

Tegan lightly touched my face. "I can see you." I knew what she meant. I was finally becoming the woman I was always meant to be. I was meant to lead.

My family began to wander away to other rooms to busy themselves with other things rather than talk, but Grey and I remained in the kitchen. I sat on the counter, studying every feature of Grey's face. If I died in this fight, I wanted to be able to close my eyes and see his beautiful face with my last breath.

"Ashling, I love you. I want to be with you."

"No."

"I'm sorry I betrayed your trust."

"I know. But I'm not ready."

"You can't push me away so easily," he said with a mischievous grin.

I hopped down off the counter, and I ran upstairs to my room. He didn't try to follow. I closed my bedroom door, shutting out everything and everyone.

The day had already broken to afternoon. Getting comfortable for the hours ahead, I slipped off my sweater and jeans, revealing my tank top and underwear. I sat down on my bed, and I pulled out Calista's journal and all my translations to reread once again. I must have missed something.

After five hours of rearranging myself around my room reading, I knew three things for certain: I was in every way the wolf Calista had written of, the prophecy was mine to fulfill, and some wolf had to claim me. It was the last part that concerned me the most. I had no idea what wolf could possibly claim me, now that I had bonded with Grey . . . even though I hadn't yet forgiven his betrayal. Could a member of my pack claim me? Did it have to be in marriage? A life in a cage would be far worse than death.

A light knock at my door, and Grey slowly stepped inside. "I thought you might be hungry," he said, holding up a cheeseburger for my inspection.

"Thanks," I smiled. "Come in."

He shut the door and walked to my bedside table. Setting down the plate before turning back around to face me, I felt him suddenly alert to the fact that I was half-naked. I quickly wrapped myself in my blanket and sat back in the window seat.

"I couldn't bear the thought of being away from you anymore," he said, sitting on my bed facing me. "Plus, your brothers were starting to make me nervous."

The distance between us seemed like nothing in my small bedroom. I could almost feel his ragged breath on my skin ten feet away. Our hearts sped up in synchronized beats. I hadn't realized how dark it had gotten. I could make out the shape of his face, but no other details except his bright green eyes that glowed in the shadows, just as my shadow stalker's eyes did.

I quickly searched the trees for him—the green eyes I'd grown so used to seeing, my dangerous comfort. But they were nowhere to be seen. The first night in weeks that they hadn't been there. Slowly I turned back to Grey, and I jumped to my feet. My blanket fell to the ground, all modesty forsaken.

"Was it you?" I said, pointing out the window. "All this time, was it you outside my window?"

He crossed the room to me, holding my hands. His everlasting calm was more than I could take. I was confused and upset.

"You can't just hang out outside a girl's window. It's weird."

"I never left you," he replied.

"What? Why?" I said.

"At first I was just curious about you . . . and then I couldn't stand the idea of being away from you. I feared I'd lose you. I feared one night you'd just disappear. I sat outside your window every night, protecting you. It wasn't until the night you woke up screaming that I knew it was coming; I smelled them on the wind. I wanted to burst through your window to comfort you, but Baran was already there. So I fell back to my position as an outsider in your life."

He never left. I couldn't fully comprehend the depth of that statement. Even when I thought he had turned his back on our love, he had still stood watch, protecting me from harm. I wanted to scream. All this time I wasn't sure if I was good enough for love, and it had been here all along.

Mund and Quinn burst into my room and stopped dead in their tracks, staring at our embrace, but Mund took two more steps into the room.

"I let you stay in this house. I am letting her choose you. But don't be mistaken, she's still my baby sister, and I will not hesitate to take your last breath," Mund said. I suddenly realized my panties and tank top were hardly the apparel I wanted my brothers to catch me in while I was wrapped in Grey's arms. I scooped up my blanket and covered myself. Quinn's face was stretched so tightly trying not to laugh.

"Understood," Grey said.

"Ash, get him some blankets from the hall closet. He can sleep up here, but on the floor," Mund said as he and Quinn walked back out.

Quinn laughed from the bottom of the stairs. "And the door stays open!" he shouted.

18

Encounter

"I think your brothers really enjoyed that," Grey said.

I smiled and crawled into my bed, pulling the blankets up to my waist. "Will you lay by me until I fall asleep?" I asked, daring to look him in the eye. "Sometimes I have bad dreams, and it might be nice to have you here with me, instead of outside my window."

He winked and disappeared down the stairs. I lay there staring at the ceiling, at nothing, with a knotting feeling in my stomach as my nervousness filled my mind. Moments later, Grey walked back into my room wearing black fleece pants and no shirt. His muscular chest was exposed for my viewing pleasure . . . and it was a pleasure. A shiver coursed through my spine and my pulse raced. He lay down on top of the covers next to me, creating a barrier between our skin, but I could still feel his warmth.

I rolled over, wrapping my arm over his chest, claiming him as my own, and I rested my head on his shoulder. I breathed in his enticing scent, excitement filling every fiber of my body. He lightly brushed my hair out of my face. The gentle caress was sensuous.

His left wrist was tattooed with the blade emblem, his brand. Blood-sucker. An icy chill settled on my heart. It was just another reminder of the dangerous game we played. I held his other arm and carefully unlaced the leather band, revealing his other tattoo. His right wrist carried the same mark as Baran, the mark of the Killian. But it was black; it wasn't burned in the blood of his fathers. Instead, I was certain, he had been marked by his mother. It was her legacy and the only map she dared leave him.

"Why do you keep this one covered?" I said.

"I don't know what it is. My dad said my mom tattooed it on me when I was two, right before she died. I don't know what it means, and he couldn't tell me either. He said if I didn't know what it was, I shouldn't go around showing it off. So I keep it covered."

But I knew what it was, and I would bet his father wanted it covered because he knew too. I fought with the idea of telling him and decided in the end that truth always prevails.

"It's the mark of the Killian, your mother's pack."

He looked puzzled as he studied his wrist. "How would you know that?"

"It's the same mark as on Baran's wrist." I put my hand on the side of his face. "Grey, it's time you knew the truth. Baran is your uncle, your mother's twin brother."

He pulled away from me as he sat up. He studied the two very different marks. One on each underside of his wrist, each claiming its right to him.

"You are of Killian blood, Grey. You are a member of Baran's pack."

"How can that be?"

"I guess your father fell in love with your mother without knowing what she was, and they had you. They each branded one arm with their lineage."

I watched his face as the emotions raged over him. Everything he had ever known was a lie—it had to crush him. He lightly ran his fingers over his Killian Bloodmark before he lay down again, confusion clearly on his handsome face.

"I miss her," he said.

"She left you the only way she knew would lead you home."

He sighed. "So that's why your brother called me a half-breed."

"Mund can be a jerk sometimes," I smiled.

"Why don't you have a mark? I mean, that I've *seen* anyway," he said, a sexy, mischievous smile consuming his face.

I bit my lip, trying to concentrate on his question. "We are born in our human forms and branded as babies with our packs' Bloodmarks—the tattoos we have, that you have. But Father didn't brand me. He was ashamed of me. I was able to shift into a wolf from birth, unlike all other wolves who shift at puberty."

Grey just stared at me and nodded, despite the shocking information I was delivering. "Go on," he said.

"My aunt Calista foretold a prophecy that I would unite the packs. Because of this, Father hid me and Mother on the cliffs of southern Ireland, away from the rest of the pack. They even faked my death to keep my existence a secret. Father didn't want rumors of a red-haired girl with the Boru Bloodmark flying around Ireland. It would have raised suspicion," I said.

"He fears you because you're different," Grey said, kissing my bare shoulder. "It has nothing to do with you." His words floated through my mind. Was he right? Did Father's hate and rejection have nothing to do with me?

"Thank you," I said, letting his truth comfort me.

"So why does Gwyn have a tattoo on her neck and not on her wrist like Tegan and your brothers?"

"Because she's not married yet."

"What?"

I sighed, reciting what I had been taught. "Simply because a woman is property of her father's pack and then her husband's. So if you look, both Tegan and Gwyn have marks on their necks signifying their Kahedin pack heritage. Then when we marry, we are branded with our mate's heritage on our wrists. Gwyn and Quinn aren't married yet, so the ritual hasn't been performed, but Tegan's wrists are branded with the Boru Bloodmark."

His face was twisted in anger. "Women aren't property. It's not like buying a car," he said.

"In our culture, it's different. We live as the old ways," I replied. "That's the problem when no one dies. It's hard to progress as a culture when you have members who are centuries upon centuries old; they fear change. But it isn't all bad. Being a member of a pack is what we are designed for. We live as one, we hunt as one, and we breathe as one. It's in our blood."

"So you're unclaimed then?"

"Until my father brands me with the sacred blood of my fathers, I can't be branded in marriage. And I belong to no one."

"Well, I'd never brand you," he said. It was wonderful hearing him say it, but I knew what it meant if I weren't branded. It left me vulnerable to other males in our world. And it was still an honor to accept your mate's pack as your family. It was more than a symbol, it was an idea of belonging.

He kissed my forehead; I closed my eyes, breathing him deep into my soul. It was cleansing to finally tell him the truth. I hated knowing more about him than he did. No relationship could be built on secrets. Maybe now he could finally discover the truth behind his mother's death, and then we could both be whole again.

He was still such a mystery to me. Half werewolf, half Bloodsucker—but all he brought with him of the wolf was his tempting scent, glowing eyes, and the tattoo from his mother. The rest of him was all Bloodsucker, but he chose to love me.

"What do you remember about your mother?"

"Almost nothing," he said. "I can't even remember her face, only her beautiful green eyes. Dad burned all the photos of her . . . like she never existed. My dad said it hurt too much to talk about her, so I stopped asking questions and she began to fade from my mind. But I see her in my dreams."

"Do you know where her family came from?"

"Dad said she was very secretive about it," he said. Which might have been true; she was hiding from Willem's father. How could Grey grow up knowing nothing of his mother? It had to hurt him deeply to not know the other half of who he was. All this time, his father had taught him to hate, fear, and destroy wolves, and yet he ran with me and he set me free before he even knew what or who I was. He had enough of his mother's spirit to balance out his father's hate.

I let my heavy eyelids close, and I snuggled in his arms.

I woke up the next morning with Grey's arms holding my back tightly to his chest. His face was buried in my hair. He must have gotten cold because he was under the covers and his bare skin touched mine. It felt like fire arousing my body. I had contemplated what it would feel like to give up and walk away from him, and every time I thought the words, it made me sick to my stomach. I had been so naïve; no one was strong enough to turn their back on love.

Baran peeked around the door. "Tegan asked me to wake you up, Ashling. She would like you and Gwyn to go Christmas shopping with her. We are all going to hang out at the mall, to keep an eye on you," Baran said. "So up-and-at-'em, little *ylva*."

"Thanks, Baran," I smiled. Grey woke up stretching and yawning. I hopped out of bed quickly to get ready. Considering Adomnan hunted us, it seemed odd Tegan wanted to go shopping, but it was very like her to continue living life to the fullest, no matter the circumstances. It was Winter Solstice and our first Christmas.

We'd had many Yule celebrations over Winter Solstice, but never a Christmas. Yule, held on the shortest day of the year, was celebrated as a symbol of the sun god Mithras being born and involved many festivities I loved. But I found myself excited to celebrate my first Christmas with Grey too.

Once I felt content with my appearance, I walked out of the bathroom expecting to see Grey still in my bed, but he was already gone. I looked around the room, but his clothes were gone too. Only the night pants remained, folded perfectly at the foot of my bed. The only proof he had ever been there and that it hadn't been a dream. I quickly ran downstairs.

"Ready?" Tegan said. She was nearly bouncing with excitement.

"Sure," I replied

"I'm not comfortable with this," Mund said.

"Really, Mund, we are only risking our lives to buy you presents. I thought you'd love that," I said.

Mund grunted out a small laugh. "We'll be keeping an eye on you ladies," he said, kissing Nia and Tegan.

Tegan and Gwyn piled in the front of Baran's Land Rover. Nia and I hung out in the back as she cooed in her pink ruffled dress. The boys promptly followed us in Mund's Jeep. I felt strange leaving Grey with my brothers; it somehow didn't seem fair to him. But if he did love me, he had to love my family too.

"Do you think Grey will be okay?" I asked. "With Mund, Quinn, and Baran, I mean."

"I think it's just what he needs," Tegan said, "and this is just what we need—a little girl time."

"I don't get it, Ashling . . . what's with your obsession with Grey? He's not one of us. He's a human," Gwyn said.

It might have been the first time she ever actually asked me a question directly. She was never concerned with my life, at least before now. Though she asked a valid question: Why did I love him so deeply? Was it his devilish good looks, his rebellious attitude, his scent, or how he made me feel when his arms were wrapped around me? I couldn't pinpoint one thing, but I knew the moment I saw him.

"I don't know, really. It was in a look. In one moment, I was his," I said.

The moment I saw him at Baran's shop, I wanted to be with him. There was no rational explanation, but the way his soft lips touched my hand that day forever marked me as his and my heart yearned for his love.

"I guess it was the same for us," Gwyn said. "I met Quinn at a Yule celebration. I smiled at him from across the room, and the rest is history, I suppose."

"Tegan, how did you meet Mund? I've never heard the story," I asked.

"It's not nearly as romantic as Gwyn's story, nor was it as dangerous and mysterious as your story, Ashling. No. . . . I met my Mund when my father betrothed me to him. But when we met, it was instant."

"Do you think you would have been happy with anyone else, had it not been Mund you were betrothed to?" I asked.

"I would have made a life with whomever my father had chosen, but it wouldn't have been what Mund and I have. My father made an excellent choice for me. I am forever grateful to him."

Maybe I should have taken Father's choice in Brychan. Instead of seeking out what I couldn't have in Grey. I probably could have found a level of happiness with Brychan. Maybe the old ways meant a simpler love, but not everyone got as lucky as Mund and Tegan. If I had never found Grey, maybe Brychan would have been a good match. Now, no one else would ever compare.

Gwyn and Tegan continued to chatter about their relationships, and they let me quietly sink into my own thoughts. I glanced behind at the Jeep, but the tinted windows made it impossible to see Grey. For all I knew, they tied him with a rope from the back to see how fast he could run. Baran would never have allowed it, but it wouldn't have surprised me with Mund and Quinn. When I was growing up, they were always causing trouble. I would have thought the two of them would have matured in that time, but no. Quinn was two hundred years old and Mund was over four hundred years old, but the two of them were like a pair of little boys.

Father always said I needed to act like a lady. I was only sixteen years old, and my brothers were centuries old, but he never saw a fault in them. A boy could do no wrong, it seemed. I never seemed to do right in his eyes. His only daughter, and he could hardly look at me. If he could see me now, he would be furious. Dressed as a common human, befriending them, loving one. In his eyes, I would be a disgrace to our kind. Mother would be proud of me for following my heart. I would see it in her eyes, her eyes always gave her away. We had a secret connection, she and I.

We pulled up to the mall, and the boys parked right next us. Thankfully, Grey actually got out of the Rubicon and was still whole. Tegan swaddled Nia to herself, and we went into the mall. Tegan, Gwyn, and I agreed to shop one level at a time so the boys could linger near. It seemed kind of silly to me, but it made the furrowed brow on Mund's forehead relax a bit. Once we separated from the boys, we started shopping.

"What should I get Grey?" I asked as I watched him across the open atrium of the mall. They looked completely out of place. They didn't look like normal humans hanging out at the mall; they looked like golden warriors.

Not that we fit in perfectly, by any means. Tegan was always wearing floor-length satin dresses, and she was exotic. Gwyn looked as if she jumped off the runway every morning. And then there was me—no matter how I tried, I looked like a wild animal stalking its prey.

"I'm not sure," Tegan said.

"Me either, but you'll know when you see the right gift," Gwyn said.

Two levels of the mall later, our lists were being crossed off, but still I didn't find anything that made me think of Grey. Nothing popped out to me as something he needed; it all seemed so materialistic.

Without a single sighting of Adomnan, Tegan was finally done shopping, and we had more bags than we could carry. As our group rejoined the boys to leave, I noticed all the onlookers; they seemed envious of us. It seemed odd to think a human would envy creatures such as us. Our purpose was to protect *them*. But after centuries of us not fulfilling that job, they were drawn to us, yearning for what was lost. We were their connection to Old Mother Earth, and the prophecy said I was to reunite the bond. They yearned for our connection to Old Mother.

The ride home was eerie—we were always waiting for Adomnan to strike. We cherished every moment because we never knew when it was going to be the end. I hated not knowing. It was inevitable that one day he would be ready to fight—we just didn't have any idea when that would be. Today, tomorrow, a week, or a year, but it was only a matter of time before the blood of my family would be on the ground, for my life. The vision made me shudder. The only thing I knew for certain: at the next gathering at Carrowmore's Bloodmoon on my eighteenth birthday, it would all end. Someone would have to claim me. It was daunting to think about, but it was my fate, and I would have to face it.

Back at home, our gift bags and boxes overwhelmed the living room. We stopped to pick out a tree for us to decorate. The custom seemed strange to me—to cut a piece of Mother Earth from her core and bring it into your home to admire its beauty as it dies. It seemed morbid.

The boys finally hauled in the blue spruce; it had to be nine feet tall, a beautiful creature. I felt bad for her, that she had to die for our entertainment, but I had to remind myself she was just taking a faster trip back to Old Mother's loving arms.

Baran would be home soon, and our pseudo-family would be whole again. Our family felt complete with Grey in it, but he had been very quiet since we arrived home. I knew I would have to grill him later to find out what my brothers talked about. They probably scared him half to death, but he busied himself stacking all the presents under our tree. The lights glittered off his already sparkling eyes. He was ruggedly handsome.

Mund leaned close to me. "You keep staring at him like that, and you'll burn a whole right through him," he whispered in my ear, laughing at his own joke. I felt my cheeks flush red-hot, and I wanted to disappear. "Come help me make dinner," he said.

I followed him like a puppy. Just as when I was a kid, wherever Mund went, I wanted to go too. That was how it had always been. I was his detached shadow, his very own tiny protégé. We began to banter about dinner, but we finally decided on braised ribs and moved on to cooking it instead of arguing about it. It was mundane and ludicrous that we all continued with life as though there weren't a wolf huffing and puffing and waiting to blow our house down.

Baran halfheartedly smiled at us, his makeshift family, as he stood in the doorway. He seemed pensive. Then abruptly his face went fierce again, and he disappeared to his room. It must have been strange for him to live with so many wolves now. He had been alone for so long, and now he hardly an inch of space to himself. I could tell he was worried about the days to come, but he hid it well. I don't think the others noticed, but I did. I set the table, and Mund called everyone for dinner. Grey sat next to me, and everyone chatted as we ate, but neither Grey nor I spoke. I was too busy watching him from the corner of my eye. He really was beautiful, almost unbearably so. From under the table, I felt his fingers reach out and lightly graze mine. I looked up into his charming eyes and was lost in the emerald sea.

When we were looking into the other's eyes, nothing stood between us, and every time his skin touched mine, my senses shut everything else out. I felt paralyzed by his penetrating gaze. Slowly I wrapped my fingers between his, holding his hand. I smiled as I remembered the awkward moment in the woods when he first held my hand. I was so afraid of his touch then, and now I couldn't get enough.

"Ashling . . ."

My attention snapped back to the present, and my family was all staring at us. They must have asked me a question.

"The two of you are disgusting," Quinn laughed, shaking his head. "Do you mind coming out of your love trance to join the conversation?"

"Sorry," I said, looking down at my lap. My fingers were still intertwined with Grey's under the table, but our attention was back on our family. "I'm listening."

"Our family has a legacy of fighters and great battles. Even Mother Rhea herself was a warrior once," Mund said. I couldn't picture my elegant grandmother as a warrior.

"You must be mistaken," I said thinking of her silvery hair and quiet presence.

"She was in the battle at the Hills of Tara over five thousand years ago," Mund said.

"She even fought several of the Dvergar pack to protect Mother and

Lady Faye," Quinn said.

Lady Faye was one of my great-aunts, thought I'd never met her. She disappeared long before I was born. Mund said she once had incredible powers, but now she was barely a myth.

"You see, Ashling, you come from a long line of female warriors. Mother Rhea would be proud you chose to stand and fight," Tegan said.

"We will win," Gwyn said. "Adomnan can't take our freedom and happiness."

But she was wrong. He could and he would. I'd seen it all in my dreams. He would take everything from me. Quinn changed the subject, and they began babbling on about how great the battle would be and something about . . . I didn't remember. My mind wandered to Grey's perfect, supple lips and his wild hair. . . .

Before I knew it, dinner was over and Grey and I were being shooed away. Grey held up a bit of mistletoe over my head, hoping for a kiss. He couldn't have realized the mistletoe's meaning in our culture. It was considered a sacred plant, and the custom of kissing under the mistletoe began as a fertility ritual. The sight of the plant set fire to my desire. I quickly kissed him on the cheek, and we ran up to my room.

I was a love-struck mess. We sat in my window seat, intertwining our legs. I leaned my face against the cold windowpane, trying to bring my rising temperature back to normal, but my heart fought against me. He smiled at me, and my lips involuntarily slipped open and a small sigh escaped. I blushed as his warm lips captured mine, and I delighted in his touch.

My hands found his chest. I could feel his chiseled muscles through his thin shirt—he was all mine. I greedily kissed his lips; I wanted all of him. Grey leaned back against the window, and his breath continued to gust out in short bursts, stopping our lust. How could he stop? His will-power was so much stronger than mine. I wanted to devour every bit of him. My desire burned through me, filling my stomach with butterflies. "Why are you stopping?" I asked.

He shrugged. "Out of respect for your family, I suppose . . . and I just don't want to push you too fast," he replied. It was a ridiculous statement, considering I was the one trying to urge his thin shirt off his beautiful torso.

I studied every contour of his delicious body, and I noticed his leather wrist cuff was over the opposite wrist, no longer covering his Killian mark—it was covering his Bloodsuckers' mark. Had he chosen? Or did my brothers have something to do with it?

"So what did you talk about with my brothers?"

"Oh you know, normal brother stuff: threats, beatings, death. No big deal," he said. There was the slightest edge of a laugh in his words. I gnawed at my lower lip. I was self-conscious knowing they had talked to him; they could have told him any number of embarrassing stories about me.

"Did they tell you anything about me?"

Grey studied my face before answering with a naughty little smile. "This is really bothering you, huh?" he said, looking almost happy at his newfound power. Sick.

"Yes," I said. I felt my cheeks burn red. Grey laughed. Even his laugh was sensuous to me. I had the desire to lean forward again and capture his sweet lips in mine. He was my match in every way, the zesty mustard to my spicy ketchup.

"You really want to know?" he asked. He looked at me over his unnaturally long lashes. The air of danger always surrounded him, and it was intoxicating and alluring. I nodded slowly, carefully.

"They kindly explained all the ways they would end my life if I dared to hurt you ever again. Including, but not limited to, dismemberment, bare-knuckle boxing in the Bloodrealms, and a sound lashing," he said. "I don't know what most of their threats meant, but I have a feeling I should be afraid."

"Sounds like them," I said. I had to admit, it was sweet that my brothers were sticking up for my honor. At the same time, did they have to be so primitive?

"You look sleepy," Grey said.

"I'm not tired," I said, fighting to keep my eyes open. He scooped me up like a baby in his arms and held me close. I rested my head on his shoulder.

A light knock came at the door, and Baran stepped in. He was so preoccupied, he hardly noticed me cuddling in Grey's arms. "Sorry to bother you," he said.

"It's okay," I said.

He paced back and forth around my room a few times before finally sitting down on my bed facing us. Whatever he came to say, it wasn't going to be easy for him.

"Grey, I wanted to tell you about your mother," Baran said, his voice raw with emotion. Grey's body tensed, and his arms felt like solid rock around my body. His emotions crashed over me so quickly, I felt nauseous. "I should have years ago, but I never could find the way to bring it up. Now that you know what we are, I think it's time you knew who *you* are. . . . Your mother, Brenna, was my twin sister. We were the youngest of the Killian pack of Scotland, and we were inseparable. When Brenna and I were just eighteen years old, we traveled through Paris. One day, she was approached by another wolf of higher status, and he demanded she marry him. She blatantly refused, and he beat her. I broke in and stopped him, but that only angered him more. I knew it wouldn't be the last we saw of him, so we fled from the city and returned home to the safety of our pack in Scotland.

"I learned his name, Verci Dvergar, uncle to Adomnan, and that we were lucky to be alive. As was predicted, he tracked us to Scotland with his pack, and he rallied the neighboring humans in an attack against our family in the middle of the night. He brutally killed our family and the rest of our pack. We were outnumbered four to one, not even including the humans. When just Brenna and I were left, the humans went on their way, leaving us to our fate with Verci. I couldn't protect her. I was gravely outnumbered, and they had broken all the bones in my body—and as my bones healed, they rebroke them. Verci raped Brenna, but she never cried out, she never let him take that from her. She was strong like that.

"When we thought all hope was lost and the end had come, King Pørr Boru, Ashling's father, brought the Boru pack, the Kingerys, and the Kahedins to save us. They were able to exterminate most of the enemy pack, but Verci fled to his father's kingdom in Iceland."

Grey's face was calm, but I could feel his emotions. He was filled with rage. It slammed around inside of me, taking my breath away. It nearly vibrated, but somehow he kept his physical self still. He was controlling his physical being in a way I had never seen before.

"Pørr brought us to the Boru Kingdom in Ireland, but Brenna's struggle didn't end back in Scotland as it should have. She was pregnant. It was not only a dishonor to her and our family, but it meant Verci could come back and claim them. To protect her and her son, Willem—your half brother—I took Willem, and she ran. She fled Ireland and took refuge in the New World," Baran said, his voice cracking. A dark cloud of the memories washed over his face. My heart ached for his pain, and I was appalled by the brutal assault Brenna had endured, only to be separated from her son. It must have nearly destroyed her.

I hadn't noticed when they all came in, but the rest of our family had joined us, sitting around the room on the floor. Baran lovingly rubbed the surface of an old, battered, tin-tile photograph before he handed it to Grey. A beautiful woman with Grey's intense eyes stared back at us. Even in the black-and-white photo, her eyes glowed. She wore a beautiful two-leaf copper necklace at her throat.

Grey looked into the face of his mother with admiration. His muscles twitched, and he held me tighter. His rage was consumed by sorrow.

Baran continued, "Willem grew and learned so quickly, so we soon set out on our own as nomads. We traveled all over Europe into Russia and Asia, making friends as we went. We visited Brenna from time to time, but for the most part, I kept Willem away from her to protect them both. Two centuries ago, I lost Willem while traveling through Greece; he met Khepri, and that was it. They settled down in Scotland, and I found myself alone once again.

"Time went on, and I saw Brenna more often over those two centuries, though I spent much of my time in Scotland protecting the Killian humans. About eighteen years ago, I lost track of Brenna. She had moved, and I had lost her scent. It took me four years to find her, and by then I was too late. She was dead when I finally found her in York Harbor. Her body lay limp in the river by the twisted oak. Knife wounds were all over her abdomen, and her head was missing, but I knew her scent. It was the most brutal thing I've ever seen, and I have lived for a *long* time and seen many evils of humankind.

"I was planning my revenge when I caught your scent, Grey. It was all over the oak tree. I followed it up to find you still hiding in the branches—a small two-year-old boy with her big green eyes, silently crying. You weren't afraid of me. I assumed you saw it all, but whoever killed her didn't see you.

"She left her lineage tattooed on your wrist as a path to your home. I called the local police and reported finding her body while hiking, and I stayed with you until the police arrived. I followed as they took you home to your father. I thought at the time that he was too shocked to cry, but now I realize it was he who killed her; I don't know if he knew when he married her what she was, or if he had planned all along to take the spirit from her body. I was too relieved to find you alive to see the truth in Robert. I'm sorry I failed you, but I vowed that day to protect you. It's what she would have wanted. And she would have wanted you to know who she really was."

Baran cried, and Tegan held his hand, comforting him. I felt wretched, and my eyes glistened with tears. Grey didn't look at anyone—he just kept staring at the photo of his mother—but I could feel his pain. I shuddered to think of the pain she must have been in to wear that silver band on her finger. Years of wearing it would have eaten away at her strength.

Baran went on to tell us Brenna had been carefree and wild and that she had Grey's beautiful green eyes and his stubborn rebellion. She was tall and lean and beautiful. Grey's breath was ragged in my ear. I knew it was hard for him to hear. Everything his father had ever told him was a lie, but even if his father was a monster, there was still a bond between them. His heart must have been breaking. I wished I could fix his pain, but there was nothing I could do to ease his suffering.

"Grey, you are one of my pack, and if you want to join me, I'd be glad to welcome you as a Killian," Baran said.

Everyone waited for his reply. Even I wasn't sure what he would say. Had I been in his place, I would have curled up into the fetal position and wept for days. But Grey's face remained calm, and he sat perfectly still with his arms wrapped around me.

"Thank you for sharing my mom with me. I would be honored to stand with you as a Killian," Grey said. There was such pride in his voice. I admired him.

Baran nodded his head and stood to leave. "I've given you a lot to think about, so I'll leave you to your thoughts." He nodded to the others, and they left quietly, leaving Grey and me alone once again. I didn't know what to say or even where to begin. He finally knew the truth; it made my heart soar, but it also made me want to cry for him. What could I say at a moment like this?

The only thing I knew for sure: "Grey, I love you," I told him. I snuggled into his shoulder. I did love him, no matter who or what he was or where he came from. Human, Bloodsucker, or wolf, he was mine. By all the gods, I had made my choice.

I didn't want him to know what I was sacrificing, that the prophecy wouldn't be fulfilled with a human by my side, but I couldn't lose him again. There would be nothing left of me, I would just lie down and die. My heart would open up and let my soul free; only my body would remain to shrivel away with time. He was the piece of my soul I was always missing. That stupid journal had it all wrong. I chose Grey, and there was nothing the fates could do to change that. I loved every part of him, even his dark side. We all had a dark side.

"You are everything to me," Grey said.

His words washed over me. I was his, in every way possible. His love gave me hope that I would survive this. Adomnan was nothing compared to our love. He had nothing and we had everything.

19
Embrace

Grey picked me up, carried me to my bed, and swept the blankets back. I was sure he was about to kiss my lips, my very ready lips. I looked up at him through my darkened lashes, waiting for him to fulfill the unspoken promise. I wanted it more than I could have imagined. My blood boiled in my veins for the taste of his tongue. I wanted every bit of his scent swirling all around me. He sat straddled above me, with his strong hand on the center of my back as he guided me down to the soft mattress. He laid my head on my pillow, and my hair cascaded over my face, covering half of it in secret. His body was barely touching mine, but I could feel his heart beat like a sledgehammer on my skin.

My breath rushed out through my partially opened lips as his fingers lightly traced over them. His fingers were rough on my delicate skin as they continued their pursuit down around my jaw line. Leaving behind burning flames on my skin. I felt lightheaded as he continued down my neck, caressing my throat. His thumb rubbed the hollow at the base, lingering there before continuing across my collarbone to the very tip of my shoulder.

Another gust of air whooshed out of my lungs, but the air coming in was so sweet with his scent. His blood was warmer, deeper. Enticing. My eyes felt heavy with his delightful poison.

His touch continued down my arms toward my fingers. I wanted him. I wanted to touch him, to taste him, to feel him. I breathed his scent deeper into my lungs, burning them. It felt like a million little knives stabling into my lungs from the inside—and I wanted more. Glutton for more punishment and more pleasure.

He brought each of my fingertips to his lips, one by one. Lightly kissing them, leaving a moist reminder behind. His gentle kisses started to grow more urgent with each erratic breath he took. He finally followed the blazing path he had left behind, kissing up my arm to my elbow. He paused as he pressed his lips to my pulsing vein at my wrist. It was almost too much to bear to remain still, but I wanted to feel it all. His forbidden lips pulsed on my veins.

He kissed every inch of my collarbone, setting my skin ablaze. His soft lips finally reached the base of my neck, but he pulled back, watching my wild eyes. He wanted it all too. To drown in our love. His intense eyes were greedily taking me all in, devouring the very sight of me. His lips curved up to a sly, sexy smile.

His head bowed back down to my collarbone, and his warm, moist tongue touched my skin for the first time. I gasped at the unexpected ex-hilaration. He licked me up my long neck to just under my ear. I needed his kiss. I turned my head, capturing his mouth with mine, our tongues intertwining in a very personal dance. His mouth was intoxicating.

He pulled away, leaving my lips feeling raw and unsatisfied. I wanted to nibble at his lower lip. It was red from all the blood rushing through him, but his eyes were wide with fear. Was he afraid of me? Had I hurt him? I studied his face and the washes of emotions that followed like a storm.

"We should stop," he said.

I leaned up and kissed his lips again. No part of me wanted to stop. I wanted to kiss him. I wanted to touch his skin. I wanted it to lead anywhere we wanted to go as long as I was with him. I trusted him and loved him inescapably.

His lips, reluctantly at first, followed mine in another deep kiss. The energy in the room vibrated around us, but he pulled away again, but this time I pursued him, after another kiss. Unrelenting. He nipped at my lip in return, catching my plump lower lip between his teeth. Nibbling it. Stimulating every cell in my body. A mischievous smile consumed his face. It was dazzling how cruelly handsome he was, and having his lips this close to mine without being able to touch them was completely distracting.

As he studied my face, concern washed over him; something was bothering him, but he guarded his feelings well. "Did I do something wrong?" I asked. I felt uncharacteristically shy.

"Never," he said. He lightly rubbed his nose on mine, but he still seemed disconnected. Part of him was lost somewhere, somewhere he couldn't or wouldn't take me.

I felt jealous that he would keep secrets from me. The energy in the room still throbbed with excitement. "Kiss me," I said.

The corner of his mouth turned up again, showing his gleaming teeth just below his upper lip. The wolf was obvious in him. He was wild too—I could see it in his eyes. Years of his obedience were just waiting to spill over and rebel, and I wanted so much to be there with him when he let go of the restraint. I wished it would be now. I wanted to know where that could lead. But I saw plainly in his eyes—he had made up his mind to behave at least for *tonight*. Though his naughty little smile still played at his lips.

"You want me, don't you?" he asked.

I felt my face flush. I wasn't sure why I was so embarrassed by his statement, but I felt like a little kid who had been caught red-handed. "Yes," I said.

His smirk turned into a full-out wolfish grin. "Good," he replied, "that's how I like it."

"Overconfident half-breed," I said as I shoved him off my bed. My hair wildly framed my face as I leaned precariously over the edge of the bed above him, calculating my attack. He pretended to be hurt by what I had said, but I knew he was up to no good. No matter how he tried to contain his smile, it kept breaking through his reserved expression.

I leapt off the bed, landing with all my weight on his chest. He didn't even flinch. I closed my eyes and took a deep breath of his scent, holding his musk in my lungs. My eyes flashed open, and I jumped off his chest to my window. In a miraculously smooth movement, I opened it and leapt out into the falling snow. Everything was coated in white as I caught my footing on a tree branch.

It was a winter wonderland. Simply beautiful.

The snow-covered world allowed an eerie blue essence to surround the forest. I looked back to my bedroom window, hoping Grey was surprised by my stealth, speed, and grace, but he wasn't there. I crept out on the branch toward the house to peek in and get a glimpse of where he was hiding, then the hair on my neck went rigid. I heard the branch crack behind me and watched snow plop down to the ground. My gaze unconsciously followed it.

The once-pure snow was now stained red.

I could smell fresh blood behind me. It made the animal inside me scream with hunger. I worked up the courage to turn my head over my shoulder to see the predator that had made me as its prey. My hair caught in the wind, and the swirling snow around my face pierced my skin.

"Boo." I heard Adomnan's vile voice behind me. I turned to see him crouching a few feet away, holding the small, lifeless body of a little boy in his cruel hands. Blood still dripped from his cold lips. "I was hoping you'd join me for dinner."

The child couldn't have been more than eight years old, and his skin was an unnatural blue. My heart ached for his poor young soul. The sadistic look on Adomnan's face sent chills down my spine. He looked straight out of a horror film, but his clothes were pristine as always. Even with the blood on his face, his beauty could not be denied.

I looked around for his brothers, certain they had me surrounded, but to my horror, they were nowhere to be seen. My only thoughts were of them attacking my unsuspecting family. Panic raked through my body in a shudder. He smiled back at me, answering my fears with his happiness. The branch cracked again from our joint weight, and the tree groaned at our intrusion.

"You're a monster," I said.

"Indeed," he replied, licking the blood from his lips.

The sickness in him was far deeper than I could have imagined, and I knew he would never stop until he had me. This wasn't just a game to him. This was where it would all end. If I went with him quietly, maybe he would let my family live. Mund would have remorse and always wonder if he could have done more, but he would have Tegan and Nia. He'd move on eventually, and I knew Baran would look after Grey.

I just had to accept *my* sacrifice. My life for theirs.

In a blur, Grey's body flew past mine, violently smashing into Adomnan, knocking me off my branch. My body slammed into the ground, and the pain spiraled through me. The pain from my leg vibrated up into my pelvis, causing me to gag. It must have broken. The little boy's body fell in a lump at the base of the tree. Ignoring the excruciating throbs in my leg, I crawled over to the boy and held his cold, lifeless body in my hands. I didn't want to cry in front of Adomnan, but my tears ran down my cheeks for the boy. I chanted to Old Mother to welcome him to her kingdom.

When I looked back up, Grey's hand was on Adomnan's throat, holding him against the tree. "Get the hell out of here or die," Grey said. His voice murderous.

Adomnan replied with a wicked, howling laugh. Adomnan lunged at Grey, knocking them both back onto the branch, breaking it. The two dropped to the ground, landing on their feet. The branch thudded into the snow between Grey and me.

"Fleshy and stupid," Adomnan said as he dusted off his coat. "Very well, boy. We can make a game of it." Grey dropped down into a crouch. He couldn't fight Adomnan. Adomnan was a skilled killing machine.

He had hundreds of years of blood on his hands, innumerable murders of innocents. I couldn't let this happen, I couldn't let Grey die for me. I couldn't bear the idea of his blood spilling in the place of mine.

Mund and Baran came running around the front of the house. I was scared for their safety. They were all in danger because of me.

"Mund!" I screamed, but before I finished, Baran and Mund stood between Grey and Adomnan. Menacing growls on both sides. It was indistinguishable whose they were. I needed to shift to heal my leg, but I couldn't with human eyes possibly on us. I wanted to close my eyes and let it be over. I didn't dare watch, nor did I dare look away.

Grey made a mistake the day he met me. He should have seen the signs. He should have known better. I knew he couldn't live in my world. He would die because he met me. They would *all* die because of me. I should have left this place when I had the chance.

"Just give up, Adomnan," Mund said. His cool confidence calmed my mind.

"And give up what is rightfully mine?" Adomnan said staring at me.

Eamon and Bento flanked Adomnan as they emerged from the trees. Bento seemed to be sizing up Baran and Quinn. He must have seen them as his threat and Mund as Adomnan's. Eamon seemed more concerned with Grey, which seemed odd. Grey was only a human, and yet Eamon's eyes didn't leave Grey's, not even for a moment to blink.

I wanted to help them fight. I needed to help. They couldn't always just hold me back and protect me. I was a part of this family, and I needed to fight to protect them too. Prophecy or no prophecy, I couldn't live with myself if I let them all fight for me. If only I could shift so I could heal quickly. I moved to stand, but fell back to the ground, gasping from pain.

"So little boy, do you really know *what* we are?" Adomnan said.

Grey just smiled defiantly back at him.

"Your blood isn't even appealing. But I would make an exception to kill you," he hissed.

Grey's heart was beating slow and steady. He had to be controlling it somehow. He was surrounded by werewolves, growling all around him.

Was he really that unaware of what we really were and what we could do to him? Or was he really that confident? I found myself wondering if he hunted with his father and how much he really knew about us. Maybe I had been wrong to assume he understood what we were . . . or maybe I was wrong to assume he didn't.

"Leave," I demanded.

Adomnan looked at me again; I swore he was seeing me for the first time. Wild hair, barely clothed, with a broken leg in the cold snow and the little boy in my arms. "You dare to tell me what to do?" he hissed at me.

"I'd happily punish you for your crimes, but there are innocents here," I replied. My angry venom dripped from my words with hate. "So get the bloody hell away from my family."

Adomnan looked at my family around me, all ready to die to protect me. "As you wish, my princess," Adomnan said. "For now." His evil smile was still on his lips as he licked the remaining blood off. Bento reached for the boy's body, and I growled a deadly warning.

"Leave it," Adomnan said. "I was done with it anyway." He locked eyes with me as they disappeared into the trees.

My heart filled with desperate sadness as I wept for the child's soul. Grey held me in his arms as we sat in the cold snow. "Call the authorities," I said.

"We shouldn't bring the police here," Baran said.

"We could move the body somewhere they will find it," Mund suggested.

"No. We will not keep his body from his parents any longer. He wants his mother," I said, cradling him in my arms. I could feel the reverberating fear from his departed soul, and it clouded me with sadness.

Baran walked into the house and returned moments later, wrapping a wool blanket around Grey and me. "They are on the way," he said.

We waited in the cold snow in silence for the police to come. They asked endless questions. We claimed I saw the boy out the window and that I rushed to try to save him, but it was a lie. He was dead because of me. If I didn't live here, Adomnan wouldn't be here killing innocent souls. They took the boy's body with them, leaving us in the cold in our blood-soaked clothes.

My leg pulsed with pain. When Grey and Mund had fought in the parking lot at school, I hurt when Grey did. But now that my leg was broken, Grey wasn't injured. How could that be? Or was he hiding his pain? I reached out my hand and lightly touched his right leg where mine was broken, and he flinched.

"I'm sorry," I whispered. He delicately kissed my cold forehead.

"You made the right decision for the child," Baran said. "Thank you for being strong enough to choose it."

I would have agreed, but the pain in my leg vibrated through my body again, and I gasped. "I need to shift," I said.

Grey scooped me up in his strong arms, carried me into the house, and whispered into my ear, "I'll take care of you."

He sat me down on the sofa and took his seat next to mine. He watched me, expectantly. He wanted to see me as an animal. Was I just some sideshow attraction for him? The beast-girl . . . how positively horrifying. I wasn't sure I wanted him to see the wolf again.

Everyone filed back into the living room. Baran shut the door with a solid thud. He looked to me and Grey and back again. Fear and exhaustion were clearly on his face. He wanted to say something, but he didn't have to. I already knew I had been reckless and had endangered the whole family with my actions. No one had to tell me how stupid and irresponsible I was; I was already ashamed of myself. I had nowhere to look but down at my own feet.

I heard Mund's footsteps as he walked over to me and wrapped his big, safe arms around my shoulders. A small whimper escaped from his lips, just barely audible to even me. His deep sadness rolled off him and onto me, nearly crushing my body. That one small sound was enough to break my heart. For so long, Mund had been my only friend, the only one who understood me, but now I knew he was also afraid of losing me.

"We had a great realization today," Baran said with the fierceness of a leader. "We aren't able to protect our humans—we are barely protecting ourselves. Every move we make jeopardizes them more. Ashling, is it still your decision to stay and fight?"

I looked at my family around me. "It is our duty to protect these people. We endangered them by being here, but even if we leave, it doesn't mean Adomnan won't kill them all before he continues hunting us," I said. "We fight for our family and we fight for these people."

"I fear for all our safety," Baran said. "No one is to leave the house alone. We need to fight them on our terms far from the city. This attack will take time to plan and orchestrate, but I believe we can win."

Our quarrel would continue another day. Even if we fled as a family, it would do no good. They would just track us. If I alone ran and they stayed, it would put them off my trail for a while. It would buy me a little time to hide. Somewhere like the Himalayas or Antarctica, though eating penguins didn't sound too appealing . . . they were too cute.

Grey held my hand, connecting us, and Mund gestured for Tegan to come to him. She puddled herself and Nia into his lap, and there they embraced each other, but Mund kept one hand on my shoulder. Gwyn and Quinn kneeled in front of us on the floor, and Quinn placed one hand on Grey's shoulder, creating the web of life. Still, no one yelled at me for my childish behavior. No one punished me or sent me away. Baran kneeled down with the others, putting one hand on Nia and one on Gwyn completing the connection. Their power flowed through me, and it pulsed with their strength. I had yearned my whole life for this moment, for this connection. Together we silently became one.

When we all let go, the energy still thrived inside me—it was the energy of a pack. I'd never felt it before, and it was intoxicating. Despite me not having a Bloodmark, we all connected as one pack, one heart. The enchanting feeling of it filled my broken heart with happiness. I finally belonged.

"Grey, what you did . . ." Mund said.

"I'm not sorry for what I did," Grey said.

"Let me finish. What you did was save her life. We weren't there in time to protect her—you were. I am indebted to you. Please forgive me." He quietly bowed his head to Grey. Grey put his free hand on Mund's shoulder, a silent agreement between men, stronger than any verbal bond.

"Does your leg hurt much?" Gwyn asked.

Everyone started to fuss around me again, worried about my leg and my discomfort. "But Grey, what about your leg?" I asked in the midst of all the things they said.

"Is your leg broken too, Grey?" Baran asked. Our bond was even stronger now; Grey was able to feel my pain just as I was able to feel his. Though when it was happening, when my leg broke, he didn't react or flinch with pain. Granted, my attention was briefly centered on my discomfort.

"It's not bad," Grey said. He shot me a dirty look. He seemed annoyed I had spilled his secret, but what was I supposed to do? He was in pain. We had to get him to a doctor to have his leg x-rayed and set. I wondered how he was able to carry me to the house with a broken leg—it must have been excruciatingly painful.

Baran reached down and felt Grey's leg, feeling for the break. "It's already healing," he said. "Is that the wolf in you or the *Bloodsucker?*" His voice was leery.

It wasn't human, and it was definitely not wolf. We had to shift into a wolf to feel the healing power of Old Mother's love as our body repaired. It had to be his father's presence in him. Some mutation in the Bloodsuckers, passed from one generation to another. I didn't know enough about them as a breed to know what to expect, and Grey had never opened up to me about his father. He was still a mystery, even to me.

The pungent smell of fear filled the room like sour milk. Gwyn leaned slightly away from Grey instinctively. Everyone saw the small change in her body language, but the others remained perfectly still. *Bloodsucker* meant something so much deeper to our kind, sending chills down our spines. It flooded our memories with all the stories and legends of the inexorably cruel creatures. Yet here one sat, right in front of me, more beautiful than any of our kind, and I trusted him completely. I was inescapably in love with him.

He looked down at our hands. Was he ashamed of what he was? Still no one moved, but I sensed them all watching him. They wanted to trust him for all his chivalrous deeds, but the truth behind his nature was almost too much for them to understand.

Mund stood up. "It doesn't matter how much of you is your father. You are one of us." He patted Grey on the back, moved over toward the window, and stared out at the falling snow. His back was to us, but I knew he was listening.

"Thank you," Grey said.

I felt somehow betrayed that Grey hadn't discussed all these things about himself. He knew far more about me than he should, according to our laws. Why didn't he feel safe to tell me about himself? I wanted to know. I *needed* to know.

"Grey," I paused, choosing my words carefully. "What else can you do, besides heal?"

He watched my face carefully. I knew everyone was also intently listening, but I didn't care what they heard or what they thought. I just needed to understand him. I needed to know him.

He spoke only to me. "I heal in minutes from most injuries, hours for near-death ones. I can run as fast as you. I can hear the sound of breaking skin. I can distinguish scents of familiar creatures for hundreds of miles . . . especially *you*," he said with a smile, "and I suspected you weren't human the moment I saw you."

I felt my mouth fall agape as I stared up into his perfect face. He smiled.

"And I needed to be with you," Grey said.

I smiled as he continued.

"I resisted my father's training for almost ten years. I should have been taught and inducted into the hunters when I was eight, but something didn't feel right about it. I knew he killed wolves. But I didn't realize they were people too." His voice broke as he spoke. "It wasn't until the day in the forest when I saw you in the cage. I looked into your golden eyes, and I knew it wasn't just wolves he hunted.

"Because I refused to take the oath, he couldn't tell me about your kind. I thought he was just in some kind of weird hunting club with some very old-world traditions with medieval silver weapons. They drank the blood of the wolves, and he kept all their skulls, but I guess I always knew something else was different about the hunters and me. My eyes glowed in the dark, theirs didn't. My strength surpassed that of everyone I knew, including my father. I could run faster than a human and most animals I raced. I learned, in time, to hide my imperfections from the world around me and from him. So no one would notice I was different."

"How many Bloodsuckers are there?" Quinn asked.

Grey turned his attention to the others, as though he had forgotten they were in the room with us. "There are never more than eight. One leader, three masters, four offspring. No child can be inducted without the approval of the others."

"Did they know what you were?" I said.

"I don't know," he replied. "I didn't know what I was, but I imagine they did."

"Will your father come looking for you?" Tegan asked.

He shook his head. "Maybe, but I'd be more afraid if he didn't . . ."

"Do you think he'd try to attack us?" Quinn asked.

"It's possible—he is a murderer," Grey said. A deep sadness settled on me, and I felt horrible for him. "I don't trust him."

"Why did you suspect I wasn't human?" I interrupted.

"You were too wild for a human. It's plainly in your eyes if you look for it. They are too deep; human eyes are dull. I knew something was truly startling about you, but I couldn't understand what it was. It drew me to you night after night. I couldn't leave you. I needed to be with you. I needed to protect you," he said. "I just didn't realize I was supposed to be protecting you from myself."

The shame of what he said seemed to consume him. I could barely breathe at the sight of his sadness, but I gluttonously breathed him in again. I knew he wouldn't hurt me, and I knew now that I would never hurt him. I looked up at Baran as a shudder of pain shook through my tiny frame. My leg was still pulsing with pain.

"You need to heal," Baran said, "and I think everyone needs time to think." I could hear the sadness in his voice.

They all left Grey and me alone. I didn't know what to say to him. I still had so many questions.

Grey followed me back up to my room. I knew he wanted to carry me, but I was determined to drag my own broken body despite the agonizing pain pulsing through my leg. The cold wind still whipped through the open window, a freezing reminder of what had occurred.

I closed my eyes and let the animal consume me. I felt it vibrate under my skin as I ripped through my clothes and shifted into a wolf. The pain instantly began to dissipate as Old Mother's magic wove its way through my body. I blinked my golden eyes as I watched Grey through my true sight. It felt so good to be a wolf again. He knelt down in front of me and rubbed my fur between his fingers. The sensation was exquisite.

"You are more beautiful than any creature who walked the earth before you," Grey said. "I knew you weren't a human that day in the woods, and I loved you then, even if I didn't know why. And I love you more now that I know who you are." He wrapped his strong arms around my neck, pulling me into a hug.

He thought I was beautiful, even like this. It was more than I could have ever asked for. It made my heart swell with happiness. It felt as though the weight of a thousand worlds was being taken off my back. I needed him to not hate me for what I was. I couldn't change who I was, nor would I want to. My leg stopped hurting as it finished healing, but how could I shift back with him here? I would be naked. If I had been able, I would have blushed at the thought, but my fur hid my embarrassment.

Tegan walked in the room with her silent, graceful footsteps. "Grey, dear, I need you to step out on the staircase for a moment, please."

He did as she asked, and Tegan shut the door behind them. I could hear them clearly from the other side of the door as she explained that when I shifted back I would be naked. I also heard his heart respond as it raced with excitement. I loved knowing I had such an effect on him. While they talked, I quickly shifted back to my human form and dressed myself.

We all joined in Baran's office to discuss the legends of Old Mother's hunters, the Bloodsuckers. Only Baran had ever encountered one before and I only knew of the fables. Even Grey didn't know anything about them, and he lived with one. The monster that raised him also killed his mother and wanted me dead. That had to be a heavy burden to carry.

Baran said, "When Quinn was just a babe, a Bloodsucker attacked the village. He cut the head off a wolf-child with his silver blade and drank its blood. The creature had no remorse. Nessa was running for the safety of the castle with Quinn, but he knocked them down and tried to rip Quinn from her arms. I heard her cries and leapt from the highest peak of the castle to save her. The fall broke both of my legs, but I was able to rip the Bloodsuckers' throat from his body, killing him instantly. It is unforgivable to kill Old Mother's humans, but I looked deep into his eyes, and this creature was no longer human. His soul was empty."

As I listened to Baran's story, I tried to find any part of Grey that was like those creatures, but Grey wasn't a vicious murderer—though, to the Bloodsuckers, vicious murderers was all *we* were.

Baran didn't enjoy the death of another creature, and this was no different. I could tell he was proud to have saved Mother and Quinn, but he was repelled by the idea of a human having to die at his hands. It left our souls heavy with the burden.

Christmas morning finally came, but not with a happiness any one of us could share. We were all scared. Though we still showered Nia with gifts and love, we opened presents in a sort of suspended happiness. The lightest change in the air could have changed everything. My first Christmas with Grey was tainted by fear, though we hadn't seen Adomnan since the little boy died, but we made the best of the day.

Grey handed me a black box. "Merry Christmas, Ashling."

I opened the box to find a delicate gold chain necklace with two green and gold leaves hidden inside. It was the necklace his mother had been wearing in the photo Baran had given him.

I ran my fingers over the beautiful leaves. "It's lovely."

"This was my mother's. She always said she dreamed in color when she wore it," he said. "It reminded me of you."

I gathered my hair up on top my head as he took it from the box and placed it on my neck. His fingers lightly grazed my skin, causing me to catch my breath. Every time he touched me, my pulse raged.

"Thank you, Grey," I said. "Now open my gift."

I handed him a small wooden box; I had carved the Killian Blood-mark into the cover. He studied it for a while before finally opening the box. Inside I had carved the words, *My heart is yours.*

"It's not much, but I couldn't think of anything else I wanted you to have more." I smiled.

He kissed me softly, his hand caressing my back. "It's all I need."

Baran said, "I am deeply thankful for this wonderful Christmas and Solstice with all of you. I am grateful to call you all my family."

Tegan kissed Baran on the cheek. "It is a lovely Christmas."

"We should end the year celebrating at the city's New Year's dance," Gwyn said.

"I don't think that's a good idea," Mund said.

"Sure it is," Gwyn said. "There will be far too many humans around for either Robert or Adomnan to threaten us. It would be a perfect way to get us out of the house safely."

It was odd to think how the roles had reversed, that the humans now protected us, but it didn't give me comfort. As much as I wanted to get out of this stuffy house, something urged me to stay home. I'd been to one dance, why were there so many?

"Are you sure it's safe?" I said.

"If we don't get out of this house, we will all be in more danger inside than out." Quinn laughed. The last couple weeks had been unendingly stressful, and I think we were starting to get stir crazy. You can't cage wild animals—eventually they will tear each other apart for sport.

Surprisingly, though, Grey seemed unaffected by the random outbursts from the others. He even wrestled with Mund and Quinn. His advanced healing allowed them to actually fight. It scared me to watch, so I rarely did.

"We will have to be cautious, but it is likely our only chance to leave the house until we can lure Adomnan into making a mistake," Baran said.

"You dapper fellow!" Gwyn cooed, hugging Baran.

In the days leading up to the dance, Beth and Emma had both called to see if I were going. I had neglected them for a while. Not a great thing to do to my first friends, but it was for their own safety. Emma informed me it was semi-formal like homecoming and we needed new dresses. Tegan told me she had it under control.

On the day of the dance, I still hadn't seen what Tegan had come up with for my dress, and it made me nervous. I also wondered what ugly hot-pink, glittery barf Lacey would wear this time. The visual of her in a barfed-up-Skittles dress brought a smile to my face.

"What's with the evil smile?" Gwyn asked.

"Nothing," I laughed nervously. I didn't want to admit some of the human tendencies of catty girls had rubbed off on me.

"Tegan's ready to show us what we're wearing tonight," Gwyn's voice was filled with excitement. Tegan loved fashion, especially now that she was no longer required to wear antique satin dresses. I followed her into Tegan and Mund's room. Tegan stood in front of three sheet-draped mannequins. She walked over to the far left mannequin.

"For you, Gwyn," she said, putting her hand on the mannequin's shoulder, "I have created a fantastic little dress in a silvery, winter-white fabric and an asymmetrical, ruffled collar." She pulled the white sheet down, revealing exactly what she'd described and so much more. The fabric was lovely. I knew it was from her stash of exotics. It was a short, ruched dress with an amazingly showy ruffle at the neckline. The squeal from Gwyn was more than enough for everyone in the county to know she was happy with what she saw. It really was a perfect fit for Gwyn with its bold shape and design. Not many women could pull off a collar like that. Certainly not me. Tegan winked at me as she crossed over to the far right mannequin.

"For myself, I have created a long, simply cut sleeveless gown with ruching at the bodice in the same winter-white fabric." She pulled the sheet down, exposing her dress. Also equally suited for her. She really had a knack for showing people's inner personalities with the garments she created. I wondered what she saw inside me. The third mannequin stood ominously still covered.

"And for you, my sweet Ashling, there was only ever *one* option."

The sheet fluttered to the ground, revealing a smooth, deep-red satin dress. It was off the shoulder and came above the knee with pleating along the sides. It was stunning. I lightly ran my fingers over the neckline, feeling the softness of the satin. It was dramatic and unexpected. I had never seen myself this way.

"You've grown up, Ashling. Your bold, powerful inner beauty matches your stunning outer beauty. When trying to capture your essence in fabric, I could think of no other color than red. I hope you like it," Tegan said.

Considering all the drama going on with Adomnan, it seemed ridiculous to be so excited about a dress, but I was. I wanted to wear that fierce red dress. I wanted to be the girl Tegan thought I was. "I love it," I replied. I loved her so much, but I had never deserved her, or any of them, for that matter.

"Stop being so mushy," Gwyn said. "Let's get dressed for the party!"

Gwyn pulled out gobs of makeup and hair products. Gwyn was a magician as far as I was concerned. I decided to let my hair be free. I wasn't going to tame it. The curly, red fire would frame my face nicely. Tegan sat down next to me on the bed as she put on mascara. My hands shook as I put the dress on.

"Are you nervous?" she asked.

"Adomnan will be there," I said. "You know he'll be watching. *He's always watching.*"

20
Stolen

Slowly I walked out of Tegan's room, and my nerves had the best of me. The red heels she had lent me were over four inches tall. I felt like a stork wobbling around on the tiny pegs. I rounded the corner into the living room to see Baran, Quinn, Mund, and Grey standing waiting for us, each wearing a suit. Grey was dressed in a black suit, his dress shirt unbuttoned a few buttons to expose some of his rock-solid chest. My pulse quickened at the sight of his skin. He wore cufflinks of the Killian crest. Baran had given them to him for Christmas. They were a symbol of who Grey was now.

Who he had always been.

I heard the air suck out of Grey's lungs, and his mouth fell agape. I walked quickly to his side, trying to hide from the others. His coarse fingers lightly rubbed over my exposed shoulders, and he leaned down, pressing his warm lips to my skin.

"You are my goddess," Grey said.

He could tell me anything, and I would believe him.

"Thank you," I said.

"Before we go, I have a little something," Baran said. He pulled out a large plastic box of wrist corsages with white lilies and white plumes. He handed them to each of us ladies, and even Nia got a miniature one. She looked like a tiny, little princess in her mother's arms.

I leaned up on my tiptoes, kissed Baran on the cheek, and thanked him. I was thanking him for far more than he knew, more than the simple flower that wrapped my wrist. I was thanking him for everything he had done for me. I thought back to the day I first caught his scent, when I thought he was sent to end my life. I realized now he gave me my life instead. He saved me when I didn't even know I needed to be saved. If it hadn't been for him, I would never have found Grey. I owed Baran so much.

We were off to join the town debauchery, and I couldn't keep my eyes off Grey. He looked good enough to eat . . . well, not quite. I stifled a laugh. The nine of us arrived with the festivities already bustling. The place was packed; the entire town had to be in that one tiny community center. A local band played in the corner, and the whole place pulsed with the beat of the music. Grey wove his fingers with mine, and I felt his strength in his touch.

Emma and Beth shoved their way through the crowd to us. "Where have you been?" Beth said.

"Family stuff," I said with a shrug. That wasn't entirely the truth, nor was it a lie.

"What are you doing here?" Beth asked Grey rudely.

He smiled at her. "I'm sorry, Beth. We both know I made some mistakes, but I'm working to earn Ashling's forgiveness—and yours."

Beth laughed. "Yeah, okay. Whatever you say."

Baran secured a large table at the edge of the dance floor. Soon Kate, Kelsey, and Ryan found us too. The whole town was in constant chatter. I could hardly hear myself think. Even Claire was babbling Baran's ear off, though he didn't seem to mind . . . he even asked her to dance. It felt so good to get out of our house and be a part of life again. I loved seeing the smiles on my friends' faces and hearing them laugh.

"May I please have this dance?" Grey asked with a slight bow.

I couldn't stifle the giggle that came out. "It would be my pleasure."

Grey led me to the dance floor to a slow song. I didn't hear the words; all I could hear was the beat of his heart as he spun me around the room. The feeling of his strong arms around my tiny body filled me with a happiness I couldn't put into words, but I felt safe when Grey was with me.

I leaned up and captured his lips with mine. We were lost in our own world of the other's touch. Somehow everything would fall away when I was with him. Every worry in the world disappeared, and all that remained on the empty dance floor was our two bodies, pressed dangerously close together, swaying from side to side.

"You're beautiful," he said.

"Thank you. Tegan made my dress."

He smiled. "Ashling, all of you is beautiful to me."

The song must have ended because everyone started thrashing around again. He looked down at me. His face was filled with admiration, and he kissed the very tip of my nose before he slowly led the way back to our table.

With no sign of Adomnan, we chatted on about nothing in particular for hours. Grey straddled the bench behind me with his arms constantly surrounding me. It was the best feeling in the world, *being in love.*

Ryan strutted over in his charcoal dress pants and blue shirt. "Grey, may I ask Ashling to dance?"

I coughed out a laugh. "I think you had better ask me," I said.

Everyone laughed. I felt Grey's arms possessively hold me a little tighter. He was jealous of Ryan. What did he have to worry about? I was lovingly, intoxicatingly bound to him.

Ryan cleared his throat. "Ashling, may I have the honor of this dance?"

I smiled. "Yes."

I kissed Grey on the cheek playfully and skipped after Ryan onto the dance floor. Ryan nervously put his hand on my hips. He stepped on my toe and blushed. He was a good friend. Simple in a way, but loyal and sweet. I was thankful to have him as one of my friends. Though he wasn't much of a dancer. He stepped on my toe, again. "Sorry," he mumbled.

I giggled. Suddenly Ryan stopped dancing.

I opened my eyes to see a girl watching us. She had messy long blonde hair and black makeup all around her eyes. She wore a strapless black leather dress, and the language of the Bloodmoon was tattooed down her pale arms all the way to her fingertips. She was beautiful and frightening; I had never seen anyone like her. Her expression was cold, and her scent swarmed around me, burning my senses. She was definitely wolf.

Mund, Quinn, and Grey were next to us in a blink of an eye. Ryan seemed bewildered by my family's sudden presence, but he was too relieved they were there to question how. It was written all over Ryan's face that he saw the girl as a threat, unlike Grey, who seemed eager to fight Adomnan.

"Who is she?" I asked.

"I'm not sure," Mund said, "but I don't think she's here to dance."

I took a step forward, and her expression mocked me. What did she want with me? I was just a girl. I wasn't a prophecy. I wasn't the key to our culture's survival. I was simply a girl. The taste of hatred was on my tongue.

Grey wrapped his arm tightly around my shoulders, claiming me. The girl smiled, but there was no kindness in her eyes, and she walked through the crowd away from us. I tried to follow, but the crowd swallowed her. I knew I would see her again. I could feel it on the back of my neck where my hair stood on end. Grey led me away in the opposite direction toward the main exit, weaving through the masses of people.

"We'll leave this place," he said. Questioning what I had heard, I looked up into his beautiful green eyes. He nodded. "Together."

I nodded my head, almost mindlessly. I knew I would follow him to the ends of the earth without question. We were leaving. It sounded so final. I had been right all along . . . I was going to have to run away. I just hadn't realized Grey would leave with me. I hadn't dared to dream that dream, but I was thankful to have him by my side.

We were separated from my family in the crowds of people. I could still sense my family following us out into the cold night air. The snow crunched and squeaked under my feet as my heels made contact with the bitter earth.

The air stung my lungs as I tried to calm my worry. Out of nowhere, Lacey came barreling out after us in her horribly pink, glitter-covered dress. She looked as if a fairy princess threw-up on her. Her bleached-blonde hair was in ringlets like a porcelain doll's. Really, when she wasn't talking, she was quite pretty.

"You're such a slut, Ashling!" she said.

Well, that ruined the effect. What else could possibly go wrong to-night? A crazed werewolf was stalking me, and now I was a slut. My first boyfriend ever—whom I had never had sex with—and I was a slut. Girls were ridiculous creatures. It's not as if I had better things to deal with than this silly little girl. I rolled my eyes. Lacey's little fists were all balled up on her hips. She was pretending to be tough, but she looked absurd—a powder-puff princess weighing no more than a buck-five wanted to pick a fight with me, a real-life werewolf. Even if I weren't a werewolf, which I was, she was picking a fight she couldn't possibly win. She had to see that.

"Go back to the party, Lacey," I said, dismissing her. I turned my back on her and wrapped my arms around Grey's neck, pulling his sweet lips to mine, capturing them in a kiss. I wanted her to see he was mine now, and that was never going to change. Maybe that would help her move on. Maybe it was cruelty, but regardless, she needed to see it was over between her and Grey. He was mine now.

She grabbed my hair and yanked me back, away from Grey. I caught my footing barely before hitting the ground. My eyes flashed with rage. I had enough of her for a lifetime. I spun around, punching her right, square in the face, knocking her down into a pile of snow with a poof. I stood over her, watching as blood started to trickle out of her lower lip. It smelled good. I could have so easily killed her, a tasty little morsel. My mouth subconsciously filled with saliva. I had to stay focused—she was one of Old Mother's humans. I could understand she was in pain, but this had to stop. I was too old for silly little-girl games.

"Lacey . . . don't make me break your pretty little face," I said. I walked back over to Grey as he wrapped his fingers with mine and we walked away from her without a second glance. I heard her cry softly, and my heart ached for her. I wanted to go back and hug her and tell her I was sorry, but what good would that do? I would be endangering her life if Adomnan knew she was important to me. It would be best to leave. Then no one would be at risk. I still ached for her.

"I wish she could see outside herself," Grey said. "I'm sorry for everything."

"I hope she'll forgive me one day," I said.

I leaned against the Land Rover as we waited for the others. I wanted to know who the tattoo girl was. She was obviously a wolf, but what side was she on? Grey picked me up easily and slid me up onto the frosty hood. He stood between my legs with his hands still at my waist; I could feel his warmth through the thin layers of my dress. Steam rolled off his skin in the bitter cold air. It made him seem even more mysterious and sexy.

The others walked painfully slow across the parking lot, trying not to draw attention from the humans. No one said anything as we piled safely in, one after the other. We looked like one of those little clown cars with all the people getting in—far too many of us for the human laws, but a car accident wouldn't hurt us.

"Nice punch, Ashling. I was waiting for that," Quinn said.

"Waiting?" I asked.

He smiled. "I knew you had it in you to fight back."

"Who was that blonde girl with the Bloodmoon tattoos?" I asked, changing the subject.

"Æsileif, she runs the Bloodrealms," Baran said. "She's not to be trusted."

"Something has to change. We can't keep living like this," Mund said. "If Æsileif has found us, it's only a matter of time before more wolves come prowling."

"School starts soon. The humans will notice Ashling missing, but we can't send her back without protection," Tegan said.

"We'll have to fight Adomnan," Mund said. "And soon."

It was so matter-of-fact, cold even. It had come to this: my loving family would have to die to save my life. It didn't seem quite fair that they should have to sacrifice so much for me. The moments when we were happy and having fun lately were heavily outweighed by the cold reality of fear.

Grey and I would have to leave soon. I seemed to be trying to convince myself that it was right to abandon my family, but what choice did I really have? Stay and endanger them, or leave and abandon them? I was a liability—to everyone. Even Grey, but he made his choice, and I was selfish enough to let him stay with me because I needed him too. At least with Grey, as long as we were touching, no one would be able to follow my scent.

It would have to be tomorrow night, before Adomnan could escalate things further. I would have to say my goodbyes without actually saying goodbye. With me gone, they could all return home to the safety of the Rock, and Mother could watch Nia grow. They could be a whole family again. I would just have to avoid Mund. He would see right through my lies, he knew me far too deeply. The others I could fool.

When we returned to Baran's house, Grey and I resigned to my room. "I have to get something from my house before we go," Grey said. "I'll be back tomorrow."

He silenced my questions with his lips and disappeared out my window. He looked up at me in the blue light of the night. It cast a cold hue onto his skin that made him look sad. I watched until he was far gone, hidden by the trees. It felt final, watching him leave. Would he be able to return from his father's, or was this goodbye? Every move we made seemed like the end.

"Tomorrow," I said.

I kept myself busy by sorting through my things so I wouldn't worry about him. Anything to set his face out of my mind and let me be blank until he returned. It didn't work. Everything I touched was a reminder of him or what I was leaving behind. I set out the necklace Grey had given me, the ring from mother, and Calista's journal. I decided that was all I would need on my journey.

I slipped the photo of Grey's mother inside the journal and disappeared downstairs to hold Nia in my arms for the last time. Her tiny body warmed my mood. She opened her blue eyes and smiled. "Sweet Nia, I'll love you forever," I said. She understood. I knew she did. "I will find you again one day."

I decided to hide in my room until Grey returned for me. My window was still open, inviting the cold inside. I went to close it, but a note lay on the sill in Grey's handwriting.

Tonight at dusk. I'll meet you at our spot in the woods.

He must have thought it was risky too return and then leave together. It would draw too much attention from the family. Hopefully, they wouldn't come looking for me until morning.

I stood in front of the mirror as I put on the leaf necklace. I ran my fingers over the metal, feeling its sweet song. It filled my heart with warmth. What had Brenna felt when she wore it? Had it reminded her of Grey, as it did me? I closed my eyes tight and saw Grey's chiseled face looking back at me; he haunted my thoughts.

I unzipped the red dress and let it fall to the floor, puddling like blood around my feet. It felt like a metaphor for the death of this chapter in my life. I looked into the mirror at the stranger before me: part woman, part child, and every bit wild. There was fierceness in my eyes I had never seen before—that of a killer. All I was missing was my family lineage on my neck to prove I was an animal.

I chose my favorite pair of dark jeans, a brown mock-turtleneck hiding my necklace underneath, and my sage-green cropped sweater. I secured my sweater with a bronze pin Baran had given me for Christmas, holding the sweater shut at my bust. All unremarkable pieces of clothing, nothing that would draw attention or be memorable. I didn't want to leave any sign of where we went.

The journal was still on the bed with my leather jacket. It was nearly time. My breath caught in my throat time and time again. I was sick with the thought of leaving my family behind. I told myself it was the only choice, and I knew it was true. I had to go. I had to protect them. This sacrifice was mine and mine alone.

The light slowly crept out of the sky as I left notes for them on my pillow. One to Tegan and Mund, thanking them for being my only friends for so long; another for Gwyn and Quinn, for coming to my aid; one for Mother, as she was the light in my life; one for Baran, to whom I left my dowry so the riches would elevate him back to his royal status; and finally, I left a note just for Nia, telling her how much I wished I could watch her grow.

I breathed in my home one last time; the warm smells of family swirled around my senses, intoxicating me with their memories. Each scent a reminder of them. With that, I silently crawled out onto my windowsill, closing the window behind me, and I dropped down into the snow. Disappearing in the swirls of fog that rose off the ground, I ran through the trees slowly at first—my heart heavy with the choices I had made. But soon my need to see Grey overwhelmed my sadness.

The brisk run passed quickly, and I found myself at the waterfall. It looked as if it had been frozen in time. The icicles stabbed down toward the earth below, and the fog swirled around my body with every small movement I made. I became deathly still as I studied each crystal of ice that angrily reached out toward me—each different from the ones before, but each dependent on the others for its survival, like a freeze frame of a war.

I heard Grey's quiet, careful footsteps as he approached from the south. All my worries washed away with the knowledge that I was his. The sweet escape of his love. I turned to the direction of the sound, but the fog was far too thick to see more than his silhouette as he approached. The swagger of his step made my heart beat with anticipation. I ran to him, eager to close the distance between us, the snow crunching under my feet with each step. Then I came to a screeching halt.

I was no more than ten feet from being face to face with Grey's father. Over his strong back was a crossbow with silver-tipped arrows. A variety of silver knives hung at his hip, each one etched with the Bloodsuckers' mark. There was almost a medieval beauty to the sharp objects that would likely seal my fate. His dark eyes looked back at me with contempt; it was clear he hated my kind, our breed of human—as we feared his.

"Beg for your life," he said, his eyes burning into mine.

"Oh, I'm sorry, should I be scared now?" My lip curled up slightly in a smile as my eyes narrowed. I was ready for this fight—he deserved to die. But my mind repeated one question over and over again: What had he done to Grey?

His face didn't flinch at my retort. Instead he emptied the space between us, standing no more than a foot away, towering above me. I had to crank my head back to see up into his face. I couldn't step back to get a better look at him; it would be seen as weak. I swallowed hard. I wouldn't back down to someone so inexplicably cruel to the one I loved.

"Grey will be here," I said.

His laugh was malicious. I growled so fiercely, it almost startled me. His face returned to its cold, emotionless appearance as he studied my face and tiny frame—sizing up the fight, no doubt. But I was ready.

"Grey finally sees you for what you are. A dirty animal that needs to be euthanized." Every word he said came out dripping with sickness, and it pierced my heart. It was the truth; I was an animal, and maybe I didn't deserve Grey's love. Still, I knew our love was true.

"You're wrong. Our love transcends space and time. No culture or creed could ever keep us apart. Even death is just the beginning."

His hand flew back and firmly struck the whole side of my face. I fell to the ground. The sharp ice cut the delicate skin of my hand, and my blood seeped from the wound. His silver ring cut my lip. My vision flickered. I held my face as the throbbing started in my cheek. I marveled at his strength. I didn't know what hurt more: what he said or what he did. But I hated him to the deepest part of my soul, and I blinked back the tears that threatened to spill over.

"Grey can't save you. I already took his life for being a traitor. He wasn't pure, his blood was tainted."

Was Grey really dead? I couldn't feel him anymore. I tried desperately to feel Grey's emotions, his anger, fear, anything, but I couldn't feel him. It was as if his soul had been ripped from mine, and I was left to die at his father's hands. I tried to shift, but my body just shook. Robert admired his eight-inch silver blade and the detailed etching for a moment before placing the cold metal at my throat, instantly causing my body to seize as it poisoned me.

"*The power of your enemies lies in their blood,*" he read. "And I will take your blood and let its warmth flow through my veins, and with it, your power."

He grabbed my bleeding palm and licked the blood. His eyes sparkled with hunger as his fingers tightened their grip around my wrist. Who was really the predator and who the prey? He lusted for our blood. My blood foamed and burned where it mixed with his saliva.

"Grey confused his urge to drink your blood with the passions of love," he said.

"Just like you did, Robert? You loved Brenna, but instead of following your heart, you viciously murdered her and drank her blood in front of *her* son. You're disgusting, and Grey is nothing like you. He is not a killer. He is a wolf."

He pierced the skin of my throat with the very tip of his blade, causing my body to convulse in tiny tremors. The silver blade wove its trickery in my mind. I shook my head, trying to shift, but I couldn't connect my mind to my body. Pure silver caused enough short-term paralysis to make shifting temporarily impossible. Not only had the silver touched my skin, but it had mixed directly into my bloodstream. The effects would take even longer to wear off, possibly even days.

Suddenly, Adomnan smashed Robert's body into the rocks. Robert screamed with hunger and annoyance, but Adomnan held his throat. I watched the fight as though it were far away, a memory, not something happening right in front of me.

"You dare to touch one of us? To taste our blood? To take what is rightfully mine?" Outraged flowed through Adomnan's still-calm voice.

Robert smiled. "I'd be happy to take your blood as well, though it's not as powerful as hers," he said. There was no fear in Robert—he didn't seem to realize the monster he was up against. Robert had murdered too many, and his confidence blinded reality. Even I knew how this would end.

With one swift move, Adomnan's fingers curved around Robert's esophagus and tore it from his body, using it to lift Robert's body like a duffle bag. There was the smallest gasp from Robert's lips, but it was only residual air left in his throat—there was nothing left of his forsaken soul.

Adomnan wasted no more time with the human. There was no saving his soul, either. It was clear no life mattered to him. He left Robert's limp carcass at the base of the rock, painting the snow with his dark blood. He truly had broken his vows to Old Mother. Eamon and Bento stood above me, watching me as they had many times before. But this time, there was something else behind Eamon's blue eyes.

"You were easy to capture," Adomnan said, bringing my mind back to the present. "Do you realize how many times I could have taken you?"

"Why didn't you then?" I asked.

He replied dryly, "I enjoy the hunt too much, but this time I had to intervene. I couldn't let a human taint what is mine." He wrapped his long fingers around my arm at my armpit, pulling me to my feet. "Even in these rags, you are truly something to behold. I'm sorry it has come to this, but you'll learn to love me. In time."

"Come to this?" I said. "You chose to hunt me like a dog."

"We tried to negotiate for you with your father. I would have made you a proper wife, but he denied us. But I always get what I want in the end," Adomnan replied. He looked around the trees, nervous suddenly. "We must move."

He began pulling me by my wrist through the trees. I ran as fast as I could, but I stumbled to keep up with their long strides. His grip didn't falter. The hole in my heart was deeper than any hurt they could inflict. I was already dead, they just didn't realize it. Without Grey, I felt desperately alone, and the silver poisoned my blood. The fog swarmed around our bodies, almost consuming us as we fled through the forest toward the north. I couldn't see Eamon, but I felt his eyes on me and could hear the light bounds of his steps in the snow. Their light steps didn't make an impression as they ran, but my stumbling would look like a wounded animal wandering through the forest, looking for a place to die.

Which wasn't far from the truth.

21

Captors

I carefully set Calista's journal in the snow on one of my falls, quietly leaving it behind. It had far too many secrets that would destroy a pure soul, much less Adomnan's evil heart. He could annihilate the entire world with the knowledge in her journal. Adomnan's strides pulled me back to my feet, nearly dislocating my shoulder in the process. I looked back in the direction we came, but the fog ate our path. The journal was lost to the wilderness.

Grey had betrayed me. Our souls were meant to be together, but he left me on the earth alone to die at his father's hands. It was as much as I could endure. Instead, Adomnan would take my life—maybe not in blood, but he would take my being. Grey's soul abandoned mine, and now I was left to the wolves. I almost had to laugh at the cruel irony. Instead of the Bloodsuckers taking my life, I seemed to have handed myself over on a silver platter to Adomnan. I couldn't yet say which was worse.

I fell to my knees, tripping on uneven ground. The pain vibrated through my knee. "Clumsy little thing," Adomnan said, dragging my body back to my feet without ever missing his own stride. "It's a good thing you have me to save you," he said. His smile was as repulsive as his anger. I could see only glimpses of his brothers through the fog, but I could smell them.

My heart was miraculously still beating despite the fact it was broken. I was lost in despair as the trees continued to whip by. If I cared, I could have noticed the small differences between each tree, each one a unique life. But to me in those moments, they were nothing more than a repeating pattern. I was less and less aware of my surroundings, how many hundreds of miles we had run, and even less concerned with the cuts and bruises that covered my body with each fall. My body ached with the pain, but my mind disregarded it.

Soon, we ran across the border into Canada, and dawn broke as we reached the east coast of Newfoundland. The icy water was frozen at the shore. I should have been trying to escape, but I just didn't have the will. I had nothing left to escape to.

I had lost everything. Grey was gone and I was alone. He couldn't have survived—he would have stopped his father. He would have come for me. I used to hear his heartbeat, and now there was silence. The place in my soul where he used to live was numb.

"I'll be back, my beloved," Adomnan said as he pushed me down to my knees in the cold snow. "Watch her," he said to his brothers. He disappeared into a small wooden shack.

Eamon walked to my side, but Bento kept his distance as he searched the horizon for anyone who might have followed us. Eamon seemed fascinated with me. It was almost creepy. If he didn't blink, I would have thought he was the walking dead. His velvet jacket was still smooth and perfect, as though he hadn't just run eight hundred miles through a forest.

"You loved that human, didn't you?" Eamon said.

I heard the words, but I didn't understand the question. I felt an icy chill from him. But if they were going to sacrifice me, it would be at Carrowmore, not here on this desolate, frozen ground. I was safe, for now. I just stared wide-eyed at Eamon.

Adomnan returned moments later, and Eamon stepped away. It was eerie how closely he watched my every movement. Why did he want to know if I really loved Grey? What did he know of love? It was obvious none of them had ever felt love and their lives were empty. My mother loved me with everything she had; I couldn't imagine growing up without the shelter of her admiration. What was it like to never feel the love of a parent, a friend, a partner?

"I have arranged a plane to take her home," Adomnan said. I shuddered to think what their home might look like. "Eamon, take her inside and find her something to wear that isn't covered in blood. Bento, you come with me." He spoke as though I weren't there. That was typical of his kind. Women weren't to be talked to when other males were present. How our kind survived for so long with such ridiculous rules, I would never know.

I followed Eamon toward the shack. It looked like nothing more than an old abandoned building, no more than one room with a rusty, snow-covered roof and an outhouse. It was a trade post. The smell of the smoky fires surrounded us inside. It was filled with animal furs, spices, and meats. Two wrinkled old human men sat at the counter. They looked up at us, startled at first—they knew what we were—but they quickly went back to milling about, trying not to pay us any mind. Eamon flipped back a thick bearskin rug on the floor to reveal a hidden door. With a creak, he lifted the wooden panels, and the floor opened up. From what I could see, it was well lit down the wooden plank ladder, but I couldn't see how big the room was below.

"After you," he said. His voice was welcoming in a way.

I carefully put my foot onto the first rung of the ladder, expecting it to break under my weight. I slowly continued down, step after step, into the cavity below until I could no longer see daylight.

Eamon quickly shut the door behind us, but there was plenty of light coming from below. Reaching the last step, I turned around and saw what had to be miles and miles of a city. It stretched on for as far as I could see. Every building and home was hobbled together with random parts. This was an entire hidden world with inhabitants that may never have seen the light of day.

"Welcome to the Netherworlds," Eamon said.

It wasn't that different from the Rock of Cashel, with its hidden labyrinth of tunnels and rooms, but this was poor, damp, and dark. The shacks went on as far as I could see down earthen tunnels. Hundreds of poverty-stricken wolves must have lived here. Two elderly women sat scrubbing old rags in dirty water, their skin gray with filth. A group of three men leaned against a tin shack with a holey roof. They appeared to be in their mid-twenties and they had horrible clawed scars all over their bodies. They wore ripped jeans and no shirts, but one wore a necklace of wolf teeth. An Asian man stood a few shacks down, pretending not to watch us pass. Though they all saw me, I knew they wouldn't intervene with Adomnan's plan. Eamon was halfway down a block before he realized I was still standing there, staring like a child.

A thin man stared back at me, not even trying to conceal his gaze. His greasy, long black hair draped over his shoulders in a slight wave, and he wore a black top hat. He had a large gray wolf's hide draped over his grimy T-shirt, the wolf's lifeless head lying limp to one side. The wolf had been so large that his tail dragged on the ground behind the frightening man. He watched me without subtlety. He walked toward me, emitting a low growl as he grew nearer. I subconsciously took a step backward, but he followed, filling the space between us once again. His rough, scarred hands reached up and touched my hair, rubbing it between his forefingers. He pulled out a knife, cut a lock of my hair, and smelled the scent.

His mouth opened wide in a sickly smile. I flinched away from the creature. I didn't want to watch as he killed me and added my skin to his coat. I breathed in deeply, trying to clear my mind. Suddenly, his scent was overpowered by Eamon's, and I dared to open my eyes.

Eamon stood between us. I was oddly comforted by his presence. The two stared at each other for what felt like an eternity. I wanted to run away, but I didn't know where to go. Finally, the stranger looked down and walked away, a sign of resignation. There was something horrible about the stranger; it was clear he wanted something with me. I could feel it in the pit of my stomach. Eamon had won, but I was certain it wasn't the end of that wordless discussion. Something told me I would be the prize for the benefactor. *The spoils of a man's war.* Eamon walked down the street, and this time I didn't linger. I felt the stranger watch us as we left, but I didn't dare look back. I was too afraid to see his sickening face again.

We turned the corner to an area where the buildings looked in more repair. Not nice, but cleaner somehow. We stopped at a two-story hut that had dried lavender on the door. We didn't knock; we just stood there waiting. For all I knew, we were waiting for the world to open up and swallow us whole. So many unbelievable things had happened, I was almost numb to the surreal nature of my surroundings.

Without a sound, a small, ghostly woman opened the door and stood before us. She had almost pure-white skin and snow-white, pixie-short hair. There was almost no pigmentation to her at all, except her large, dark eyes. Her irises were so dark, it gave the appearance that she didn't have them at all—like two giant pupils looking back at us. Even her eyelashes were white. She was nothing like the place that surrounded her. She looked pure. Her white gown flowed to the floor, creating a puddle of fabric around her. Eamon bowed to her, and she nodded in return, motioning for us to follow her inside.

It smelled of lavender and mint inside, and everything was glazed in white, from the wooden chairs to the rugs on the floor. Even the wallpaper was white damask. The only color in the entire house was dried lavender above the hearth in the living room. She stood watching us.

"Lady Faye," Eamon said, bowing.

"Why do you stand before me today, Eamon?" she asked.

The glow from the fire made her look more alive. The flames danced on her skin, making it look warm, though her expression didn't soften. There was something very old behind her perfectly smooth skin. I wondered if she were one of the Elder Gods, like Mother Rhea. Most of the others were nothing more than myth and song now, but I felt a kinship with her.

"I come to you seeking a cloak for this woman."

She turned her now-stunned gaze to me. "A mere child," she said.

Eamon nodded his head but didn't reply any further. My clothes were torn and covered in my own blood, and despite my best efforts to look strong, I knew I appeared weak. She circled around me like a predator circles its prey, stopping directly in front of me. I averted my eyes, too frightened to look at her. She leaned forward, curving her head around mine, and breathed in my scent.

"The only daughter of King Pørr and Queen Nessa Boru," she said. I looked up at her, astonished. She knew me without my name, without my father's Bloodmark, though I was certain I had never met her. "What happened to you, child?"

I glanced at Eamon while weighing my options. I didn't know what side she was on, nor what Eamon's anger could look like.

"I fell down."

She looked at me, yet I was sure she was seeing inside me. "Your heart is pure," she said, smelling me again. "His love surrounds you still."

"Grey?" I blurted.

"His soul is searching for yours, but he can't see you," she said. "The silver poison is still in your veins."

I could only stare at this beautiful creature before me. She held more magic than I had ever imagined existed in the whole of the world. When the silver poison finally left my body, would Grey's soul haunt mine? She held her soft hand palm-up above her shoulder, as were the old ways, awaiting mine. I placed my hand in hers, palm to palm, and she led me behind a white curtain into an empty chamber. There were white-framed mirrors all around us, each frame different. She let go of my hand at the center of the room, and I stopped moving. It was easy to see what she wanted me to do. She walked to a mirror framed in white fire at the far side of the room and reached her arm inside, through the glass. It seemed to pool and ripple around her arm as she pulled out a warm, brown drape of fabric.

It hung across her forearm as she began to remove the clip from my sweater. She studied the bronze pin in her hand. I knew by her glance that she knew who gave it to me. She pinned it to her gown. I slid the sweater off and let it fall to the floor as well as my now-torn shirt. She touched my necklace, running her fingers over the delicate metal, and she smiled. What secret she found there, I didn't know. I quickly slipped off my tattered jeans as she slipped the fabric over my head. As it fell to the floor, it braided and twisted itself into a dress around my body at her whim, forming around my every curve. I looked at myself in the mirror, expecting to see my wild-haired self. Instead I saw someone who looked like a goddess . . . but she had my face.

The gown dipped to the end of my sternum between my breasts, exposing my cleavage. It had a braided fabric belt low around my waist that created a train down the back. A large hood hung behind me, covering the racer-back style of the garment. She pinned the bronze clip to my hip, returning it to me without a word.

"Unclaimed child, know that you are the dream."

She turned away from me before I could question her, and she raised her hand again and led me back to Eamon. He was pacing back and forth until he saw us enter. His mouth fell open as he studied me in my new gown. He gently placed my hood over my face. It covered my eyes and nose; even my wild red hair was contained in its shroud. Only my mouth remained visible.

This wasn't subtle. Even in this world I would be noticed, much less flying on an airplane with humans all around us.

"My lady," he said to me with a nod. He bowed to Lady Faye, and I followed him back out onto the dirty underground streets. It was easy to forget where we were, inside her clean, white sanctuary. We were once again in the bleak Netherworlds. I glanced back over my shoulder, but her door was already closed.

The way she touched my necklace must have meant something to her. Could she have known it was Brenna's? Or that Grey had given it to me? Oh, Grey. I missed him with every fiber of my being. I wished for a chance to just sit down and cry instead of being dragged all over North

America as a hostage. I needed to mourn for my love. With every step I took, I felt as though I were dying.

I wondered if Mund had found me missing yet. Would he try to find me? Would he find Grey's lifeless body? That realization shook me, and I gasped for air. Eamon looked at me quizzically but didn't inquire. Instead he offered me his arm as he led me back the way we came. We passed all the sad little wooden shacks and the variety of werewolves who hung out near them, but they didn't pay attention as we walked down the street. I heard children playing nearby, their small laughs echoing off the earthen walls. I felt like a ritual sacrifice being paraded down the streets . . . which might not have been far from the truth. The stale air was filled with the filthy scent of the squalor.

I saw the mummified human-form bodies of werewolf warriors displayed for each pack. Their eyes were replaced with black glass, and their skin was leathery. It was a sign of strength to worship their dead. Eamon nodded to one of the mummies as we passed by. I found myself wondering more about him. Who was Eamon without Adomnan? Was he a brutal killer too? Or was he a gentle soul? It was hard to see him beyond his family's stain. We were all viewed as a total sum of our pack, not its parts. But each individual part was like a single snowflake, exquisitely different from the one before.

"Whose body was that?" I said, my curiosity getting the best of me.

He looked at me, startled to hear my voice. "The great warrior Tizheruk of the once-great Inuit pack."

"Where are his sons?"

"Dead."

"All of his pack?"

"Adomnan doesn't leave survivors."

I didn't ask any more questions. I blindly followed Eamon; I didn't care where he took me. There was nothing left of me to punish; the part of me who cared what happened was gone. All that remained was this empty shell of who I once was. I caught the scent of the greasy stranger as we neared the ladder, and my heart pounded with fear. I peeked past the hood to see he stood between us and the way out of this underground tomb. I was afraid of him, but I didn't know why. I involuntarily took a step backward. Eamon looked at me, and his eyes filled with anger. I was stunned by his sudden distaste for me. He growled at the stranger. I could feel its vibration in my bare feet on the dirt floor.

"You have no business with us," Eamon said.

"I have *business* with this lady," he said; he didn't look up as he answered. He just continued wiping his knife with a torn piece of leather. Over and over again. Methodically following the edge of the blade.

Eamon growled a terrifying sound. He pushed my body farther behind his, shielding me from the stranger who looked up, watching us both. I wanted to run away, back to Lady Faye, but my feet were frozen in the dirt. The stranger took a step toward us, filling half the gap. Eamon prepared for the fight, and the stranger threw his dagger into the ground at Eamon's feet. Still Eamon didn't react.

"I know who you are," he said to me.

I peeked around Eamon's shoulder, watching the stranger as he paced forward. The lifeless creature on his shoulder told a strong warning as to what fate might await us. I wasn't sure who was stronger between them, but I didn't want to find out.

"If you have any sense to you, *wolf*, you'll leave the lady be," Eamon said.

The stranger laughed as he moved only a few inches from Eamon, who was the only barrier between me and the disgusting man. I could smell the grease that covered him, but it covered his true scent. The two growled, but neither showed any fear. Before it could escalate, Adomnan's large figure dropped down the hole. When he stood to his full height, he towered over both Eamon and the stranger.

I wasn't sure if I were relieved to see Adomnan or not. Watching male wolves fight was like watching the dance of devils. Adomnan crouched down, as ready to attack the stranger as Eamon was. They both arched their bodies at him, ready for the kill. There was no question in my mind that Adomnan intended to kill the wolf without a single spoken word between them.

Panic rippled through me, and I cringed away from them. I just wanted to be home on the cliffs with Mother or back in my bed at Baran's house with Grey's warmth surrounding me. I wanted to be away from this violence. I covered my ears with my hands, desperately trying to block out their growls.

The lights above started to pop and explode, raining shards of glass down on us like glitter. The entire city was dark in a matter of moments. I felt a hand touch my arm lightly as the stranger leaned in close to my ear and whispered, "They cannot take what is not rightfully given." Was he trying to protect me?

And with that, he was gone into the darkened streets, leaving the three of us lost in the dark. I shivered from anxiety. Reserve lighting kicked in, spotlighting every one hundred yards. I quickly stood over the blade the stranger had thrown into the dirt, hiding it in the fabric of my gown. I didn't know what the stranger truly wanted, but I didn't want Adomnan to find the dagger, either. A lot could be told about someone by his things, and I strangely felt the need to protect everyone from Adomnan. Even though I couldn't protect myself.

"Quickly," Adomnan said. "We have lingered here with her too long. We have not gone unnoticed."

Eamon looked back at me, and I followed them to the ladder. As I put my foot on the lowest rung, I glanced back at the dagger. The stranger was now crouched by it, his hand gripping it tightly as he pulled it from the earth. He dashed off and ran between the houses.

Bento met us outside, and he looked twitchy. Something had spooked him and Adomnan, though I didn't think it was only the presence of the greasy man. Something was coming. I could feel it on the unnatural wind. My hair stood on end, a warning. Something was coming—or someone.

22
Darkness

"*Take her to the airport.* I will meet you on the plane," Adomnan said, looking back to the south as the wind whipped us.

My arms were bare to the rough wind, though I didn't feel the cold. Without a word, Eamon held my hand, and he started running inland with Bento flanking him. Miraculously, I was able to run in my dress, though I was certain Eamon kept a slower pace for my sake. He was much kinder than Adomnan, but really, that wasn't saying much.

Eamon's hands were noticeably softer than Grey's. A life of royalty verses that of real men like Grey. Grey had been rugged. Eamon was refined and proper and respectful. He was still Adomnan's brother, but I did feel safer with Eamon than any of my other options, so I just followed along and tried to keep up. And what chance did I have as a mortal? The effects of the silver from Robert's blade wouldn't wear off for a couple of days, and I wouldn't be able to shift until then. If I couldn't shift to heal my wounds, it would be harder to survive.

Did Grey's heart still beat? Did mine? Were we even able to live and breathe without the other? Or did I die in the woods? If this were all just a nightmare, why could I not wake? A pain that couldn't heal deep in my chest reminded me I still breathed. I was completely and forever bound to Grey, even after death. Nothing changed the fact that I was still his. His father's body was cold and dead, strewn about in the snow where my body should have been; but I died in that moment too.

We arrived at the edge of the Natashquan airport, and a small aircraft waited on the runway. We approached the pilot slowly, and Eamon didn't release my hand, though we both knew I wouldn't bother running. The pilot eyed us for a moment before speaking to Bento.

"Are we still waiting for one more?" he said in a thick French-Canadian accent.

Bento nodded.

"I'd like to get the lady out of the elements," Eamon said.

"Yeah, sure," the pilot said, backing away.

Eamon led the way onto the empty plane. He chose the farthest-back seats, sitting me next to the window.

"Keep an eye out," he said to Bento and sat down next to me. Eamon leaned over and whispered in my ear, "You can't hide from your destiny."

Why did everyone talk in riddles? No wonder nothing ever got done—no one knew what anyone else was talking about. None of them made any bloody sense. My destiny was for my only love to leave the earth ahead of me and for me to be taken against my will. That was *my* destiny. I was tired of being pushed around all the time.

I glared at him. As he looked into my eyes, I got the feeling he saw far more than other wolves—that he might be a soul reader, that he could read my past. I felt as if all my secrets were open to him. I pulled my knees up to my chest, hugging them tightly, and I turned away from him. Whatever he was looking for, he wasn't going to get it. This freak show was closed.

I stared blankly out the window at the desolate wasteland. The winter's cold bite made everything look bland and lifeless. It mirrored how I felt—left behind to die. I heard Adomnan and the pilot get on the plane as they exchanged pleasantries that weren't pleasant at all, but I didn't bother to listen. It didn't matter anymore. Whatever happened to my body was no longer a concern of mine. I had nothing left to fight for. As the plane took off, I watched the trees disappear below us. Everything I had grown to know and love was gone. I couldn't feel Grey's heart anymore. I couldn't sense his emotions. Every sign of him had been torn from my soul, and it left it naked.

Adomnan came out of the cockpit and approached us. I was suddenly happy Eamon didn't take the hint and move seats. His body next to me meant Adomnan couldn't get any closer to me, and for that I was thankful. I hid my face under my hood, hoping it would conceal my fear from his watchful eye. I held my breath until he finally sat down several rows ahead of us. The air whooshed out of my lungs in a rush, and I shuddered.

The flight went by slowly as fear consumed my heart. We were getting farther and farther away from my family, and I didn't want to realize this nightmare. I didn't want the plane to land. Landing meant it was over and I was lost. No one would come for me. I finally knew what it felt like to be truly alone.

Hours later, the plane landed in the cold landscape of Iceland. I resigned myself to my fate and continued to follow them blindly. We walked away from the plane into the surrounding forest, disappearing into the darkness and fog. Adomnan was no longer in a hurry; it was obvious that whatever we ran from in Canada no longer trailed us here.

"We are nearly home, princess," Adomnan said, smiling. His words made my skin crawl.

The trees here were reminiscent of those back home in Ireland, but there were far more of them towering above us here, like a shield from the heavens guiding our path to their hell. Not a single other creature left its footprints in the new snow, an unnatural warning. As white as the snow was, the darkness and shadows still loomed all around. Ice and fresh snow coated the branches of every tree, creating a harsh reality.

I followed them for miles and miles in my bare feet, but I didn't feel the cold. We finally broke through the trees to a clearing where a white stone palace stood at the center of the snow-covered wilderness. The fog rolled around us, giving the already frightening baroque palace an even eerier appearance. A frozen moat surrounded it, keeping it safe in the summers; in the winters, the water froze everything still in time. We walked across the frozen water as it cracked and gurgled in disapproval under my feet. I watched the ice splinter its web as I saw faces frozen still in terror under the ice. My breath caught in my throat as I stared at their open eyes. I felt their fear, and it crushed what little confidence I had left. This was a land without hope.

We slowly ascended the frozen steps up to the black palace doors. All the windows stood dark. Not a soul seemed to live here. Adomnan pushed the doors open with a thunderous crack. The palace was a reminder that they were once a society of immense wealth and power, but now were only rebels. They were the night kings of this dungeon. Bento shut the doors behind us, securing them with a side bar, shutting us away from the outside world. Eamon lit the wicks, illuminating the darkened space with dramatic shadows.

Adomnan led the way down the dark corridor into the center of the palace. The baroque architecture seemed to be built in the 1800s—which was rather new for werewolves—though parts of it seemed to be much older. The walls were covered in paintings of their family. Their unnatural eyes seemed to follow our every step. Did King Crob himself still live here in this empty castle? Were they bringing me to cower at his feet? I was filled with dread, and my skin prickled. I didn't want to meet my father's oldest enemy.

We turned down a dark, damp passage. Looking around, I realized it was surrounded on both sides by barred cages, and to my horror, they were filled with humans. They huddled together in their tombs, watching Adomnan walk by. Men, women, and children all stared up at me, their eyes blank and deadened from all the pain and fear they had endured. Their clothes were nothing more than rags, but they were well fed. No doubt, they were stored for eating.

I was disgusted by it all. Everything here was surrounded by death. I was nauseated just thinking about all the lives they had stolen.

We entered a long throne room, and the ceilings were adorned with paintings of their family history. Each one told a gruesome tale of their conquests and death inlaid in gold. There was no mercy here. At the end of the room stood an enormous throne carved from human bone. The fierce head of a wolf was carved at the top, protruding out, teeth bared. It was meant to strike fear into all those who dared to enter this place. Adomnan touched the face of the creature with respect, bowing his head to it.

"Leave us," he said. Bento bowed immediately and walked out a side door. Eamon looked nervous, but he bowed and left, leaving me standing before Adomnan, whose back was still to me. Slowly he sat down in the throne, looking far older than I had seen him before—instantly aged by the chair he took. His eyes were cold and judging as he looked down on me.

"We are finally alone, my princess. It has taken much time to get you all to myself."

My hood still hid my eyes from his inspection, but my quivering lip was exposed. I would've given anything to have died in the forest instead of standing before this creature.

"How do you like my throne?" he asked.

"Do you dare disgrace your father's rightful throne?" I said. This was Crob's palace, and he wouldn't take lightly to his son playing king in his absence. It was forbidden.

He slammed his fist down on the armrest. His face twisted with indescribable hate. He bared his teeth to me as he slipped leather gloves over his hands and eliminated the space between us in an instant. He wrapped his long fingers into my hair. I felt his breath on my face as he spoke.

"I drank his blood as he died in my bare hands."

I turned my face away from him, repulsed. He had killed his own father and desecrated his body. I felt limp in his arms as he violently shook my tiny frame like a rag doll.

"What do you think of that, little princess? You are now in the presence of a real king." I didn't look at him. There was no greater sin than that of taking one's father's blood. He was inexorably evil and I was at his mercy.

"You *will* submit to me!" he screamed as his spit spattered on my face. He dragged me from the throne room by my hair. I grasped my fingers at his wrist, trying desperately to stop the pain. My legs writhed to right myself as he pulled my body up several flights of stairs into an empty marble room.

He pulled my battered body up to his as he tried to crush my lips with his. I gagged at the thought as I scratched at his face, my nails tearing into his flesh and releasing a trickle of blood from his cheek. "You little bitch!" he screamed in my face.

He yanked me farther into the room, locking silver shackles around my wrists, dangling me from chains. The instant the silver touched my skin, my mind began to swim with the poison. It had finally come to this. I would die here. The cold finality of the metal around my wrists devastated me. I could never shift here . . . not with the sliver poisoning my blood.

"I told Redmund I would train you, my love." He lightly ran his fingers over my breasts as I wrenched my body away from his touch, but the chains just swung me back into his grasp. "Such beautiful skin," he said, running his finger between my breasts up to my lips. I bit his finger, digging my teeth into his flesh.

He yanked his hand from my mouth and backhanded my face with a strength that vibrated through my bones. I hung lifelessly from the ceiling. "You are nothing without me," he said and walked out, slamming the door behind him.

I wiped the blood and tears from my face with my shoulders as I looked around the room. I knew this room. I had been here many times in my dreams. Other than the black, ornately carved ceiling, a claw-foot bathtub, and an enormous chandelier, the room was empty. The chandelier contrasted against the blackness of the room with its carved-bone wolves covered in cobwebs. The light from the windows cast the dark room in an ominous glow.

The hours passed slowly as my body ached. My toes barely touched the floor—just enough to keep the pressure off my wrists. The agony made me want to die. I just wanted it to be over. Exhaustion must have lulled me to sleep because I awoke to Adomnan's loud voice echoing.

"Have you come to your senses?" he sneered.

I looked up into his horrible face, at the bloody scabs on his cheek. "I will never submit to you," I said, spitting on him.

To my horror, he smiled in return. "I was hoping you'd say that," he said. A leather whip uncoiled from his hands like a snake. "I do love to punish you." He dragged it behind him as he circled me. I tried to turn to see him, but the chains wouldn't allow it. The first crack of the whip sliced into my back, releasing the most unholy sound from my lips. The gown protected only some of my skin, but the exposed pieces of flesh opened with each blow. I hated him. With every crack, I cried out again until I had no more tears to shed and my body had gone numb.

I didn't hear him leave, but I was alone again.

I felt my blood dripping down my back onto the floor. I don't know how long I dangled there, but the silver shackles were cutting into my wrists, and a river of my blood ran down my arms. I didn't fear death, I knew Old Mother would welcome me home, but I had never imagined it would be like this. I tried to think of a better time, but I couldn't force my mind past the pain. Even if I got out of the shackles, it would be days before the silver poison left my veins. Escape was hopeless.

I woke again to Eamon unchaining me, and my body crumpled into his arms. My face fell forward into his hands, and my tears broke free. Everything I had felt poured out into the hands of my enemy, and I was helpless to stop the flood.

"Do what he asks of you, and he won't hurt you anymore," he said.

I looked for salvation, but his expression was blank. There was no safety for me there. He wanted to me to obey Adomnan to survive, but what survival was that? Submission wasn't in my blood. I wouldn't bow to a false king in this land of eternal night. Through my tears, I shook my head no.

He nodded to me. "I will try to protect you," he replied as he left.

I curled in a ball in the pools of my dried blood as I sobbed. When my body stopped trembling, I crawled to the corner of the room near a window, soothing my back with the cold walls, and there I waited for the end.

By now Grey's soul would be with Old Mother. We never stood a chance. I had led him to his death by choosing to love him. It was my fault he was dead. If I hadn't interfered in his life, he and his horrible father would both still breathe.

Several nights passed by, and I saw no one. No sound of another living thing moved in this marble casket. Whether day or night, the light never changed through the windows, as though the whole land was frozen in an untimely death. I was grateful to be unchained. The silver started to lose its strength over me, and my mind started to clear. I kept trying to shift, but it was still useless.

Suddenly, the sound of footsteps and whimpering approached my door, and I stood. Bento entered, dragging a young human girl no older than me across the cold marble. He dropped her at my feet. Her blonde hair was matted with tears, and her arms were bound behind her back. She'd been bathed and wore a simple ice-blue slip.

"His majesty thought you might be getting hungry," he said.

The girl flinched as the door slammed closed. She was pretty. I leaned down to untie her, and she screamed, squirming away from me like a caterpillar. It was a pathetic attempt to save herself, though I had to admire her strength to try.

"I'm not going to hurt you," I said softly. She had nothing to fear from me. "When you are ready, I will untie you." I walked back to my corner and stared out the window at the ice-covered wilderness.

She lay where he had left her, but I wasn't going to push her and frighten her more. Eventually she would realize on her own that I wasn't a threat. I tried to pay her no mind, though I did peek at her. Her eyes were light blue and her skin as pale as mine. She was Nordic.

"Will you untie me?" she whispered. It wasn't a request as much as a question. I could smell her fear. Her voice was soft and barely audible, but I could hear her clearly.

I moved over to her and knelt to untie her. I was a servant of Old Mother, and I would protect this girl, though I didn't know how. "My name is Ashling."

"Svana."

I gave her a weak smile and touched her shoulder. I returned to my corner to stare out the window, giving her what little privacy I could. Soon she sat beside me, but her heart still raced.

"Why aren't you going to eat me? You are one of *them,* aren't you?"

"I have no interest in taking your life."

"But you are a werewolf?"

I nodded.

"Why are you here?"

"I am no more a guest here than you."

She considered what I said as she studied my face. Her eyes gave her away easily; she wasn't fully convinced that I wasn't going to eat her flesh, but she was willing to find out. Not that she really had a choice. Humans were interesting that way. They thought they were making choices when really they didn't have one to begin with. Fate seemed to have a way of sneaking up on us all.

"Where is your family?" I asked.

"I am the last."

I nodded sadly.

We slept that night huddled together for warmth. She seemed thankful to be with me, but what she didn't realize was I couldn't protect her from anyone but myself. She was as much at risk here as she was in the cages, but I thought it best not to tell her. It would only unnecessarily frighten her more. I wished I could set her free to live her life, but we were both captives.

As the false day dawned, Adomnan entered our chamber. I moved forward, leaving her behind me in the corner. I would protect her as long as I could, but it was a useless fight, I feared. He looked at her still living and breathing.

"Did you not enjoy my gift?" he asked. "Perhaps she's not to your liking, perhaps something younger? Children have such tender flesh."

I didn't answer him. I merely stood my ground between him and Svana. He surveyed my response before erasing the space between us.

"Did you not smell her sweet blood? Her nectar?"

Still I didn't respond to his crass questions. He leapt across the room to Svana, and she was trapped in his rough hands; he dragged her back to me. "Will you not enjoy her flesh?" he asked, forcing her body toward me. Her scent swarmed around me once again. Svana screamed.

I stared up into his angry face with contempt.

My lack of response was filling him with rage. Before I could conjure an answer, he grabbed her and bit her throat, ripping the flesh from her body. The cracking and popping sickened me. Her blood was smeared across his angular face, and her lifeless body fell to the ground at my feet. Her warm blood poured from the wound, soaking into my dress. I dropped to my knees, putting my hands over the wound, trying to stop the bleeding, but it flowed freely past my fingers—her soul was already gone.

"You soulless bastard!"

He wrapped his bloody hand around my neck, forcing my face down to Svana's dead body, smearing my face in her blood. "Does it not call to your soul? Just submit to the beast within, and we can be one."

I was torn between the animal that did desire her flesh and my love for her human soul. I forced myself to turn away from her open wound. He lifted me up and suspended me above the floor. My feet dangled in his murderous grip. Her warm blood dripped from his lower lip as I gagged for air.

"I own you!"

"The hell you do," I croaked, barely a whisper as he closed my airway.

My eyes fluttered from the lack of oxygen, making his face seem like a strobe. His menacing expression started to fade until I could no longer see. I smelled Eamon before I heard the crack and splinter of my body colliding with the glass window and felt my body sliding down on the broken glass, lifelessly to the floor.

23
Wild

Tears spilled over my cheeks as oxygen flooded my lungs. The marble floor shined like black glitter. I ran my fingers through the cold liquid and lifted my hand to inspect the beautiful blood that coated my skin. It dripped down my hands—it was all around me. It was the scene from my dreams, and the smell made me want to vomit.

My hate for Adomnan writhed like worms under my skin. He stole Svana's life as if it were nothing. This wasn't the way of our kind, the way of Old Mother. All life and death was part of the earth and was to be respected and protected.

My shoulder oozed blood. I couldn't focus on the wound, I kept seeing double as the blood poured out of my arm. I pulled a piece of glass from my flesh and wrapped my fingers over it, squeezing it shut as best I could. Sound finally started to return to my throbbing ears. I couldn't make out what Adomnan and Eamon were saying over the high-pitched ringing, but I knew they were fighting. I could only guess Eamon was fighting for me.

Adomnan walked past Eamon toward me, his footsteps echoing off the walls like thunder. Nothing he could do would ever be as bad as losing Grey. I tried to center my mind on Grey, to shut out this nightmare, but Adomnan stood over my broken body, laughing, delighting in my pain.

Eamon pulled Adomnan away from me, throwing him into the doorway as Bento stood to the side, away from allegiances. Eamon stood alone between Adomnan's fury and my broken body. I needed to shift before I lost consciousness; I needed to heal these wounds. I tried to shift, and my body began to vibrate. I could nearly feel my blood warm, but as quickly as it began, it ended, and I was still human. I was losing too much blood, and the silver poison still lingered inside me. I felt desperate and scared.

"What are you doing, Adomnan?" Eamon said.

"Get out of my way. I killed Father and won't question doing the same to you."

Eamon growled.

It was clear on Adomnan's face that he was fully willing to rip the life from his younger brother's body without any concern. Bento jumped between the two.

"We have her, why would you kill her, Adomnan?" Bento yelled. "You already have the power over all the packs."

"I'm not going to kill her."

"Than what are you doing?" Bento asked.

Adomnan grabbed my arm, pulling me to my feet. My head throbbed and I was dizzy. He rubbed my shoulder under the strap of my dress. I squirmed from his touch, but his fingers dug into my skin, holding me in place.

Adomnan laughed. "I will break her. She *will* be mine."

"This isn't right, Adomnan," Eamon said, "you know this isn't right."

"She's of the Boru line. Royalty. You can't take what isn't rightfully given," Bento said.

"She's unmarked. *Ripe* for the taking," Adomnan said as he pulled my dress down, exposing my naked body. I tried to cover myself from their stares, but he held my wrists. I felt violated and terrified. "My lovely queen," he said.

I finally understood what he wanted. He intended to consume all of me, claiming my body and soul for his, and his alone. To stand as his queen. If he raped me, I would belong to him by all our laws. I would belong to him. No one could take me from him, and I couldn't be saved. Our laws were clear and absolute. An unmarked female wasn't her father's property. Once Adomnan mated with me and his scent filled me, I would belong to him. By not branding me, my father had thought he was protecting me, but instead he gave Adomnan my life.

I wanted to throw up. I felt sick with the idea of his body touching mine. Losing Grey, losing everything—to die even—I could endure. But to be raped? I couldn't stand the thought. It made every inch of my skin burn with hate, but I felt too weak to fight or shift. I wanted to live, but I didn't know if I could fight this to the end.

Maybe Grey and I would meet in another life. I wondered what kind of creatures we would be. I believed with all my heart that he loved me, that he still held onto my heart after his death, and that I would be with him again. With the amount of blood I was losing, I would be dead soon anyway.

"Come to your senses, brother," Bento said. "You will be starting a war."

"I won't let you do this," Eamon said.

"You won't *let* me?" Adomnan laughed, letting go of my arm. I crumbled to the floor.

"No. I will not let you do this."

The two squared off in human form and lunged at each other. Their bodies clashed together, and their growls echoed off the walls. The sounds dripped with their hatred for one another. It stemmed deeper than this one moment, I was sure. Eamon threw Adomnan into another glass pane, and Adomnan broke through the window. The glass rained down two stories below into the snow. Adomnan's body dangled outside the window, bent out awkwardly and faltering, as though he might fall, but he caught his footing and lunged back into the room. He slammed Eamon's body into the iron bathtub.

Eamon cried out in pain as his right arm broke, hanging unnaturally at his side. A twisted laugh escaped Adomnan's lips. Eamon retaliated, ramming his body into Adomnan's chest, slamming him to the ground. His lifeless arm still hung at his side as he crushed several of Adomnan's ribs.

But Adomnan wrapped the chains from the shackles around Eamon's throat as he kicked him in the back. A cracking sound came from Eamon's neck. With the sound of an animal dying, Eamon finally fell to the ground in a heap, gasping for air. It was all over so fast, a clash of gods in mere moments. Bento rushed over, helping his fallen brother back to his feet.

"Will you not stand by me, brothers?" Adomnan said.

Neither brother answered Adomnan's call to fight. They just stared back at him. He was once their brother, their leader. Now they had to decide if they stood with him or against him.

"Choose!" Adomnan screamed at them. "Choose!"

Eamon's head fell with shame for his elder brother.

"We can no longer protect you from yourself, Adomnan," Bento said. "We cannot stand with you."

Adomnan nodded and turned his back on them. After centuries of loyalty, their blood bond was broken. It was almost heartbreaking to imagine, but it wasn't so different from what I had done to my family, fleeing from them as I did.

Eamon was too wounded to fight again. I could see it in the way his limbs hung unnaturally at his sides. With the silver poisoning him, making him temporarily mortal, he needed to escape, or he would die easily at his brother's hands, like his father before him.

"I failed you," he said to me as Bento led his broken body out of the room.

There was nothing and no one left to stand between Adomnan and me. No one left to protect me. The truth of his imminent rule over me made me sick.

After studying his wounds and torn garments, he turned to face me. "There are no more fleshy bodies standing between us," he cooed, his voice soaked in a false admiration. "It's just you and me, and now we can finally be together."

He said it as if it were *my wish* to be with him, as if he were fighting for what I wanted. He reached out tenderly to touch my cheek as a lover would, but I flinched away. He grabbed my chin, nearly crushing the bone with his force, and turned my face back to his.

"I *will* grow my pack from your womb, and you will *not* question my rule again."

He rubbed his thumb roughly over my lower lip, splitting it. A tiny bead of blood formed in its place. He leaned down and sucked the blood off my lip as I squirmed away with a whimper. The smell of his sickly sweet breath made me gag, and his saliva pooled on my lower lip, mixing with my blood.

Lust and power filled his eyes as he devoured the taste of my blood's lineage. His soul dwelled in perpetual darkness. His large hands slid to my shoulders, gripping my small frame as he caressed my skin. He wanted to break me, to own my body. His touch made me feel filthy. I wanted to peel my skin off my bones to remove his touch. Every part he touched became his. I couldn't bear the idea of having to carry this tainted flesh for the rest of my life. The shame of it was almost too much. His hands made their way down to my stomach, lingering where his hateful seed would grow. His touch was soft, but it may as well have been a knife. I wanted to hide inside myself, to stop feeling what was happening. I could let my soul die with his touch, but if I did, it would never return. A dead, soulless trophy at the side of a killer.

His fingers lightly grazed over my sex as bile quickly filled my throat. I wasn't going to let him hurt me. Not this time. Not like this. The wild animal inside me filled my blood with adrenaline. I felt my golden eyes fill with hate as rage consumed my flesh like wildfire, burning away his unwanted touch. I slapped his chiseled face, leaving a red welt in the shape of my small hand on his cheek. He turned back to me laughing.

"Don't act crazy," he said.

I bared my teeth with a smirk. "You haven't seen me crazy yet," I sneered.

He threw my body across the room, and I slid into the base of the cast-iron tub, cracking my ribs and splitting open my shoulder wound again. I leapt up onto the edge of the tub on all fours. Crouched like the animal I was, waiting to attack. A cry escaped my lips—it was a cry from hell itself. My body shook and trembled as I lunged into the air, shifting into a wolf. My body filled with the blood of Old Mother as I crashed into him without leaving a single mark. He easily blocked my attack and slammed my body back down on to the floor, knocking all the air from my lungs.

"It's nice to see you in your proper attire," he said.

He was just trying to get under my skin, but he was already there. Already fueling my hate. My hackles stood on end. I wanted his blood. I wanted to see him take his last breath. I wanted him to die.

"I have been waiting for you to accept what you are. You are a killer. And you are my queen," he said.

He slowly stalked toward me. Every step he took made me hate him more. He was trying to break me, but I wouldn't obey him. With each step he took, I measured my next move. I remembered everything Mund had taught me about fighting, and I lunged forward, clamping my teeth into the flesh of his arm, tearing away at the muscle. He screamed in pain as he dug his fingers into my shoulder wound. The pain was nearly unbearable.

Involuntarily, I released my jaw and backed away, but he pursued. I tried to calm the pain and panic as I watched my opponent. He was older, stronger, and a merciless killer. I had to be precise and calculating. I sat back, pretending to submit to him, luring him to me.

"Good girl, accept your master."

He kneeled before me, looking deep into my eyes. With a flash of my sharp teeth, I bit into his face, ripping his left eye from the socket. He let out a violent scream and held the bleeding socket where his eye had just been. With his other hand, he slammed me across the room with the force of a sledgehammer. I slid to a stop as I watched his hand desperately feel his empty eye socket as the blood seeped over his cheek.

I felt weak from starvation and injury. Blood still poured from my shoulder—it wasn't healing fast enough, and I was so very tired. This was my last chance to survive. I had to be his killer. Saliva pooled onto my dry tongue at the thought. The animal inside me consumed my soul. The girl of Ashling was all but lost in my rage. Suddenly, I felt stronger than I ever had before. He was still kneeling on the floor, pieces of him missing. He stared into my golden eyes with rage. Did he know he was locking eyes with his murderer?

"There is no one to save you now," he said. But he was wrong; there was no one to save *him*. I didn't need to be saved. I would save my bloody self.

I lunged forward, knocking his body to the ground. His throat was in my mouth before he knew what was coming, and I ripped the life from his body in one sharp snap of my neck. The smallest gasp came from him as his soul left his body. His blood coated my fur, matting it down in its sticky, sweet scent.

I stood over his lifeless, decapitated body, still growling at his flesh. As though he could still hear me—hear my rage. I wanted him to know how he had hurt so many, but there was nothing left of him. He couldn't hear my hate. My soul would never be darker than it was in that moment. But I didn't allow him to touch me or anyone else ever again, and that was the only thing that mattered.

Adomnan's guards came barreling into the room, ready to fight. When they saw me standing on their master's chest with his blood coating my fur, they stopped dead in their tracks. I had beaten their false king.

They looked as though they could be brothers, bred for this life. Both were bulky, muscular men. Which meant the same in wolf form. Both had hair as black as night and dark circles under their deep-set, sinister eyes, though one was clearly younger than the other. They were trained killers. Their sole purpose was to protect Adomnan and kill any who threatened him. But Adomnan had made a mistake. Thinking he would be able to take me with ease, he instructed them not to intervene. They had failed him, and I delighted in that fact. It was my duty to put nature back in order and protect Old Mother's way of life.

The older one lunged at me, grabbing hold of my front paw before I could get out of the way. He broke it with his bare hands.

I wiggled my broken paw free from his grip and limped backward as the two pursued me. I had no way out of this room. With my shoulder still bleeding, a broken paw, and cracked ribs, I was in no condition to beat these two guard dogs.

"I will crush your bones," one snarled.

I took another few steps back, keeping weight off my damaged paw. The ache throbbed up my leg into my chest. It was hard to keep my killer instincts with the pain in my body screaming at me.

I growled at them as my body finally backed into the wall. There was nowhere to go. I was trapped and they knew it. There was no time left to reflect on my short life, but I had accomplished one great thing, and my fur was still coated in his revolting blood to prove it. I had saved the world from one sadistic murderer, and that was enough for one lifetime. My suicide prize.

One of them reached his hand toward me, but I snapped at it. He laughed at my attempt to hurt him. My death was nothing more than a game to them, and it was only a matter of time before they won. So many had died for Calista's vision. It seemed unfair that so many lives had to be destroyed because of an idea of unity.

"Come here, little red. I won't *hurt* you. I always wanted a pet."

He grabbed my neck, pulling me forward. My nails dragged and ripped at the marble floor, but he held me tight in his steel grip. No matter how I writhed, I couldn't free my broken body from his tight restraint. I had expended my energy in killing Adomnan.

Finally, I was able to turn enough to sink my teeth into his cheek, ripping his skin. I spat out his disgusting flesh, but the potent flavor remained, tainting my tongue. He easily threw my body into the corner of the room, splintering my broken ribs into my lungs. The pain burned through me as I struggled to breathe. The thunderous ringing in my ears made it impossible to hear. I tried to stand, only to fall back down in pain. Broken. I was on the ground, bleeding for all I loved.

I wanted to breathe Grey in one last time to fill my mind with the happiness I had once felt in his arms. I closed my eyes to the pain. It was as though I could really smell him. His earthy scent intoxicated my mind, swirling into my senses and shutting off my ability to feel any of the physical pain. The overpowering feeling of Grey's love filled my animal heart, melting away any remaining hate. His love consumed all of me. I breathed him in again and again, thinking of his deep green eyes, his chiseled jaw, and his delicious lips. Oh, to kiss his lips again. I would let go of this life just to feel his warm lips on mine one last time. I knew I should fight to live, for the pack, but I was exhausted, and my only thoughts were selfishly of Grey. Suddenly, I felt a hand lightly touch my matted fur and search for a pulse. I opened my eyes to Grey's beautiful face.

It was impossible, but there he was. He was just as I remembered him, though his eyes were deep with sadness and fatigue. Was I already dead, or had he followed me all this way only to be too late? I was dying—I could feel the end was near. I could feel my soul slipping away.

"Ashling," he said. My name was only a whisper in my ringing ears.

Grey turned his attention back to the two startled guards as he pulled broken glass from his hands, casting it to the ground. His blood was all over the broken window he had crawled through. A deep, unrelenting growl ripped from his chest. His body naturally curved, and he lunged forward as the two attacked him. He meant to kill them, but he was only a human. He couldn't win this fight. I tried to stand to protect him, but my body was too badly broken, and it wasn't healing as it should. I fell back down with a whimper. The younger one had a hold of Grey and started repeatedly punching him in the chest. I could hear his ribs snap one by one, but Grey didn't cry out, and my body was too broken for the new pain to register.

Satisfied with his brother's abilities to win against the mere human, the older one lunged at me, shifting into his wolf form. Smashing into me and pushing my body back several feet, he smeared the floor with my blood. The giant black wolf stood above my broken body, and his dark eyes glared down at me. He stepped down on my broken paw, and I cried out in pain.

Grey's growl grew even more inhuman; it was a sound I had never heard any other creature make. He broke free from the grip of his captor and lunged at the older black wolf who was hurting me. Grey's body vibrated, and his head cocked to the side as his bones began cracking. His golden chest ripped through his shirt, exposing his bare skin as his arms tore out of socket. I was petrified with fear watching his body break apart. Suddenly Grey's growl changed to a haunting howl as he shifted into a wolf, right in front of my eyes, landing on my attacker's back.

It happened so fast. I had to be hallucinating from the pain and shock. But there he stood, nearly three times my size—my Grey, a dire wolf. A large gray wolf with bright-green eyes that danced with hate. He tore into my attacker's throat. With a horrible gurgling sound, the dead wolf fell to the ground, blood pouring from his wounds.

The stench of blood filled the air, smothering out life. The younger wolf had shifted, and he leapt onto Grey dominantly and bit into his back. Grey let out a desperate howl. He flung his head around, biting the guard in the face, crushing his skull. My sight started to flash and flicker. I blinked hard, trying to keep my eyes on Grey, to stay alive for him, but it was a lost cause. My body involuntarily shifted back into my human form, and I curled my naked body into a ball, gasping for air as I lay in the cold pools of blood.

Two more wolves rushed into the room howling, but it was too late. My eyes closed to the pain. I could hear the fight raging around my lifeless body. My breaths came out in small gasps, barely getting oxygen into my lungs, but with each breath came Grey's fantastic scent, and it comforted my pain.

I wanted his arms around me. I wanted him to hold me and tell me it would be all right, that we could finally be together. He had followed me around the world and fought to save my life, to see me this one last time.

I love you, I thought. Before I could imagine the words on his sweet lips, I drifted into unconsciousness.

24
Survivor

"I won't leave her," I heard Grey say.

I blinked hard, trying to get my vision to focus. I could see Grey's handsome face in the center of the darkness. He stood by the bed, rage rippling through his strong body, shaking his core—like a young wolf learning to control his shifting and anger. His black dress shirt was open a few buttons, revealing his deliciously golden skin. I wanted so much to call out to him, to scream his name, but no words would come out. I needed to touch him, to know he was real, to know I was alive.

"You have no place here," Flin said. "You're not one of us."

Grey stood his ground against my eldest brother. His back was to me as they faced off. He couldn't see my face as I silently screamed for him. I tried to scream again and gagged for air. Flin's face was filled with distaste; he wouldn't tolerate insolence from anyone.

"Listen, man, I'm not going anywhere. Why don't you just get used to looking at my pretty face," Grey said, his voice filled with sarcasm.

I had missed the sound of his voice, and it sent tingles down my spine. I loved the way he stood up to anyone who stood between us.

Flin shoved Grey, but he was unwavering to Flin's anger. Grey was fighting for the right to be with me, and frustration overwhelmed me. My body was unmoving and my voice was lost. I couldn't break through to them. This time Flin hit Grey with all his strength, sending Grey flying backward into the nightstand next to me, smashing it. The pain shot through my body like flames licking at my skin. Grey growled territorially. His body curved; he was readying himself to attack my brother. My hand searched for him with all my strength, and my fingers barely touched his.

Grey jumped away from me, startled by the gentle touch. His green eyes were wide with concern as he knelt at my side. He held my limp hand in his, rubbing warmth and life back into it. He studied my pale face as though he hadn't seen me in years. I smiled weakly, touching his cheek with my other hand, and he kissed my palm with his warm lips. His touch was my salvation.

My brothers ran in surrounding Flin. Mund smiled, and his acceptance was all I needed to know we would survive this new battle. I looked around the room and finally realized I was at the Rock of Cashel in Calista's bedchamber. No one used this room. It was preserved the way Calista had left it on that fateful day. The beautiful gold chandelier with inlaid rubies hung above me, lit in all its glory, casting its golden glow onto our skin. The room was exquisite.

Quinn, Mund, Felan, and Flin were all here, but where were the girls? Where was Nia? Why was Baran not here to see me? Would Flin not let him in?

"I will not ask you again, servant—remove yourself," Flin said to Grey.

I looked to Mund in a panic. They couldn't take him from me. Not now. Not after everything we went through. We needed each other. I just held Grey's hand tighter as my strength began to return to me. He leaned forward to my earlobe, lightly pressing his burning lips to my cold flesh.

"I will never leave you," Grey said.

Flin stalked toward Grey and punched him in the jaw, but Grey didn't fall this time. He simply licked the blood from his lip and continued to hold my hand. Angrily, Flin crouched down, preparing to escalate the fight.

My jaw ached from the impact, but I dare not show the pain. Not here. I had to keep our love a secret . . . for now. I closed my eyes, trying not to cry.

"Flin, stop this," Mund said.

Baran stepped out of the shadows of the room beside Grey. "You will not touch him again, Lord Flin."

"Stand down, Killian. I speak for the king," Flin dismissed him easily. "Do you?"

"This isn't your fight. This is between *this dog* and myself."

"Grey is my kin, and you would be wise to choose your words more carefully, little prince. I do not fight for your king. I fight for Ashling."

Flin's face was red with outrage. I could only imagine the horrible things that were running through his mind.

"Flin, why don't you go do something useful, like tell Mother that Ashling is awake," Mund said.

Quinn walked boldly past Flin to my side, sitting next to me as he roughed up my already messed hair. Mund sat at my feet and turned his back on his eldest brother. I had never seen my brothers take action against Flin. He stormed out, cussing up a storm. Felan stood back at the doorway, looking lost.

"It's good to see your golden eyes again," Mund said. "We thought we'd lost you."

Quinn held a cup to my mouth, wetting my dry tongue. I coughed and sputtered unattractively, but my voice started to return, though it was barely a whisper.

"What happened?" I said.

Mund nodded to Grey.

Grey lightly touched my face. "I went to our meeting spot, but I was too late. All I found was my father's body. I couldn't have imagined my father was capable of such treachery. I tracked you north through the forest, but as more time passed the less I could feel you; it was as if your soul had left your body. I almost caught up with you, but I followed the wrong trail—Adomnan must have left it as a decoy. By the time I found the airport, your scent had faded and I couldn't feel you anymore. I thought you were dead."

"I thought you were dead too!" I said. "I couldn't feel you, your heart, or even your pain. It was the poison of the silver blade—it blocked our connection and my ability to shift."

Grey continued, "It took me days to track Adomnan's scent in Iceland. I'm sorry I didn't get to you sooner. I tried. The gods know I tried." Grey hung his head.

Mund said, "When Grey saw your broken body in Dvergar Castle, his repressed natural state ripped free, and he shifted into a werewolf—he's more of his mother than we thought. He saved your life, Ashling. If it hadn't been for him, we would have lost you." He shook his head. "Baran and I tracked Grey, but he moved quickly and didn't leave a strong scent. So we were unable to catch up to him. When we finally reached the castle, the battle was all but won. What we didn't realize was that it was Grey fighting, so we attacked him. It wasn't until he shifted back to a human by your side, endangering his own life, that we knew what we had done."

"Thank you for coming for me. I tried to wait for you, I didn't want to die. I want you." I touched Grey's chin so he would look at me again. His face was filled with regret. I saw a glimpse of his bare chest—it was scarred. I ran my fingers over the claw marks that had ripped through his chest. He now carried the mark of a warrior.

"I can't lose you again," I said.

My beautiful mother ran into the room and laid her head on my knees, sobbing. She smelled of vanilla musk and white wood. My mind swam with all my memories of her. I had desperately missed her. "Ashling. Oh my sweet, beautiful Ashling," she cried.

I pulled my sweet mother into my arms, holding her tightly to me. There would never be a day that I didn't think to myself, *I need my mother.* "Mother" was the word of love on the lips of every child.

As I held her, Mund explained, "You've been sleeping for two days, since Grey found you. Your body was extensively broken. We brought you here, and he hasn't left your side once, much to Flin's dismay," he chuckled.

Mother slapped his leg, shaking her head in playful disapproval. "Ashling, my angel, if it weren't for this boy, I would have lost my baby girl," she said, squeezing Grey's face as only a mother could.

Flin walked back into the room. Instinctively I grabbed hold of Grey's arm. I wasn't going to let him be taken from me. He was mine and I was his. No one could break that bond. He saved my life—it had to mean something to them.

Panic rippled through me as Father's large body filled the doorway, blocking the light from the hall. I was still angry for all he had done to betray me, but I had to admit, if it weren't for his decisions, I might never have found Grey.

"Ashling," he said. "I have a gentleman to present to you."

He couldn't even visit me without tainting the memory with his absurdity. Anger slid through me. I could see Brychan standing behind him. I hadn't seen him since he offered to marry me. The anxiety of that day came flooding back, and I was that scared little girl again. I forced myself to breathe as I studied him.

He was dressed in a full suit that was tight across his broad chest. He was handsomer than I had remembered—the years had done him well.

His offer of marriage was still open. Mund had only bought me time; he hadn't really won me a choice. Now that I was out of hiding, it would be appropriate for him to court me. There was no hint of playfulness to him, as he was here on business—the business of a bride.

"Dear," Mother interrupted, shaking her head disapprovingly, "Ashling is in no condition to see someone of Brychan's status. It would be hardly appropriate."

Father nodded to her and led Brychan away from my chamber without another word. I was thankful for my mother's keen observation of etiquette. She winked at me as she followed after Father, shooing Flin and Felan out with her. It was a temporary solution, but I was happy to have it.

"Where's Nia?" I asked.

"The girls are all in the sitting room," Mund said. "They're safe. We're safe."

I nodded. "What of Eamon? He tried to protect me from Adomnan. Is he healed?"

"He is."

There was something Mund didn't want me to know, something he was hiding from me. I could see it on his face. Had Eamon demanded my life for his brother's? He was the king now, in his father's and brother's absences. It was his right to demand payment of a life for a life, for a king lost. But Mund wasn't ready to explain whatever secrets he held, so I didn't push him.

"Baran, you really shouldn't have kicked Flin out," I said. "He will find a way to punish you."

"We all stand with you, Ashling," Mund said. "Grey saved your life, he has proven his worth."

"But it's dangerous to turn your back on Flin," I said.

"I will always serve *you*," Baran said.

Baran leaned down and kissed my forehead. I knew what he left unspoken—that he loved me as though I were his own and a member of his pack. I felt the same. I was honored to be at his side. I wondered if Grey would join in the Bloodbond of his pack and with it take his rightful place as a Killian? They were once a powerful pack, equal to the Boru.

I looked up into Grey's eyes again. He knew what Brychan's presence meant, and his eyes showed his sadness. Underneath his rebellion, I think he only wanted to be accepted by my family. His father never accepted him, and even now that he was finally surrounded by his own kind, he still wasn't their equal—he was a servant to them. I knew what the pain of rejection felt like. At least Mund and Quinn considered him family.

"Let's leave these two wolves to talk," Mund said playfully as he pushed everyone out of the room. It was crazy to think Grey was now one of us.

The door remained open. It was already scandalous to be left alone with Grey in a bedchamber. If the door were closed, I couldn't even imagine what would happen to us. It would be Grey's blood as payment for the offense. But I could smell Mund outside the door. He was giving us as much privacy as we dared take here. Grey lay on the bed next to me, listening to my heartbeat as he ran his fingertips over my pale skin. His breath was slow and steady. His strong arms were wrapped around my small body, protecting me from the outside world.

"I gave up, Grey. I'm so ashamed." I cried.

"You fought back. You killed Adomnan. You didn't wait to be saved, you fought," Grey said. He was right; I had fought back and I won. I smiled. "It wasn't until I reached Iceland for my revenge that I felt your rage rippling through you and I tasted foul blood. I knew then you were alive, but I still couldn't track your scent. The snow hid your scent from me. I dropped to my knees in the forest and closed my eyes, trying to decide which direction to go. I had come so far and was so close to you, but still I couldn't find my way. Then I smelled the faintest hint of your scent on the wind, and I knew your blood had spilled. I didn't know how long I had to save you, but I knew there wasn't much time. I followed your scent for miles. By the time I scaled the wall and got to your side, you were so badly injured . . ." Grey shook his head at the memory. "I thought I'd lost you again. I wanted to die too.

"That bastard dared to hurt you, and the reality of your pain broke down the walls I had spent my life building around my rage—and it ripped free. The feeling was incredible, like I was tearing through my own skin. As I killed them, I thought there was no sweeter feeling in the world—until I felt you in my arms again. It melted away my anger, and only my love for you remained.

"Mund and Baran rushed in to save you. They couldn't have known it was me, so they attacked. I refused to fight them and shifted back into my human form, but not before Mund split open my chest."

As he told me about his journey, I ran my fingers over the scar again, feeling each of the places the nails had torn into his flesh. He had exposed his human form to two wolves to touch me one last time. Was that love—or insanity?

"I'm sorry about your dad," I said.

"He's nothing."

"But he's your father!"

"He betrayed all of us. You are everything to me. You are my family now. Ashling, I would follow you to the ends of the earth to be with you. I don't care what any of them say—you were meant for me," he said.

As I looked at his loving face, despite all the desires I had coursing through me, I knew he was wrong. "You realize that when I was in your world, we couldn't be together? I was the wolf and you the hunter. And now that you're in mine, you aren't even allowed to speak directly to me. All this time, I compared our love to that of Romeo and Juliet, but now I see ours is a love of far worse fate." He looked into my eyes, the hurt I was causing was clear, but I had to continue. "Grey, we were never meant to be. We have to fight to be together."

Relieved, he smiled and kissed my shoulder where the scar remained from Adomnan's hate. "I'd fight the gods themselves to keep you in my arms."

I captured his sweet lips with mine, kissing my love for the first time in weeks. The power of the connection pulsed through my body, reviving it. Every inch of my nerves ached for his touch. We lay there in each other's arms for what felt like hours—though it may have been only a few beats of our erratic hearts. Our love was stronger than any bond I had ever seen between two mates, but Grey was only half werewolf. I worried the Bloodsuckers would come for him.

"Grey," Mund said. "It's time." He nodded to the door.

"Mund?" I said.

"We've been noticed." Mund glanced out into the hall as footsteps approached. His eyes were filled with fear.

Grey hopped off the bed and knelt next to it. "Rest, Ashling, we have dinner with the packs tomorrow."

Grey kissed my wrist before following Mund out to meet Father as the door shut behind them. I couldn't see them, but I could hear and smell them all.

"What is the meaning of this?" I heard Father ask.

"We were just making sure Princess Ashling had everything she needed before we left her to rest," Mund said.

Father grunted. "I'm leaving a guard by her door to keep her safe."

But it wasn't my safety that concerned him—I was trapped. With that, I heard them all walk away, and I smelled my new guest who lingered outside my door. It was Dillon, the head of the guard.

Servants brought food into my room but left just as quickly as they came. I didn't mind, really. I needed the time to process everything that had happened and accept what I had done. Most of all, I needed to find my path through the games ahead. Father was up to something—I just had to find out what.

The next evening, Tegan swayed into the room with the aura of a goddess. "Ashie, don't you dare ever run away from us again," she said, tears filling her eyes.

"I'm sorry, Tegan. I thought it was the only way to protect you."

"Well, you're plainly wrong," she said, laughing lightly. "We are a pack, and we protect *each other.* Now let's get you cleaned up for dinner." She gestured to the closet.

I followed her into the bath chamber adjacent to the room. It was equally as beautiful as Calista's other things. I didn't belong in a room so exquisite. Underneath my family name and birthright, I wasn't the slightest bit royal. But that never mattered to Tegan; she had never treated me any differently. She had always seen past my lack of elegance to the scared girl underneath.

But the only thing I feared now was fighting my father for Grey.

"All of our packs are here to receive you, to honor your life," she said as she picked my dress from the vast closet. "Grey is being permitted to eat with the packs as one of Baran's guests."

"One?" I asked.

"Willem and his wife, Khepri, are here to receive you as well. I think Baran asked them here to help protect Grey from getting himself killed. If he acts too boldly or claims right to you in front of the council, your father will have no choice but to exterminate him." Her words were soft, but their dark truth was a cold blow to my already unsteady confidence.

"What do I do?"

"We just have to get you through tonight. Your father has agreed it's in your best interest to finish your education as well as not cause any more unwanted notice from the humans, so he's going to send us all back to York Harbor. Tonight, be careful not to look at Grey too often. If your father senses you've bonded with him, he'll be outraged. We have to hide this . . ." she said, "for now."

I nodded my head numbly. "Does Grey know of this?"

"Baran is informing him of the appropriate behavior."

There was something else she wanted to say. It was on the tip of her tongue. By the stress on her face, I could tell she wasn't supposed to tell me, but she wanted to intervene.

"Tegan?" I asked. "What is it?"

Her small lips pursed as she considered her options. "I think you have a right to know what you are walking into. Brychan is here. His offer still stands to court you."

"I know. I saw him yesterday."

"That's not all. With the announcement of your safety, Channing Kingery has also asked to court you. As well as Eamon Dvergar. All three will be at dinner, and Mother Rhea intends to have a formal offering. Eamon has vowed his pack to the council and with your hand would prove his loyalty. Grey has a lot of royal and noble competition. Now that he's a wolf, the stakes are even higher," she said, shaking her head. "Slip this on while I tame your hair."

She handed me an ivory strapless gown that formed around my curves. The thick gold trim accented my hair as Tegan pulled it back into a Grecian style. It reminded me of my mother's pack, the Vanirs.

"Tegan, I just want to love Grey."

"Chin up, Ashie, I can smell them."

She stood next to me as the door opened. Her posture was rigid but feminine. Mother and Father stood there in their finest. Father nodded to us as they continued past the door. Flin and Bridgid followed behind Father with their three sons. Mund was behind them; Tegan quietly joined him, scooping Nia into her arms. Felan, Cadence, and their son walked slowly past the door without the slightest notice of me, but as Quinn and Gwyn passed, he gave me a big smile and she gestured for me to follow them. I had never been to a council dinner, nor had I ever met most of the packs. I was walking into an unknown wolf den, and I was afraid. I wanted Grey by my side, but that would mean his death.

I would have to learn to stand by myself . . . and I would have to learn to play their games better than they did.

The doors to the grand dining room opened, and I could hear the entire room stand as Mother and Father appeared in the doorway. "King Pørr and Queen Nessa," was announced as they entered the chamber. Father and Mother gracefully walked to the head of the table, taking their seats, as all others remained standing. I could see some of them through the crack in the door. I peered inside, looking for Grey, but I couldn't see him from where I stood. Each of my siblings and their mates were announced one by one as they entered the chamber, until only I remained in the darkened hallway. I felt anxious.

Father stood, getting everyone's undivided attention. "I present Princess Ashling Boru," he said.

The sound of everyone's heads snapping back toward the doorway was like the crack of a whip. They all inspected me as I stood there, and I stared wide-eyed back at them. They scrutinized my every movement as I walked awkwardly to the open seat across from Quinn. As father sat for the second time, everyone around me sat. I followed a few beats behind their mass movements. Down at the end of the table, I recognized Grey's handsome face sitting with Baran's small pack. At least I knew he was safe with them. I forced myself not to smile at him and instead busied myself with counting all the gems on Gwyn's amethyst-covered dress.

I could feel all their eyes on me like burning flames on my cheek. I didn't even know whom I was sitting next to. I was too scared to look up for fear of catching Grey's eye and putting his life in danger. My neighbor leaned in close, whispering in my ear.

"These dinners are always more show than anything," said a kind, masculine voice.

I looked up into Brychan's dark eyes. Though his regal face didn't soften, his voice was reassuring. I wondered now how I had never noticed how handsome he was. I suppose I didn't know what handsome was then. I dared a glance down the lengths of the table, and I spotted Eamon immediately, his eyes burned into mine. I couldn't hide anything from his watchful eye, so I looked away. Dinner went on for three courses, mostly of raw animal flesh, without me looking up from Gwyn's dress. I was thankful for the distracting gems.

"It is time for declarations," Mother Rhea said.

Mother Rhea was a werewolf who had lived fifteen centuries but only appeared in her seventies. She had seen many battles and had been near death many times, all of which aged her physically. I knew very little of her history, only what Mund had told me. She was so elegant; I loved her British accent. Her silver hair was curly and sculpted beautifully atop her head with a few ringlets on the right, but it was her pale skin and beautiful blue eyes that everyone always spoke of. For me, it was her smirk and her pointy eyebrows—just like mine—that made me want to fold myself into her arms. She was refined in every way, but I knew underneath that exterior she was one tough lady. She used to visit Mother and me on the cliffs from time to time.

As first in line for my hand, Brychan stood facing my father. "I, Lord Brychan Kahedin, Beldig-son of Wales, declare my honor and will court Lady Ashling at your will," he said.

Father nodded.

I felt as if I were being auctioned off to the highest bidder. I was sick to my stomach. I had been here for no more than a few days, and I was already being drowned in pack laws.

A tall blond man stood. His strong jaw held his mouth firm in his decision. He had piercing pale-blue eyes, and his strong body rippled beneath his black suit. He looked like a spy from one of those *007* movies Baran loved. "I, Channing Kingery, Karik son of Switzerland, declare my honor and will court Lady Ashling at your will," he said. Channing was the elder brother of Cadence, Felan's wife.

Father nodded again.

I knew Grey stared at me. I could feel his rage at other men talking this way about me, Grey's rightful mate. Publicly, my father showed him where he stood—no more than a witness to these proceedings. Baran was doing all he could to keep Grey in his seat. He was being torn apart by this spectacle. And his pain was my pain. I wanted to cry for us both.

Eamon stood up; his body was all mended from his battle with Adomnan. Bento sat by his side. "I, King Eamon Dvergar of Iceland, declare my honor and will court Lady Ashling at your will."

There was a hush among the guests as they awaited father's rule. The son of his greatest enemy now asked to court his only daughter, and not only that, but he was now King of the Dvergar land and pack. There was something about the way Eamon stared at me that made me uneasy. Despite everything he'd done for me, I still didn't trust him. Father nodded, reluctantly. There was a smile in Eamon's eyes; I was sure only I could see.

The room grew quiet. No more offers were spoken. I knew, from what I had read, that this was the only time declarations could be made. A female of mating age was either betrothed to someone or open to declarations. If Mother Rhea closed the offers, no more could be made. I could never be with Grey without breaking a Bloodbond with my family. I felt as if my soul were being smothered. Suddenly I needed air, and my head began to spin. I stood abruptly, letting the chair scrape across the floor as I stumbled backward. Trying to catch my balance, I crashed down toward the floor.

Grey's strong arms caught me. He was faster than the others—most weren't even out of their seats. Even Brychan didn't have time to react to catch me. I breathed Grey in again. He had scooped me up in his arms like a child cradled against his strong chest. When he didn't put me down, I knew he wanted to run away with me in his arms. Mother Rhea offered me her hand, to intervene before he could take such rash actions. Grey set me back on my feet carefully.

"Perhaps . . ." she said, studying Grey. She seemed to be reading our connection. The Elder Gods could see the energy between two bonded souls as though it were a colored fiber dancing around us, our own personal aurora borealis wrapping around our bodies and connecting us together. When she finally looked back to me, it was clear she knew what Grey and I were and that we had already bonded. Neither of us could ever live without the other. "Perhaps Grey of Killian should make an offer," she said.

There were grumbles and curses around the room at the idea of a nomad courting me, their high princess. It was beyond words, and had anyone but an Elder God suggested it, that person would have been put to death. I held my breath.

"Mother Rhea?" Father said.

"As Lady Ashling's savior, he has earned this right, if he dares claim it." Grey squared his shoulders to my father. "I, Grey Donavan of Killian, declare my honor and will court Lady Ashling."

A small smirk was hidden at the corner of his mouth. I knew he had intentionally left out the statement, *at your will*. He was stating his right to me, not asking for permission. Mund was fighting down a smile, as he had caught the defiance too. Mother Rhea turned to father. He didn't dare question an Elder God again. He nodded solemnly to Grey's offer.

"And so it shall be. The sons of our packs Dvergar, Kahedin, Kingery, and Killian will court Princess Ashling of Boru for the right to be her one true mate," Mother Rhea said. She held her hand out for Grey to escort her back to her seat.

Brychan stood, helping me back to mine. He poured my water, setting it in front of me. He studied my pale face as the color started to return.

"It can be overwhelming at first, but you get used to all the silly rules after a while. Don't worry, I'll help you," he said, smiling for the first time. It softened his masculine features.

"Thank you, Lord Brychan," I said. My voice was barely a whisper.

"As the suitors of my only daughter, I must be sure of your strength as an ally and your ability to protect her. You shall all fight in a series of matches in the Bloodrealms to prove your worth," Father said.

There were some rumblings and whispers around the room before each of my suitors started knocking his metal goblet on the table and all cheered at the prospect of the matches. The testosterone nearly dripped off their skin as they sized each other up.

"Princess Tegan, I think my lady is still feeling a bit faint. Would you kindly escort her back to her room?" Brychan asked.

I wasn't sure if he was trying to be nice or just separating me from the other suitors, but I wasn't going to ask. I was willing to flee before this evening got any worse.

"Would the ladies care to join us in the sitting room?" Tegan said.

As though it weren't a question, the other women and children stood and followed us out, leaving the room filled with testosterone. I suddenly wasn't sure that was a good idea, either.

Tegan sat me on the small sofa in the corner of the room where Mother Rhea joined me. She didn't say anything as she watched me carefully. Her indiscreet eyes didn't leave any inch of me unmarked. She knew all my secrets, even the ones I had yet to discover in myself.

"Thank you, Mother Rhea," I said.

"For what, my dear?"

"Grey," I whispered his name.

"He earned his place. It is his right to fight for you. But you must also learn your place. You will save the humans. As a species, they can only be saved by love." She patted my hand thoughtfully. "You must protect Old Mother; she is the soul of nature that gives life to the universe. Her love is poured out upon the earth, and it is she who links us to the land and the cycles of the seasons and the moon. It is she who created the humans." She spoke of the humans' lives as though they were more important than her own beating heart. Her love for them was deep in her bones.

I finally understood the humans' need to fight—it stemmed from fear. Fear that resulted from us not protecting them and not fulfilling our duty to Old Mother. We were meant to balance them and protect them from the fear of darkness.

"Each pack was created with a purpose," she said. "The Boru brought wisdom, the Vanir brought life, Kahedin brought balance, Killian brought protection, the Kingerys brought compassion . . . even the Dvergar have a place in the elements. They are strength, though strength in the wrong hands can become corrupt. But all along, Old Mother's work was flawed. She never gave them love. That is why she created you—and why you're so wild. You are filled with the love and passion the humans so desperately need because one cannot contain love nor stop it. It is the greatest strength in the world. It overpowers evil, fear, and hate."

I now knew the brightest of lights would always attract the darkest of nights, but love would outshine the darkness. If love was allowed in, it would save souls.

I felt so overwhelmed. Everything had changed. I was no longer just a silly werewolf princess in love with a human; I was the survivor of a ruthless attack, a daughter of a king, a princess with four suitors, and the key to the prophecy. In less than a year, my whole world had changed forever.

Brychan, Channing, and Eamon would likely move to York Harbor, and they wouldn't go unnoticed by the small town. Their persistent closeness to me would stir suspicion from the humans.

"Shall we retire?" Tegan asked.

The room emptied as I was lost in my own thoughts. "Sorry," I mumbled as I followed her out. "Where's Grey?"

"He'll meet us in the library."

I couldn't stop the smile from taking over my face at the thought of being with him again, to feel his strong arms wrapped around my body. I yearned for his touch.

25
Bloodmark

We walked into the library, the room where I had started my journey down this twisted path of mistaken love. The books still filled the shelves as they had before, but now they did not hold my escape—they held the past. I had lived life away from everything, and my tale had only just begun. Grey leaned against one of the pillars. His black shirt and jacket were open again, and his black tie hung loosely around his neck. He smiled as I approached him. I wrapped my arms around his neck as he kissed me.

"We have to talk," Mund interrupted.

Grey loosened his grip on my waist as I turned around to face my brother, but his hands remained resting on my hips. His touch awakened my body.

"Grey, I know you are Ashling's one true mate, but you will need to win not only her choice, but our father's. You must beat all three of the others in the Bloodrealms. If you don't do this, you will leave Ashling to her death, as I know she will not accept any other choice from our father," Mund said.

"I understand."

"The Bloodrealms are an old-world werewolf tradition. It started out as bare-knuckled boxing leagues for royal and noble packs to blow off steam, show strength, win a bride, and occasionally settle disputes. After the split, the forsaken packs have made it a much darker place of unspeakable treachery, violence, and slavery," Mund said. "There is one more thing you must know. Ashling, before we leave in a fortnight, Father has one more ceremony that will be performed during the Bloodmoon, and no one can interfere. No matter how she screams in pain, Grey, you cannot interfere." He turned his attention to my obviously worried face, and his voice softened. "You will be branded as a Boru. You will finally receive your Bloodmark."

A shiver involuntarily ripped through my body. The brands were tattooed in the blood of our fathers. Tegan said it was the most excruciatingly painful thing she had ever endured. I knew it was for my own protection from other competing packs, but the idea of it being burned into my flesh didn't bring me any comfort. Still, I was honored to finally earn my mark and my place in the pack.

"As she wasn't branded as a child, you will have to bear witness to our father's right to her, as you are a potential suitor. And if you show any pain or in any way try to interfere, you will be put to death."

"Does everything lead to death with you people?" Grey said.

His dry sense of humor didn't make anyone else smile the way it made me. I agreed with him. Our laws seemed so ridiculously ancient. You annoy someone, death. You speak to someone above your station, death. You breathe in the wrong blood direction, death.

"Etiquette dictates that you shall escort Ashling to her chamber as we follow behind," Tegan said. "Remember there are eyes everywhere here, and they are watching you, Ashling. Until we are home in York Harbor, we aren't safe from their inspection, and even then, there will be eyes on you. We must behave accordingly."

We walked the halls as slowly as we could, dragging out every possible moment we could together without drawing attention from the others we occasionally passed. I wanted to be alone with him. I wanted to pour my heart out to him. To tell him every feeling I had without him by my side. But I knew it couldn't happen as long as we remained at the Rock.

He kissed my cheek lightly, and my blood warmed at his lightest touch—he fueled my wild abandon. Tegan shooed him away to the chamber he shared with Baran down the hall. Once I was finally alone in my chamber—as Dillon, the head of the guard, stood watch oustide my door, I climbed into my giant bed. I was still in my beautiful gown. I curled myself into a ball and subconsciously touched my cheek where Grey's lips had been moments ago.

I couldn't stop thinking, *I'm alive.*

Grey saved my life in more ways than one. When I thought I had lost him, I had let go of who I was. But he came for me and brought me back to myself. I closed my eyes, letting all the emotions of the day slip away into the night.

Ancient rituals filled my days leading up to the branding ceremony. One particularly annoyed me. I wasn't allowed out of my room nor was any male allowed in. It was devastating knowing Grey was on the other side of my stone prison. I busied myself with reading, but in every story I read, the characters became Grey and me. Their love transformed into our love. Grey's every move and breath besotted me. Even when I couldn't see him, I still couldn't get him out of my mind.

Finally, one night while I lay awake staring at nothing, a small note slipped under my chamber door. I bounced off the bed and picked up the folded piece of parchment, and Grey's scent saturated the paper. I quickly unfolded the message:

I dream of you.

I held it tight to my chest as I fell back onto the bed. He was as desperate for a glimpse of me as I was for him. A wave of calm washed over me, extinguishing my rebellion. Only a few days remained until I would be free to wildly love him once again.

Every night continued in the same way. I waited, leaning on the door for my knight to come, and every night he slipped the tiny notes under my door.

You are the fire in my soul.

As long as you are mine.

I lie awake missing you.

The notes became our only moments together in those thirteen days. Our only way to communicate. I wanted to rip the wooden door apart that dared to separate our warm bodies. I wanted to taste his sweet lips once more.

The Bloodmoon finally came, illuminating the night of our sacred ceremony. Mother dressed me in the gown Lady Faye had given me; through the assaults, it hadn't been damaged or bloodstained in any way.

"Mother, how did this dress survive?"

"The Elder Gods, like Mother Rhea and Lady Faye, are the weavers of souls. They see everything, know everything. Lady Faye spun this cloak with her hands from a piece of Old Mother's soul, and it is yours by birthright. It will not and cannot be destroyed. It was created by Old Mother for her wolf daughters."

"But what does that mean?" I said.

Her light laugh filled the room. "That you have to find out for yourself," she replied.

I scowled.

"A lady does not make such a face."

I laid my head on her shoulder, and I breathed in her scent. I had missed her. Her softness gave me such strength. For all my life, I could remember only one other time I had been away from her. Only one time darkened my memories.

"I don't like being away from you," I said.

"This was our first time apart. It's always the hardest."

I looked up at her, confused by her statement. "When I was two, you left me," I said, my voice breaking with strain. "You left me alone on the cliffs. They said you'd chosen another life."

"I can't believe you even remember that."

I whispered back, "I remember everything."

She lightly cupped my chin. "Ashling, I did leave you. I didn't think you would remember it." She shook her head lightly. Her scent drifted down on me from her woven hair. "Your father sent word that Crob Dvergar was searching for me. He believed you still lived and that finding me would lead him to you. I fled to protect you. To lead them away. I would never have left you if it had been anything less than life-threatening."

"I stood on the cliffs all night until you came back for me. I didn't move."

"Redmund told me how you didn't cry. You didn't make a sound. You just watched me flee over the hills. He tried to convince you to come inside after darkness fell, but you just stood there. Unmoving. Your bare feet on the cold stones. You were a stubborn girl." She smiled. "It's good you didn't move. It's as if you knew something we could not. Crob was waiting at our house . . . you would have walked right into his trap, and I would have lost everything. He was so close to taking everything I held dear from me," she said, tears welling in her eyes.

I held her tight to me as she wept. My throat tightened and I felt helpless. "And if it weren't for Grey, I'd have lost you again, Ashling, and I can't live through that."

"You will never have to."

"I know he loves you," she said, changing the subject.

I just smiled. I knew something like that wouldn't go unnoticed by my very perceptive mother. She saw all my unspoken thoughts, like beautiful calligraphy on the walls of my heart. Her head turned sharply toward the door.

"The ceremony is about to begin. You have to play their game. Promise me," she said. I nodded. She kissed my forehead and stepped aside, letting me walk out into the hall. My brothers were positioned like four pillars around me, escorting the family's greatest treasure to the branding ceremony.

Father sat at the head of the stone circle with two seats open on each side of him for my brothers. Across from father sat my four suitors. They all circled the center stone as I walked with my brothers. They stopped in front of the blood-stained stone. My stomach recoiled. The smell of old blood burned my lungs.

Father approached the stone; as the leader of our pack, it was his duty to brand me with my Bloodmark. My brothers moved to their stone seats, and I knelt before the great stone, bowing my head to him. My wild red hair cascaded around my face like an ocean of fire. The cold stone calmed my raging mind; the unnatural calm before the storm.

"Daughter of the Boru," Father said, "you are one of us."

I gasped as the gold quill broke the delicate skin on the back of my neck with its intrusive, piercing opinion. The ink of my fathers' blood pooled into the wounds the quill created. It burned and bubbled into my flesh, scarring deep. I felt my face contort into indescribable pain. I could no longer hold back the screams of agony that consumed my body, shattering any solace I had when I had entered. I had never felt a pain so deep in my bones, in my soul. No living creature should have to endure this marking, and yet I felt pride to have it.

Grey's eyes were almost lost of all color as he endured my Bloodmark. His eyes were locked on mine without blinking. He stared in horror at my anguished face. I knew by his clenched jaw he felt every pain I felt, but he dared not cry out. Our bond would be exposed and our lives would be lost.

I gagged at the cold air, trying to stay conscious as the quill continued to gouge out my skin, leaving behind the mark of my fathers burned into my flesh—a reminder to all whom I encountered that I was no longer alone. I was a member of the Boru.

I felt my body go numb as my father finished our family crest. Nausea followed the numbness as the blood continued to burn into my flesh even after he had finished. I knew the ceremony wasn't complete until I stood on my own and left the circle.

My hands searched for the ground, pushing me up to my feet. The world spun around me, and I couldn't focus on any of the faces that surrounded me. I stumbled backward toward the door; I just had to get back through it. I walked unsteadily away from them. As I made my exit, Mother and Tegan waited there for me. As the door closed behind me, I sunk to the floor at my mother's feet, choking for air to breathe. They would carry my limp body back with them—as long as father didn't see my weakness.

"You have powerful strength in you," Mother said. Her voice was filled with concern as she scooped me up like a baby in her strong arms.

By the time we reached my chamber, the burning had subsided. I looked in the mirror at my mark. It had already healed and was now a part of me. "I will keep your father away. Rest, *m' eudail*," Mother said. I loved the Gaelic words on her tongue—she always called me *m' eudail*, which meant "my dear." Mother left me at the door of my room, and Tegan and I sat on the edge of my bed.

"I'm sorry for the pain you endured," she said. "I know how awful it is—and to have so many watching and for Grey not to hold you."

"I'm fine," I lied. I didn't have the strength to talk. I was tired and wanted to close my eyes and sleep.

"Goodnight, Ashie."

"'Night, Tegan."

"Grey can carry you all the way home if you like," she said with a smile.

I couldn't sleep. I was too excited to leave this stone prison. The night resisted the dawn that I waited all night for. My eyes were wide open, and night persisted.

I smelled Grey and jumped off my bed to crouch at the door, waiting for his next note, but it did not come. A chuckle came from behind me, and I involuntarily jumped to my feet, staring back across my room. Grey was leaning against the stone wall next to a small opening that hadn't been there moments before.

A hidden passage.

I ran to his open arms as he whirled me around, then we crumbled to the floor as I kissed every inch of his face. He wasn't wearing a shirt, and I could finally see his entire scar. It tore from his collarbone to his sternum. I ran my fingers softly over the damaged skin, and I pressed my moist lips to his flesh to heal his hurt.

His lips kissed my Bloodmark.

"I love you," he said in a raw whisper.

"And I you."

I curled up into his lap, pressing as much of my body to his as possible. Selfishly trying to consume him with my touch. My heart crashed into my chest, it beat so hard. Having Grey's touch again made me feel whole. His hands lightly moved my hair aside as he inspected my Bloodmark with its fierce Celtic knots, heart, and wolves' heads. His fingers lingered over the tender skin before he kissed it again.

"I can't wait to get you home," he said.

"How did you get in here? Where does that lead?" I asked, interrupting him.

His wicked smile curved around his wolfish teeth. "To my room."

I couldn't hide the shock as I stared into his perfect face. "Your room?"

"Baran showed it to me. Apparently your great uncle thought Calista needed extra protection, and so a secret passage was made between her chamber and her guard's chamber. I'm just using it for *my own* purposes."

He nipped at my nose.

"Care to run away with me?" he asked. A gleam of mischief danced through his eyes.

"Always," I giggled. "When we go home, where will you live?"

"Baran is my legal guardian now, so I will live with you."

"And where will you sleep?"

"With you," he said with a smile.

I pushed him down, straddling him. My skin tingled as I imagined him in my bed every night. I leaned toward him nearly touching his lips, but a spark still pulsed between us. My heart pounded in my ears. His scent filled me with primal need. I captured his lips and our tongues met.

How easy it was to lose ourselves in that moment, but footsteps approached my door. I climbed off Grey and sat next to him.

"The dawn breaks," I said.

"Goodnight, my love," he whispered as he slipped through the passage door, closing it behind him. I sighed as his scent still masqueraded through my mind. Making it impossible to form a coherent thought. My chamber door opened as I still lay on the floor, and Baran stepped barely inside.

"Princess Ashling, it is time to pack your things. Our flight awaits," he said. His words were all proper decorum, but the wink he gave on the way back out told me he knew of my secret rendezvous.

I glanced through the carved chest at its elegant contents of priceless jewels, including the ring that represented Brychan's claim to me. I moved on quickly to the bureau. There was nothing in there that belonged to me. The closet was filled with gowns, each more elegant than the last.

As I quickly flipped through them, one caught my eye. The dress was simple in design, but the details were delicate and precise. It was the softest shade of golden-ivory crocheted lace. It was elegantly shaped into a V-neck gown with keyhole back and fluted hem. It was exquisite. I knew from family paintings that it dated back to Calista herself.

I quickly zipped it into a garment bag with the notes from Grey and ran down the halls to the gates. I was more than ready to break free from this stone tomb. I never thought any place would hold more hope for me than the cliffs, but now everything for me was with Grey.

I burst into the foyer and froze in terror to see Flin pin Grey to the wall. They didn't react to my presence. The hideous sound of their growls echoed.

"I don't know what you're playing, but you have no place here," Flin said.

"Déjà vu," Grey replied.

"What did you say, slave?"

"You have a lot of *interesting* qualities in common with your brother

Mund."

"That fool has chosen to trust you, but I see through your deceit."

The dress slipped from my numb fingers, falling to the cobblestone floor as I stared at my eldest brother attacking Grey. His forearm was cutting off the air to my lungs as well. Although Grey didn't act aware of it, I couldn't breathe. I gasped for air. Grey's eyes flashed to mine and raged consumed him. My eyes flickered from the lack of oxygen, and the cold air did nothing to return my breath.

I fell to my knees. Grey threw Flin easily aside and held me as the air filled my lungs. Flin stood back up with rage in his eyes. We would all pay for betraying him. Channing ran in and knelt with Grey beside me.

"Are you well, Lady Ashling?" he asked as he took the opportunity to touch my hand.

Grey clenched his jaw tight with jealousy. I knew he wanted to rip Channing's arms free from his body for daring to touch my bare skin. Even though Grey wasn't from my world, he knew how intimate the gesture was.

"I seem to have tripped," I replied.

Channing helped me to my feet cordially and bowed. He didn't even question the lie. "I'd be happy to accompany you safely to your home in York Harbor," he said, smiling.

I smiled back nervously.

"That won't be necessary, Lord Channing," Mund replied before Grey could. "It would be best if we went back and settled for a month or two before you and the others arrive."

Channing bowed again. "Lord Redmund."

Mund bowed his head as he took my hand, leading me away from the fray. I felt Channing's eyes on my body as we escaped. Grey gathered up my dress and followed behind us to the car. The rest of my pack was already nestled inside for the trip to the airport.

I quickly hugged my mother. If I lingered too long, I wouldn't be able to let her go.

"*Tha gaol agam ort,*" Mother said.

"I love you too." I smiled. "I will see you at Gwyn and Quinn's wedding at Castle Reglan, won't I?" Mother nodded as she watched me go. I wished she could come with us, but I knew her heart always walked with mine.

26
Lies

The eight of us sat quietly on the plane as it crossed the ocean, away from all the laws and ridiculous rules of our kind. We all had grown to love the freedom away from the council, though I don't think any of us knew how much so until we went back to that caged life.

Grey's head fell onto my shoulder as he finally welcomed sleep. I snuggled my head into his hair. Every breath took me deeper; our love was unquenchable.

I hadn't realized how much time had passed since I had jumped from my window at Baran's house to run away with Grey. It was already into March as when we arrived home. It felt so good to be back, but it also meant I would have to go back to school on Monday, and I didn't have a clue what I would say to everyone. Grey, Mund, and I had been missing from school for two and a half months, Robert had died, and Baran's shop had been closed since we left. There were bound to be many curious people. Though my bruises from Adomnan had healed on the outside, I wasn't ready to face the firing squad of high school.

Once we were home safe, Baran sat down across from me at the dinner table. This was where it all began with us only nine months earlier. So much had changed since then. I was free, and no prison would be acceptable ever again. I studied Baran's rugged face. I should never have run away and let him worry as I did; I had been childish. I should have known they would all follow me. I put my small pale hand over his large scarred hands. We were so different . . . and yet we were just the same.

"What are we going to tell everyone? They'll gossip and suspect something," I asked.

"You worry too much," Mund said.

He didn't know half of the worrying I did. I worried about everything. I worried about things that could happen, things that did happen, things that I caused to happen. I worried about decisions I had to make and the ones that were made for me. I worried at an Olympic level. I rolled my eyes in mockery of myself.

"As you know, Grey's father died that day in the forest, and he was put to rest while we were all away," Baran said. "Unfortunately Grey missed the funeral. His reputation for being rebellious helped create speculation that he ran away after learning of his father's death. With your father's help, we fabricated Robert's missing last will and testament to leave Grey to me."

"As for us, Claire helped with the damage control, saying your grandparents were ill and we had returned to Ireland so you and Mund could be with them."

I nodded my head as his words sunk in.

"But please, don't cause quite so much trouble at school this time. I don't need any more phone calls from the principal."

I blushed, thinking of Grey and I getting caught kissing in school that day.

"We are going to help Grey collect all his things from his father's home tonight. Then we should be all settled in, and the rumors should die down quickly."

I felt nervous to return to school. The last time everyone saw us, we made quite the spectacle. I had even hit Lacey. I regretted hurting her.

My pack set out on what would be one of the hardest emotional battles we had ever faced. I didn't want to go back in Grey's house. The thought of it made my skin writhe, but Grey and I walked hand in hand inside, both knowing there would be unspeakable horrors inside. I didn't want to see what was upstairs, but we weren't doing it for us, we weren't even doing it for Old Mother. We were doing it for *them,* for each of their souls.

I had felt their pain when I had entered Grey's home the first time. I knew now I had to set them free. Our family followed us inside; I could tell they were scared and angry. I could smell it on them.

"Wait here," I said as Grey and I continued to climb the stairs. His thumb rubbed the back of my hand. I could feel his nervousness and anger.

We left them all in the entryway as Grey and I faced our gruesome fate. We walked up to an ironwood door burned with the Bloodsuckers' mark. The door had eight different silver locks, each hand carved, on both sides of the doorframe.

"A lock for each member of the hunters' clan," Grey said. "One of these should be mine." He let go of my hand; it was instantly cold. He ran his fingers over one of the locks. Silver terrified me, but Grey was immune to it. He rested his forehead on the door, and his sadness rolled over me in waves. Grey then leaned back and kicked the door with a fierceness that splinted it. The broken pieces clattered to the floor. We entered a large, darkened room. Not a bit of light seeped in. Even I could barely see anything in front of me, but I smelled their blood and their souls called to me.

Grey walked over to the dark drapes and tore them from the wall. Metal clips snapped and clattered to the floor as the cascade of the dingy fabric rippled down. The bright sunlight burned my eyes briefly until they adjusted. And then the sight before me finally took its toll. I fell to my knees with my face in my hands. I almost couldn't look, but I had to. Hundreds of human and wolf skulls were displayed on ornate iron shelves from floor to ceiling, filling the room. It was a display tomb. Disgust filled my soul, and I could hear their cries for help. One in particular caught my attention. A young girl no more than five—her fear vibrated in the air. I placed my hand on her small skull, letting my energy calm her.

Grey stood in front of the only skull in the room that was truly on display. It was under a domed glass cover on a hideously beautiful stand in the center of the room. It was clearly the pride of Robert's collection. Grey removed the lid, letting it fall from his fingers and shatter on the cold floor. Slowly he picked up the human skull and held it to his chest. Tears glistened over his cheeks, and I wrapped my arms around him, holding him tightly as he cried. He didn't have to say a word. I could smell a mix of Grey and Baran on the skull. It was his mother.

I heard her soul filled with so much love and pride for her son. I wished he could have heard it too. We removed all the skulls and hides from the house and stacked the skulls high into a pyramid on top of the skins. Grey kissed his mother's skull as he placed it on the very top. We lit the pyramid on fire to return them to the earth as ash with our pack around us.

Baran, Mund, Tegan, Nia, Quinn, and Gwyn danced with us around the fire that night—not in sadness or mourning, but to celebrate their lives and their freedom as Old Mother welcomed them all back to her. We all stayed with them until all that was left was a pile of ash. And with a big gust of wind, Old Mother took her children home.

As nightfall came, the boys moved Grey's belongings into our home. He didn't take much with him, only his clothes, guitars, and books. He took nothing of his father's, and Grey's motorcycle was already at our house.

We bolted sheet metal over all the windows and doors to Robert's house and left it alone in the woods. Grey had said the silence was deafening as he left all his father's things behind. I had never known loss as he had. It had to leave a hole deep inside his soul.

Killing Adomnan left its own mark on me. The weight of him followed me around. I had never realized what the warriors had meant when they said the dead followed you, but now I understood. You couldn't upset the balance of Old Mother without her leaving a mark on you. The taste of Adomnan's blood still lingered in my senses, reminding me of what I had done.

But I had survived.

I awoke the next morning to Tegan's beautiful voice calling up the stairs. It was time for school. Dread filled my stomach, making it feel like a bowling ball hung inside it. Almost as bad as facing my death was facing a school full of hormonal, gossipy teenagers.

Finally, I willed myself to get out of bed and swallow my pride.

The three of us rode together so we could answer inquiries together and make sure our stories matched up. I personally liked the idea of safety in numbers.

The day wasn't as bad as I had imagined it to be. We arrived at school to excited, relieved friends. All except Lacey, who avoided us. Even Beth and I picked up right where we had left off as though our friendship had never been put on hold. I learned Emma and Kate were heading up the prom committee, and they filled me in on all the juicy details I had missed from the day-to-day high school rumors.

"Some people even said you and Grey had run away to elope!" Emma exclaimed.

I hadn't thought of that. The runaway part was true enough, though I would marry him any day. I smiled to myself. Mund rolled his eyes at me.

"Sorry, Emma. Nothing that terribly interesting. Our grandparents were very ill, and we went to spend time with them," Mund replied. "And luckily, Baran was able to find Grey and convince him to come back home safe and sound."

Grey punched Mund in the shoulder far harder than a human could have withstood, but Mund barely budged. And he punched him right back. Human bones would have crushed under the blows. It was unreal to think Grey was one of us now.

"Grey, I'm terribly sorry for your loss. Your father was a great man. And to die so horribly at the mouth of such a beastly creature . . ." Emma's voice trailed off as she shook her head. Little did she know *we* were the same beasts she referred to and her blood smelled just as sweet to us.

Mund offered his elbow to escort Emma to class. Pulling the attention off Grey's emotionless face—well, emotionless to everyone else. I could see the storm of emotions that flickered through his eyes. I lightly touched my fingers to his, and he grabbed on as we followed the others to class. He didn't say anything—he didn't have to. I knew he was torn up.

It got easier after that. Still, we faced endless questions about where Grey went when he had "run away." He claimed he drove to California on his bike. Everyone bought the rebel-without-a-cause scenario.

They didn't know him at all.

He had followed me to the ends of the frozen earth. To save me. He wasn't selfish and unsure, as they all assumed, but I couldn't possibly tell any of them the truth. They could never fathom the depths of the truth that surrounded us.

The morning hours passed by quickly as we repeated our story over and over again. So many times, I almost began to believe it myself. Lunch soon came as they continued to grill us. I started to tune them all out as I studied my tasteless lunch.

"So Grey, did you ask Ashling to prom?" Beth said in her less-than-subtle way. She had him for a brief moment. He looked honestly shocked, but he recovered quickly. He dropped to his knees at my feet, right there in the middle of the cafeteria, exaggerating the movement as he pushed up the sleeves of my sweater. He lightly kissed the back of my hands with his warm lips.

"Oh sweet and beautiful Lady Ashling, will you do me the honor of being my lady at prom?" he asked, loud enough for the entire room to cease talking and watch the spectacle.

I felt my face blush to match the color of my hair. I tried to pull my hands away from his grip, to hide my face and embarrassment in them. But he didn't release me.

"Please, Lady Ashling, wilt thou leave me so unsatisfied?"

A laugh burst from my chest, a most unladylike sound. He was playing it all up for our audience of eager youth. He flipped my hand over, kissing my wrists one and then the other—where his crest would one day go. Only Mund and I recognized the subtle gesture. My flesh smoldered where his skin touched mine.

I snatched my wrists away as I nervously pulled my wild hair out of my face and up into bun. Twisting and untwisting it. I had to find a way out of this ridiculous display.

"Ashling! You got a tattoo!" Kate said.

They leaned in to see the mark. Kate's thin hands pulled mine free from obstructing her view. She examined the intricate crest. I would have been happy their attentions had been redirected from Grey's prom spectacle, if only they had not been redirected to me.

"It's beautiful. It's almost the color of blood," Kate said as she ran her small fingers over my skin. "What does it mean?"

"Family crest," I mumbled and sat down.

"Did it hurt?" Emma asked.

"Like you wouldn't believe." I shivered at the memory.

Grey, now standing, grabbed my hand and pulled me back up into his rock-hard body. "You can't get away that easily," he said with a smile. "What say you to my proposal?" His scent danced with mine around our bodies, and I could feel his heart beating in my chest. Underneath his overly confident exterior, I knew he still needed my confirmation.

"With all my heart."

He smiled as he released me. I quickly gathered my books. I had enough public displays for one day. I was willing to be early to class to avoid this nonsense.

"Is that a yes?" he asked.

A naughty little grin curled my lips. "Figure it out," I replied and walked away to class—leaving him standing there in the middle of a room full of our curious peers. I could almost hear their heads turning back and forth, watching him and watching me walk away. I felt triumphant. But I knew he would get me back later . . . I yearned for it.

At least now I had a reason to wear the dress I had brought home with me, I grinned to myself. I heard Emma, Kate, Kelsey, and Beth's footsteps behind me as they ran to catch up. I could identify each of their individual footsteps; it was as individual as their fingerprints to my keen ears.

"You should have seen his face!"

"It was perfect."

"I can't believe you walked away from him like that!"

I laughed.

"Oh, but you should have seen Lacey," Emma said. "I think she may have burst into flames."

Kelsey replied, "She hates you something fierce for stealing Grey away from her."

I stopped dead in my tracks and abruptly turned to face my friends. It was obvious some of them didn't approve of Grey and me, but I didn't care.

"You cannot steal someone who doesn't want to be stolen."

Kelsey slowed down her pace and didn't keep up with the rest of us. I noted the change in her but didn't have time to figure it out. I glanced at her as we ducked into class. The others were continuing to jabber on, but Kelsey kept her distance, pretending to read.

I was about to walk over to ask her what was going on, but the teacher walked in and brought the class to order. Had I been too harsh? Perhaps I should have been more apologetic for Grey and me, but why should I have to apologize for falling in love? You can't help whom you love.

I didn't hear a word the teacher said. Looking back, it was hard to even say what class I was in. It wasn't until I was back home with everyone that I realized I was still worrying about it. Something had changed between Kelsey and me. My bold remark had hurt her in some way. I still didn't understand girl logic well enough to comprehend what sacred crime I had committed. In some way, I suppose Grey and I had broken up the group of friends I had first met in Ryan's garage. Now they felt they needed to choose sides. If the tables were turned, whose side would I have chosen?

If Kelsey chose Lacey, I couldn't blame her for her choice, but it still hurt.

The division between us grew over the next few weeks as she started sitting with Lacey and Nikki on the other side of the lunchroom. The others commented on it but didn't dwell. Lines had been drawn and sides chosen, and thus high school continued in its adolescent way.

Grey and I were inseparable. Almost losing him really changed me. I felt as though I had grown old in one single breath, and there was no turning back the clock. I knew, without a doubt, what fear truly felt like. Before, I might have fretted over silly things like a teenager. Now I knew love, loss, and true horror.

I had lived through Adomnan's torture. It was my real-life nightmare, and it didn't stop after I took his breath. It continued, playing over and over again in my mind. He dared to think he could touch my body without my permission—the thought still sent chills down my spine and filled me with pure rage.

I had never killed before. It was surprisingly easy to make the decision to take his life, as though he were nothing more than a common thief. But that was all he was. He may have been born to power, but royalty he was not. He had forsaken his sacred vows to Old Mother and could no longer say he was one of us. Releasing his soul from his body made me feel as though my own soul had aged. I was no longer the innocent six-teen-year-old I once was. I felt different now. My hatred of him did end with him, but protecting myself from his attack had a haunting effect.

Grey slipped his body behind mine, pulling my back into his chest, as he sat down on the window seat. His warm arms made me feel safe again, easing my pain.

"What are you thinking about?" he asked as he kissed my earlobe.

"Nothing," I replied, smiling at him.

27
Perfect by Nature

Prom finally came, and the snow had melted. Beth, Kate, and Emma decided to get ready at my house again, but this time Tegan, Gwyn, and Beth's mom helped us get ready with pedicures, manicures, and styling our hair. I actually started to feel confident for the first time since Adomnan's attack, and I was surrounded by people whom I loved. I couldn't imagine my life without all of them.

I was in awe of my beautiful friends. Even though my friends weren't werewolves, they still each had a unique beauty I admired.

I stepped into my gown. The keyhole back framed my porcelain skin, and the fluted hem danced around my feet. The gown was completely constructed by hand of crocheted lace over cream satin.

One by one, we went down the stairs to meet our dates. Grey kneeled at the bottom of the stairs waiting for me. He wore a charcoal-gray suit with an almost metallic sheen and a gray dress shirt he left open a few buttons to reveal his sexy skin. The very top of his scar showed—it would endlessly remind me of his sacrifice and his unending love for me.

"Looking into your eyes is like swimming in warm honey," he said, kissing my wrists.

Baran gave me a hug and whispered in my ear, "You are perfect by nature," then loudly added, "don't you be staying out too late!"

I almost laughed.

Beth and James looked adorable together. I was so happy for her, and James doted on her. Kate and Clint looked bored as they waited for the rest of us to go, but it was Emma who had snagged Ryan's interest. They giggled quietly together as he put her corsage on. Eric had asked a freshman to prom, and he was picking us up with the limo.

It was a weird feeling to be going out with Grey and our friends without having my brother as a chaperone. He and Tegan had decided not to go to prom. Tegan didn't want to leave Nia behind, but I think they finally trusted Grey and me together. It felt good to have the trust and love of my family.

We took pictures in the yard for Mother. I wished she could have been here with me, but Gwyn captured the moment for her.

We finally arrived and danced the night away like fools with our friends, but time hadn't erased my pain. Grey felt my pain with me as it washed over us. He wrapped his strong arms around me, holding me tightly in his love, as we slowly turned around the dance floor. I buried my face and my fears into his shoulder. I wasn't ready to forget.

"Let's go home," Grey said.

I nodded my head as I let him lead me out the door. No one noticed our silent escape. I was suddenly filled with a sense of urgency to get home, and we darted across the parking lot.

I stopped dead in my tracks a few blocks from home. I smelled an unfamiliar, smoky scent. We slowed our pace to a walk. The stranger's scent was thicker with every step. As we turned onto our street, I saw him.

The greasy stranger from the Netherworlds stood between us and our family.

He was leaning causally against the porch. This time he wasn't draped in a wolf's skin—instead, he was dressed in a full black tuxedo, but he still wore his top hat. With or without the wolf's skin, he looked just as menacing.

We stopped on the street in front of the house. I knew he could certainly close the space between us in a heartbeat, but the distance still gave me a sense of security. Grey wrapped his arm around my waist as though he knew my knees were considering falling out from under me.

"Lady Boru, I greatly regret being tardy to the prom. I would have liked to have had a dance," he said with a smirk.

Grey growled in return.

His hair still held the same wave, but the smell of grease no longer lingered about him. The smoky air of his scent was like strong incense, and it made my head hurt.

"You're in our way," Grey said.

He studied Grey again; this time it was clear he was observing him as an opponent. My stomach rolled at the idea. What did this killer want? He turned his attention back to me as he held open his jacket. "I have something of yours," he said. Inside his coat, I clearly saw Calista's journal.

He must have tracked my scent back here and found the journal where I had abandoned it in the woods to keep it from Adomnan. But why track the path back to where I began, rather than follow the one on which I left? And why were Baran and the others not confronting this stranger? It didn't make sense.

"Leave the journal on the porch, and get out of our territory," Grey said. His voice was authoritative. He would make a great leader one day.

"I admire what you're doing here, but you are far out of your league."

"Where is my family?" I said.

He smiled. "Inside. They have been waiting for you. So have I."

"Let me pass," I said.

"You look just as she said you would, you know."

"Who are you?" I said.

"My greatest apologies, my lady." He bowed in respect. "I should have introduced myself in the Netherworlds, but I didn't get the chance. I am Odin, son of Jarl of the Norse Lands."

Baran's large body came out the door and stood next to the stranger. His large hand clapped the stranger on the back. "And the guard of the late Lady Calista," Baran said, bowing his head to Odin.

"Do you trust the half-breed?" Odin asked Baran.

I felt Grey's body tense as the anger rippled through his skin. I knew he didn't like being called a half-breed, nor did he appreciate having his honor called to question. I wrapped my small fingers through his, claiming him. I straightened my shoulders in front of Odin and steeled my face. I wouldn't succumb to his unwanted inspection with fear. Grey's tension eased with my touch.

"He is one of my pack," Baran replied.

Odin nodded and walked into the house. Baran held the door for us, and we walked nervously past him. As we entered, I saw Odin talking quietly with Mund and Quinn. Did they know him as well? Gwyn, Tegan, and Nia were the only ones not in the room. It was a council of men.

"Is she ready to lead?" Odin asked Baran. "She is nothing more than a child."

Baran nodded.

"I am right here, and I would appreciate if you would have the decency to address me directly," I said.

"You are the wild one she said you would be," Odin said.

"You dare to speak to me that way?" I growled. "If you have no real business here, I demand you leave the journal and be gone."

He smiled. "You have her strength." His face softened for a moment, as though he were lost in a memory, but it quickly faded, and the seriousness of his expression returned. "I have come to swear my allegiance to you, Princess Ashling Boru. If my life can serve you, you shall have it."

Grey spat, "Guard of Calista—great job you did protecting *her*."

The devil himself couldn't have had a more menacing face than what consumed Odin's. "There are moments that distinguish between men and boys. Warriors and the dead. One breath separated me from saving her life. You will not question that again," he said. His eyes shot to mine, piercing them. "The wolf's hide I carry with me is Calista's killer. His body is a reminder to all who cross me. I will not fail again." Turning to me, he said, "My lady, my soul is yours."

A territorial growl came from Grey's chest. He didn't trust Odin.

"Why do I need your protection, Odin, son of Jarl?"

His head remained bowed as I stood in front of him. The fierceness of Mother pulsed through my veins as I waited for his answer. I felt a surge of strength I had never felt before. My childish fears were slipping away, and a fierce woman was taking her place.

"One whom you trust will betray you. Lady Calista foretold it. I gave my sworn allegiance to protect you when that moment came, and I will not forsake her rule."

"Why did you not protect me in the Netherworlds?"

He looked up at me with his black eyes that filled with regret. "Until you accept my allegiance, I cannot fight royalty, even to save your life."

I gagged, remembering Adomnan's sickening expression as he touched me. "You chose not to stop him, because of some archaic covenant?"

"My vows to Calista do not allow me to step outside the order. Her words still control my actions . . . until I swear my allegiance to you. I wanted to break them, I wanted to shelter you from them, but I didn't have the right. Even after her death, my vows still rule my actions."

I turned my back to him with disgust. Laws and rules stopped him from saving me. Saving me from the memories that were burned so deeply into my soul, from having to take Adomnan's life. The taste of his blood still embodied my mouth. I shook my head.

"I don't trust you," I said before turning around to face him. I studied his face, but nothing reassured me of his character. "I need to consult with my pack."

I gestured my family into the kitchen, where I knew the girls waited. I looked to Baran for answers.

"He is the only one of Calista's guard who didn't betray her. I have known him for centuries, but he has been to hell and back. His soul is dark with her death, but I would trust him with my life," Baran said.

Mund said, "You have to follow your heart with whom you trust."

Grey didn't say anything. He simply held my hand. His lips were firmly drawn together with worry. I knew now what I had to do. It wasn't about the childish dreams of a girl, but of the greater good of the pack. With a small tug of his hand, we walked back into the living room to face Odin once again.

"I accept your allegiance to myself and my pack," I told him. He nodded and handed me Calista's journal in return. I felt the warmth of the leather in my fingers. "You will not cross me," I threatened.

He kneeled in front of Grey and me, completely submitting to us. I didn't know what part he had yet to play, whether good or evil, but his life was already intertwined with mine. The fates had already decided our paths must cross.

I now knew the sacrifices I had to make. The prophecy called to my soul, like a link to my heart. I was the chosen one. Only I could bring balance to the earth and unite us for Old Mother. As Grey and I went to face the Bloodrealms, I wasn't afraid. No matter what hidden evil lurked there, I had faith in our love, and I could see our future.

Don't miss *Bloodrealms*
the next book in the Bloodmark Saga.

bloodmarksaga.com

Pack Reference

Boru – Ireland
Ashling Boru
Bridgid Boru
Cadence Kingery-Boru
Donal Boru
Felan Boru
Flin Boru
Mund Boru
Queen Nessa Vanir-Boru
Niamh Boru
King Pørr Boru
Quinn Boru
Ragnall Boru
Tegan Kahedin-Boru

Kahedin – Wales
Lord Beldig Kahedin
Brychan Kahedin
Gwyn Kahedin

Dvergar – Iceland
Adomnan Dvergar
Bento Dvergar
Crob Dvergar
Eamon Dvergar
Uaid Dvergar
Verci Dvergar

Kingery – Switzerland
Channing Kingery

Killian – Scotland
Baran Killian
Khepri Killian
Willem Killian

Vanir – Greece
Calista Vanir
Lady Faye Vanir
Mother Rhea Vanir

Norse Lands – Finland
Odin Pohjola (son of Jarl)

Bloodrealms – Valhalla
Æsileif

Bloodmark Glossary

Beltane
Gaelic festival halfway between the spring equinox and the summer solstice.

Bloodmark
A pack symbol tattooed in blood.

Bloodmoon
A red moon that comes once during each season.

Bloodrealms
Underground city in Valhalla.

Bloodsucker
The clan of humans that hunt werewolves.

Carrowmore
Carrowmore is one of the passage tomb cemetaries in Ireland. In Bloodmark they are the resting place of the humans in the battle of 4600 BCE.

The Dream
The prophecy foretold by Calista Vanir.

Elder Gods
The original werewolves.

Foresaken Packs
Werewolves that broke their vows to Old Mother.

Hills of Tara
Location of the Vanir and Dvergar battle commemorated by ancient monuments in Ireland.

Netherworlds
Underground werewolf city in Canada.

M' eudail
Gaelic for 'My dear'.

Rock of Cashel
The home of the Boru pack.

Samhain
Gaelic festival marking the end of summer and the beginning of winter.

Tha gaol agam ort
Gaelic for 'I love you'.

Winter Solstice/Yule
Gaelic festival for winter solstice.

Bloodrealms
Rodane, Norway

Rock of Cashel
Cashel, Ireland

Bloodmark

Ashling Boru by: Aurora Whittet

Special Thanks

Thank you to my husband for his endless support and love; my son for showing me the world anew; my mother for teaching me how to love; my father for teaching me persistence; and my family for putting up with me all these years. I love you.

Thank you to my dearest friends and family who took the time to read the first awful draft of *Bloodmark* and shared their enthusiasm and constructive critisim with me. I'm in a circle of brilliant minds. Sarah DeYoung, Jessica Epp, Heidi Gayle, Jennifer Rich, Melissa Robinson, Kourtney Rose, Jennifer Sandstrom, Sarina Sandstrom, Sylvia Sandstrom, Sandy Showalter, Christopher Ryba-Tures and Brian Whittet.

To Cory Bauer for lending me his talent and creating a Kickstarter video for *Bloodmark*. Thank you to my Kickstarter Pack, your pledges and faith in me are priceless. A special thank you to Emily Adams, Adam Boltik, Rothanak Chhoun, Marian Deegan, Sarah DeYoung, Jessica Epp, Michael Green, Shashi Lo, Rhonda J. Luschen, Kevin & Laura Pankratz, Darin Pfeifer, Jennifer & Leslie Rich, Jerry Sandstrom, Sandy & Brad Showalter, and Steve Whittet.

Thank you Jessica Flannigan Consulting for your amazing PR talents and attention to every little detail of the fancy life. Eliesa Johnson you are the goddess of photography.

I would like to thank my editor for all her guidance, patience, and sense of humor. Amy Quale and the entire Wise Ink crew.

Music for Bloodmark

Thank you to Leslie Rich and Caleb Peterson for writing and performing the beautiful song *Bloodlines* for the Kickstarter project. And thank you to Leslie Rich for writing and performing *Heart Strings* that touches the very soul of *Bloodmark*.

facebook.com/themusicofleslierich

Be a part of Bloodmark

aurorawhittet.com

bloodmarksaga.com

goodreads.com/aurorawhittet

twitter.com/aurorawhittet

facebook.com/bloodmarksaga